Grant Sutherland was born in Sydney and brought up
in rural Western Australia. After studying at the London
School of Economics he worked as a money broker
with Exco in Sydney. He now lives in Oxfordshire with
his wife and daughter.

Due Diligence

Grant Sutherland

HEADLINE
FEATURE

First published in 1997
by HEADLINE BOOK PUBLISHING

First published in paperback in 1998
by HEADLINE BOOK PUBLISHING

A HEADLINE FEATURE paperback

10 9 8 7 6 5 4 3

ISBN 0 7472 5693 4

Typeset by CBS, Felixstowe, Suffolk

Printed and bound in Great Britain by
Mackays of Chatham PLC, Chatham, Kent

HEADLINE BOOK PUBLISHING
A division of Hodder Headline PLC
338 Euston Road
London NW1 3BH

Due
Diligence

Department has been strangely becalmed. The bread-and-butter work, the underwritings and flotations, have kept coming in, but the big deals that Vance once pulled off so regularly, the takeovers and defences, have dried up. The fees and bonuses have gone elsewhere. The simmering discontent in the department had begun to break into open revolt before the Meyer deal came along: three of our best employees walked. Vance promises me the Meyer deal will mark the beginning of our renaissance, but reading his memo now I'm not at all reassured: the Meyer brothers don't want to raise the bid. If they don't raise their bid they won't get Parnells, and if they don't get Parnells we won't get our success fee. No success fee, no bonuses, and a full-scale meltdown in our Corporate Finance Department will follow: then everyone in the department worth keeping will walk.

Rubbing my eyes, I put the memo aside. I came in to work early to escape the heart-numbing silence that I wake to each morning these days. My daughter no longer comes into our room and crawls into bed between us; my wife no longer turns on the radio and listens to the morning prayer. They have left me. Theresa has taken our daughterAnnie, and gone. I came in to escape, and now this. Looking down at Vance's memo, I try very hard not to contemplate what might happen to the bank should the Meyer bid fail. Troubles, they come not single spies. Coffee. I need a mug of coffee, black and strong.

The Corporate Finance offices are still empty, but inside the Dealing Room alcove I surprise a dealer from the nightdesk blowing smoke-rings into the steam from the urn. He's young, twenty-two or -three perhaps.

'Morning,' he says, pushing away from the bench.

'Busy night?' I ask, and he shakes his head. 'Jimmie, isn't it?'

'Jamie,' he says.

But he doesn't seem troubled by my mistake. And I remember him now, one of last year's graduate intake, a first in Medieval French History. Making myself a coffee, I ask what the US dollar did overnight.

'Down a bit.' He stubs out his cigarette. 'Big-figure on the Mark.'

Someone calls from the Dealing Room and he hurries away. I stir my coffee, sip a little and follow. Including Jamie, there are three of them down on the nightdesk, they sit in a small pool of light at the far end of the Room. The other desks are still in darkness, all empty. Very early. I glance at my wrist, but there's only a bruise where my watch should be.

'Hey! How was the party?' Owen Baxter, the loud braying voice is unmistakable. 'Big night?' he bellows. He's a senior dealer, usually on the proprietary trading desk, and depending on your point of view either the team-joker or the biggest bore out here in Treasury. He trades like the rest of us breathe. When the real markets fall quiet he gets involved in those quirky parallel markets that ripple across the City from time to time: Christmas trees at Christmas; at Easter, chocolate Easter eggs. Last week it was bananas. Owen bid too high, and a barrowload of rotting fruit was subsequently dumped at the Carlton Brothers reception. Daniel, our treasurer, wasn't impressed. As a punishment for the misdemeanour, Owen's now in temporary exile on the nightdesk.

'Not bad,' I answer, approaching down the aisle.

Overhead, on the big wall-screen, the closing numbers from Tokyo glow in the darkness. Endless lines of numbers go flickering across the Reuters screens, and the PCs hum quietly, unattended. The dragon sleeps.

'Becky go?'

Becky, my secretary, falsely rumoured to be sleeping her way towards a trial as a trainee dealer.

'Didn't notice,' I say.

Owen smiles and the two younger men avoid my eyes. I really don't need this. They've been watching over the bank's currency exposure; I ask how it went. Owen reaches across and gives me the deal-sheet. There's one big number buried there, a Yen trade. I look up.

'Who gave you the ton?' One hundred million US.

'Bunara,' he says, and I wince.

Bank Bunara, a heavyweight from the Far East, the rogue elephant of the currency markets.

'Dumped it quick as I could,' he adds unhappily. 'Bloody pricks.'

'Expensive?'

He shakes his head. I ask him what the Profit and Loss was for the night.

'Even, pretty much. Ten grand up,' he says.

But without the disastrous Yen deal they'd be up two hundred thousand. Expensive enough, and I'm surprised he's been caught like this. I hand back the deal-sheet. Owen keeps his eyes lowered. He tells me about some revised growth figures due out later, and then gives me a quick summary of some statement the German Chancellor made at a conference in Beijing. Owen's second offsider plays with a Gameboy; watching him, my mind drifts. I see moonlight on the Thames, and hear laughter and the clink of a glass.

'Raef?'

Pinching the bridge of my nose, I ask if Bunara were trying to stuff us.

Owen turns to the other pair. 'Sure they were trying to stuff us, right?'

The one with the Gameboy mutters, 'Dollar–Yen just dived.'

Jamie continues ticking off deals, checking them against the slips in his hand.

'Leave it with me,' I tell Owen. 'I'll have a word with Daniel.'

The big glass doors swing open, and the first few of the day-shift come in. Suddenly the electronic ping from the Gameboy turns musical. The lad whoops and pushes the toy up near Owen's face. He calls Owen a loser.

Owen swears. He grabs the Gameboy and smashes it on the desk, the thing bursts into a shower of shattered plastic. Jamie keeps his head down, but the other lad stares at the mess in disbelief.

'What the fuck?' he murmurs.

A smile rises to Owen's lips. 'Unlucky bounce,' he says.

Hilarious. I push away from the desk and head for the door. Around the room the squawkboxes, the speakers that sit in rows on each desk, are coming to life. The brokers at the far end of the lines are putting together the first bids and offers of the day. The Dealing Room is two floors deep, and up on the next level, through the glass wall of the bank's in-house restaurant, a cleaner waves down. I nod in return. When I hit the switches by the door, the whole Dealing Room is awash with light, and Owen cheers. More of the day shift arrives.

Back in my office I sip my coffee and glance at Vance's memo again. I must get a grip. I tell myself this quite firmly. Pull yourself together; snap out of it . . . all the clichés. Zero hour is approaching for the bank, and I'm only half here. My ship is drifting towards the rocks, and I – the man with his hand on the tiller – I am still gazing astern, looking backwards, stricken by the sun. Get a grip. I sit down and take a breath; gather myself. I draw a jotting pad near and pick up a pen. The desk calendar, six hours late, ticks over. Thursday morning, and for me, the Honourable Raef Carlton, Deputy Managing

Director of Carlton Brothers, the phoney war is over. Alone at my desk it comes to me quite clearly: the real battle at the bank has just begun.

2

Most of the paperwork is in the OUT tray before Becky arrives. The Meyer memo, the sole piece of any interest from the pile, sits at my elbow.

'Sore head?' I ask as she enters.

She frowns. The last time I saw her last night she was dancing on a table, bottle in hand.

'Can you get Stephen to come in for a word?'

'Sir John's in the Boardroom,' she tells me. A New Zealander, her voice lilts, so when she adds, 'He wants to see you,' it comes out like a question. 'Something's happened,' she says, reaching for the OUT tray.

'What happened?'

She shrugs. She doesn't know.

On my way to the Boardroom I put my head in at Stephen Vance's office and ask him to come and find me in half an hour. He says he has a meeting with the Meyers later, and invites me to tag along. I tell him I'll see.

Life out in the open-plan Corporate Finance section is stirring. About fifteen young men and two women today, the rest of them are scattered in hotel rooms across the globe. Some of those who remain are helping Vance with the Meyer bid, and most of the

7

others are preparing a big mining company float for later in the month, and two upcoming bond issues. But right now they're checking their E-mail, sipping their coffees and chatting. Until three years ago, one of these desks was mine. I was Vance's deputy then, and many times since I've wished myself back out here in the fray. At times like this, the Meyer bid running down to the wire, the yearning to be part of it again is almost physical. A few of them nod to me as I pass.

When I enter the Boardroom, Sir John looks up and I stop, surprised. Since I saw him yesterday evening he appears to have changed, buckled somehow, he's showing every one of his sixty-four years. He drinks to excess these days, but this looks to be much more than a bad morning after.

'Daniel,' he says.

I turn back to the door, explaining that it might take me a minute to find him.

'Daniel's dead.'

I check. The words echo. Then slowly I turn. He looks straight at me, and his moist eyes hold something I can't quite understand. But then I feel it: sorrow; deep and heartfelt sorrow. It sweeps towards me like an incoming wave.

'Raef,' he says, 'I'm so sorry.'

The wave breaks over me warm and deep, my mouth stops its ridiculous twitching smile.

'Daniel?'

'Go home, Raef.'

'But he was there,' I say stupidly, my voice suddenly husky. 'Last night.'

Sir John can't look at me now.

I raise my eyes to my grandfather's portrait on the wall. There is a sense of unreality, of profound disconnection. Far away, glowing in the endless summer of childhood, I hear two young boys laughing.

'How?' I say.

Sir John drops his eyes. He tells me the police will be arriving here soon.

'What happened?'

'We're not sure.' then he looks up and past me. 'Raef. It seems Daniel was shot.'

'Shot?'

He lifts a hand, frowning. 'I've only just heard myself.'

'You're sure he's dead? Where was this?'

'He's dead, Raef. He was shot down on St Paul's Walk. Some Inspector called me. He'll be here shortly.'

St Paul's Walk by the river, just fifteen minutes' walk from the office. I bow my head and stare at my hands, suddenly adrift from the things of the world.

'The Inspector wants to question everyone who was at the party last night.' Sir John turns his head. 'Terrible thing.'

I find myself nodding. Is this real? Had it happened?

'Was there anything untoward at the party?'

'No.'

'I just can't understand it Raef. Who would do a

thing like that? And Daniel.' Sir John looks bewildered. 'He must have been mugged.'

'Could it have been an accident?'

Sir John regards me with sympathy. 'Raef, he was shot.' He rises and comes toward me. 'If there's anything I can do, Raef. Anything.'

Nothing to be done, I think, the phrase rising unbidden. Everything to be endured.

He touches my shoulder. 'Go home. If there is any more news, I'll let you know.'

After a moment his hand slips away. The door opens and closes just behind me.

Alone now I try to face it: Daniel Stewart, the man I once loved as a brother, has been killed, he is no more. I should feel something. I should be weeping, but my eyes remain stubbornly dry.

'Raef?'

I pivot. Stephen Vance has come in.

'I couldn't wait,' he apologizes. 'Reuben Meyer just called, he wants the meeting ASAP.'

Stepping past, I tell him to check my diary with Becky. 'Fix it for tomorrow.'

'What's wrong with now?'

Going out, I repeat that one word quietly. Tomorrow.

3

After giving my driver his instructions, I turn and

mount the steps to my home. These moments, a hand in one pocket, grappling for the keys, are usually the most dismal of my day. There's no one to greet me on the far side of the door – I know that – yet I still get this surge of expectation, as if my mind hasn't convinced my heart that they're gone. And today? Turning the key in the lock, I shoulder the door wide open. Home in Belgravia. Daniel is dead, my wife has left me, and here I am at 9.00 a.m. returned to my big, empty home.

Mid-morning, and I still wander the house like a wraith. How much more can I lose that is dear to me? In the bedroom I brush past Theresa's dressing table, moving a small mahogany box out of place. Carefully I push it back with my finger. Back into the line of her combs and hair-clips; everything in order, all just as she left it when she took Annie down to Hampshire two months ago.

Then I resume my aimless wandering, room to corridor, corridor to room, stalked everywhere by a feeling of dread. At last I stop outside Annie's door. Then I reach, and the door opens. Warm winter sunlight pours in through the window, slanting across the giant panda by the cupboard, and the doll's house upended in the corner. Above the bed, a mobile of smiling moons and silver stars begins to turn.

I should leave, I think. But instead I cross to the bed and sit studying the cartoon elephants stencilled in neat rows on the wall.

Daniel, Daniel, what has happened? I bow my head

as the memories rise and break over me. I see him as a schoolboy, sitting on the riverbank and laughing. I see him in the attic at Boddington, jumping from the table and teaching me how to fly. And older now, going up to receive the maths prize at Speech Day, the headmaster shaking his hand. The trip we made to Italy that last summer of university; seeing him off at the station when he went to Sandhurst, and watching him walk through the door of my office the day he joined Carltons. I see him in the only way I'll ever see him again, in the random light of memories that will fade with the years and grow dim.

I lie down. There are stars and bright smiling moons just above me. It should be night. I rest my cheek on the pillow. Dear God. Dear God, this is not how I thought it would be.

Later, Celia calls.

'Raef,' she says tearfully. 'Will you come round?'

When she starts to cry, I close my eyes.

'Raef?'

'I'll be there in half an hour.'

4

Celia presses her face to my chest, and I wrap my arms round her shoulders.

'The police,' she says, then she falters.

I turn her and walk her inside.

It's been ten years since Daniel brought Celia to my house and announced his engagement. She was vivacious then, always smiling, but the years between have drawn heavy lines on her face. Marriage to Daniel has aged her. As we enter the sitting room she wipes the backs of her hands over her eyes. Everything here is just as it always is, neat and newly cleaned, and there's a faint smell of wax on the air. She slumps into the sofa.

'He was shot,' she says.

She looks straight ahead, eyes fixed, and it occurs to me she might still be in shock. But when I ask if I can get her a drink, she shakes her head.

'Why would someone shoot him?'

'I don't know, Celia.'

'The bank?' she says, wiping her eyes again. 'Why?'

I can't bring myself to face her. I ask what she's heard from the police.

'They said they'd talk to me later. They had a policewoman bring me home after I saw Daniel.' I glance down the hall. 'Gone,' she says. 'I sent her away.'

She gestures for me to sit.

'He said he'd be late,' she tells me, meaning Daniel. 'That's what he always said. I wasn't worried when he didn't come back. He said it was no wives. Was that true?'

Not true at all, as I think Celia sees from my expression.

'Theresa didn't come either,' I remark lamely.

'Right.' She looks absolutely wretched. 'I got a call at five this morning. I thought it was Daniel but it wasn't.'

'The police?'

'They came and got me. I had to identify him.' Tears come to her eyes again but she holds them back. She explains that Daniel's body was found on St Paul's Walk. His wallet, it seems, was still in his jacket.

'So he wasn't mugged?'

'They don't think so.'

'Who found him?'

'Some policemen found him. I heard them talking at the morgue. They said they thought he was a tramp, drunk or something. They tried to wake him up.'

She stares into space. When she starts to tremble I go and sit by her, an arm around her shoulders.

I never thought I'd feel close to Celia, not when I first met her. But after my marriage to Theresa all four of us became close friends; we even took holidays together before Celia's first child, my godson Martin, was born. And as Daniel's peccadilloes have become too brazen to ignore, I've found my fondness for Celia turning to admiration and respect. Now she leans forward, her face in her hands, and I feel as close to her as I've ever felt to anyone.

'How do I tell the boys?' she whispers. Her two sons, they're up at Eton, and for one horrible moment I think she's asking me to break the news to them. But then she says, 'I'll have to go out and see them later.'

I ask if she wants me to speak with Daniel's lawyers. She looks surprised.

'Daniel's will,' I explain. 'I'm an executor.'

When she understands, she seems relieved. She doesn't want to be seen reading the will over Daniel's unburied body. Then I ask if there's anything else I can do and she pushes her hair back and holds it there. Her face is red now and twisted with pain.

'Who would want to kill him?'

'I don't know, Celia.'

She shakes her head and fixes her eyes on mine. Beneath her pain there is a real perplexity. Her lips tremble: she is on the verge of tears again.

'Why?' is all that she says.

5

Cocktails at my father's flat in St James's. One of the catering staff ushers me in and I take a glass from a passing tray and look around. Not as many here as I'd expected; maybe not even thirty, and a good few of those I don't recognize. I sip my champagne and steel myself for the evening ahead. If I could be anywhere else at this moment, I would be, but I have a duty to fulfil: to the bank, and to my father.

Charles Aldridge nods to me from near the fireplace.

'We missed you,' he says when I wander over.

'Thought you wouldn't make it.'

This, it seems, is my invitation to mention Daniel. I let the opportunity pass.

'Where's my father?'

'Edward?' Charles looks around. 'Haven't seen him for a while. Quite shaken up by the news.'

Ignoring this second opening to unburden myself, I sip my drink. Charles Aldridge handles our family's legal affairs and has done for as long as I can remember. He also sits on the Carlton Brothers Board. He gave up practising as a barrister some years ago, when he turned sixty, but he's retained his obliquely probing manner. Normally it doesn't trouble me, but right now I could do without it. Picking up the signal, he gestures around the room.

'Into the fray?'

'How's it looking?'

He runs a hand up through his thick mane of silver hair. 'Not good. There isn't much chance of twisting arms if they aren't here.'

'Where's the Chairman?'

'Couldn't make it.'

'The other Committee members?'

'Two.' He nods across the room. 'The other five couldn't make it either.'

Wonderful. Tomorrow the Treasury Select Committee sits in public to ask questions about three recent privatizations, one of which was handled by Carlton Brothers. The signs are that we'll be singled out for particular attention. In Westminster and

Whitehall the knives are out for my father.

When my grandfather died my father became chairman of the bank and took up the family seat in the House of Lords: but unlike my grandfather, who attended the House rarely, my father has become increasingly active in Westminster. He now sits on several parliamentary committees dealing with the Ministry of Defence. When Carlton Brothers were in the running for the privatization there were rumblings from our competitors in the City about unfair advantage, rumblings that were seized on by the Opposition. A suggestion came through from the Cabinet that my father might like to downgrade his role at the bank to non-executive chairman. My father bridled, but complied. Carlton Brothers was subsequently awarded the privatization.

But now his enemies have re-emerged. If the Select Committee focuses on Carlton Brothers tomorrow, there'll be ample opportunity to smear the non-executive chairman. My father will never get the junior Ministry of Defence Procurement post he has been promised, in fact he'll be lucky to retain his current committee seats: his political career, to all intents and purposes, will be over.

'Another?' Sir Charles offers to take my glass.

I down the last of the champagne and he goes to fetch more. The chatter from the guests is quite loud, they must have been here a good while. How many of them, I wonder, know about Daniel? More than a few, judging by the sympathetic and rather awkward looks I'm getting. Soon the condolences will begin, but for the time being I gaze fixedly into the middle distance, holding them off.

The end of my father's political career is not by any means our worst problem. If the Select Committee launches an assault on him tomorrow it will rebound on the bank. It's too late for him to resign the chairmanship now – that would simply be a tacit concession of defeat. An attack on him will hurt Carltons, no question. But worse, Vance thinks it will harm the Meyers bid. What that means for us we know only too well.

Tonight was to be our last-ditch effort at containment, but most of those we were to threaten and cajole haven't come. The day seems set to finish as it began: another disaster.

'You needn't have come over, Raef.' Mary Needham. She touches my arm. 'Edward's in his study.'

Frail but formidable, that's how Theresa describes her. A widow, Mary's been a frequent guest at Boddington, our Gloucestershire estate, lately. She's my father's first female companion since my mother passed away. A good woman, and I won't be sorry if, as he's hinted, he finally marries her.

'You needn't have.'

'I look that bad?'

'My dear' – she rests her hand on my arm – 'You look awful.'

'What have I missed?'

'Here?' Her change of tack is masterly: she scans the room. 'Not the most inspiring collection.'

She begins putting names to the faces I don't know. Charles Aldridge returns with my glass and completes the picture: a master of the influence game, he knows everyone. It seems we've ended up with several makeweight MPs and their wives, a scattering of industrialists and their wives, a handful of bureaucrats – Treasury and Department of Trade – unaccompanied, and in the far corner of the room a cluster of my father's friends from the Ministry of Defence.

'Not quite the turnout we'd hoped,' Charles remarks dryly, a knuckle resting on his chin. 'Still. Do what we can.'

Undaunted, he moves off to mingle. Mary touches my sleeve.

'Edward,' she says, and when I follow her gaze I see my father in the doorway of his study, watching me.

Time to face the dreadful moment.

The study door closed and locked, he sits behind his desk and gestures to a chair. He looks up and I see the puffiness around his red-rimmed eyes. My heart lurches.

'Terrible business,' he says.

His eyes flicker down again and he studies the desk in silence. Even the reflection of his grief for Daniel is painful. Looking around at the leather-bound books, I wait for him to regather his composure.

'John called,' he remarks finally. 'Apparently the police were at the bank asking questions.'

'Daniel was shot.'

'Yes. Do they know any more? I've tried to phone you.'

'I went to see Celia.'

'All day?'

'I went for a walk.'

His look becomes searching. This afternoon I walked for hours down by the river, past Chelsea; just walked and remembered.

We must have been nine years old when Daniel spent his first summer down at Boddington. By then we'd become friends at school and the holiday turned into an extended exploration of the estate. My parents had given me a spaniel pup, Sergeant, at the start of summer; he went with us everywhere: we swam down at the weir and played in the barns, plunging like stuntmen from the loft onto broken bales of hay. We'd rise early to go and watch the dairymen, and the gamekeeper took us on his rounds, checking crow traps and shooting squirrels.

And then something happened. One afternoon my mother sent me to fetch Daniel back to the house for tea; he'd gone down to the river to play. When I got down there I heard splashing so I knelt in the grass and crept forward, meaning to scare him when I crested the riverbank. He was there all right, but I froze when I saw him. He wasn't playing. He was crouched on his haunches at the water's edge, long forked stick in hand, and he was using the stick to fend Sergeant away from the safety of the bank. There was no other way up from the river. Sergeant was drowning.

Hey.

Daniel turned as I scrambled down the bank; immediately he dropped the stick.

What are you doing?

He was dirty, Daniel said.

Sergeant, tiny chest heaving, clambered whimpering onto the bank.

Was not.

Was so, Daniel said.

And he looked at me then in a way I've never forgotten: burning with some inner rage, hurt, and yet behind it all deeply remorseful. I picked up the pup and scrambled up the bank, Daniel at my heels.

You won't tell, he said.

I didn't answer at first; I made him suffer till we got near the house.

We'll say he fell in, he said. You won't tell.

Next time I'll tell.

I put Sergeant down and he shook himself; he was shivering, but he wasn't going to die. Daniel prodded him with his foot.

He's not yours, he's mine, I said.

That look came back into his eyes: hurt and remorseful. I didn't understand it at all then. But he was nine years old, his father was dead, and for some reason his mother didn't want him over summer. When my mother called us inside, Daniel crouched and tickled Sergeant's ear.

We'll say he fell in, he said.

Did I sense even then how much he wanted what I had, the warm affection of a family? But if I did, why in the world, when we went inside, did I calmly explain to my mother that Daniel had just tried to drown Sergeant in the river?

'Are you all right, Raef?'

I look up, returned to the present. 'I'm all right.'

'I called Stephen,' my father says. Stephen Vance. 'He seems to think it won't derail the Meyers bid.'

'No.'

'Good.' He lowers his eyes. 'Good,' he repeats faintly.

This is even worse than I'd feared. I explain that I'll be giving Vance a hand for a while, but this doesn't seem to register.

'Shocking business,' he murmurs again. He peers down at the desk.

Years ago, Daniel was like a second son to him and he seems to have slipped back there now, to those earlier times before disappointment with Daniel set in.

He served with Daniel's father during the War, they remained friends, each becoming godfather to the other's first and – as it turned out – only child. But Daniel's family lived down in Dorset, and I don't recall ever seeing Daniel until my third year of prep school. I was an adult, about twenty-five, before my father thought it appropriate to tell me most of the story.

Daniel's father, after bankrupting the family business, had committed suicide. It was reported in the papers as a shooting accident, and in Daniel's presence that's how it was always referred to: your father's accident. But the life-insurers proved beyond doubt that it was suicide. The family was ruined. My father felt honour-bound to take over responsibility for Daniel's education. He never explained why this entailed moving Daniel out of his old school, or why Daniel spent so many holidays with us instead of returning to Dorset to his mother.

My own mother came to treat Daniel like a second son, too. Perhaps my father is remembering both of them now. His shoulders sag.

'Charles doesn't seem hopeful,' I say, gesturing back to the door. A feeble attempt to move us on.

But to my relief he grasps this straw. He pushes a list of names across the desk.

'Tonight's guest list. A red dot by the refusals.'

The red dots are liberally scattered; everyone of consequence has declined. I hand the sheet back, and he regards it thoughtfully. We both know that just ten years ago, when my grandfather was alive and Carltons was still a real force in the City, there wouldn't have been a single no-show.

'There's no need for you to stay, Raef.'

'I'm here now.'

'Have a night in with Theresa.'

'She's still down in Hampshire with Annie.'

He lifts his eyes from the sheet.

'Her father's quite ill,' I explain.

He nods without comment. He knows me too well not to have realized over the past few weeks that something is amiss with my marriage; he knows, but tonight all other concerns are dwarfed by the memory of Daniel. He passes a hand over his face.

'What have the police found?'

'I haven't spoken to them.'

'The whole thing,' he says quietly, brow furrowed. 'So bloody pointless.'

We drift into silence again. He stares at the guest list, unseeing. He's thin and pallid, on the backs of his hands the veins stand up pale blue. We have had our differences – most, though not all, about the bank – but right here and now I want to feel that we're together in our grief. I want to feel that every one of the walls between us is down.

'Father. Remember when I told you Daniel was going to blow the whistle on Odin?'

He rises slowly and comes round the desk. He stops by my chair.

'Let it go, Raef.'

'The other night—'

'Let it go.'

A moment later and the door is unlocked and

opened, and the sound of chattering guests breaks in.

'They're expecting us,' he says.

By the time I turn round he has gone.

Half an hour later, and I regret not leaving while I had the chance. The women all want to discuss the latest Impressionist exhibition at the Royal Academy and their husbands seem fixated on the cricket. England are touring the West Indies; to everyone's amazement we've won the first Test. And every five minutes someone feels it necessary to turn me aside and offer a few discreet words of personal condolence. Inevitably there are questions: Where? Who did it? Why? To all of which my answer is a silent shake of the head and a long blank gaze into my glass.

Charles Aldridge comes over to save me from my current persecutor, a woman I barely know who goes back to discuss Cézanne with her friends. He asks me if I've spoken to Gerald Wolsey yet.

'Wolsey?'

'Like the Cardinal. Big wig in the DTI.' The Department of Trade and Industry. 'He's over there with Lyle.'

Charles nods to the terrace windows and I freeze. Darren Lyle.

'What the hell's he doing here?'

'Who, Darren?'

'Yes,' I say. 'Lyle.'

'He's giving evidence at the Select Committee

tomorrow. Edward thought a little courtesy wouldn't go amiss.'

I make a sound. The idea that courtesy might have any effect on Darren Lyle is faintly absurd.

'Yes,' Charles murmurs. 'Your father does have these notions.'

Like most who have had dealings with him, Charles is well-acquainted with the more unpleasant aspects of Darren's character. Darren Lyle once worked for us at Carlton Brothers: for two years he was Vance's deputy in Corporate Finance. It's since leaving us that his career has really taken off: through a fierce application of his Darren-Lyle-first policy, he's risen to the Managing Directorship of Sandersons, another independent merchant bank much like ours. As it happens they're running the Parnells' defence against the Meyers. I'm not sure how much of his smiling insincerity I can take tonight.

'If you want to slip away,' Charles suggests, 'now might be the time.' But just then Darren spots us; immediately he leads Wolsey across the room.

'Too late,' Charles murmurs.

'Raef.' Face fixed into show of sorrow. Darren Lyle thrusts out his hand: 'I can't tell you, I mean Daniel, Jesus, do they know what it's about?'

'No.'

'I heard he was shot, is that right?'

'Darren,' I say tightly, freeing my hand: 'not now.'

He nods, straightening his tie. 'Right. Right. Unbelievable.'

Charles intervenes, introducing me to Gerald Wolsey, and the conversation turns. Wolsey, it seems, was one of the mandarins behind the push to set up a committee in the City to promote 'best practice' standards across the Square Mile. This committee has become one of Lyle's pet projects. He chairs monthly meetings in the Sandersons' Boardroom. In tribute to the chef at Sandersons, and the hopelessness of the committee's task, it's now referred to almost universally as the Best Lunches Group. I wonder if anyone's ever mentioned that to Gerald Wolsey. An earnest-looking man, one of the grey legion that swarms into Whitehall from the suburbs each morning, I have a feeling he wouldn't see the joke. When Charles begins to quiz Wolsey on some internal politicking at the DTI, I take Lyle by the elbow, drawing him aside.

'Why did you come?'

'Your old man asked me. Why, what's the problem? I shouldn't have come?'

He is a picture of innocence; I restrain a sudden impulse to punch him.

'You're not welcome.'

'I'll get you a drink.'

He wanders across to the nearest waiter. Darren Lyle. Amazing, after all these years, how even the sight of him can make my hackles rise. The man exudes vigour, like some cannibal who's devoured more than his fair share of enemies; several years ago he made an attempt on Daniel and me.

Now he chats to the waiter and smiles in my direction.

Daniel was Deputy to the Deputy Treasurer then, and I'd been in Corporate Finance for just a year. Lyle, answering to Stephen Vance, was my senior: he seemed to take me under his wing. Darren. Darren bloody Lyle. He came within an ace of finishing me.

We were working on the defence for Azart Industries at the time, a Midlands manufacturer. Lyle seemed to get cold feet about the price we'd recommended they accept. He made quite a show of it, trailing his doubts in front of me every hour. Eventually he suggested we might ask someone from our Treasury whose discretion we could rely on; someone who could give us a feel for what the market thought. I mentioned Daniel. And the rest, as they say, is history: I broke the rules. With a nudge and a wink from Lyle, I spoke to Daniel about Azarts, breaching the Chinese Wall between the two departments. I reported Daniel's thoughts back to Lyle, who surprised me by pointing out that I'd broken the bank's internal rules. He seemed annoyed. And that afternoon the Azarts share price took off. Before close-of-trade Darren was quizzing me on Daniel's integrity, implying that I'd made an horrendous mistake. The next morning, after a sleepless night, I was confronted by another barrage of questions as the Azart share price continued to rise. Was I sure, Lyle wanted to know, that Daniel and I weren't buying for our own accounts? I swore we weren't. He told me not to tell Vance or there'd be real trouble. He suggested I have a quiet word with my father, still Carltons' MD, and have Daniel dismissed. The world seemed to be caving in.

Then Stephen Vance called me into his office. He'd seen Lyle and me in whispered conference; he'd been watching the Azart share price; and he'd noticed me sitting in distraction at my desk.

Perhaps you might like to tell me, Vance said, exactly what the hell is going on.

And I did. To this day I'm not sure why. When I finished my story, Vance had Daniel come in. Daniel confirmed what he knew, and swore, like me, that he'd spoken to no one else about Azarts.

Vance ordered us to take the rest of the week off while he looked into it. When we returned to work the next week, Darren Lyle had already resigned and gone to head the Corporate Finance Department at Sandersons. Later Vance told me what he thought had happened. Darren had his sights set on the MD's chair at Carltons, but he knew I'd always stand in his way. Vance suspected, but couldn't prove, that Lyle himself had been behind the rising Azarts share price. Had Vance not intervened when he did, Lyle had ready everything he needed to blacken my name for ever. It was a rough awakening to the dirty realities of corporate politics.

But Lyle, in the years since, has prospered. He now has his coveted Managing Directorship, and access to some of the best boardrooms in the country.

As he returns across the room with the champagne I notice that he's put on a good deal of weight lately. His flat, broad face and squat build give him the look of a prizefighter gone to seed.

'So,' he says, handing me a glass, 'who gets Daniel's job?'

'You think I'd tell you?'

'You might.'

I sip my drink and gaze past him. Have I ever really had anything to say to Darren Lyle?

'Quin's going to blow Vance out of the water,' he remarks. Quin is Vance's opposite number at Sandersons, the man working on the Parnells defence. 'You want money on it?'

'No.'

'Lost faith in Vance, eh?'

'Darren. You're a prick.'

For a second his look turns icy. Then it softens, and his eyes narrow. He raises his glass and smiles up at me. 'To Daniel,' he says.

FRIDAY

1

The first thing next morning, I find Becky placing a vase of flowers on the bookshelf by my desk.

'I thought it'd brighten the place up,' she explains. 'You know.'

With an effort I try to return her smile.

'We had to give statements,' she tells me as she arranges the flowers. 'The police came. Just us from the boat.' The boat down by Blackfriars she means, where the party was held. I go and sit at my desk. The paperwork, as usual, is inches deep. When Becky faces me there are tears in her eyes. 'Who would want to shoot him, Raef? Why would they?'

But what can I say? Fate? Was it the stumble of a blind and senseless universe? Or dare I tell her the unpleasant truth, that Daniel might actually have deserved it?

'I don't know, Becky.'

Frowning, she returns her attention to the flowers. Sir John appears in the doorway.

'One of the Inspectors is here,' he says. 'If you're free, he'd like a word.'

When I enter the Boardroom, the Inspector's over by the rear wall studying my grandfather's portrait. He turns and drops his hand from his chin. 'Mr Carlton?' Shaking hands, he tells me his name: Ryan. 'Strong family resemblance,' he says, glancing back to the portrait.

I explain that I don't have much time. He gestures to a chair.

'Won't take a moment.' We sit facing each other across a corner of the table. 'I understand you and the deceased were friends.'

'Do you want some kind of statement?'

'That shouldn't be necessary.' He raises a brow. 'Unless you want to give one, of course.'

I tell him, no, not particularly.

'I need to know a bit more about Stewart,' he says.

It jars to hear Daniel's name like this from a stranger; but Ryan seems to expect a response, so I nod.

'Anything that might give us some inkling why he was shot.' He pauses. 'You did know he was shot?'

'Yes, I spoke with his wife.'

Ryan takes out a notepad. Pencil poised, he asks, 'When did you last see him?'

'At the party, on the boat.'

He jots this down. 'Didn't say or do anything out of the ordinary? Didn't seem worried?' He glances up. 'This isn't a statement, Mr Carlton. Just a few notes to aid a bad memory. Don't let it put you off.' He repeats his questions.

'I'm not sure,' I tell him. 'I didn't get much chance to speak with him.'

'Was he drunk?'

'He'd had a few, but he wasn't drunk. Who said he was?'

The Inspector smiles. 'It was just a question. I understand his position here was quite important.'

'He was Head of Treasury.'

'Which entails what?'

'Haven't you got this already?'

He taps his pencil on his notepad. 'Bear with me,' he says.

I want this over with, so I give the Inspector a brief description of Daniel's responsibilities as Treasurer. He was in charge of Carltons' whole trading operation, responsible for a daily turnover of several hundred million pounds. Foreign exchange, gilts, bonds and equities, he oversaw them all, both interbank and into the international exchanges. A major position at the bank. Ryan listens, but writes none of it down.

'And he answered to you,' he says when I finish.

'That's right.'

'His position was likely to make him enemies, I understand.'

I remark that any position is likely to make a man enemies. Ryan takes a moment with that.

'Not just here,' he says. 'Among the other banks. And your clients, possibly?'

'Nobody's in this business to make friends, Inspector.'

He looks at me very directly. 'How did he get on with the Meyers?'

The Meyer brothers? Where do they come into this?

'They're Vance's clients,' I say.

'Some takeover, I'm told. The Meyer Group for Parnells?' Ryan flicks back through his notebook but can't seem to find what he wants. 'That's the biggest piece of business you're involved with just now, isn't it?'

'Probably.' In fact this bid is the biggest deal the bank's been involved with for almost two years. I rest my forearms on the table. 'That bid's in the balance, Inspector. I don't think the Meyers would appreciate being drawn into this without good reason.'

He glances at his notepad. 'They've been quite cooperative, actually.'

'You've spoken to them?'

'An hour ago.'

Christ Almighty. I'll have to take Vance over there to reassure them. Soon.

And this Ryan, I've read him completely wrong. The heavy moustache and the prop-forward's build give the impression of lumbering slowness; a fake impression, I realize now. Sitting up, I start to pay a good deal more attention.

'Cast your mind back over the past year, Mr Carlton. Any particular deal went badly wrong? No major dispute Stewart was involved with?'

'Dozens.'

'No particular one?'

I shake my head. I ask if he'd like a tea or coffee, but he politely declines. He rises and studies my grandfather's portrait again.

'More like you than your father,' he remarks.

Surprised, I ask if he knows my father.

'Telly,' he explains. 'Rather out of my class, Lord Belmont.' This comment lands like a fly on a still pool of water. I let it drift by. 'Sir John tells me he might be retiring soon,' he says, turning. 'You'll replace him?'

'That's the board's decision.'

Ryan looks sceptical.

'It's likely,' I concede.

He asks what the change would have meant to Daniel.

'I don't follow.'

'Well presumably your own position would become vacant. Could Stewart have expected to replace you?'

'He would have been considered.'

Ryan leans against the wall. 'Who else was in the running?'

And then I see what he's getting at. 'Are you serious?'

He looks at me, waiting for an answer.

I hold up three fingers and tick them off one by one. 'Treasury, Funds Management, Corporate Finance. The head of each department would normally have his hat in the ring.'

'Not this time?'

I explain that Tony Mannetti, the boss of Fund Management, joined less than a year ago from New York. 'He wouldn't even be hoping.'

'And now Stewart's dead,' he says. He lets the implication hang there: the way's now clear for Stephen Vance. 'Who was likely to take over Stewart's job?'

'Me, for the time being.'

'And when things settle down?'

When things settle down. This seems such an impossibly distant prospect right now that I find myself smiling hopelessly. I tell him that the question of Daniel's replacement is still open, to be sorted out later with my father and Sir John.

He repockets his notepad, telling me he's expecting the full autopsy report later in the day.

'I thought Daniel was shot. No?'

'Three times, close range. We've found two of the bullets; they're being run through ballistics.' Ryan pulls at the flesh below his chin. 'I doubt the autopsy'll tell us anything, but we live in hope.'

He asks if I can show him to Vance's office. I rise and go to the door.

'You wouldn't know, would you,' he says as we go

down the corridor, 'if Stewart had any serious private problems?'

'Not that I know of.'

He nods, unperturbed. 'If you have any ideas . . .'

'Sure.'

Back in the privacy of my own office, I sit awhile replaying the interview in my mind. What kind of man is Inspector Ryan? Persistent? Lax? Overworked? Looking southward, I watch the dark clouds building: there will be rain again later. Persistent. Definitely persistent. I swivel back to my desk. Becky's moved the vase down from the bookcase; already the flowers are wilting. How well, I wonder, has Odin been buried? I blow on the flowers, and ever so gently they stir.

2

'I'm sorry you were dragged into it,' Vance tells Reuben and David Meyer. 'If we could have done anything to prevent it, we would have.'

Vance and I agreed on the way over that an upfront apology would be best; it isn't a situation either of us have dealt with before. Now Reuben, the older brother, looks thoughtful. But David stands and points.

'Don't wait for our thank-yous,' he says. 'How do you think it looks, police inspectors here? It's your problem.'

Reuben says something in Yiddish. David reluctantly retakes his seat. The profiles in the press say David is fifty-five, but up close you can see he's older by a good ten years: journalistic error, I wonder, or vanity?

'Mr Vance,' Reuben says evenly. 'How does this affect the bid?'

'It doesn't,' Vance tells him.

David Meyer mutters. He wants us to know he isn't happy. Vance told me weeks ago that David was difficult, but this is the first time I've seen him in action. Already I feel like throwing something heavy in his direction.

'If we stick to what we planned,' Vance continues, 'there's no reason for any disruption.' He nods towards me. 'Raef'll be acting as our Treasurer for the duration of the bid.'

I see this catches David by surprise.

'Yes,' Reuben says. 'Good.'

Before David can raise an objection, Vance takes two folders from his briefcase, handing one to each brother. He gives a verbal report on progress to date and Reuben Meyer listens. David studies the folder. I heard all this in the taxi, so now I let my eyes wander. There's a faded kelim hanging on the wall, and a brass bowl on a stand in the corner. Reuben's desk is old rather than antique, and the whole place has the feel of a counting house in some Middle Eastern souk. But as far as I'm aware, neither brother has ventured much further east than Canary Wharf since the family fled from Poland to London during the War. The decoration is Reuben's taste, I'd say.

When Vance finishes, David looks up. 'You still think we must raise the bid?'

As soon as possible, Vance tells him.

'Monday?'

'Monday morning if we can. Drive the holding up over forty per cent fast and keep the pressure on.'

The talk moves on to a possible number, the amount the bid should be raised. Not having spent weeks ploughing through the relevant spreadsheets, there isn't much I can contribute here. Nothing, in fact, so I listen. Vance does most of the talking, David makes frequent interventions, and Reuben stays as silent as me. All four of us desperately want this deal to go through. For the Meyers it will be an emphatic statement that in the premier league of property developers they've risen to the top of the table. But for Vance and me the matter is much more urgent. If the Meyers get Parnells the simmering revolt in our Corporate Finance Department will die. But if the Meyer bid fails . . . Listening to Vance now, I squeeze my forehead. It's just occurred to me that the only thing between Carltons and calamity at this moment is Stephen Vance's silver tongue.

After twenty minutes the talk reaches stalemate. Vance wants them to raise their bid from a 160p cash equivalent to 180p: the Meyers think 170p is enough.

'180 if you want to be sure,' Vance says.

Reuben smiles. 'If we really wanted to be sure we'd

bid 200. What we want, Mr Vance is not to waste our money.'

Vance looks suitably chastened. David Meyer turns to me.

'Who killed your Treasurer?' Before I can collect myself, he goes on: 'I mean, who had reasons to kill him?'

'That's what the police are trying to find out.'

'I'm not asking the police,' he says. 'I'm asking you.'

I feel Vance and Reuben both watching me.

'I've no idea.'

'Someone just shot him – your Treasurer – and you've got no idea?'

'Has this got something to do with Parnells?'

'I don't know,' says David Meyer, folding his arms. 'Has it?'

Beneath my breath, I count to ten. 'The police are pursuing their inquiries. In the extremely unlikely event of the murder having even a remote connection to your bid, we'll let you know.'

'Please do,' he says, unsmiling.

A frosty silence follows, then I rise and there's a round of perfunctory handshakes. Vance and I are passing out the door when David calls after us. 'And in the extremely unlikely event that we agree to a raised bid, Mr Carlton, don't call us, we'll call you.'

He closes the door firmly at our backs.

'What's up with him?'

'He's been like that from day one.' Vance steps after

me into the taxi. He gives the driver Carltons' address. 'Nothing personal. David's got rudeness like the rest of the world's got manners.' He rests his briefcase on his lap and his tanned hands on the briefcase. His week's holiday in Mauritius last month must seem an eternity ago. 'What did you think?'

'If anyone can convince them, Stephen, you can.'

'Vote of confidence noted,' Vance says, facing me. 'Now, what did you think?' Even after I'd worked with him for years I could never match Vance's relentless and absolutely focused attention on the deal. Now it's like being taken in the grip of a creature whose power I'd long forgotten.

'They're not idiots,' I suggest. 'They'll come to the party.'

Vance doesn't reply. A hollow feeling forms in the pit of my stomach.

'Stephen?'

'Let's hope so,' he says tapping his case. 'Why do you think he was asking about Daniel?'

The name hovers between us a moment, a spectral presence in the taxi; the nether world intruding on the everyday.

'I don't know. Just being bloody?'

'Maybe.' He flips open his briefcase and digs through the paperwork, handing me two sheets: the current acceptances on the bid and a copy of a Sandersons' press release issued this morning. When a bid for a public company is launched, the clock starts ticking: the bidder has sixty days in which to win

41

control, and if they haven't succeeded after that, they're obliged by the Takeover Code to withdraw for twelve months before trying again. Right now we're weeks into the Meyer bid and, looking at the sheet, it's clear that acceptances remain low. As Vance has been telling the Meyer brothers, they'll have to raise their offer. The second sheet, the Sandersons' press release, is a masterly piece of innuendo. It manages to call into question the competence and integrity of the Carltons' analysts who did the numbers on Parnells, and concludes – this must be Lyle's touch – with condolences on the unexplained death of our Treasurer. The impression it leaves is of a bank gone rotten at the core.

I hand back the sheets. 'What now?'

'On Clover?' Clover, the code name we're using for the Meyer deal. 'We wait,' he says. 'Nothing more we can do until they decide a new number. Are you sure you shouldn't be taking some time off?'

'I'm okay.'

He nods, unconvinced, and considers me a moment. 'I don't want to sound like a hypocrite, Raef, but I'm sorry about Daniel.'

My throat constricts. I mumble a few words of thanks.

'I wasn't in Daniel's fan club,' he says, 'but something like that . . . Has that Inspector got any ideas what happened?'

'He was shot.'

Vance looks thoughtful, he closes his briefcase. 'I

mean, does he have any idea who did it?'

'He doesn't seem to.'

'No idea why?'

I turn my head, and gaze out at the passing City buildings, things of the world, all strangely diminished this morning.

'Take some time off,' Vance suggests quietly.

'I don't need it.'

'I think you might.'

His simple consideration touches me more than I thought possible. 'What happened to Carl?'

'Carl, my brother?'

I nod. Vance looks at me uneasily.

'He's still in Canada, lecturing at McGill. Raef,' he says, 'you don't have to come back to the office.'

The City buildings hang over us now, oppressive and grey.

'When you write,' I say, 'send Carl my regards.'

Vance holds my look a moment longer, then his glance slides politely away.

3

After lunch, Karen Haldane comes into my office and places a folder on my desk.

'I think we've got a problem,' she says. She's our Chief Compliance Officer, her remit is to ensure both in-house and general market regulations are adhered to by everyone at the bank. An accountant by profession, she also sits on the bank's audit committee: not a woman to be worried unduly.

Opening the folder, I take out the only page and read. It's a few lines of Daniel's almost illegible scrawl.

'From Daniel's office,' she tells me. 'I needed last week's numbers, I found this—' she points to the note '—on top of the file.'

'His office is locked.'

'I've got a spare key.' I look at her. 'Well, was I meant to ring Scotland Yard?' she says.

I tell her it might be an idea if she stays out of there until Inspector Ryan's finished.

She isn't pleased. 'What about this?'

The note. I manage, eventually, to decipher it. And when I do, my heart sinks. I drop the page back into the folder. 'Bin it.'

'What?'

'Karen, it's just a few numbers and a few question marks.'

She reopens the folder and points. 'Did you see that? "Speak to Henry"?' Henry Wardell, presumably, our Chief Dealer. 'And see these other numbers, they look like losses. See this?'

I don't look down.

'Why did he need to speak to Henry if it wasn't about the Dealing Room?' she asks.

'No idea.'

'They could be Dealing Room losses.'

'We're a bank, Karen, it happens. But if you want to follow it up, have a word with Henry.'

Becky comes through on the intercom, reminding me I'm due in Westminster: the Select Committee hearing. I assure her I'm just leaving.

Annoyed now, Karen picks up the folder. I reach over the desk, open hand extended.

'Just for safe-keeping,' I say. 'Daniel's spare key?'

4

My father's office in Westminster is small and dark. His secretary informs me that he's already gone down to the Committee Rooms, so I head down there too. Walking the corridors like this reminds me of the times my grandfather brought me here as a child. My boyhood memories of the place are fond ones but, more recently, the place has taken on a rather different aspect: a gilded Victorian dream of the Medieval world, its mock-Gothic fantasy now leaves me cold.

A servant of the House opens the Committee Room door to me.

The hearing has already commenced. Up near the Committee, a bank of camera lights shines fiercely. The rows of seats around the room are nearly all full, but just down the aisle my father has kept a seat free.

Slipping in beside him, I ask in a whisper, 'Lyle said his piece yet?'

He gives a brief shake of the head. Glancing around

the panelled room, I recognize a few faces, but only a few; this is my father's world, not mine. But the man answering questions I do know. It's Roger Penfield, even with his back turned he's unmistakable: broad shoulders, a well-tanned scalp that gleams beneath the camera lights and a voice as smooth as velvet. He's the Deputy Governor of the Bank of England. But I seem to have arrived just as the Committee Chairman's thanking him for his time. Penfield rises and buttons his jacket. As he walks past me on his way to the door he grins and rolls his eyes: Westminster, apparently, isn't his favourite place either.

The Committee Chairman consults his agenda and asks if Darren Lyle is here. While Darren makes his way to the table up front, there's a general stir as everyone stretches, or talks with a neighbour; some – Bank of England colleagues, I presume – follow Penfield out of the door.

I cover my mouth. 'Daniel left a note on the Odin loss.'

My father acknowledges someone across the room. 'Yes?' he says, smiling with his teeth.

'Our compliance officer found it.'

'Is it a problem?'

'I don't think so. It's just the numbers. Odin isn't named.'

My father considers a moment. 'If you can stop it without a fuss, stop it. If not, don't worry, it can't be traced.'

Nodding, I drop my hand. Darren has settled into place before the Committee, the room falls quiet now. The Chairman welcomes him, and asks him to give a quick outline of the work done by the 'Best Practice' committee. Darren complies, but when he starts to ramble the Chairman cuts him off.

'Thank you. Now perhaps we can move on to some specifics, Mr Lyle. If you don't mind.'

'I don't mind.'

The Chairman doesn't like it, but Darren's riposte draws a titter from the room. Maybe there really is some substance to the rumours that Lyle's considering a move into politics: playing to the gallery is something he does well.

A series of questions and answers follows. The Committee members try to score points off one another, while Darren remains polite and helpful; a side of him we never saw much when he worked at Carltons. My gaze wanders down to my watch. I'm tired, but when I find myself drifting into thoughts of Daniel I take a deep breath and look up. I can't afford to dwell on it. Not now.

It's fifteen minutes later before they finally touch on the matter that concerns Carltons.

'I understand your "Best Practice" committee produced a series of guidelines for those banks which wished to tender for Government business.'

'Yes, that's right,' Darren Lyle says.

'The guidelines would cover privatization business too?' the Chairman prompts.

Lyle nods. 'Among other things.'

The Chairman asks when the guidelines were published. Lyle tells him.

'So they were published before tenders were invited for the privatization of the Government Laboratories, then. Is that right?'

'Months earlier,' Lyle agrees.

Carltons was the Government's main adviser on the deal; we underwrote the flotation. It must be clear to a good many in the audience just what this is building up to. Darren Lyle, we all know, is no friend of Carltons.

'And would you say, Mr Lyle,' the Chairman enquires, 'that your committee's guidelines were respected in this particular case?'

This is Darren's big moment, he pauses as if he's actually considering the question.

'No,' he says at last. 'No, I wouldn't.'

I sense the eyes turning towards my father and me. After all Lyle's innuendo, we really don't look good. But this damaging moment is suddenly broken when a northern MP on the Committee remarks, 'Aye. But 'twould 'a' been with proper law, not daft guideline rubbish.'

The Chairman goes scarlet. Another Committee member chokes back a laugh, and a murmur of amusement ripples around the room. It becomes louder when Darren cranes round and everyone sees how cross he looks. More than cross, he is absolutely livid.

'Mr Lyle,' the Chairman says, trying to reassert himself. 'Would you tell us exactly how the guidelines were breached?'

Darren obliges. He does his best to maintain a note of shocked surprise at how the privatization was carried out: he even mentions Carltons by name several times, but the sting's been taken out of it now. After the northern MP's gruff intervention, all Darren's fine phrases about probity, self-regulation and integrity just sound like so much City cant. He shifts uncomfortably in his seat as he speaks.

'It appears a horse and cart were driven through the guidelines,' the Chairman says.

'My committee's job was advisory, not regulatory,' Darren responds. He's defensive now.

Unexpectedly, we seem to have been carried over the worst of it. The Committee asks more questions, but Lyle answers with a good deal less enthusiasm than he showed earlier. The subject moves on from anything that might concern Carltons.

'Not so bad,' I whisper to my father.

He smiles, thin-lipped. We sit through another ten minutes of questions to Lyle before the Chairman looks left and right. 'Nothing else then? No? Nothing?' It appears to be over. He begins thanking Darren for his time, and I've half-risen from my chair when the only woman on the Committee speaks.

'Just one thing before you go, Mr Lyle.' She smiles disarmingly at the Chairman, who stops mid-sentence. I sit down. 'With your experience in the

City,' she says, 'perhaps you might suggest any other City-to-Government links that deserve this Committee's scrutiny.'

Darren pauses. 'The privatizations? I'm sorry, I'm not with you.'

He isn't the only one. The Chairman is looking at her curiously, this wasn't on his agenda.

'I'm thinking of particular areas,' she says. 'Departments. For example, the Department of Social Security and the City, links like that.'

Lyle drops his head to one side. She elaborates.

'If you could give us a specific department to focus on, it could save us some time.'

Beside me, my father stiffens.

'A particular department?' Lyle asks.

'Yes,' she tells him. 'If you can.'

Darren thinks a moment, trawling for some hidden reef, then he seizes the opportunity. 'Defence,' he says.

'Thank you,' the Chairman breaks in.

'And the general rule,' the woman concludes, 'is to keep Government and business apart?'

Darren turns in his chair, smirking. 'One time it doesn't pay to keep things in the family,' he says.

The eyes are on us again, and this time no one is laughing. Rage, pure rage, wells up in me. I feel the restraining pressure of my father's hand on my knee. The Chairman suggests a fifteen-minute break. There's no time to gauge how damaging Darren Lyle's last sally has been: the Committee rises, then we all rise, my father guiding me out ahead of the crush.

'Don't hang about,' he says in the corridor. 'We'll look ridiculous.'

'What's he playing at?'

'I'll speak with Charles.' He nods to the exit. 'Go on.'

But at the exit I look back to see Lyle in the corridor chatting amiably with that woman MP, and right beside them is Gerald Wolsey. Westminster games. Turning sharply, I walk from this shadowed place, out into the cold afternoon.

5

Sir John pours us both a drink. 'Stephen tells me you'll be working with him on the Meyer bid. Be like old times for you.'

I rest my arm along the back of the sofa. Sir John's office has no Reuters or Blomberg screen in here, and no PC; it feels more like a country-house library than a place of work. The Turner watercolour behind his desk is a piece from his private collection.

'That's not what I came about.'

'No,' he says, handing me my drink, 'I thought not.' He slumps into his favourite armchair. 'How were things at the Select Committee?'

'Penfield was there.'

'Darren Lyle?'

'Star of the show.' Running a finger around the

rim of my glass, I add: 'That's not what I came for either.'

He sips his whisky, then sighs. 'The arrangement?'

Yes, I tell him, the arrangement.

He takes a real swig this time. Carlton Brothers, under Sir John's instructions, and in my absence, has borrowed money from one of the clearing banks and used the funds to buy that same clearing bank's shares. Privately, at his club, I shouldn't be surprised, Sir John has agreed to warehouse this parcel. A cosy arrangement: they get protection from predators, and we get a powerful friend. The money has passed through enough intermediaries to make the transaction opaque, but in principle the deal is illegal. I want it undone.

'Useful friends,' he remarks of the clearing bank.

'Not once the Stock Exchange gets its teeth into us. They'll run a mile.'

'I don't believe so.'

'I don't want a debate, John. I just want us out of it.'

We've had this conversation once before. Then I suggested he undo the deal: now I'm telling him. Still nominally my superior, Sir John looks peeved.

'They'll be furious, Raef. They're relying on us.'

'Then you've got some work to do.'

Our eyes lock for a moment before his gaze slides away. He sips his drink. When my father resigned the Managing Directorship of Carltons nine years ago, there was some soul-searching before he appointed Sir John to replace him. I was ruled out early – still too young, my father thought. My turn, he promised me, would come. But the other candidate was Charles Aldridge, eminently suitable, and it cost my father a good few sleepless nights before he made his final decision. Sir John, Deputy Manager at Carltons then, got the nod. Charles seemed to take it well enough, but relations between him and Sir John have never been quite the same since. And more than once lately I've wondered if my father didn't perhaps choose the wrong man. I've nothing against Sir John, not personally. But professionally I've lost all faith in him. Nine years ago he was a good banker, exceptional even, but changes in the City and an over-fondness for alcohol have steadily clawed him down. The days when I admired him as much as I admire Stephen Vance are well and truly over. Yet for the man he was I retain a vestigial respect; next to my grandfather and Stephen Vance, Sir John has taught me more about banking than anyone.

I certainly don't enjoy seeing him hanging his head before me now. To help him over his embarrassment, I ask if he's coming down to the shoot at Boddington tomorrow.

'Wouldn't miss it,' he says. 'Wouldn't miss it.'

He seems relieved by the change in subject, and for a few minutes we discuss the shoot. But as soon as I feel I've soothed the bruises raised earlier, I set my glass down.

Disappointed, he urges me to stay.

'Just five minutes, Raef.'

Looking into his eyes, I see something I'd rather have missed. Sir John, the mentor of my youth and caretaker of my inheritance, doesn't want to be left drinking alone.

6

Noise crashes over me like a breaking wave; the markets are in full cry. Henry Wardell's behind his desk in the Dealing Room, almost hidden by a bank of screens and squawkboxes. His hands are cupped to his mouth, and he's shouting. The Chief Dealer at Carltons, this room is his domain.

When he pauses, I ask: 'What's the news?'

He points to a screen. The US Discount rate has risen half a per cent. The equities screen is awash with red numbers, but as I watch the numbers start turning blue: the bargain hunters moving in.

'Were we set?'

'We'll do okay this time.' Henry gives me a look. The last Rate rise we were caught flat-footed: our Chief Economist was convinced it wouldn't happen, and when it did we took heavy losses across the board. Our Chief Economist's name is William Butler: here in the Dealing Room they call him Billy Bullshit.

'Heard anything on Daniel?' Henry asks me.

I turn my head; no. He hits his keyboard and bonds replace equities on the screen.

'That fat bastard came to see me,' he says.

'Who? Ryan?'

'The Inspector guy.' He lifts his eyes from the screen and shouts at the bond desk. 'Dump it!'

'What was he after?'

'Christ knows.' Henry scribbles a number on his deal-sheet. 'Was Daniel different lately? Stuff like that.'

'What did you say?'

'Nothin'.'

There's another flurry of activity, an increase in volume. Henry shouts at the proprietary desk this time. In here Henry has none of the awkward self-consciousness he displays outside. Here in the loosely-reined chaos of the Dealing Room he's completely at home. In his mid-thirties now, he joined the bank a year or two before me, straight out of sixth form. Initially a clerk in Settlements, he convinced one of the desk managers out here to take him on as a trainee. Since then his career has been a steady rise, the past few years under Daniel's tutelage. He has a gaunt look, prominent cheekbones and sunken cheeks, and his voice now as he shouts across the room is surprisingly loud coming from such a small frame. But he doesn't bully, he commands: here in the Dealing Room he has earned their respect.

I ask him if Karen Haldane's been down.

'What for?'

I explain about the scribbled note Daniel left behind.

'Ahha,' Henry says.

Then Owen Baxter comes over. Owen tells Henry that one of our trading lines is full, not an unusual problem for a small bank like ours. We have limits on our exposure to all the counterparties in the market, other banks and institutions, and at busy times like this our trading lines fill fast. Generally we have to convince others to increase their exposure to us: this time, Owen explains, it's a small Canadian bank which needs our limit for them increased.

Henry asks by how much.

'Fifty in the one week.' Fifty million US, one week forward. 'They're the only decent bid we've seen,' Owen says.

Henry glances at me. The extra exposure will roll off in a week, and Owen looks like he really needs it. I nod.

'Okay, give them fifty,' Henry tells Owen. 'But that's it.'

Owen punches a fist in the air. He strides back to his desk and shouts, 'Stuff that fuckin' moosehead!'

Henry toys with his deal-sheet. 'What's this with Karen then?'

'Karen thinks Daniel's note looks like some losses we took out here.'

'So?'

'Your name was on it.' At this, Henry looks up. 'It said, "See Henry",' I tell him.

He shakes his head unhappily. 'Last time she was

chasin' a problem down here, I was stuffed in two nights runnin'. 1 a.m., 2 a.m. Me and Daniel both.'

'She's conscientious.'

'She's a fuckin' zealot.'

'Just make the right noises,' I say. 'Keep her happy. If she pushes too hard, let me know.'

'Can't you put her off?' There's a note of real despair in his voice.

I tell him I've delegated that particular responsibility. When he asks me who to, I just smile. Henry groans.

A hand reaches over the screens and dumps a pile of deal-sheets in front of him.

'Fuck,' Henry says. He picks up a pen and flicks through the deal-sheets, countersigning each one as he goes.

7

The rain has stopped. I send my driver home, telling him I won't need him till Monday. It's cold and dark, the wet pavement lit by streetlamps and the headlights of passing cars. The Square Mile is winding down now, the push and shove of commerce following daylight to another part of the globe. The other pedestrians are just like me, huddled in their coats and bowing their heads against the chill wind. A bleak night in the City of London.

Lights shine from some of the office buildings, but

most are unlit. It was like this when Daniel and I used to pace these streets over a decade ago. I don't know how many hours we spent wandering the City and scheming: too many, I suppose. We thought the future was something we'd make, a blank page to be written on. He'd rise through Treasury, become Treasurer one day, and turn our Dealing Room into something special. He did become Treasurer, and our Dealing Room grew, but the truth is it remains what you'd expect of a small British merchant, nothing special. And me? I was going to take over from my father and drive us into the world, re-make Carltons into what it was last century, into what my grandfather believed it could still be: a player on the international stage. One year short of my fortieth birthday, I can finally admit to myself that some of this might not happen. Sir John still holds the reins at Carlton Brothers, the big international players have arrived in the City, and on the home front, within the Carlton family, life has intervened.

Mounting the church steps, I hear the organ: something by Bach. Evensong is over now, but two old women have stayed, they sit up by the altar and listen to the organist practising. I slide into a pew near the door. A clergyman, grey-haired and shuffling, is reordering the hymn books. There's no haste in his movements. Time isn't money here: time is God's, a fragment of eternity. It's the kind of place my mother would have liked, but though I've passed it often, I've never been inside before.

'Can I help you?' The clergyman has paused, hymn books in hand.

I turn my head, and he goes back to his gentle task. Then the music stops. There's the sound of turning pages, and the two old ladies crane round and look up to the choir loft above my head. After a moment the organist finds his place and the music continues. A hymn this time. The women turn back to the altar. The clergyman makes his way down to the front and disappears into the vestry.

As the organ note swells for the refrain, I take a kneeler from the pew and place it on the floor. And this time when the music stops, I get to my knees and I pray.

SATURDAY

1

I tell Margie 'no eggs,' but she slides two onto my plate anyway. Our guests at the big kitchen table talk as they eat, and Margie, the housekeeper here at Boddington, goes back to the stove. The Duke has brought his two youngest daughters; and the girls sit on the high kitchen bench. I wink and they turn away giggling. Voices ring across the kitchen: the families and friends of those shooting have all crowded in.

Charles Aldridge leans over to me and says quietly: 'All right?'

I don't know if he means the business with Darren Lyle, or breakfast, or if he's enquiring about my state of mind. But when I nod he seems satisfied.

As usual lately, I haven't slept well. The bed Daniel used on his boyhood visits still sits beneath the window in my room; and on the landing this morning

I noticed the cracks in the old Chinese vase, the results of our hasty glue-work after Daniel misjudged a slide down the banister. I'd hoped for some respite here at Boddington but there are just too many signs that remain.

'Gentlemen?'

My father. He produces a leather pouch, and those of us shooting step up to draw our numbers. I draw between Charles and Mahmoud Iqbal, the Lebanese owner of a neighbouring estate, and ten minutes later, in a convoy of battered Land Rovers and four-wheel drives, we set out.

Ours isn't the largest estate in Gloucestershire, or even the most profitable, but the roots of my family run deep here. There were Carltons on this land in Elizabethan times when the peerage first came to us, and now, driving up the valley, I look back to the house – Cotswold stone, eighteenth century – and beyond to the five acres of garden that roll down to the river. Daniel and I fished that river last May. We skirt the arable fields, finally stopping by a hedgerow where the gamekeeper waits. Walking to the first pegs, the frosted ground crunches beneath my boots, and I feel life – real life – returning.

'Theresa did not come today?' Mahmoud.

'No,' I tell him. 'She's at her parents'. She'll be down tomorrow.' There's a memorial service for my mother, it wouldn't look right for Theresa to stay away.

Mahmoud, dressed in tweed, touches his

moustache absentmindedly. 'Good shot, Theresa.'

But when the gamekeeper signals us up to the first line I try to forget about my wife. I try to forget the bank and Daniel too. My father gave me an air-rifle when I was seven, a .22 when I was ten and a shotgun three years later; even as a boy I took my troubles out into the fields.

Now it begins. The beaters drive the pheasants from cover and we stand by our numbered pegs and fire; behind us there are compliments from family and friends. The gamekeeper blows his whistle – silence as the last shots fade – then the dogs race to gather the fallen birds. We switch to safety, unload, and exchange polite banter down the line. The last bird picked, we move to the next stand.

So it goes on, our idleness structured into the semblance of purpose all morning. My head gradually clears, and by midday I'm shooting quite well. An hour later and I've bagged more than ten brace.

Walking across to the barn for lunch, Charles steps up beside me.

'Plenty of birds,' he says.

There'd need to be the way he shoots, but I keep this uncharitable thought to myself.

'New keeper,' I explain. 'He put them down early.'

'Lyle gave quite a performance, I hear.' The Commons Committee. 'Made things rather uncomfortable for your father.'

I remind him that I was there.

'Quite,' he says ruefully. 'Has to be dealt with.'

Then he pockets an unused cartridge. 'We hoped you might have some thoughts, Raef.'

'I don't want Carltons involved.'

'After Lyle's little effort?' A significant pause, then he touches my elbow. 'We'll talk this evening.'

A misty rain has begun to fall, I feel the world closing in. The clean, clear morning is over.

2

Sir John considers the whisky in his glass. 'Vance is the obvious choice.'

Then he looks from my father to me. There are only four of us here by the drawing-room fire. Mary Needham left after dinner: business in London, she said, a tactfulness my mother would have appreciated. Sir John's wife has retired upstairs.

It's my job we're discussing, a possible replacement: after Daniel's death there'll have to be a reshuffle at the bank.

'Raef?' my father asks.

'It has to be Vance,' I agree. Then I face Sir John. 'This isn't a question until you fix a date.' The date of his retirement, not a subject he broaches easily. He keeps his eyes lowered. My father does too: it was his move into politics, his early retirement from Carltons, that first raised Sir John into place. Sir John has held this supposedly temporary position for three years now, and I'm more than a little tired of waiting for my chance to take over.

My father wonders aloud who will become Head of Treasury. I suggest Henry Wardell.

'You could look outside again,' Aldridge says. 'That Mannetti's worked out, hasn't he?'

In fact Tony Mannetti has worked out well, certainly better than I expected. He came to us from American Pacific, an aggressively expanding US bank with which we recently crossed swords. At Carltons we tend to promote internally, there was much debate before we decided to elevate Mannetti to head of Funds Management. I was the major opponent of the move, but the department seems to be responding, albeit sluggishly, to his pushy style. Still, I'm not entirely convinced. He has a short fuse and a temper which he occasionally unleashes on his subordinates, a trait I find less than endearing.

We toss a few more names around, other possibilities, but nobody mentions Daniel directly: it's always the title, Head of Treasury, as if Daniel's name is taboo. After a few minutes I can't bear any more of it and I stand and wander off around the room. It's dark in the far corners where the family portraits hang, but nearer there's a small Breughel, one of those winter scenes: peasants, snow-covered houses and a broad river of ice. My mother bought it in Paris: it was one of her favourite pictures. The flickering firelight plays across the human warmth and conviviality of the scene, a stark contrast to the disagreement developing between

Charles Aldridge and Sir John behind me.

Between my father's two friends there's always been a certain antagonism. They're very similar in many ways, but their disagreements these days seem to become more and more heated. Sir John's being selected for the Carltons' Managing Directorship certainly didn't help, but it runs deeper than that. They seem, at times, to be competing for my father's friendship. He's a few years older than them, and despite their both being over sixty they seem to look up to him. I'm sure it's more than just the title. In recent years Sir John's star has been on the wane, and now it's Charles my father generally turns to for advice over a quiet drink in the evening.

Their sallies go back and forth till the mantel-clock strikes ten. When I return to the fireside, Sir John, who's been flagging, takes himself off to bed. My father stokes the fire.

'Charles put some feelers out in Whitehall,' he says. 'About that Select Committee business.'

'Wolsey's in it up to his eyeballs,' Charles puts in. 'He and Darren Lyle both. That woman, what's her name? The MP?'

My father mentions the name.

Charles nods. 'Ex-CND ratbag. Got a bee in her bonnet about Defence. Wolsey primed her, had to have done.'

So it was a set-up, just as it seemed. But any illusions I harboured about Whitehall and

Westminster were dispelled years ago. I ask where Lyle comes in.

'Wolsey's chairing the DTI Committee that's been working with Lyle's City Committee,' he tells me.

I'm out of my depth here: any problems we have with Westminster I leave to my father; Charles takes care of Whitehall. Now I ask him what he thinks Wolsey's after.

Like an otter into the stream, Aldridge plunges in. He sketches the outlines of a battle currently raging between the Ministry of Defence and the Department of Trade and Industry. It seems the President of the Board of Trade is pushing to grant the tender for the next-generation sea-to-air weapons systems to a failing British manufacturer: the Ministry of Defence wants to buy American. Wolsey was the man who convinced the DTI President to nail his colours to the mast over the issue, and now he is pulling every string to make sure this particular ship doesn't go down. If the Ministry of Defence win the debate the DTI President will be acutely embarrassed. Heads will roll; most notably Gerald Wolsey's. Charles elaborates on the complex web of pressures: he loves all this; it's meat and drink to him.

I raise a hand to stop the flow. 'Does Wolsey get anything if they win?'

'If he pushes the policy through?' Charles raises a brow. 'Promotion. A seat at the High Table.'

'That doesn't interest Darren Lyle.'

Charles turns to my father with a significant look.

'Raef,' my father says quietly. 'We think Lyle might make a bid for the bank.'

It takes a moment for this to register. 'Carltons?'

My father nods stiffly. There are dark rings, I now notice, beneath his eyes.

Charles goes to the fireplace to warm his hands. He explains that if Lyle raises enough questions, Wolsey can justify sending a team of DTI investigators into Carltons.

'Where'd you hear this?'

'Once they're in,' he continues, ignoring my question, 'Wolsey will use anything they find as ammunition against your father. He'll also pass it to Lyle. Lyle will use it against you.'

I put down my glass. I still can't believe this.

Charles gives a world-weary smile, pushing a hand through his thick silver mane. 'No love lost between you two, is there?'

'There's a lot of people Lyle doesn't like.'

'The man's poison,' my father remarks. He knows about my run-in with Lyle. 'He's not all there. He might do anything.'

'It is possible, isn't it?' Aldridge asks me.

'A bid for Carltons?'

'Yes. I mean there's nothing to stop him, is there?'

'It's possible,' I concede. 'Unlikely, but possible.'

'And what if he can drive your share price down first?'

I consider. It's standard practice for a bidder to

talk down a target company, but with a small bank like ours the collateral damage might escalate uncontrollably.

'Any thoughts, Raef?' my father asks.

'Unlikely, isn't it? Where's the gain? Two British independents, what does that make? A bigger minnow?'

My father sniffs. Agreement? Dismissal?

'Wolsey won't let go of this,' Charles warns. 'It's probably his best chance for promotion before he retires. He'll make waves.'

But Wolsey's Whitehall not City. 'He's your department.'

'Not quite,' Charles says sipping his drink. 'I take your point though.'

The fire crackles in the grate and sparks fly upward in a shower of burning stars. I glance across to my father. This time last year, he and I sat right here discussing another bid for the bank. We'd been approached by American Pacific, they'd built up a small stake in us. They wanted to take it further, a full takeover. A sum of three hundred million pounds was mentioned; negotiation might have driven it to three fifty or more, a good price. My father was inclined to consider it, but I refused; the bank meant too much to me. It still does. And I certainly have no intention of letting it fall to Darren Lyle.

The wood shifts in the grate and the sparks fly upwards again.

'It would be useful,' my father says, 'if we knew a

little more about Lyle's intentions.'

He looks at me. My task, it seems.

The conversation continues, but we're soon in the realm of speculation, the economists' wasteland of Let-Us-Assume and What-If.

After twenty minutes my father rises to pour another whisky, but Aldridge has had enough. 'Country air,' he remarks yawning.

There's a round of 'Good nights' then he leaves us.

My father drops back into his chair. The crackling fire sounds very loud.

'How's Celia taken it?'

'Not well.'

'And the boys?'

'I haven't seen them.'

He nods, staring at the flames. After university, when Daniel was turned down by the Air Force, my father pulled strings to ease Daniel's way into his own old regiment, the Irish Guards. But when Daniel resigned his commission early my father took it personally: I'm not sure he ever forgave him. Even when I wanted to take Daniel on as a trainee at the bank, my father conceded with reluctance. Daniel was a big success at Carltons, but it never quite restored him to the favour he enjoyed as a boy.

My father is silent. There'll be no further mention of Daniel tonight.

'I'm not going to let Lyle get Carltons,' I tell him.

He closes his eyes. The firelight plays over his face, unforgiving.

'I'm tired,' he murmurs. 'You'll be tired too. Get some rest.'

A spark leaps onto the rug. I kneel and flick it back into the fire. But when I turn to speak, the words die on my lips. Lord Belmont, my father, suddenly looks like a very old man.

I take up my whisky and consider Darren Lyle: What if? But my thoughts soon slide into a deeper channel. Tomorrow I see Theresa and Annie.

my grandfather, his likes and dislikes tended to become mine: and my grandfather's life wasn't here at Boddington, his whole being was tied up with the City. I remember him taking me into his office as a boy, something my father never did. Edward's boy, Raef, he'd say, nudging me forward to shake a colleague's hand. He was a big man: this isn't a trick of memory, his portrait in the Boardroom confirms it. He was the kind who leaves an impression, gregarious and able: the family folklore has him besting Maynard Keynes in a public debate on the gold standard, and Keynes returning in private for advice.

My father isn't like that at all. He's self-effacing and diffident, people don't warm to him easily. In the City, I see now, he could never escape my grandfather's shadow. Only when my father inherited the title and a seat in the Lords did he really find freedom. He resigned the Managing Directorship of Carltons almost immediately. These past nine years there's been a change in the house-guests down here at Boddington; as my father's moved on from orchestrating votes and key speeches among the peers, the industrialists and bankers have been replaced by politicians and senior civil servants. The cartoonists draw my father as a wraith-like Victorian figure in top-hat and tails, a fair representation of the outward man I suppose. But what goes on behind this public façade even I find hard to understand. After almost forty years as his son, years in which he's passed on every material blessing he can give, the deep places of his heart remain a mystery to me. But I'm sure of this: Boddington, the ancestral seat of our family, he truly loves.

Nearing the stables now, I see Charles in the yard talking with someone. It looks like the groom, but then the groom appears from the stalls.

My father notices me squinting. 'Gifford,' he says. Eric Gifford, President and leading light of American Pacific. 'I asked him down.'

'Why?'

'He was in town. Charles thought it might be a civil gesture.'

I feel my shoulders tighten. Twelve months ago I would cheerfully have strangled the urbane Eric Gifford. Twelve months ago he was accumulating a stake in Carlton Brothers, and we were wondering if we'd have to mount a formal defence. At my insistence, Charles was sent across to New York and a truce was organized: Gifford stopped buying at five per cent. But Sir Charles was so impressed with what he saw of their operation, and by Gifford himself, that he suggested we turn the unasked-for connection to advantage. Our joint venture in Funds Management is the first fruit of this uneasy transatlantic alliance.

'Apart from that?' I ask.

'Hmm?'

'Apart from the civil gesture. What's he doing here?'

'It can't do any harm. Raef.'

I put a hand on his elbow and we stop in the open field. I ask him why he hasn't told me about this.

'It's nothing formal,' he says. 'With Lyle making trouble we thought it might be an idea.'

'Meaning what? You think we need a white knight?'

'Raef. Please.'

'I've got a right to know.'

He seems to draw into himself. He doesn't like open confrontations, especially with me.

'A precaution,' he says. 'That's all.'

A precaution: in his own mind he really believes that. But his thoughts are turning in a direction that I don't like one bit. He thinks that if Lyle makes a move on Carltons, it might be useful to have a cash-rich ally close by; a possible white knight who could save us from the clutches of Sandersons. But being saved like this would mean disappearing into American Pacific's great maw. My father, though he would never admit to it, is preparing to lose.

'Edward! Raef!' Charles calls.

We turn to see them both mounted and looking our way. In silence, we go down to join them.

2

Later, back up at the house, I'm putting on my dark jacket when Margie passes the bedroom door.

'Raef? Theresa and Annie just come.'

A jolt of confused impulses rushes through me: happiness and recrimination; behind these a good deal of pain.

'I'll be right down.' I continue to check myself in the mirror, and a minute later I feel ready to face my wife.

Theresa's in the dining room; she comes across and pecks my cheek. Sir John and his wife stand near by.

I draw away gently. 'Where's Annie?'

Theresa gives me a piercing look. 'Out in the garden.'

'How's everything down in Hampshire?'

She says her parents send their love. We exchange a few more banalities – isn't the house looking good, aren't the willows growing well – all as if nothing has happened. Not a word of regret for Daniel. At last Sir John and his wife come over to join us and I excuse myself, stepping through the high french windows. The tension eases. I fill my lungs with air.

My wife is a beautiful woman. This isn't just my opinion, I couldn't count the times I've been congratulated on my undeserved good fortune. Even my mother, a hard judge of the feminine, conceded that Theresa was more than just pretty. And my father adores her. She has an elegant grace, a natural ease, that no amount of effort could counterfeit. But I married her for another reason. I married Theresa, if it doesn't sound too ridiculously old-fashioned, because I loved her, and because I believed that she loved me.

What changed? For the first few years it was fine, we were happy. Very happy. But then she started talking about children, and I wasn't ready, there was still too much to do at the bank. We discussed it, mature adults being reasonable, and she agreed to wait. Reasonable. What chance does reason stand against nature? In the last few years before Annie was born I'd sometimes wake in the middle of the night to find Theresa crying quietly beside me. And I knew why. Yes, I knew. But I was sure that once I had the bank sorted out we could put things right again. Would that have happened? I don't know. Maybe.

Annie's on the lawn, stamping patterns into the melting frost with her tiny galoshes. She drags her heels, joining patterns, then she takes a long stride and looks back. A moment's uncertainty, then she laughs.

'What is it?'

'A house,' she says.

'A doll's house?'

She shakes her head sternly and I bend down and rub my cheek against hers. She laughs again and pushes me away. My hand slides over her back, an instinctive movement, nothing remains now but the one small scar. Beyond the walled garden the churchbells begin to toll.

'What's that?' she says.

But before I can answer, Theresa calls from the doorway. 'Annie. Come and put your shoes on.'

Annie stomps, making patterns again. I scoop her

into my arms and she wriggles and shrieks with laughter as I carry her back inside. It feels wrong.

Theresa and I enter the church together, Annie clinging shyly to Theresa's left hand. Scores of people have come, friends of my mother's I haven't seen for years, every pew in the small church is taken. There's a low murmur of conversation, and the heads turn our way when we pass. As we slide into the family pew near the pulpit I wonder what these others see when they look at the three of us. A family? Only my father, who enters behind us, knows something is wrong. He knows Theresa's spent many weeks down in Hampshire lately, and he knows I don't bring Annie, as I always used to, when I visit him in St James's. My excuse, Annie's cancer, has become rather worn. But even he doesn't know that for the past three months Theresa and I have barely spoken, nor that we no longer share the same bed.

The churchbells ring out, and through the stained-glass cross of St George the refracted light shines down on the altar. Theresa hands me a prayer book and the Order of Service without looking up. Amidst the many troubles of our lives, we must try now to remember the dead.

3

'So that's it, they agreed to raise the bid to 180.' Vance

has been pacing his office, a bundle of nervous energy, and filling me in on his meeting with the Meyers. Now he pauses. 'I did call you. No answer the first time.'

He flicks through another file then puts it aside. I've never seen him this worked-up before.

'Stephen, if you've got any worries about this I'd like to hear them now.'

'Worries? Raef, we're almost there.'

It was three o'clock before he got through to me at Boddington; lunch over, my father had just suggested a walk with Theresa and Gifford. Vance's call was timely; I got in the car and came straight here.

He opens his hands. 'What can we lose?'

'If we get it wrong? How about our reputation?'

He shrugs off this feeble platitude. Our reputation, as we both know, will be shattered anyway if our Corporate Finance people decamp *en masse*. Scrambled, cobbled together, hurried, whatever way we can manage it now, we have to win this bid. I lean across his desk and punch up last week's closings on the Reuters. He starts in about David Meyer, but I interrupt him, tapping the screen. 'You saw this?'

On Thursday the Parnells' price took an unusual jump, not dramatic, but quite noticeable against the background of a sliding market.

'More buyers than sellers,' he says. 'So what?'

I point to the Thursday closing on the Footsie, the Stock Exchange's primary index: thirty points down.

'Parnells weren't the only ones up,' Vance protests.

'Some up, some down, it's a market.'

'Who's worked on the new offer documents?'

'Haywood and Cawley.' Two hot-shot MBAs.

'You warned them?'

'They both know the rules.'

The rules are that insider knowledge is untradeable, but there are degrees of knowledge, and wide grey areas where fortunes are made each year. Parnells is in our Red Book right now, the in-house list of companies no Carltons employee can dabble in. Definitely off-limits.

I look out through the window, into the evening. Only a few lights burn in the buildings on the far side of the river. It's Sunday: all the sensible men are at home with their families. And here am I with Stephen Vance, talking business.

'How are the boys?'

He glances up from his reading. 'Fine. Jennifer's bringing them up next weekend.' Jennifer his ex-wife, they've been divorced several years now. 'What about Annie?'

'Better. She seems okay.'

Vance's grey eyes are sympathetic. He isn't one to bare his soul or to pry into another's personal affairs. Now he looks at me and waits.

'They think she's over the worst. We get some more results back in the next few days.'

'How's Theresa holding up?'

'Not bad.'

'You?'

'Honestly?'

He nods.

'I feel,' I say, 'like the mine caved in, and I'm the only survivor.'

He drops his head to one side. 'You shouldn't be here. Annie's still getting over those tests. Now Daniel . . . Maybe you should have a break for a week. Take Theresa and Annie away somewhere.'

If only, I think. If only my life were that simple again.

'They're down in Hampshire already. Seeing Theresa's parents.'

'Well, go and join them.'

'Did I ever introduce you to my mother-in-law?' At this Vance smiles. 'I'd just be on the phone to you here all day,' I tell him, 'I'd rather stay.'

He offers to have Jennifer call Theresa, but I politely decline. He looks pensive.

'Do you see her much?' I ask. 'Jennifer?'

'Not much.'

He rocks in his chair and stares out across the river. We seem to have drifted near to a subject I've never broached with him before, his divorce. And I feel that I could ask him now, that he's even expecting it: What went wrong? How did the boys take it? Did he gain a new freedom, or only loneliness? Was it, in the end, a huge mistake? But I hesitate, and the moment passes. He turns back to his desk.

'Daniel's death wasn't your fault, Raef.'

I draw back. 'My fault?'

'Sir John thinks you're blaming yourself. I'm not sure that I don't agree.'

'Me?'

'For organizing the Treasury party. Choosing the boat.' He raises his eyes. 'It just happened, Raef. You're not to blame.'

Me. I'm not to blame. Face burning, I reach across his desk for the printout from Parnells' registrar: the latest list of shareholders.

'You're not going to take a break, are you?'

'No.' I scan the list: the usual pension funds and investment houses, and below these a cluster of nominee accounts. 'But you can tell Sir John you tried.'

Vance laughs. 'I told him it wouldn't work.'

I hand him the printout. 'Can't see any of these causing trouble, can you?'

Vance reads the signal. Back to business. He goes on to give me more details of this morning's meeting. Diplomatic and businesslike, this is more like the Vance I know. After quoting some remark of David Meyer's, he says, 'I wouldn't be surprised if he was the brains.'

'I thought that was Reuben.'

'So does everyone.'

'Don't get psychological on me Stephen, let's keep them both happy.' I turn his glass paperweight over in my hands. 'You're confident we're going to win this?'

'Now they've raised the bid. Sure.'

'No cock-ups?'

'Raef,' he says firmly. 'There won't be a problem.'

A phone rings somewhere down the corridor. Vance points to his console. 'Your line.'

I pick up the receiver. Roger Penfield. He has something to discuss with me, he says, but not on the phone. He would like to see me now, in his office.

'Twenty minutes?'

He says he'll be waiting.

When I hang up, Vance looks at me askance. 'Roger Penfield?'

I pull a face, picking up my coat as I head for the door.

'I'll save you a seat for breakfast,' Vance calls.

Standing at the lifts, I hear a quick tapping at the keyboard start up behind me. The life of a man parted from his family. Sunday evening, and Stephen Vance, the corporate banker's banker, is settling down to work.

4

Nationalized in 1946, the Bank of England has been a pillar of the City for centuries. Apart from its responsibility for the currency it has a duty to maintain stability in the banking system, an obligation overseen by Roger Penfield. A security guard accompanies me up to the office. The vast spaces of the building are meant to impress, fifty years ago they probably did, but nowadays the marbled caverns seem an empty extravagance. The functionality of the Bundesbank offices, their German counterpart, could belong to another world: the real world, Daniel always said.

Penfield comes round his desk to greet me. He notices me glancing about. 'Redecoration,' he says. 'Three months' worth of meetings. Drop your coat over there Raef.'

I would ask why I'm here, but that's not how things are done in this place. Instead I take a seat. Like me, Penfield's dressed casually. Without his suit and tie he seems strangely diminished, incongruous even, as he leans against his desk. The bright yellow Ralph Lauren jersey, I suspect, was chosen by his wife.

'Ski tan?' I venture.

He tells me about his winter break in Canada; heli-skiing apparently, his latest big thing. Behind his smugness there's a boyish enthusiasm that redeems him. He's reputed to have a fierce temper, but I've never seen it myself. We move on to City gossip: the Fed rate rise last week, who's doing what to whom. And just when I'm wondering if the direct approach might have been better after all, he mentions that he's spoken with Inspector Ryan.

'Hasn't made much headway, I understand.'

I remark that the Inspector seems a capable man.

Penfield never really knew Daniel, but he knows that Daniel and I were friends. He gives me a sympathetic look, but to his credit he spares me any hollow condolences. He hands me a sheet of paper. 'What do you make of this?'

The sheet bears the Carlton Brothers letterhead: the family crest, a stag rampant on an azure shield, and the family motto, Loyal in Adversity. Beneath these, there's a short note.

Dear Sir,
    A fraudulent trading ring has been operating at Carlton Brothers plc over the past twelve months. Details of several transactions are enclosed for your perusal.

No signature. I turn the page over, but the other side's blank.

'Where's the rest of it?'

'That's it. No enclosure.'

I read the note again. 'You're not taking it seriously?'

'Wouldn't normally. These things come in from time to time. Cranks. Someone with a grudge.' He goes to a cabinet in the corner. 'Drink, Raef?'

I turn my head. I ask what makes this note different.

'Timing. We received it Friday.'

He leaves the obvious unspoken. Daniel died Thursday night.

'Ryan never mentioned it,' I say.

Penfield returns from the cabinet with a glass of

port. 'Rather our fault, I'm afraid. The letter wasn't opened till late Friday. It went to the Investigation Unit.' The Bank department charged with investigating questionable activity at City-based banks. 'The head of the Unit takes his work home. He found it this afternoon. Rang me straight away.'

I fill in the blanks. Penfield asked to see the note himself, and after meeting with the Head of the Investigation Unit, and still not satisfied, he called me. Probably at home, before trying the office. And somewhere along the way he's spoken to Ryan.

I hand back the note. 'You think this is tied up with Daniel?'

'Odd coincidence, wouldn't you agree? This isn't Moscow, Raef. It's not every day a senior banker's shot dead in the street.'

'So do you want me to look into it?'

'We were thinking in terms of our people.'

'The Investigation Unit?'

'We thought perhaps early this week.'

'Roger.' I look at him in disbelief. 'It's an unsigned note.'

He tells me there are certain pressures. 'I haven't much choice, you understand.'

But I'm too alarmed to understand anything just yet. Pressure? From Ryan?

'Our Treasurer murdered one week, and the next week the Investigation Unit's crawling all over us? Roger, you'll know all about pressure if the rumours start. Christ. How do you think this'll look?'

He studies the space above my shoulder. He knows exactly how it will look. It will look as if Daniel, Carltons' Treasurer, was involved in a fraud. Overnight, Carltons could become a leper in the City.

'You can't want that.'

'Of course we don't want it.'

'Then stop it,' I say.

There it is, what he must have been expecting to hear. Stop it. Don't investigate. Help me defend my bank. In my grandfather's day this conversation would have gone no further; a handshake, my grandfather's assurance, and there it would have ended. But my grandfather's day is gone.

Penfield rises, the worry-lines ploughed deep. 'Not that easy, I'm afraid. You saw that bloody Commons Committee the other day. Half a dozen of the elect, and not a brain cell to share between them. There are noses being poked in here I didn't even know existed.'

'I could speak with my father.'

'I wouldn't encourage him to get too involved.'

'He's Carltons' chairman.'

'Keep him informed,' Penfield demurs, 'by all means. But for the time being an active involvement on his part might be' – he searches for the word – 'counterproductive?'

I turn that one over. 'Are we talking about Lyle's testimony before that Committee?'

'It's been mentioned. Not an opportune moment for your father to be making waves on Carltons' behalf, I shouldn't think.'

'You know what an investigation might do to Carlton Brothers?'

'We won't do anything foolish.'

'A formal investigation over nothing? An unsigned note?'

'I'll make sure they move quickly. It won't be a long-drawn-out business.'

He looks a very worried man. And then I suddenly realize why; the real cause of his concern. Roger Penfield, as the whole City knows, wants the Governorship of the Bank when the current incumbent retires, and this note is an unwanted obstacle in his path. Either the note's true, in which case his Unit will uncover a fraud that's been perpetrated during his stewardship of the banking system: a serious black mark against his name. Or the note's false, and his Unit's public intervention will serve only to give Carltons' enemies a stick with which to beat us. Given our current problems – Daniel's murder, which he knows about, and our Corporate Finance staff problems which he's no doubt heard about on the City grapevine – the last thing Penfield wants is to weaken us further. A banking crisis would finish him. He wants a public investigation as little as we do.

'What choice is there?' he says.

'Roger, it doesn't matter how long it goes on. The rumours'll be in Tokyo before your lot have been in our office ten minutes. What good does that do?'

'I can't ignore this, Raef.'

'Ignoring it's not the issue. I'm talking about the best way to handle it.'

He goes back to his chair and picks up the note and stares at it. Then he swears.

'Give me a fortnight,' I say. 'Whatever I find, you'll get.'

He seems to weigh this up. The Investigation Unit – immediate exposure to the public gaze, and possibly disastrous consequences for both Carltons and him – or my proposal: a private inquiry over a limited time-frame; the chance of a discreet resolution.

He puts the note aside. 'It's specialist work. And a fortnight's beyond the bounds of my discretion.'

'What's within the bounds of your discretion?'

'It's still specialist work.'

'So I'll get a specialist.'

He looks at me curiously. He asks if I have someone in mind.

'Hugh Morgan. Acceptable?'

Penfield takes this on board. He knows the name. 'Could you get him?'

'He owes me a favour.'

A partner in a small but expensive accountancy firm specializing in City fraud, and an old university acquaintance, Hugh Morgan is a depressingly busy man. In his time he's done work for every regulatory body in the City, including the Bank of England. I can tell by Penfield's silence that my proposal appeals. Hugh, discreet and professional, is ideal.

'A fortnight's too long,' he says.

'Ten days.'

He smiles grimly. 'Rather a long time in banking.' Then he rests his forearms on the desk. 'If you get Morgan, you can have till close of trade Friday.'

'Friday?'

'The Bankers' Association do.'

Five days? What chance do I have of sorting this out in five days? But when he sees I'm about to protest he raises a finger.

'I can't do any better, Raef. That's it. And if I'm not satisfied by Friday evening I really will have no choice.'

He rises and offers me his hand. The interview is over.

5

At home I ring Hugh Morgan, but he isn't in so I leave a message. Next I call my father and explain about the note.

'Lyle?' he says.

'I don't know. Maybe.'

Then I tell him about Penfield's warning that he shouldn't become involved. There's a pause.

'Very well,' he agrees finally; but he isn't happy. 'Raef? It couldn't be genuine, could it?'

My eyes wander across the kitchen walls and stop on the calendar. Friday. A fraudulent trading ring, the banker's worst nightmare: there could be a great gaping hole where Carltons' assets should be.

'I don't have a clue,' I tell him.

After a few more moments' desultory conversation, I hang up and reach for the fridge.

My house here in Belgravia is empty. The maid has gone home and the nanny's down with Theresa and Annie in Hampshire. I close the fridge door, and one of Annie's pictures comes free and flutters to the floor. I prop it against the fruit bowl where I can admire its kaleidoscope of messy swirls as I eat my cold bacon sandwich.

It must have taken Annie quite a while, this picture: she's a girl who has to get everything just right. When she learns a new word she repeats it again and again, then we don't hear the word for weeks, but the next time it comes there's no hesitation. And this picture, I can imagine her standing on the chair, leaning over the table and moving her crayon with infinite care. Her brow furrows comically when she concentrates, but she won't allow us to laugh. On the summer evenings of her first year we often walked her through Green Park, she'd rock in her pram when the wind stirred the leaves overhead. Complete strangers would stop to look in at her; simple pleasures, yet even now their memory lingers. I turn Annie's picture one way, then the other. A tree?

What would I say to her now? How much of this unjust storm could she even begin to understand? That look of puzzled innocence when I first found the lump on her back, the memory of it still fills me with fear for her. But if that was all, I could have coped. My mantra these days: I could have coped. Lying awake at 2 a.m., staring at the ceiling, this is what I tell myself. If Annie just had cancer, if that was all, I could have coped.

The phone rings. Vance. He tells me McKinnon wants to see me for lunch tomorrow.

'Fine. I'll book it in. Anything else?'

'David Meyer,' he says. He explains that David isn't happy we haven't managed to establish meaningful contact with the Parnells' Boardroom yet. Vance asks if I have any suggestions.

'I suggest we buy David Meyer a new dummy.'

Vance laughs and rings off.

Finishing my sandwich, I head out through the drawing room. Here there's another picture, a framed photograph on the side table of Annie, Theresa and me. I pause, running a finger over the frame. In that distant place five months behind us there is happiness; and ignorance. Annie smiles, the tumour already growing inside her. Theresa holds back Annie's windswept hair and looks at me – how? With love? And me, a hand resting on each of them, confident and secure. My life is good.

Now, five months later, what wouldn't I give to have the world as it was? What wouldn't I give to have Annie unblemished, what Faustian pact wouldn't I make? Unstoppable time. My finger slides from the frame. I turn out the lights and go up.

I tell him not to bother. No need to add another sleep-deprived zombie to our number.

From down the table Gary Leicester enquires languidly if there'll be many more of these early starts. He's the head of Leicester and Partners, the PR firm we're using on the bid. 'I mean this won't become a habit, will it?' he says.

'It's all business.' Peter Fanshawe, our stockbroker on the bid. 'What's your bitch?'

Leicester laughs. 'Some business.'

Smiles all round. Vance has called in everyone to discuss tactics and make sure they're singing from the same songsheet when the Meyers' increased offer is announced later this morning. Four years ago we had a highly embarrassing débâcle when someone working on the Blackwright defence was accidentally left out of the loop. He was busy telling the *FT* that Blackwrights weren't considering the offer while the rest of us were at a press conference on the other side of town drinking toasts to the company's new owners. One of the few times I've seen Vance really angry. Nowadays when anything fundamental on a deal changes the policy is to gather everyone together face-to-face, just like this. Win brings two jugs of orange juice from the kitchen, the smell of bacon drifts out, and suddenly I feel very hungry. I'd just put dinner into the microwave last night when Celia phoned. We talked, but I'm not really sure what she expects of me now. She mentioned Daniel's will, but I don't think it's just that. And I noticed she can already speak Daniel's name calmly. Compared with some of us she's coping quite well. She talked for almost an hour. My shrivelled dinner is still in the microwave.

Vance arrives: he's slicked back his hair, and he's wearing a different suit to the one I saw him in yesterday. At work, no matter what day, it's always a suit with Vance: he keeps three or four in his office. Around the table everyone sits up a little. He takes a chair opposite Cawley and opens a folder: the battle plan. 'Shall we start then,' he says.

Beyond the glass wall, the Dealing Room clock ticks over: 6 a.m.

'The new number's 180.' Vance glances at me then the others. 'I'm confident that will get us there. Quite quickly, with any luck.'

'Walkover,' Gary Leicester murmurs.

Vance gives him a look. 'Let's save the gloating till it's done, shall we.'

Leicester's cheeks flush, his eyes wander down. Like everyone he picks up his pen now and listens. Vance runs methodically through his checklist, confirming his instructions: the day's documentation is prepared, Leicester has the press-releases ready, and our broker knows exactly what we want him to do when the announcement's made. Minutiae, endless details, but every piece a potential stumbling block to the bid. As Vance talks, an air of expectation builds, it seems to stir something deep in us, almost primeval, when one company moves to devour another. After three years away from it I'd thought this feeling might have abated in me. I was wrong. For the first time since I woke, Daniel moves to the back of my mind.

'I've prepared a summary.' Vance passes me a sheaf of photocopies from his folder. Taking one, I hand the rest down the table, a single sheet each. 'Para one deals with the management record,' he says.

Vance gives us a moment to read the litany we've been reciting since the first day of the bid. The Parnells' board, comprised mainly of Parnell family members, has presided over a decline in the company's fortunes for decades. Built up in the late nineteenth and early twentieth centuries, Parnells were once one of the country's great transport giants, their operations reaching into every corner of the Commonwealth. No more. The business acumen and sheer energy once so prominent in the family has died out, a fact the current Parnell patriarch, Richard Parnell, fails to see. Ever since his father's tenure on the Board the company has shown an infallible instinct for backing the wrong horse: Parnells were still building passenger ships long after the airline boom began; they missed the growth in the oil tanker business, finally buying out one of the Greeks just in time to see that market collapse; more recently they turned up their noses at the bus business, then found the highly profitable bus companies outbidding them for rail franchises. Every single strategic decision the Parnells have made for decades has been wrong, and every one has cost money.

'Para two,' Vance says, 'recaps the Meyers' record.'

Another pause as we read. This paragraph, as one might expect, gives a much rosier picture: the Meyer Group has an almost unblemished record of growth. Sandersons have raised questions about how this was achieved – stories of violent union-busting on Meyers' building sites have re-emerged in the press – but the profit record as given in this second paragraph is the story the City fund managers want to hear.

'Finally,' Vance says tapping his summary, 'rationale of the bid, and final offer.'

Here we have a reprise of the deal's logic, the bid's bottom line. Parnells retains a few overseas interests, shadowed remains of its glory days, but now it's primarily a European trucking business, a husk of the company it once was. But it owns a string of warehouses and depots on the outskirts of most major European cities between Aberdeen and Vienna, and it's these properties the Meyers are after. If they win Parnells, Reuben and David will sell off the subsidiaries and the trucking business, and develop the increasingly valuable sites. The logic of the deal, even at the new offer price, is sound: the Meyers should make money. But the sticking point in all this is Richard Parnell. He still thinks he's a transport magnate, and as long as he can keep the rest of his family, and a few fund managers, in line, he might yet retain control.

I set the summary aside.

'Peter.' Vance turns to our broker. 'Any remarks?'

'180?' Peter Fanshawe tips his hand from side to side. 'Close, but, yeah, that should do it.'

There's a murmur of agreement around the table, a sage nodding of heads. The number we've wrung from the Meyers gives the bid a good chance of success. Vance rests his forearms on the table.

'One way or another this'll be over within a fortnight.' He pauses; a long pause, and everyone seems to lean towards him, waiting. Suddenly he smiles. 'England expects every man to do his duty.'

This draws a burst of laughter from everyone, a noisy release that brings Win from the kitchen. Vance orders a fresh jug of coffee, and a minute later he has moved the meeting on.

Don't bore the audience and don't confuse them: he drummed these two rules into me remorselessly all the time I worked under him. Two simple precepts, and I see them broken every day of my working life. We've all been there: the mind-numbing presentation at which half the assembled company dozes off; the chemicals analyst who mistakes himself for a comedian; the speaker who keeps losing his place, the frantic search for a missing page, and puzzled looks all round. But never with Vance. Listening to him now, I'm reminded of just how good he is. Cawley, I see, is hanging on Stephen's every word. Vance has to give everyone here confidence that we're moving forward with purpose. If they have doubts, these doubts could communicate themselves to others, and market sentiment might turn swiftly against us. But even as he delivers his pep talk, he's aware that nothing can be counted as certain. I know it too, yet I feel myself responding to his words. Like so many of the best bankers, Vance would have made a fine confidence-man. With nothing more than words he's built this deal; and words, as he's taught me, are the insubstantial foundations of our world.

2

After seven thirty I get half an hour to myself which I spend at my desk catching up with the weekend's E-mail, and generally clearing away paperwork. When I sat at my grandfather's knee and listened to his stories about the City – a kind of *Arabian Nights* set in London, the way he told them – I never imagined these wasted hours. Daniel once tried to calculate how much time each year we poured into this bottomless pit. Six weeks I think it came to.

Before I've finished the last memo, Karen Haldane comes in.

'Henry won't see me,' she says.

'Good morning.'

She looks annoyed, but no more than usual. I finish with the memo and toss it in the bin.

'Henry's got a lot on his plate this morning. Unless it's important, see him tomorrow.'

'Who'll explain that to Inspector Ryan?'

'Ryan?'

'Coming to see me in ten minutes,' she says.

'About what?'

'I'm the Chief Compliance Officer, Raef. Our Treasurer's just been shot. What's your guess?' She puts a hand on her hip. 'Ryan called five minutes ago, I got straight onto Henry. Good old Henry told me to bugger off.'

'You don't need Henry.'

'Raef, I can't lie to them.'

Silently I count to ten. I knew what Karen Haldane was like when I hired her. Honest and trustworthy. Fearless too, not someone to be steamrollered easily. But she doesn't accept any grey areas in her dealings. A useful quality in the person charged with overseeing the bank's compliance with regulatory and internal rules, but one that makes her difficult to manage. During the five years Karen's been with us she's averaged one major row with each Head of Department per month. When she worked with Daniel and our IT department last year, designing the new settlement system, her obstinacy nearly drove him crazy. He took to referring to her as That Bitch. Eventually I had to ask him to refrain.

Now I ask Karen what she's told Ryan.

'That I'd have something ready for him in a few days. P and L to last month. Balance sheet. They won't do him much good.'

General accounts. She's right, they won't tell him anything.

'If that's what he wants, give them to him.'

Becky calls over the intercom; David Meyer has arrived.

As I go to the door, Karen says, 'Raef,' and I stop and look back. 'If Daniel's murder had anything to do with the bank, Ryan should have access to our records.'

'I don't want the bank turned upside down for no reason,' I tell her.

She gives me a cool look then steps by me. 'I'll make an appointment with Becky,' she says. 'We have to talk.'

3

The Dealing Room's off-limits to our clients so Vance has taken David Meyer up to the restaurant. From there they have a clear view over the trading desks. Vance is pointing out various traders through the glass wall when I enter. Glancing around, I find that Reuben hasn't come.

David notices me. 'How soon do we see you down there?' he asks.

Vance tells David I'll be going down later.

Big Win asks if we want coffee, and David Meyer waves him rudely away. Win turns to me, I nod, and he goes back to the kitchen. I hope David Meyer hasn't seen that look in Win's eye.

Then David asks about the unusual jump in

Parnells on Thursday. I assure him that the Stock Exchange haven't queried it, but we're keeping our eyes open.

'You don't need a telescope,' he says. 'Ask Mr Leicester.'

He looks down to the Dealing Room again. Vance raises a brow at me. Leicester? But this is news to me too.

Below, the noise level is rising. David gets to his feet and paces along the glass wall: he's more nervous than I expected. The Meyers' increased bid was announced ten minutes ago, by now our broker will have waded into the market. I phone down to the room below.

'Henry? Raef. How's it looking?'

'Quids in,' he says. 'They can't give us the stuff fast enough.'

I give David Meyer the thumbs-up.

Down below, Henry peers at a screen. 'Market's picking up a bit, but we're still getting it in at 172.' Then he looks up to the restaurant, smiling. 'What do I do, wave?'

I pass the phone to David. The increased offer seems to be working. While Henry explains the situation to David, I take Vance aside. For a forty-eight-year-old man who hasn't slept properly in weeks, he looks remarkably spry.

'What's this about Leicester?' I ask.

'First I've heard of it. But he knew early enough. What do you think?'

'Get him back over here.' I turn and head for the door.

'Where are you off to then?' he asks.

Waving a hand over my shoulder, I keep right on walking.

In my office I pick up a box of discs, then I take the lift to Ground and walk the few hundred yards to Cannon Street where Hugh Morgan has his office.

4

Hugh's hair has gone completely white, the last traces of grey finally faded. He studies the note a moment then looks up.

'Some nut,' he says. 'Anyone could have got hold of the letterhead.'

'Roger Penfield isn't convinced.'

A flicker of interest appears. 'Penfield's seen this?'

'He gave it to me. I've got till close of trade Friday to find out what's behind it.'

'What if you can't?'

'He sends in the Investigation Unit.'

Hugh whistles quietly through his teeth, a discomfiting reaction. But he seems puzzled.

'Just for this?' He hands back the note.

'This and Daniel,' I tell him.

Hugh looks blank, and it's a moment before I realize why: he hasn't made the connection. Daniel was up at Cambridge; Hugh never knew him. I ask

Hugh if he was away somewhere last week.

'Morocco,' he says. 'Why?'

'Our Treasurer was killed last Thursday. He was shot.'

Hugh purses his lips. 'Not an accident I take it.'

Briefly I explain the circumstances.

'They haven't found who did it?'

'No.'

'But Penfield thinks this note might be tied up with a motive? Raef?'

'I don't know.'

Hugh makes that whistling sound again. Being what he is, the matter has just become interesting. In our Oxford days I was never particularly close to Hugh, and after university he went straight to work at the US Securities and Exchange Commission, so I never saw him much then either. He was helping put fraudsters behind bars while the rest of our crowd were struggling with MBAs. But when he came back to London I helped him get his face known around the City. I've even helped him out on one of his cases, and this I trust, is the pay-off.

I place the box of discs on his desk. 'Our Treasury records for the last twelve months.'

But Hugh's mind is elsewhere. 'Stewart,' he says to himself. He snaps his fingers, trying to remember, then he does. He points at me. 'Daniel Stewart. I did a course with him a few years back. Derivatives.' He smiles. 'That's right. There was a female tutor; he was knocking her off after two days.'

'I don't have much time, Hugh.'

'You don't have much time, so I panic?'

'I need a favour.'

'Yeah. I see.' He thumbs through the discs. 'Three sets?'

'One forex, one money market, one miscellaneous,' I explain.

'Miscellaneous?'

'Commodities, equities and anything else.'

Hugh considers my request. I hope he's also considering the help I gave him on the Arnold Petrie case. A one-time client of Carlton Brothers, Petrie relieved thousands of his own clients of their pension plans and disappeared to South America two years ago. Just months earlier, Petrie had disputed our fees and bounced a cheque on us. We dropped him as a client and now the bank to which Petrie took his business after leaving Carltons has two senior executives awaiting trial. Vance told me he had nightmares for days after those two bankers were charged. Petrie was so secretive, Vance said, they wouldn't have known a thing about it. The Serious Fraud Office think differently: those two bankers will never work in the City again. Hugh's the man the Serious Fraud Office called in to help with their investigation, and Hugh – when he discovered Petrie's earlier connection with Carlton Brothers – called on me.

He looks up. 'And that's all you've got, this note?' he says.

'That and Daniel.'

'No suspicions?'

'Like?'

'Well have any dealers been wearing balaclavas lately?' He grimaces. 'Anybody left unexpectedly, that kind of thing?'

I tell him no, not that I'm aware of.

He flicks through the discs. 'I'm meant to be writing a report on Habibi.' He explains about Habibi, a Moroccan fraudster who's just decamped to his home country. I can see he's wavering, he owes me, but he isn't a man to waste time on lost causes.

'I wouldn't ask, Hugh, but I need someone I can trust.'

'What you need is a dozen forensic accountants you can trust.' He flips the disc box closed. Looking at me straight in the eye, he delivers his verdict. 'And they wouldn't have a prayer of getting through this lot by Friday.'

My stomach turns over. I hold tight to the back of the chair.

'Look,' he says, 'leave this stuff with me. I'll make some time to have a browse. If I have any bright ideas, we'll see. Okay?'

Slowly, I return to myself.

He repeats it, 'Okay?'

'Penfield wants to know you're working on this. You personally, Hugh.'

Hugh raises an eyebrow. 'Flattered.' He rocks back

in his chair. 'If you speak to him you can tell him I'm working on it.'

'I appreciate this Hugh.'

He smiles, amused by some private thought. I ask him what's up.

'Keep this happy moment in mind,' he says, 'when you get my bill.'

5

Back at Carlton House, I find Vance waiting in my office with Gary Leicester. Leicester starts a spiel about some feature on the Meyers he's lined up with the *Telegraph*. I let him talk for half a minute before cutting him off.

'The Meyers want you sacked.'

Leicester stops dead.

'You've upset them,' Vance says.

'Me?'

Then I follow up with the question that counts. 'Gary, did you buy any Parnell shares on Thursday?'

'Fuck no.'

'Before Thursday?'

'What is this, an inquisition?'

Vance tells him it's not an inquisition but a question.

'What about your employees?' I ask.

'It went by the rules: what am I, an idiot? Bullshit like that and I've got no company.'

'No one's accusing you,' Vance tells him.

Leicester crosses his arms. 'If I find out who's spreading the story I'll sue the bastard.'

He has a brooding look. He's PR to the fingertips, and I don't really trust him, but right now he appears to be telling the truth. David Meyer got it wrong.

'Gary,' I say reasonably, 'if you know any reason why Parnells went up Thursday it might be better if we knew now.'

'No idea,' he says. It is like a great door slamming closed.

I look at Vance but he has nothing to offer. I turn back to Leicester.

'All right, this one goes through to the keeper. But should anything occur to you – anything – let us know.'

Carefully Leicester does up his jacket buttons, the very picture of offended dignity. Problems like this we just don't need. To smooth his ruffled feathers I ask about the PR campaign. Churlishly, he gives us a ten-minute report on how his company is cutting a broad swathe through the media: TV, press and radio, he has them all covered. Parnells have made no response to the increased offer yet; it will be a while before they can muster anything credible, and by then City opinion should be moving our way. Such, at least, is the plan. He finishes the update.

'Good,' I say, turning to Vance. 'That's it?'

Vance nods.

Then Leicester says, 'It wasn't David Meyer was

it? Who fed you that bullshit?'

I pause. 'What if it was?'

'Jesus. That man is a prick.'

He tells us the story. He and David had an argument last week, a disagreement over the number of interviews David's been giving the press. Leicester asked him to be a little less forthcoming, and David didn't take the advice kindly. This present false accusation, Leicester suggests, is David Meyer's way of getting even. He repeats his judgement. 'What a prick.'

The three of us look at one another. Then Leicester rises and goes and shakes Vance's hand. Solemnly. Next he comes and shakes mine. Not a word is spoken. A strange scene.

But when he crosses to the door he glances back. 'You weren't to know,' he says.

This is his exit line. The door closes behind him and finally I get it. Magnanimity. Gary Leicester our PR man, that model of moral rectitude, forgives us. I squeeze my temples to ease the pressure.

'What do you think?'

'He didn't buy the shares,' says Vance. 'He knows we can check. And to tell you the truth, I wouldn't put it past David bloody Meyer to use us like that.'

So we're back where we started: waiting to hear from the Registrar on the 212 we've filed to uncover the buyer. We can't waste more time on this now. I ask how the broker's going with Parnells, and Vance gives me a brief account. So far, no problems.

'Stephen, the other day Inspector Ryan was with you quite a while.'

'Waste of time.'

'What was he chasing?'

'Daniel's murderer supposedly. Who knows?'

His tone is offhand but I see that the interview with Ryan has disturbed him.

'You weren't even on the boat that night.'

'I was here,' he says. 'Working late.'

I offer to speak with Ryan, but Vance waves the suggestion aside. He tells me we have a bid to attend to.

'Real work,' he says.

Once he's left I try to settle down to the backlog of paperwork: a note from Gordon Shields, our Finance Director, about an Audit Committee meeting later in the month, a summary of our positions in the Dealing Room, this one thoughtfully prepared by Henry; memos and letters, most of them absolutely pointless. I notice that there's nothing from Sir John. My mind keeps drifting to Annie.

Out on the Thames the barges pass silently by, and the low dark clouds scud east. Raindrops strike the windowpane, tracing broken patterns down the glass.

6

When I put my head round Karen Haldane's door

she's studying a printout. She looks up and takes off her glasses. 'Got a moment then have we?'

'What did Ryan have to say?'

'He asked some questions. He wasn't here long.'

'What was he after?'

She lays a ruler across the printout and scores a red line. 'He thinks Daniel was involved in something.'

'Involved?'

'I'm only telling you what he thinks. I'll tell you something else too. He's not going to give up on it either.'

'Involved in what?'

'I don't know Raef.' She hesitates. 'Fraud, I suppose. Ryan asked about our procedures: who has authority for what, all that. He said he's coming back to you later.'

Fraud? Daniel? And why is Ryan coming back to see me?

'I can't block them,' Karen adds flatly.

I should be angry but her obstinate honesty is solid ground in this widening mire, one point of certainty from which I can take my bearings. She isn't like Leicester or Darren Lyle; not even like my father, if it comes to that: with Karen Haldane I know exactly where I stand.

I tell her to keep me informed.

My next stop is Sir John's office where I spend fifteen minutes filling him in on the progress of the bid. He holds himself a little too squarely, and gives my words an unusually careful consideration. He has been drinking. I don't like these occasions at the best of times, and now when I've said my piece I rise and head for the door. Sir John checks me.

'Raef, do you think Stephen's quite steady just now?'

'He's got it under control.'

'Not the bid. I was thinking of Inspector Ryan. He's heard about the two of them. Stephen and Daniel.'

'The two of them what?'

'With the best will in the world, Raef, they never saw eye-to-eye, did they?'

'That was work.'

'Yes, I told Ryan that.'

'Why's he asking you about Stephen?'

'I've no idea.' He frowns. 'But I mentioned it to Stephen just now. Asked him what he wanted me to say. He nearly bit my head off.'

I tell Sir John it might be best if he steers clear of Vance for a while. 'He's under enough pressure with the Meyers, he doesn't need us on his back.'

'Stephen was here on Wednesday night, wasn't he?'

'Yes?'

'I was just wondering,' he says tentatively. He strokes his nose, a habit he's developed since the red veins there became quite visible.

'Wondering what?'

He looks at me from the corner of his bleary eye. 'How far do you suppose we are from St Paul's Walk?'

* * *

Back in my own office I try to call Hugh but all I get is his answering machine. Then Becky comes in. She fusses with the papers on my desk, and I'm about to ask her what the problem is when she asks, 'That Inspector's all right, isn't he?'

'Sure.'

'He spoke to me again, about my statement and that. You know. What I saw that night on the boat.' She looks down. 'I had to say.'

The Antipodean approach defeats me. I reach across for our loan agreement with the Meyers.

'I mean, I told him how Daniel stood back up and everything.'

My hand freezes on the folder. A great chasm seems to open wide beneath me. Looking up slowly, I ask Becky what it is, exactly, that she has told the Inspector.

'Well,' she says apologetically, 'I told him I saw you hit Daniel. I'm sorry Raef, I had to.'

She saw me hit Daniel the night of the party, the night Daniel died. I stare at her.

'What did he say?'

'He wants to see you. He made an appointment.'

'When for?'

Becky opens her hands helplessly. 'Now?'

7

Ryan eases himself into the chair. He looks at me

stone-faced, and the first thing he says is, 'Why didn't you mention it?'

'It wasn't important. Nothing.'

'You hit him.'

'We scuffled. Schoolboy stuff.'

'Six hours later Stewart was dead.' Then a claw clicks out from his paw. 'Mr Carlton,' he says. 'You know I don't want a media circus.'

A cold shiver runs through me. The tabloids: if they pick up on this I'll be crucified, we both know that, but I hold his gaze.

'Talk me through it,' the Inspector says. 'The scuffle.'

'We argued. We'd had a bit to drink.'

'And then?'

'Look, Daniel was shot. I don't see that this comes into it.'

'I'm not suggesting he was beaten to death Mr Carlton. I'm trying to understand why two supposed friends were brawling in public just hours before one of them was murdered.'

I tell him it wasn't a brawl. He asks me what I'd call it then.

'Is this where I demand to speak to my lawyer?'

But this foolish quip falls into silence. Worse, the Inspector's gaze wanders down.

'There's the phone,' he says.

He isn't just some banker or client; he isn't here to negotiate. He wants to discover the truth.

'Friends fall out,' he says. 'It happens. Then again,

men your age, in your positions, they don't duff each other up in the street just for fun.' He drops his head to one side. 'Why?' he asks.

The blood pounds in my ears.

'Mr Carlton?'

'Daniel thought I was having an affair with Celia.'

'Celia Stewart?'

Yes, I tell him, Daniel's wife.

Ryan's eyes widen a little. 'Was it true?'

'No.'

'He accused you, then you hit him.'

'We scuffled.'

'Your secretary saw him fall.'

'He took a swing and I grabbed him. We wrestled a bit; he wasn't hurt.'

'Were you?'

I hold up my wrist. 'Broke my watch.'

He asks why he's only hearing about this now.

'Because it isn't important,' I say.

He stands and takes a turn round the office, pausing by the window.

'You and Stewart were friends a long time. Back to Eton.'

I incline my head.

'You might help me,' he says.

'If I could.'

His look immediately darkens. I know at once that I've made a mistake.

'I hope you don't think this investigation can be deflected, Mr Carlton, because I won't let that happen.' He goes to the door. 'I'll call on Mrs Stewart. If you contact her before I do, I'll regard that as an obstruction of my inquiries. Thanks for your time.'

The truth – the simple truth – is all that he wants. But the simple truth is the one thing I can't give him.

I pick up the phone and dial Hugh Morgan.

8

Before lunch there's a gathering of the corporate finance team in Vance's office. The atmosphere is cheerful, almost partylike, everyone discussing different angles on the bid. When Henry walks in with Peter Fanshawe, our broker on the bid, young Haywood claps theatrically and cries, 'Bravo.' Peter takes a bow. The backslapping done, I draw Henry aside.

'How much have we got?'

He gestures back to Fanshawe. 'They're still doing the numbers. Looks like we're over forty per cent, thereabouts.'

As Vance hoped. From here on in, Parnells will find it extremely difficult to shake us loose.

'Dried up a bit after ten,' Henry says.

'Last bid you saw?'

'177.'

'Last trade?'

'Same. Just hanging round there.'

Vance, overhearing, leans across. 'Maybe the arbitrageurs might stay out of it for a change.'

Henry tells him to keep right on dreaming.

I touch Vance's arm and we step out into the corridor. Behind us Henry regales the others with a Dealing Room story; it would turn the Equal Opportunities people apoplectic if they heard.

'What do you think?' I ask Vance as we walk down the passage. 'Forty per cent enough?'

'Could be worse. You've still got lunch with Brian McKinnon today?

Brian McKinnon, the manager of an investment fund that's one of Carltons' major shareholders: they own a large parcel of Parnells too. Over lunch, I will try to convince McKinnon that 180 is a worthwhile bid.

I tell Vance it's still on. We stop by the coffee machine and he leans against the wall and stifles a yawn. At last the sleeplessness is getting to him; he's human after all.

'This Inspector Ryan's getting on my pip,' he says.

'Humour him, Stephen.'

He rubs his eyes. 'I keep thinking about Daniel. I was checking my diary just now: Daniel and Celia were meant to be coming round for dinner tonight.'

'At your place?'

He sees my surprise. 'Burying the hatchet,' he explains. After their last big argument I told him to do just that. Apparently he intended to try. 'Now?' He shrugs. 'You know what I mean?'

I know exactly what he means. Mortality weighs heavy on us both.

'Just like that,' he says. 'How old was he, forty?'

'Thirty-nine.'

'Jesus, his boys too.' Vance shakes his head. He asks if I've spoken to Celia.

'She's all right.'

'That Ryan, the Inspector.' Vance lifts his head. 'Did he say anything to you about Daniel and me?'

'If he's bothering you, Stephen, I'll have a word.'

Becky calls me from down the corridor, we look down there.

'I'll ring you after I've seen McKinnon,' I tell Vance.

'He asked about you.'

'McKinnon?'

'Ryan,' he says.

'Raef?' Becky calls.

I back away down the corridor, telling Vance I don't want to keep McKinnon waiting.

He gives a dry smile. 'Good life for some,' he mutters. Turning he retreats to his office.

9

'They're saying it was a hit,' Hugh Morgan tells me. When I look blank, he adds, 'Professional.'

'Who's saying?'

He waves his hand airily. 'Contacts.'

'The police?'

He nods, tapping at the keyboard of his portable. We're in Darcy's, a coffee bar in a cramped City alley, Hugh asked me to meet him here. We have a rear table, Hugh has his back to the wall. The few customers who enter don't stay long, they buy what they want and move on. Hugh turns the screen a little so that I can see: the Carlton Brothers numbers appear.

'What does that mean?' I say. 'Professional?'

'Like it sounds. Someone who knew what he was doing. Someone who got paid.' He glances up. 'This is just between us, by the way.'

'A hitman killed Daniel?'

'You remember a few months back that dealer at Shobai?' Shobai, one of the big Japanese banks. 'He didn't show up for work two days running. Police broke in and there he is, suicided all over the floor.'

'What's the connection?'

'Maybe none.' He sips his coffee. 'The Shobai managers asked us in to take a discreet look at the books. Seemed okay. But the Inspector on the suicide didn't like the smell of it. He turned up so many questions the coroner brought in an open verdict.'

'Meaning?'

'Meaning maybe it was suicide and maybe it wasn't.' He concentrates on the screen again. 'I don't suppose you know how much business your Treasury does with Shobai?'

'Not offhand.'

He hits a key and a long list of last month's Shobai–

Carltons deals comes up in black and white. The list is in three sections. Hugh points to the smallest. 'Miscellaneous,' he says. 'Equities and commodities, you don't do much.' His finger runs over the other two sections. 'Forex and money-market, a bit more.'

'Which tells us what?'

'Bugger all.' There's a certain look Hugh gets when he wants to be serious: he goes quiet and seems to sink into himself, thinking. He gets that look now. 'Actually, we should drop your miscellaneous file. You want something by Friday, I'll have to narrow the field.'

'You're assuming this is connected with Shobai?'

He shrugs. 'One possibility. We've got too much information anyway. We do some pruning now or we'll be thrashing around the data jungle for the next four days going nowhere.' He puts up a hand and orders two more coffees. 'I've scanned all the files you gave me, the pattern's similar. Plenty of forex and money-market deals, a lot less equities and commodities. Most of these frauds rely on burying crooked trades under truckloads of real ones. If you want to hide a tree, plant it in a forest.'

'So we drop the miscellaneous file?'

'You agree?' he says.

It's Monday. Only four full days left. I tell Hugh I'm completely in his hands.

He bends over his keyboard, explaining how he spent half the morning reformatting the Carlton Brothers discs. 'Compatibility,' he says in that

American accent he sometimes affects. 'Such a bitch.' A female customer looks sharply our way. Hugh doesn't seem to notice. He points to the screen and the list of miscellaneous details disappears: if the fraud was buried there, we won't find it, not by Friday.

Our fresh coffee arrives.

'You don't take this hitman business seriously?' I say.

'The name Roberto Calvi ring any bells?'

It does. Roberto Calvi, a banker with connections to the Vatican, was found hanging by his neck one morning beneath Blackfriars Bridge: coincidentally, a stone's throw from where Daniel was found. Another open verdict.

'I could show you half a dozen more, just from our own files.' Hugh finishes typing and looks at me. 'A friend at Scotland Yard, he's been there thirty years, he says every murder he's ever seen was over money or love. In the City, Raef,' he touches the numbers on the screen, 'no shortage of money.'

I ask him what happens now.

'I fly by the seat of my pants.' He stares at the screen. 'I'll look for patterns. Counterparties that never take a loss, deals that don't fit. Needles in haystacks.'

'How can I help?'

He pushes a pen towards me. 'Do me a list of who does what at Carltons. Just money market and forex. You know. Who's trading gilts, Spot Yen or whatever.'

I explain that there are scores of faces in the

Dealing Room I know only by sight.

'OK, just the senior dealers. When you get back to the office you can send me a fax with the rest.'

As I jot down the names and job descriptions, Hugh plays with the numbers on his screen. When I'm done, I read the list I've made. Almost twenty names, and I find it alarmingly easy to suspect more than half of them. I hand the list over.

'Something else,' he says. 'I need an outline of your security. Who signs what, when. Who answers to whom.'

I suggest that a chart might be helpful.

'Chart's fine. If you've got one, fax that over too.'

I nod to the PC. 'How long did it take to sift out the Shobai deals?'

'Push of the button, once I'd done the reformat. Software's tailor-made, one of mine.'

Hugh was the computer whizz in our Oxford days, the one everyone called on when a poorly written program went haywire.

'What if I give you another name?'

'Fire away.'

'Try Sandersons.'

'Sandersons?'

I nod. Hugh's fingers go dancing over the keys.

'What's the story here?' he says.

But so far our suspicions about Sandersons are a private affair, just my father, Charles Aldridge and me. For the time being, I think, it's probably as well to keep it that way.

'Daniel had a problem with their Treasurer,' I lie.

Last month's deals with Sandersons appear. Hugh scrolls forward two pages to the end: there are many more deals than with Shobai.

'Didn't stop you dealing with them,' he remarks.

I've seen Hugh's suspicious mind at work on others, the last thing I need is for him to turn it against me. I force my eyes to the screen and the numbers. Beyond these there are thousands more deals with other banks and corporations worldwide. Alone I'd be lost, but with Hugh there's at least a faint ray of hope. He scrolls back and forward over the Sanderson deals, chewing his lip.

'Four days,' he murmurs.

I stir my coffee bleakly.

'Who's the Inspector on Stewart's murder?' he asks. He sees that the question surprises me. 'Four days, Raef. I'll need all the help I can get.'

'Inspector Ryan.'

Hugh hunches up his shoulders. 'Moustache? Stocky build?'

Warily, I nod.

'Handshake like a vice?'

'That the one,' I say.

'That Shobai business. The Inspector who wouldn't buy the suicide?'

A cold feeling creeps up my back. 'Ryan?'

'Yeah,' Hugh says thoughtfully. 'Ryan.'

10

There was a time when boatmen ferried passengers across the Thames all day long. Now looking out from Butler's Wharf I see just the one solitary craft. As it passes, I read the black lettering: River Police.

McKinnon booked this table with a view; he isn't one to stint himself on the perks of City life. We're onto the cheese and port before our conversation, City gossip till now, moves to the business at hand.

McKinnon slices the Stilton. 'Richard Parnell wasn't too happy with that piece in the *FT*.'

'The truth, wasn't it?'

'Come on.' He smiles from the midst of a full black beard. A Scotsman, and one of the best fund managers in the business, he's excused the hirsute eccentricity. 'They went way overboard. There's bloody hundreds as bad as Parnells.'

'Not too many in your portfolio, I hope.'

'You buy one, you buy another one. How was the salmon?'

'Good.'

He tells me he owns ten per cent of the fishery that supplied it: conversation the Fund Manager way.

But I respect Brian McKinnon. Most fund managers are part of a herd: when the markets are abuzz about Latin America, they all rush to set up Latin American Growth Funds, their hapless investors climbing on board just in time to run off the cliff. Then the fund manager hears technology stocks are booming; he sets up a Hi-tech Fund and invites the survivors from the Latin American disaster to join him. And this is the strange part. Many of them do.

In this world Brian McKinnon stands out like a beacon. He can be cantankerous and rude, sometimes very funny, but whatever else he is, he's definitely not part of a herd. He's the London end of an Edinburgh-based operation, part of the Scots mafia. Even Stephen Vance respects him, a rare tribute.

'Richard Parnell's been onto you then?'

Brian misses a beat before he nods.

'A bit late in the day for him to be thinking of shareholder loyalty,' I say. 'Did he make any promises?'

'Usual story. Hang on, the upturn's coming next quarter. Your name was mentioned.'

'Compliments?'

'Not exactly.' A waiter comes our way. With a turn of the head, Brian warns him off.

It's no surprise that Richard Parnell has been trying to secure Brian McKinnon's allegiance. McKinnon's fund owns one of the last large parcels of Parnells that might still fall into the brothers' hands. Vance has given me the job of ensuring it does, hence lunch here today.

'Not a bad old goat,' Brian says referring to Richard Parnell. 'Just stayed around too long. The Meyers are doing the rest of the Parnell family a favour.'

'They're doing every Parnell shareholder a favour.'

'Look, if I bale out of Parnells I'll be underweight in industrials. And what's to buy out there in UK industrials?'

'Come around to the office. Our analysts will be happy to help.'

'Your bloody analysts wouldn't know their arse from their elbow,' he remarks cheerfully.

'Brian, without the Meyer bid, Parnells is a dog.'

'Stephen gave me the flim-flam last night, Raef. Save your breath.'

We stare at each other. Carltons wants something, he has it; I can't walk away.

'So tell me about precious metals,' he says. 'You've heard the Central-Banks-building-gold-reserves story?'

I have. We all have. This old chestnut comes by as regularly as Christmas. A story like that doesn't normally register with a man like McKinnon: he's trying to tell me something else.

'What's the McKinnon yearly special on gold?' I ask.

He taps the side of his nose significantly and gives me a look. Now I know what he's after.

'Remind me, Brian. Did you come to the Crest presentation?'

His eyes open a little. Crest? Had he mentioned Crest? But as I have.

'The African crowd. I dropped in for a wee look. Weren't too bad.'

'They were better than that.'

He laughs. 'You've been reading your own PR bullshit.'

'No, I've been reading the subscriptions list. How much are you down for?'

'None,' he says.

'None?'

A look of belligerence comes over him. His voice rises. 'None. Zero. Half of fuck-all.'

I glance across to the other tables, mainly men in suits, talking quietly. In one corner an old woman dressed as a young woman shakes her gold bangles and throws back her head and laughs. No one is looking our way.

'Half of fuck-all,' I say turning back. 'That's not much.'

He smiles now. He tells me good-naturedly that I'm a cunt. We're on familiar territory here. When a company brings its shares to market the shares are underwritten, pre-float, by a bank or a broker which then places the stock with investors: usually institutional funds managed by the likes of Brian McKinnon. Crest has been an easy sell for Carltons, money for jam, the institutions have been clamouring for the stock. But somehow Brian's fund has failed to apply for an allocation: it seems we have something he needs. We can trade.

'Say someone was interested in a decent-sized parcel,' he says. 'That'd be useful to you.'

'We're oversubscribed.'

'Say a ten per cent parcel?'

'Not a hope in hell.' I remind him of the five per cent limit the Crest vendors have placed on individual subscriptions, they don't want the shares manipulated post-float. 'Why the late rush?'

He takes up his glass. He tells me we've all got our problems.

Problems, I think. Brian, if only you knew.

'We can look at numbers up to five per cent,' I offer. 'But that's it.'

'Five per cent.'

'Maximum.'

'No,' he says. 'Five per cent.' He has me, and he knows it. He looks over the grey river to the City. 'Someone might trump the Meyers' bid.'

'It's their final offer.'

The choice is clear. He either accepts the Meyers' offer for his parcel of Parnells, and gets an allocation of Crest from us; or he doesn't accept, in which case he has to buy his Crest shares after flotation, an expensive proposition.

'Five per cent of Crest's available today, but don't expect the full amount tomorrow. By then it'll be down to four per cent.' Brian takes this calmly enough, so I add, 'Three per cent by Thursday.'

He nods, businesslike. We understand one another.

How many hours of my adult life have been spent like this? Sometimes the dance can go on for days and reach no definite conclusion. Days? Sometimes months. I'll show you mine if you'll show me yours. And endless meetings later you discover that you don't want what the other party has anyway. At least with Brian McKinnon the whole ritual can be concluded over lunch. Small mercies.

I signal for the bill now, ignoring Brian's offer to pay.

While we're waiting, he toys with the cheese-knife. 'Any idea why your Treasurer was shot?' he asks.

The question hits me like icy cold water. I make a sound.

'You looked at your own share price lately?' He points to the floor. 'Going down. I've got seven per cent of Carltons at the moment. I'm starting to wonder why.'

Carltons' share price has been slipping since last Thursday. I'd thought nothing of it, but Brian seems concerned. I ask what he's heard.

'I've heard all's not well in the House of Carlton. I've heard the murder investigation's centred on the bank.' He studies me. 'True or false?'

'The Inspector's been in a few times.'

'And?'

'And nothing. He's been in a few times. What do you expect?'

'When I hold seven per cent of your company,' he says, 'I expect to know what's happening.'

A nasty thought occurs to me. 'Darren Lyle hasn't been in touch has he?'

Brian's eyes stay fixed on mine, unsmiling. Not yet, he tells me.

A cold hand seems to close over my heart. A hard

knot forms in the muscles of my stomach. If Lyle were to get hold of McKinnon's stake in Carltons, we could be in very serious trouble.

When the bill arrives, I pay cash.

11

Back at the bank, our Finance Director, Gordon Shields, corners me in my office. An accountant by both trade and nature – married, two children and one grandchild, a house in leafy Surrey and golf on the weekend – he's the butt of every boring-accountant joke they dream up in the Dealing Room. He takes it all with good humour. He knows as well as I do that without his antlike attention to detail, and his careful diligence, Carlton Brothers would grind to a halt within days. Now he gives me a fifteen-minute lecture on the latest recommendations from the Accountancy Standards Board; he says I should know about this before our audit committee meets next month.

I find my eyes wandering to the phone. Should I call Hugh Morgan now, or wait?

'Raef?'

Gordon offers to go through it again, but this just isn't a priority.

'Leave the notes. I'll have a look at them later.'

He places the folder on my desk.

'Who'll replace Daniel on the audit committee?' he asks.

Daniel again. No escape. I mumble something about decisions-pending, and, unsatisfied, Gordon leaves.

I reach for the phone. Becky comes over the intercom: Ryan is here. My hand hovers then hits the button.

'Send him in.'

He has on the same heavy grey coat he wore earlier; he doesn't bother to take it off. Raindrops shine on his shoulders.

'If you want to see Vance, I think he's out.'

'I came to see you.'

Unlike McKinnon, Ryan has no need to follow any long and circuitous rituals: immediately we're just where he wants us to be.

'I've been to St Bartholomew's,' he says.

Bart's. With every ounce of will I possess, I hold myself steady. The shock leaves me dumb for a moment. He's been to Bart's. When I recover, all I can manage to say is, 'Why?'

He waves this aside.

'You told me you didn't know of any private problems Stewart had.'

Get up, I think. Get up now, walk out. Contact a lawyer.

But all I do is sit here. I can smell the wards of the hospital.

'Mr Carlton, how long have you known Stewart was the father of your child?'

133

12

'Mr Carlton?'

'Three months.'

'Only after she went into hospital?'

I nod, still stunned. I ask him how he found out.

'My sergeant was checking Stewart's holiday records,' he explains. 'He noticed an overlap with yours.'

'Who told you Annie was at Bart's?'

'No secret was it? What exactly happened at the hospital?'

'They ran some tests.'

'It wouldn't have told you who the father was.'

'It told me who he wasn't.' The words escape me with a real bitterness, but the Inspector stays pointedly silent. I rise and go to the window. On the street below, people are going purposefully about their business. That feeling hovers over me again now. Fear; that was the first thing, fear for Annie. Then the tests and the waiting. At last, knowledge. 'Do you want me to say I didn't kill him?'

No answer. When I turn I catch a fleeting glimpse of sympathy in his eyes, but the shutters go up immediately.

'How did you find out it was Stewart?'

'My wife. She wasn't a compatible donor either.'

'So she told you Stewart was the father?'

I nod.

'Who told Stewart?'

'She did.'

'Was he reluctant to go in for the tests?'

'No idea.'

There's a pause. Looking at Ryan I have a sense of deep disconnection. Where am I? Four months ago Daniel was my friend, I loved my wife, and Annie was my daughter. Now a police Inspector sits in my office and wants to know if I killed Daniel. How did I get to this place?

'Who else knows about this?'

'Theresa. The doctors.'

'What about Stewart's wife?'

I shake my head. There's never been the slightest hint from Celia that she suspected anything between Daniel and Theresa.

'Did Stewart actually say he hadn't told her?'

'He didn't actually say much of anything the past three months. Not to me anyway.'

'You had to work together.'

'We sat in the same meetings. He got memos from me, I got memos from him.' Retaking my seat, I tell Ryan, 'We didn't seek out each other's company.'

'Not an ideal situation.'

'No,' I agree. 'It couldn't have gone on much longer.' I'm far from comfortable, but the initial shock at Ryan's discovery seems to be wearing off. I smile crookedly. 'So much for doctor-patient confidentiality.'

Ryan doesn't bother to apologize.

'That scuffle by the boat. Stewart didn't accuse you of an affair with his wife, did he? What was it about? Your wife?'

'I don't know. I said something. He said something.' I truly don't remember how it started. I look over Ryan's shoulder now at the books I seem to accumulate but never have time to read. 'I didn't kill him.'

Ryan makes no comment on my unsolicited plea.

'How's the girl?' he asks. 'Annie.'

I feel an almost ungovernable urge to strike him. What right has a stranger to go stumbling through the most private places of my life? But as the angry words rise to my lips I notice Ryan's eyes: they've changed.

'You have children?'

'A daughter,' he says.

A daughter. Momentarily we're just two fathers, hostages to the fortunes of our children. 'She's in remission,' I say, returning to my desk. 'The doctors seem hopeful.'

He studies me a moment, then rises from his chair. 'I'll be speaking with your wife, later.' At the door he looks back. 'And in the meantime you might like to consider if there's any way of verifying that you went straight home from the boat last Wednesday night. It could be helpful.'

Parting, he nods to me in a very Inspector-like way.

13

When the pressures of work became too much, I would go and talk with Daniel. After my first few years at Carltons I realized the City was changing fast, and that we weren't keeping up. After my grandfather died it got worse, I had to fight tooth and nail to get even the most necessary changes past the watchful eye of Sir John. Daniel, early on, became my ally in Treasury. Nothing was off-limits between us, a fact that Darren Lyle guessed, then used, when he tried to bring me down. Immediately after Lyle's resignation Daniel and I became more circumspect, but we soon drifted back into the old routine: Daniel in my office or, after he became Treasurer, me in his, relaxed and giving voice to frustrations and ambitions we both kept well-buttoned outside. Even with Vance I've never had that kind of freedom.

Now I step out past Becky and glance up and down the corridor undecided. Sir John will be in his office but it's past three o'clock: his drinks cabinet, I'm sure, is already open. Anecdotes about the Old Days don't appeal right now, so I turn and head the other way.

Trust, that's what I had with Daniel. A trust deep and familiar, its roots in our childhood, a thing unquestioned. At nine years old we cut our thumbs with my pocket knife and pressed the bleeding cuts together. Walking the corridor at Carlton Brothers thirty years later, I nod calmly to the young corporate bankers, while the boyhood memory pierces inside.

Vance steps from his office in front of me, looking harassed. Immediately he turns on his heel. 'I need a word,' he says, going back in.

Curious, I follow him. Tony Mannetti, the head of Funds Management, stands by Vance's desk; he looks grim. It seems I've walked into something.

'There's been a cock-up,' Vance says.

'There was no TV,' Mannetti tells Vance, apparently restarting the conversation Vance walked out on. 'No papers. Nothing.'

'Must have been very pleasant for you.'

Mannetti stabs a finger at Vance. 'Get a fucking life.'

I intervene. 'Okay. What's up?'

There's a knock at the door, Karen Haldane comes in.

'Just in time for the good news,' Vance says, turning to Mannetti again. 'That parcel of Parnells that went through before the bid. Guess who bought them?'

We all look at Mannetti now. He looks at the floor.

'No,' Karen says, appalled. 'You fucking didn't?'

Mannetti's head jerks up, he rounds on Vance. 'This is bullshit.'

Karen speaks over him. 'You know the rules, Tony. You buy shares, you buy through us.'

She's less than pleased. And so am I. If he's been insider trading he'll have to resign or be sacked. Then I notice Vance slowly shaking his head.

'Tony wasn't buying for Tony,' he explains, directing

another withering glace at Mannetti. 'He was buying for us.'

Mannetti passes a hand across his forehead. Karen swears.

'For Carltons?' I say, the magnitude of it finally registering. 'You bought for one of our funds?'

Mannetti screws up his face. 'Johnstone bought them for the Alpha Fund while I was on holiday last week. He got his wires crossed.'

'He couldn't have,' Karen protests. 'He couldn't have got it past the systems.'

Mannetti erupts. 'He did, all right? We own a piece of Parnells, what the fuck you want me to do, pretend like it didn't happen? Jesus Christ, I've got enough with fucking Johnstone, I don't need you up my friggin' ass.'

I tell him, very firmly, to shut his mouth.

He sways forward on the balls of his feet, the muscles of his neck bulging. Karen looks furious. Vance too. And well they might. Johnstone's purchase of Parnells has placed us in clear and serious breach of the Takeover Code: we're in serious trouble here.

I ask Vance if he has told the Meyers yet. He says he hasn't.

'The Stock Exchange?'

'Not yet.'

I ask Karen if she's heard from the Stock Exchange's surveillance team. She shakes her head curtly. Policing this kind of infraction is her responsibility, the slip-up makes her look bad. She calls Mannetti a name.

'Karen.' I raise a hand. 'This isn't the time.'

She can barely restrain her anger, her hands are clenched into fists.

'Maybe we can unwind it,' Mannetti suggests, dolefully.

For a moment we all look at one another, four erring children wondering who will tell the teacher. At last I speak to Mannetti.

'Pull those Parnells shares out of the European Fund and stick them in an empty account. Book them out at the purchase price and don't let anyone else know. Do the paperwork yourself.'

He nods unhappily. I jerk my head towards the door and he goes.

Then I face Karen. 'I'm not even going to ask how this got past you, we'll sort that out later. You and Stephen are going to see the Meyers. Get your coat.' She makes to speak, but I cut her off. 'Now,' I say.

Still furious, she retreats. The door slams.

Vance drops into his chair. He props his elbow on the desk and rests his head in his hands. Quietly he swears.

'This isn't good, Stephen. We look like half-wits.'

He massages his temples.

'Who else knows?' I ask him.

'Nobody. Mannetti came straight in. He's only just found it. Unbelievable.' He looks up. 'How was McKinnon?' he asks distractedly.

I tell him about the Crest shares. He nods, but we both know it will take more than McKinnon's acquiescence to save the bid now.

'David Meyer will go ballistic,' he mutters. 'What the hell did Johnstone think he was doing?'

I offer to take Mannetti down to the Stock Exchange; our only hope is to throw ourselves on their mercy. Vance agrees. He suggests I speak with Sir John before I go. 'His cronies on the Panel might help,' he said. The Takeover Panel. Sir John has two friends on the executive and one on the Panel itself.

I clap my hands to my pockets and look around.

'You didn't bring anything in,' Vance says; and then as I'm heading to the door he asks, 'What the hell do I tell the Meyers?'

This question rises from the midst of the whole sorry disaster and catches me raw. When Darren Lyle hears what's happened, he'll laugh his fat head off. Brooding, I go out to fetch my coat.

14

The Takeover Code is overseen by the Takeover Panel, a collection of worthies selected from the City's self-appointed top drawer. The day-to-day running of its affairs is conducted by an executive of bureaucrats. Mannetti and I sit outside the closed doors of the Executive office. We've made our wretched pitch to them, thrown ourselves on their mercy, and now we await their verdict in silence. The minutes tick by.

'Go on,' I tell him. 'I'll see you back at the office.'

'I can wait.'

I turn my eyes towards the exit.

'I think it went okay,' he says.

When I made no response he starts rehashing the whole stupid episode: who misunderstood what, and when, but I'm already thoroughly sick of it. I give him a warning glance; his voice trails off.

'As soon as you get back there, have Johnstone's swipecard number wiped off the system.'

'I already fired him.'

'Good.' I look at my watch. 'If Vance is there, tell him I'll be back within the hour.'

Mannetti wants to say more, but he knows that this isn't the time. He gets up and departs down the corridor, touching his hair into place as he goes. The golden boy at bay.

I turn back on the closed door. I'm on the outside for once, the wrong side, not a very comfortable place. It feels a bit like the night of my seventeenth birthday: I spent it in a police holding cell, waiting for my father to come and bale me out. Those hours haunted my nightmares for years. Seventeen and drunk and foolish, Daniel and I were relieving ourselves against a parked car when two policemen happened by. They were quite amused at first. But then Daniel started. I was still struggling with my flies as he gave them his opinion on harassment and his 'Why weren't they

looking for real criminals anyway' speech. He asked
for their names, he said he was going to report them.
When I tried to lead him away he clapped me on the
shoulder. 'Don't you know,' he asked the increasingly
annoyed pair, 'don't you know who his father is? And
his grandfather?'

They didn't, so he told them.

Twenty minutes later we were enjoying the
hospitality of the local police holding cells. For the
next three hours, before my father arrived, I sat and
listened to Daniel snoring: the lessons of life.

Now the door opens. The Chief Officer of the
Takeover Panel Executive beckons me in.

The office is spartan, strictly functional, there isn't
even a picture on the wall: the unadorned workplace
of the City referees. Earlier there were four of them,
but two must have retired to the adjoining office: the
Chief Officer takes a seat by his younger deputy.

The deputy who reads aloud, from his notes, a
summary of the situation as narrated by Mannetti
and me.

When the deputy finishes, the Chief Officer says,
'Fair?'

Yes, I tell him, to the best of my knowledge, that's
how it happened.

'It's a serious breach. You realize the Panel will
have to be convened.'

'It was an honest mistake.'

'I don't doubt it,' he says in a tone that tells me he
doubts it very much. 'But I don't feel that the

gentlemen from Parnells or Sandersons will be inclined to let it pass. Do you?' He opens a folder, and launches into an explanation of where things will go from here.

The Takeover Panel and the Stock Exchange are at the top of the list of those to be informed, but right now I really don't care. All I want is to get out of here, to speak with Vance and prepare for the onslaught that's bound to come when Darren Lyle gets wind of this. The deputy appears to be enjoying my discomfiture. When the Chief Officer finishes, his deputy pushes a sheet of paper across the desk to me.

'Just as a token of good faith before they convene. The Panel Chairman's requested that you sign it.'

Two paragraphs. A guarantee that Carlton Brothers will pay difference cheques to those Parnells shareholders who sold to our Alpha Fund, a total of half a million pounds perhaps. I sign. When I hand back the sheet, the deputy doesn't bother to thank me.

'You can go now,' the Chief Officer says.

And it's there in his eyes too, the same thing I glimpsed in the eyes of his deputy. How long has it been like this? And is it just me, or all of us out in the land of seven-figure bonuses?

I offer my hand; he reaches over his desk without rising.

'Goodbye,' he says.

His cool look was hardened, it's quite obvious now:

he doesn't respect me. But only when I've left his office do I let the proper word form in my mind. It flares up, one more piece of unwanted knowledge. What those two men felt for me was contempt. Not just disrespect, not even envy, but contempt.

Down on the pavement I stand disorientated a moment. I have spent the best part of my adult life trying to prove myself to be more than the sum of my inheritance. I have done the eighteen-hour days, and the countless nights in anonymous hotel rooms across the globe. I have neglected my wife and my family. I have – God help me – poured seventeen years of life away in the struggle. And now, what am I? A rich man? But I would have been rich if I'd done nothing but play polo for seventeen years. A happy man? Next question. A good banker? Yes, I would have said so, certainly better than the average. But what does that amount to? I'm successful in a game which brings more and more money and increasing disrespect. Contempt even. Is this what I wanted? Is this the way I meant my life to go?

The river of pedestrians breaks and moves round me. Someone calls my name and I look up. My driver waves from the kerb, and I jostle numbly through the push of humanity to my car.

15

'The arrangement's still in place,' Sir John says.

I move past him and pull my dog-eared copy of the Takeover Code down from the shelf. Stephen Vance has just left us; his meeting with the Meyers was apparently a very sobering affair. If the Parnells bid fails, he thinks David Meyer might even try to sue us for professional negligence.

'Are we expecting to need some help?' Sir John enquires.

'Let's hope not.' I mention the names of his cronies on the Takeover Panel and Executive. 'I'd like them to know our side of the story before Lyle gets to them.'

Sir John nods. This whole business is sliding into the great grey territory of City life, the place where he does his best work. Then he frowns, thinking. I turn the pages of the Takeover Code.

'Raef,' he says. 'I'm worried about Stephen. That Ryan fellow's been in to speak with him three times already. People are saying some odd things.'

'Let them.'

Sir John grimaces, he thinks I'm being pig-headed. Annoying, but over the years I've learnt to pay his opinions some heed.

'Inspector Ryan doesn't know Vance,' I said. 'He's got the wrong end of the stick. And Stephen's got enough trouble with the Meyers right now without having us on his back.'

'I thought I should mention it.'

'So you've mentioned it. Thanks.'

Karen Haldane knocks and puts her head in.

'Oh, yes,' Sir John says to me, snapping his fingers,

'and Penfield called. Wants a chat when you've got a minute.'

He goes out past Karen.

'Penfield?' she asks me, coming in.

'Don't worry. Nothing to do with Mannetti.' I toss the Takeover code aside. 'Or our Compliance Department. How were the Meyers?'

'Thrilled.'

I tell her Vance said she handled herself well at the meeting. She shrugs this off, determined to stand proof against flattery. She really doesn't mesh with the normal give and take of the world: it's not surprising she's so unpopular.

'Becky copied some discs the other morning,' she says. 'For you.'

'Ahha.'

'You might have told me. I'm meant to book stuff in and out, remember. That's my department. I'm responsible.'

'I needed them, Karen. When I called through, you weren't there.'

She rests her hands on her hips. 'Needed them for what?'

'To check. Fair enough?'

'I'd like them back.'

'Not yet.'

'Why?'

She looks at me with real challenge now. It takes an effort, but I control myself.

'Karen. I'm answerable to a few people, more than

I'd like sometimes, but you're not one of them.'

This rebuff, like the earlier compliment, makes no visible impression. There are times I regret ever hiring Karen Haldane.

'Okay, I should have told you about the discs. It was an oversight.' I push some papers around my desk. 'If you want me to say sorry, Karen, okay, I'm sorry.'

She makes a sound.

'Christ.' I gesture to the sofa by the wall. 'Sit down and have a drink.'

She glares a moment more, but then the anger gradually drains from her. Was that all she was after, my apology? The tension dissipates, we seem to be colleagues again.

She goes and sits on the sofa, and I prop myself on the corner of the desk, facing her. This is one very strange lady.

'I was worried,' she says. 'You know, Becky strolls in and gets copies of everything, nobody even questions her.'

'She's my secretary.'

'That's hardly the point, Raef.'

Her gaze wanders off around the room.

'When's Daniel's funeral?' she asks.

It jolts me. 'They haven't released the body yet. Maybe next week.'

She nods, but she seems to have something else on her mind. She asks if the drink's still on offer.

I go and mix two gin and tonics. It occurs to me

that she's worrying about that Johnstone business, so I explain that Vance has gone to see Gary Leicester. Together they're preparing a response for when the accusations start flying from the Parnells camp. We've decided on a full and frank confession, the same approach we took with the Takeover Executive. Vance believes we can ride out the storm.

'Bully for us,' she says, taking the drink. 'Becky says the Inspector's been back to question Stephen.'

I'll speak with Becky later, she can be a little too forthcoming at times.

'He came to see me again too,' Karen says.

'Busy man.'

'He wanted to know what connection Daniel had with Compliance. I got the impression he's trying to tie the murder in with Carltons.'

'He's just asking questions.'

'He seemed to know a lot about it.'

'Our Compliance Department?'

'No. In general. Treasury procedure. Chinese Walls, and all that.'

Knowledge he no doubt picked up during his work on the Shobai suicide.

'Basically he wanted to know if Daniel was on the fiddle,' she says.

When I laugh, she shoots me a sudden caustic look.

'He wasn't joking, Raef. He told me if I thought of anything I should let him know.'

'Like what?'

'Had Daniel ever tried to override the system, how

much access he had to the other departments. You know.'

I tell her not to worry, it's probably just routine.

'A couple of weeks ago Daniel asked me some pretty odd questions,' she says.

I give her a blank look.

'About our systems,' she goes on. 'Where I thought we might have weaknesses.'

'He designed them with you. Why ask?'

'It was all pretty casual, he didn't make a big thing of it. I don't know, I'd forgotten about it till Ryan poked his nose in.'

'You mentioned this to Ryan?'

'No.' She considers. 'If Daniel thought someone else was on the fiddle, it makes sense. He would have asked me then, just to check. Maybe he was looking into some deal he didn't like the look of. Maybe—'

'Karen, get serious.'

'If he asked me about it,' she says, 'he must have told you too.'

She's guessing here, but it's a very good guess.

'He mustn't have thought it was that important,' I tell her.

She studies me a moment, then sips her drink.

'Were there any weaknesses?' I ask. 'In the system?'

'People.' She pulls a face. 'Look at this thing with Becky. Waltzes in, waltzes out, who knows?' Her head lolls back against the cushions. 'I gave the girls a blast. They'll know better next time.'

With any other woman I'd say the pose was deliberate: head to one side, hair framing the profile, and the grey skirt riding up towards her thighs. But not Karen.

'Why did you need those copies?' she asks.

'Nothing particular.'

'Mind my own business?'

I pistol my fingers in her direction and to my surprise she smiles. I finish my drink. Then I go round to the other side of my desk and I lock all the drawers. I flick off the desk lamp, the heaters and the PC. It's past six o'clock and I've had more than my fill of today. Karen takes the hint, she finishes her drink too, and puts down the glass.

'Listen Karen, if you think Daniel asking questions about our systems has anything to do with his death, then tell the Inspector. If not, then leave it.'

When she joins me by the door, I reach for my coat, my other hand poised over the light switch.

'You think it does?'

'No.'

I flick off the light. 'Then leave it.'

16

No sound from the alarm. When I call the maid's name down the hall, a voice answers from the drawing room.

'In here, Raef.'

My heart jumps. Not the maid, but my wife.

She hangs up the phone as I enter. A trick of the mirrors reflects her in an endless receding line.

'We've just come for some things,' she says.

Her eyes are dull, she looks drawn and tired, and at first I think 'Good', but in the next moment I'm ashamed of my pettiness.

'We were up at the hospital.'

'Where's Annie?'

'They're getting some clothes.' She glances upward and now I hear the movement in Annie's room. The nanny must be with her.

I ask Theresa if she's heard from Ryan.

'Ryan who?' she says.

Not so very long ago I'd have driven this into her like a knife, but not now. I explain quickly, avoiding her eyes. Ryan, the police Inspector, knows.

There's a long silence, then she asks, bewildered, 'Who told him?'

'He knew about the tumour. He went to Bart's.'

'Why?'

'I don't know, look' – I slice the air with my hand – 'it's happened, he knows, now he wants to see you.'

'Me?' She seems startled. 'Why?'

A burst of laugher comes from upstairs, we both look up. Then I cross to the side table and flick through the mail, separating Theresa's letters from mine.

'See what he asks,' I advise her, 'but I wouldn't tell him any lies.'

When I hand her letters over, she drops them into her lap. She tells me that Annie isn't sleeping well. A retort rises to my lips but I manage to quell it before it escapes. I really can't trust myself yet. Turning my back, I go out to the hall and lean against the banister, breathing steadily. How much longer this can go on? How much more can I take?

Upstairs, I surprise the nanny coming out of Annie's room, the zip on her bag is open and a white-laced sleeve hangs free. We hold a quick whispered conference by the door. She assures me that Annie's just fine. Inside the room I find Annie in the corner, kneeling and digging through a low drawer.

'A blue one for the blue,' she says with childish earnestness. 'The red one, that's for red.'

Innocent and clear, her voice shines into my heart like light. But it's not as it used to be, nowadays the light casts a shadow.

She reaches into the drawer, almost topples in, then cocks a leg, ready to climb.

'Hey,' I say gently. She turns, one hand holding fast to the drawer. 'Remember me?'

She presses her chin on her neck; her shoulders rock back and forth.

I ask if she's been good. She nods in that same way again, stretching her neck forward to open her mouth.

'Ah-ah-ah,' she says.

I kneel and reach, but she shrieks with laughter and swerves clear. It's a game to her. She's still laughing as she runs to the door. I make a mock-grab and she shrieks again and disappears into the hall.

I shuffle forward on my knees. In the drawer there are two mop-haired dolls, one red and one blue. The blue doll rests on a blue shirt, the red doll on a red. Annie. She has brought order to one small part of the world.

Downstairs, Theresa sits just where I left her. But she's smoking now, a habit she gave up soon after we married. Standing in the doorway a moment unnoticed, the usual questions assail me. What went wrong? How did we, a gilded couple with the world at our feet, beneficiaries of every kind of material blessing, how did we manage to fall so desperately far? And Daniel. Why Daniel? With the passing months the questions have lost their first brutal power, now they merely fall on me in dreary and remorseless strokes.

This is where we were when she told me. She was in that same armchair and I was over by the window, every detail of that awful moment remains etched on my memory. We'd just come back from the hospital, the day after the tests, the doctors had taken her aside for a private word.

I have to tell you something, she said.

Can it wait?

No.

I'll just call Stephen.

Raef—

154

And then it happened, she started to cry. A quiet weeping that racked her whole body, I went and put my arms round her shoulders.

Don't worry, I said. Annie's in good hands, they'll look after her there.

Theresa pushed me away, wiping her eyes. She looked at the floor.

They want to test Daniel.

It didn't register. My world had just broken in two and I didn't understand.

He might be compatible, she said. Then somehow she found the strength to raise her eyes to meet mine, the tears coursed down her cheeks. Compatible, she said, with Annie.

Compatible with Annie, so simple, just three words and I knew. From knowledge, no remission; implacable it went into my soul. I stood, turned my back and walked out. Tears. So many idle tears.

And now here we are again in this place together three months later. It seems life just will not let us go.

Theresa taps her cigarette on the ash-tray.

'What did the hospital say?' I ask, going in.

She looks up. When she speaks, there's smoke.

'Keep coming for the check-ups. It might be a full remission.' She draws on the cigarette. 'God,' she says, 'they don't know.'

'Does she need anything?'

'A father.'

My whole body goes rigid, the blood rushes to my

face. A father. Annie needs a father. Like a depth charge, it sinks deep then explodes.

'Don't push it, Theresa.'

'Raef—'

'Don't fucking push it!'

Silence. Even Annie's laughter from the kitchen now falls still. But Theresa doesn't take her eyes off mine.

'Do you want to divorce me?' she says.

My heart lurches again. Here it is. After all the shouting and recriminations in the months since we found out, here it is. This is the first time either of us has mentioned the possibility of divorce, and I find to my surprise that I can't face it, not directly. I mumble something inane about more time; I say we'll have to wait and see.

Annie comes in and wraps an arm around my leg. But when I touch her silky, white hair she releases me and goes to her mother. She arches her back against the chair.

'We can't pretend for ever,' Theresa says, pulling at the frills of Annie's dress. 'Your father rang to see if I was going down for the hunt.' The hunt this coming Saturday, at Boddington. 'I said I was. He wants to see Annie.'

'Fine.'

'I can't cancel it, Raef.'

'Daddy,' Annie says. 'Where's granda?'

I crouch and explain that granda is working right now but she'll see him on the weekend. Annie comes over and presses her little fist against my stubbled cheek. Then the nanny calls from the hallway: everything's packed, she's ready to go. Annie runs out to join her.

'Will you be there?' Theresa asks me.

'Probably.'

As she steps by me, she lowers her voice so that the nanny won't hear.

'It can't go on like this. I need to know one way or the other. You can tell me on Saturday at Boddington.'

Once they're gone, I pour myself a drink and go through to my study. And there, for two or three hours, I pretend to work.

17

'Suspicions among thoughts are like bats among birds, they ever fly by twilight.' So says Francis Bacon. When I turned twenty-one my father gave me a leather-bound copy of Bacon's *Essays*: I still take it down occasionally from the library shelf at Boddington. It has these phrases that stick, and it's this one about bats and suspicion that comes to mind as I sit with my father in his flat, going through the family accounts.

It's 11.00 p.m. He's spent the whole day down at Abbey Wood, the Defence Procurements complex just outside Bristol, but the travel and work seem to have taken little toll on him. He sits at his desk, reading the numbers. Every so often he asks me a question. Shoes off, feet on the sofa, open file resting on my knees, I give my opinions full rein. For once Charles Aldridge isn't here. Our family assets fall into three main divisions: Carlton Brothers shares, Boddington, and 'other'. 'Other' is the smallest division, negligible really: we deal with that quickly then move on to Boddington. The land agent's report for the quarter has just come in, we're received another embarrassingly large payment from Brussels. My father remarks that Adam Smith must be turning in his grave. The agent has advised us to buy a new harvester, I tell my father I agree: he jots a note. Another twenty minutes and we move on to Carlton Brothers.

I close my file. My father studies the latest list of Carltons' major shareholders.

'If you're looking for Sandersons,' I say, 'they're not there.'

He continues scanning the list. He took the news of today's disaster at the bank remarkably well, but perhaps that's because he thinks we have even more serious problems on our hands. He asks who's been selling Carltons down. I give him some names.

'There's no big bale-out,' I assure him. 'McKinnon and the rest are just covering their bets.'

'Charles seems quite certain we've got a problem with Sandersons.'

'A takeover doesn't make sense. If Sandersons get us, where's the benefit to them?'

'He isn't often wrong, Raef, you know that.'

'He isn't perfect.'

'Nevertheless . . .'

'I can handle Darren Lyle.'

He makes no comment. He peruses the list, the lamplight throwing shadows over his eyes. Suspicions.

The names on the list give a rough sketch of who has real influence over the affairs of the bank. Through Boddington Investments our family has a twenty per cent stake, by far the biggest single holding. After that come two pension funds, each with seven and a half per cent, American Pacific with five, then one of McKinnon's funds with seven per cent. A grand total of forty-seven per cent, more than enough to give us effective control provided everyone stays in line. My father sits on one of the pension-fund boards, and the other fund's chairman is my grandfather's godson. With American Pacific, we have a standstill agreement. None of these have been selling. But McKinnon's holding his slipped, and some of the smaller names, too, are offloading. My father looks troubled.

'If Sandersons want to get in there,' I say, 'they can't do it quietly.'

'That won't worry Lyle.'

'We'll see him coming. If he buys in the market we'll see him. If he starts touting around the major shareholders, we'll hear.'

'Still, I'd like to be ready.'

Precisely what I've been telling him: we're already prepared. But I don't press the point, he must be more tired than I thought.

'Have you heard any more from the Select Committee?' I ask.

He turns his head.

'Nobody's mentioned Odin?'

He looks pained. 'Raef, it's done with. As far as the Ministry's concerned, Odin never existed.'

He bows his head to read. He really doesn't want to talk about this. And me? What is it that drives me now? Why do I find myself, halfway through life, a sudden convert to the cause of truth? There have always been veiled places where my father worked, questions it was understood I'd never ask. Why now?

'Do you remember when I came to see you last Wednesday?' I ask.

No response; he continues to read.

'I told you about Daniel,' I said. 'I told you he'd found out about Odin. I mentioned he might go public with it.'

He takes up a pen and scribbles with a look of deep concentration. He isn't going to make this easy for me.

'You said you'd take care of it,' I remind him.

He doesn't look up, and I know that if I don't ask him now I never will. So I ask.

'What did you mean?'

His head stays down. He goes on scribbling for a while as if the question was never spoken. Then he

TUESDAY

1

Most of Daniel's mornings started like this: a meeting. Henry and William Butler, our Chief Economist, would go to Daniel's office, and the three of them would put their heads together for twenty minutes comparing notes on the overnight news: modern-day priests, digging through the entrails. But today it's my office they've come to. And being the first Tuesday of the month, Tony Mannetti's here as well. We discuss some recently published economic figures – trade balances, interest and inflation rates, and the US unemployment number due out tonight. This is going on all over the City right now, everyone trying to second-guess the markets before trading begins. Henry has the trader's view, he knows all the rumours and has a keen eye for when the big corporates are likely to move. He makes his points succinctly. William, on the other hand, is a chartist.

He believes that with a handful of repeating patterns he can read the mind of man. And he makes his points with painful slowness. Mannetti doesn't even try to disguise his disdain, he examines his fingernails, occasionally clicking out an imaginary speck of dirt. The meeting doesn't take long. The US dollar picked up after last week's rate rise, but William's sure it hasn't broken out of its primary downtrend. He shows us the chart. Henry says he's heard that two oil majors are moving money offshore, funding Far Eastern investments: Sterling might come under pressure this week. William makes a note. Without Daniel to bounce their ideas off, the pair of them are unusually subdued. Mannetti stifles a yawn.

'If that's it?' I say.

'What's the news on Daniel?' Mannetti's hand drops from his mouth. 'The clients are asking some questions.'

'Tell them to sod off,' Henry mutters.

Mannetti shoots a cold look at him. William intervenes, saying that he is being asked about Daniel too.

'Henry?' I say.

He nods reluctantly. 'Yeah, same in the Dealing Room.'

To be expected, I suppose. And there is absolutely nothing we can do about it.

'Just tell them the police are following up some leads. Say it was a mugging if you like. Whatever it was—' I look at the three of them '—it was nothing to do with the bank.'

'Right,' Mannetti says.

Henry turns on him. 'What the fuck does that mean? Right. You sayin' somethin'?'

'Henry.' I raise a hand and he stops. We have enough problems without these two falling out. 'I'll let everyone know as soon as the police find anything more. Until then, anyone asks, they get the same answer. Clear?'

Avoiding my eyes, Henry nods; then the other two. Tapping my new watch, I suggest they get on with their day.

William gathers together his charts and heads out to the Dealing Room to spread the morning's gospel: Sterling weak, Dollar strong.

Mannetti stands, pushing a loose curl from his forehead. He's a good four or five inches taller than Henry, and handsome. But his Adonis-like look would be more attractive if he wasn't quite so conscious of it.

'Sometimes,' he says to Henry, smiling frostily, 'right just means right.'

Henry watches him go, then turns sharply to me. I raise a hand again. Henry smiles wryly. 'Didn't say a thing.' Then he wanders across to the shelves and takes down a book. 'Mind if I borrow this?'

'Take it.' He turns a few pages, but he isn't reading. 'What is it?' I ask. 'Dealing for Beginners?'

He grins. It's been a very long time since Henry was a beginner. He started out with us as a clerk in

Settlements, and got his break as a trainee in the Dealing Room more than ten years ago. Talent and hard work have raised him to the Chief Dealership, but someone like him, without a degree, wouldn't normally have a chance of moving higher. Daniel's death might have changed that.

'Something up?'

He closes the book. 'Well, yeah,' he says. 'Maybe I shouldn't ask, but, you know, what's gonna happen with Daniel's old job?'

'There'll be a decision this week. Come Monday there'll be a new Head of Treasury.'

'Not you?'

No, I tell him, not me.

His awkwardness is almost embarrassing. He entered the Dealing Room young, his whole adult life has been shaped by the place and now outside it, even here in my office, he seems strangely at sea.

'Your name's in the barrel, Henry, along with one or two others.'

'I was just wonderin', you know.' He nods to himself. 'Owen's running a book on it. Maybe I'll have ten quid on me.'

'Your money.' I pick up a pen and tap the desk, waiting for him to go. But he doesn't get the message, he just stands there. Gauche, that's what Daniel called him. I see he had a point. 'Did Karen speak to you?' I ask.

'The Ice Maiden? Yeah, she was on my back

yesterday. Ancient history. What is it with her?'

'It's her job.'

'You seen that new paperwork she dreamed up?'

I remind him that she's working for me.

'Sign three times before you take a leak?' He holds up a hand as he goes out. 'Look at this. Callouses.'

Outside the door, I hear him sharing a joke with Becky before he heads back to the Dealing Room. The prospect of promotion has raised his spirits. But it's Becky's laughter that makes me realize just how quickly Daniel's murder is slipping into the past. For most of those who knew him, the tears have dried; questions remain, but the living are getting on with their lives. Most but not all. Not me or my father. Not Ryan.

Vance comes in without knocking and drops the *FT* on my desk. 'Read the "Lex"?'

I haven't, so I read it now. The *Financial Times* sets its best and brightest loose on several City stories each day: their short, well-informed pieces appear in the 'Lex' column. Its reputation has declined lately but it remains a useful sounding board for the City. This morning there's a piece on the Meyer bid, and the opinions it offers on the Parnells' board and management are scathing.

'Malign neglect? Close to libellous, isn't it?'

'Not our worry.' Vance takes back the paper and gives it a second perusal. 'I've faxed it over to the Meyers, make sure they see it.'

I ask if the Meyers are drawing down the rest of

the credit line. He admits that he hasn't raised the subject with them yet.

'You must have mentioned it.'

'I didn't want to rock the boat,' he says. 'We're nearly there.'

I remind him that we're also nearly in breach of Capital Adequacy, the ratio of capital to borrowings, set by international statute, that governs our loan book. Gordon Shields, our Finance Director, has been onto me about it already this morning. The Meyer bid is really stretching us thin. Times without number I've seen Vance take someone on his team aside to tell them not to confuse the interests of the client with those of Carltons. Now I recite the lesson to him.

'I'll have Cawley and Haywood take a look at the options,' he says. 'See what they can turn up.' Then he fixes me with a steady look. 'We might have capital adequacy problems, but if this bid falls apart you're going to have a meltdown in Corporate Finance.'

'Whose opinion's that?'

'It's not an opinion, Raef, it's a promise. The headhunters are gathering.' He goes to the door. 'By the way, Lyle seems to be getting personally involved in the Parnells defence. Any reason for that?'

'You know Lyle.'

Vance makes a sound. He knows Lyle all right.

'Stephen, have any headhunters contacted you?'

He smiles at me but doesn't answer. Then he turns and goes out, closing the door gently behind him.

The hairs prickle up my neck.

I phone Sir John immediately. No time for the usual discursive approach, so I ask him directly if he's unwound that deal yet, the one with the clearing bank. He tries to deflect me. 'John,' I say, 'have you done it? Yes or no?' A moment's silence, then he answers, 'No.' His tardiness, for once, is welcome. I tell him to leave it in place for now, and he seems quite pleased.

Hanging up, I press my hands to my face, I can't imagine Carltons without Stephen Vance, I really can't. An old saw of my grandfather's comes to mind. No friends, no leverage: no leverage, no friends. A cynical truth that explains many of the City's dark ways. And I have a sudden queasy feeling that very soon here at Carlton Brothers we'll need all the friends we can get.

2

The Meyers have their offices in Spitalfields, behind Brick Lane. Forty years ago they rented a shopfront in the same building; they were in the rag-trade then, but after moving into property they gradually bought out the other tenants. The brick exterior is shabby, but the reception's all plush carpeting, pale blue, and mahogany-panelled walls.

As we step in, Vance mutters, 'Once more into the breach.'

We've had some more bad news overnight. Bainbridge, an arbitrageur, South African but based in London this past year, has built up a four per cent stake in Parnells. Apparently David Meyer has taken the news badly; he wants someone to blame. Stephen Vance has been summoned.

Normally I'd be content to let Stephen deal with it alone, he's easily a match for David Meyer. But when I got into work this morning, and saw him, I changed my mind. Stephen does not look well. Lack of sleep; pressures of the bid; worries about Ryan: I don't know what's done it, but today he seems to be carrying the weight of the world. He was surprised when I said I'd come with him. No need, he said. But I assured him I had nothing better to do.

On the way over he gave me the dossier on Bainbridge that Haywood prepared in the early hours of this morning. There are articles from the financial press in South Africa, Canada and Australia, the markets in which Bainbridge made his name as a player in mining stocks; pieces which related a familiar and depressing story. Bainbridge's arrival on a company's register was the signal for the canny investor to bale out. Those who didn't generally found themselves pushed to the sidelines, voiceless, as he transferred any worthwhile assets into his personal holding company before departing to perform the same stunt elsewhere. A profile from the *FT* in the dossier puts his fortune at around eighty million pounds.

As we enter the office Reuben rises to greet us. But David Meyer doesn't bother: he starts straight in.

'So tell us the story,' he says. 'What went wrong this time? Who dropped the ball?'

Reuben invites us to sit. Then he sits down himself and rests his clasped hands on his stomach. He asks Vance to explain. David paces the room.

Deliberate and concise, Stephen gives an account of the Bainbridge holding. There isn't much sign of his earlier weariness now: he seems to have this enviable ability to call up some hidden resource just when he most needs it. David interrupts, but when I hand him our dossier on Bainbridge, he slumps into a chair and reads.

Once Vance is done there's a brief silence, then David closes the Bainbridge dossier. He looks from me to Vance.

'You fucked up again.'

Vance stiffens. 'With respect—'

'Don't give us that.' David slaps the dossier down on the floor. 'We're not paying for excuses. You told us 180 and we'd get Parnells. Now you're telling us what? Sorry, you made a mistake?'

'We weren't to know Bainbridge'd get involved.'

'Wrong,' David shouts, leaping to his feet and pointing at Vance. 'Knowing when a prick like this Bainbridge is coming in, that's your job. That's why we pay you.'

Reuben says something in Yiddish. David answers

in the same language, then turns back to Vance.

'You're saying we can't get Parnells now? We upped the bid—'

'We can do it with your support,' Vance says.

'Then go ahead.'

It isn't like Vance to let things get under his skin, but I can see that he's had more than enough of David Meyer. Reuben intervenes. He asks Stephen if the Bainbridge holding has been confirmed.

Vance explains that we're expecting the Stock Exchange confirmation later this morning, then he points to the dossier in David's hands. 'One thing I can tell you, he won't be making a bid for Parnells himself. He's a spoiler, not a manager.'

Reuben asks exactly how much of Parnells we've secured. Vance tells him.

'Now Bainbridge has four per cent,' Reuben muses aloud.

'And you schlemiels,' David points at Vance again, 'have one per cent.'

At this blunt reminder of our cock-up, Vance winces. David Meyer mutters to himself, the one word I hear clearly is 'shambles'. I address Reuben.

'Stephen's appearing before the Panel this morning. Indications are, we'll be slapped over the wrists. The Meyer Group won't be dragged into it.'

David Meyer laughs. 'Why not? You've already got us answering questions in a murder investigation.' He waves a hand airily. 'Takeover, murder. Another day at the fuck-up office.'

Reuben looks from his brother back to me. I'm beginning to realize just how hard Vance must have worked to get the deal this far.

'We don't doubt your good intentions,' Reuben says. 'It's your results that concern us.'

It's my turn to wince. We have, by any measure, handled the Meyers' interests very poorly.

'We'll still win this,' I say.

But there's no reaction from Reuben. David smiles unpleasantly. And then Vance, as he's done so often before, comes to my rescue. He gives them a short dispassionate assessment of how the bid currently stands. He, too, concludes with an assurance of victory.

'Remind me,' David says. 'Have I heard that one before?'

But Vance has taken the bit between his teeth now. Unruffled, he reaches into his briefcase and takes out a file. Then he goes across to Reuben's desk and begins his performance. A minute later he has Reuben on one side, David on the other, and all three of them are bent over the open file, talking numbers. Stephen Vance really is something. When I first started in corporate finance, he used to take me along to a lot of his meetings, and I generally felt then, just as I feel now, surplus to requirements. He could talk under wet cement; and not only talk, but convince and inspire. But I think the thing I admire most about him is that, unlike so many in our business, he has standards. One of those early meetings he took me to, I've never forgotten. It was at the head office of a major industrial, and it lasted about ten seconds. The company was interviewing a number of banks, a beauty contest: they wanted to select one of us to manage their affairs in the City. It was a big deal at the time; we'd been working on it for weeks; even my grandfather was involved. When Vance and I walked in we found the company executives seated in line behind a table. There was one chair in the centre of the room, the whole thing laid out to intimidate. The Chairman didn't introduce himself. He said we should keep our presentation brief, and he pointed to a small bell on the table. When I've heard enough, he said smirking, I'll ring the bell. The rudeness was pointed and deliberate. Vance looked at me and smiled. Then he walked to the table, picked up the bell and rang it in the Chairman's ear. I don't think I've ever seen a man look more surprised. We didn't get the business, but that gesture stood ever after as a benchmark for me. It taught me that there exists a level below which even a corporate banker shouldn't sink in pursuit of the deal; it taught me to maintain my self-respect.

Twenty minutes later, on the street outside the Meyers' offices, Vance thanks me.

'What for?'

'You didn't walk out.' He pushes his fingers up through his greying hair. 'That David is a first class pain in the arse.'

The performance over, Vance looks tired again. I

ask if he's heard any more from Inspector Ryan.

'Jesus,' he says, laughing. 'One thing at a time.' Vance, the corporate banker's banker, has nothing in his sights but the bid. On the corner he hails a taxi. He steps in and gives the address where the Takeover Panel have convened their hearing. 'Coming?' he says.

I wish I was. Unfortunately my days of thinking about just one deal night and day – in the shower, on a plane, in my bed – are over for ever. My father's son, I've inherited a place at the table of an altogether lonelier and more uncertain game.

As Vance pulls away in the taxi, I glance at my watch. Hugh Morgan will already be waiting.

3

'We got a break.' Hugh beckons me into his office. 'Pull up a chair.'

There's a whiteboard by his desk. On the left side of the board Hugh's copied the details from my fax: the hierarchy of the Carlton Brothers management from Sir John on down. A maze of arrows and questions marks join the names. On the right side there's a list of deals in red lettering, and more arrows.

Looking over his shoulder at the screen, I ask, 'How bad?'

'Seen worse. Okay, from the top. We dumped miscellaneous so I churned money-market and forex from the system, looking for patterns. Zero. Too many deals. A few crooked deals a week, they'd just disappear into the statistical noise.'

'This is a break?'

'Hang on. Last night I was thinking about that note. You know, from Penfield?'

'Ahha.'

'It said over the past twelve months, right? Fraudulent trading over the last twelve months.'

I nod, unsure where this is taking us. Something else occurs to Hugh now.

'By the way,' he says, leaning across to tap the list of names on his whiteboard. 'Anyone above this line joined Carltons in the last year?'

'Tony Mannetti,' I tell him. 'He came across from New York.'

Hugh wants to know more so I explain how Mannetti came to us. It was a *quid pro quo*, part of the standstill agreement we worked out with American Pacific after they'd built a stake in the bank. Once we'd made it clear to Eric Gifford that we wouldn't offer him a seat on our board, he quickly lowered his sights. He suggested we pool some resources in selected businesses. As it happened, American Pacific had built one of the strongest funds management teams in the US while our own efforts in that department were foundering. He offered to send us one of American Pacific's rising stars for a short time. Mannetti came. Two months later, both the head and deputy of our funds management team left for greener pastures. When Mannetti offered to stay, we cleared it with Eric Gifford, then accepted. Until the past few days the arrangement has worked out well.

'Until the past few days?' Hugh echoes.

It will become public knowledge anyway, so I tell Hugh about the cock-up. 'We're in front of the Takeover Panel right now.'

'Ah,' he said. 'So Mr Mannetti's not flavour-of-the-month. What's he like?'

'American. A bit flashy. Not exactly my taste. You can rule him out on this fraud thing.'

Hugh asks me why. I nod to the screen.

'He's funds management, ninth floor; he doesn't even have access to the Dealing Room. And the cock-up happened while he was on holiday.'

'No access at all?'

'None.'

It comes out in a tone of regret. I've worked with Mannetti for the past several months but unlike with everyone else above the line on Hugh's whiteboard – Vance, Sir John, Henry Wardell and half a dozen others – I've developed no real liking for the man. It would be so convenient if he was the fraudster, but he isn't.

Hugh doodles some more with his pen. 'Okay, the note. Last night I started wondering why whoever it was only sent it now. I mean, if he's known this stuff's been going on for a year, why wait till now before he sends the note?'

'Maybe he didn't know. Maybe he just found out.'

'One possibility. But what if something else triggered it?'

'Like?'

'Like a deal,' Hugh says. 'A crooked one that just got done. One the note-sender didn't want to happen.'

I'm no expert, but this suggestion seems like a rather wild guess, and I say so. Hugh isn't troubled.

'Then allow some time for the note-sender to turn things over, or for something else to occur—'

'Daniel's murder?'

'I checked with the Post Office,' he says. 'The note could have been sent just before, or just after, Daniel died.' He types then, telling me he's narrowed the field even further. 'I concentrated on forex: there was a big surge in deals late December.'

In late December the French Franc collapsed, there was pandemonium in the Dealing Room. Our settlements staff had to work shifts to stay on top of the volume.

'If someone wanted to hide a deal, this'd be the place. There were two big days, the twenty-seventh and -eighth. I've done a search and scan on all the Franc deals your lot did both days.' He hits one final key. 'Hey, presto.'

The screen goes blank for a second, then three deals appear. Alongside each, there's a name, and though I'm staring straight at it, I can't believe what I see.

'Shobai,' I say.

But it isn't Shobai I'm looking at, and nor is Hugh. He points to the second name.

'Odin. You know them?'

What now? Christ Almighty, I think, what now? I shake my head. To give myself time, I point to the third name, Twintech. 'Who's that?'

But Hugh won't be put off, the Twintech and Shobai deals aren't a fifth the size of the Odin transaction.

'Get this,' he says. 'Someone scrubbed Odin off the main file. My software picked up the gap and I traced the transaction number. I cross-checked the counter-party code and turned up these guys, Odin Investments.' He gives me more details, proud of what he's found.

I ask about Shobai and Twintech, but Hugh's dismissive.

'Small fry. Probably statistical anomalies. Odin's the one.'

He's wrong. I know it, but how do I tell him? The Odin deal was a one-off; it can't possibly be part of the fraudulent trading referred to in Penfield's note. But how do I explain that to Hugh?

'Concentrate on Shobai.'

'Have you been listening?' Then he speaks slowly, word by word, as if to an idiot. 'Someone scrubbed Odin off the main file. Your problem is Odin

179

Investments. Are you reading me?'

'You've done good work.'

'That's not what your face says, Raef. What the hell is this?'

'Forget Odin.'

He gives a snort of choked laughter. 'I'm doing you a favour here. Now it's forget it? No way.'

'Hugh—'

'No way.'

He's becoming angry. Up at Oxford, when he got his teeth into a problem, he simply wouldn't let go; and that Petrie case, the same thing. And now?

I choose my words carefully.

'Hugh, it's not necessary to investigate the Odin deal.'

He searches my eyes. He asks me to repeat what I've just said, so I do.

'Fuck,' he says quietly.

'Listen—'

'No,' he says, stabbing a finger at me, 'you listen. You already knew about this Odin deal?'

I try to speak but he cuts me off.

'Well thanks for the information. I was up half the bloody night working this out. Consideration or what?'

He stands suddenly, his chair slides back, crashing into the wall. Then he stalks to the window and looks out.

'I couldn't tell you, Hugh. I would've but I couldn't.'

'You didn't.' He faces me again. 'Look, if you were running your own investigation at the bank, why not just say?'

His misapprehension, and the depth of it, catches me out. I hesitate. Already suspicious, he sees.

'You are running an investigation?' he asks.

He looks straight at me. If I lie now, and he catches me in the lie, he'll dump me. And with just three and a half days before Penfield's team moves in, I can't afford that.

'Odin isn't a problem.'

'Oh yes it is,' he says. 'Because if you don't tell me what this is about, I'm all finished. You wanted to find a deal that smells, I've found one. I did what you asked, and you've changed the goal posts. I haven't got any shortage of work here Raef, I'm in the world's biggest fucking growth industry. Now you tell me what this Odin's about, or that's it. You're on your own.'

'I can't.'

He shrugs. 'Fine.' Then he goes back to his desk. 'Your choice.' He starts shuffling papers around, and wiping away invisible dust. 'Do you want your discs back?'

I've been dismissed. Without revealing the truth, what more is there for me to say?

I tell him to keep the discs, I'll pick them up later. He makes no comment, perhaps he sees what's in my mind: later I might have to return cap in hand. Later, once I've had time to think, I might decide there's no choice but to answer Hugh Morgan's questions.

As I open the door he says, 'Raef?' and I turn. 'That Odin file,' he says, 'you wouldn't know who scrubbed it?'

Our eyes meet, and he looks long and hard.

'No.'

He nods to himself. 'You know where I am.'

When he bows his head over his paperwork, I back out the door.

4

The Dealing Room is chaos: dealers yelling, people tapping at keyboards, the squawkboxes rattling out endless strings of numbers. Henry is nowhere in sight. As I walk across the room it occurs to me that Hugh might have made a good dealer: he'd never let himself pay too high.

At the Spot Dollar/Mark desk I pause. Owen Baxter's running the show here: he's come across from the proprietary desk to fill in. There's a female dealer on one side of him, and on his other side that young trainee, Jamie.

Owen hits a button and barks, 'Dollar/Mark?'

A broker's voice bursts from the squawkbox. '25–30.' Then a pause. '30 paid.'

Owen makes the broker an offer. Jamie asks if he should put the offer on the dealing screen.

Owen looks aggrieved. 'Did I say that?' He nods toward the urn. 'Don't be a cunt all your life. Go make some coffees.'

Jamie, an Oxbridge graduate with a first in Medieval French History, goes to fetch the cups. Not for the first time lately, I wonder just what kind of contribution Carltons is actually making to the civilization of the world.

'30–22, your offer,' the broker says.

Owen shouts this time. 'Don't tell me, you little prick, tell the market.'

'Ten mine!' the broker shouts back.

Owen hits the button. 'Ten done. What's the name?'

He starts punching the deal into the system while the woman writes the deal-slip: 10 million US dollars sold at 1.32 against the Deutschmark. Then the broker's voice comes from the box again.

'SocGen. And for that Sandersons deal at 19, five dollars, your name's Barclays.'

I lean forward. 'What's up with Sandersons?'

Limit problems, Owen says. Apparently they've turned us down twice.

Barclays is switching the deal for us, writing retrospective back-to-back deals with Carltons and Sandersons to get us over the problem. This kind of thing is tit-for-tat, every bank gets caught out sometime, switching deals for friends is like oiling the wheels of trade. The deal remains done, but now Carltons and Sandersons both have Barclays as the counterparty rather than each other. But people talk.

And if Sandersons keep turning us down the brokers will start to wonder why. Worse, so will the other dealers in the market.

'Anyone else turned us down?' I ask. 'Or just Sandersons?'

Just Sandersons, Owen tells me.

Jamie returns with the coffees. I drift over to the Forwards desks where William, Billy Bullshit, is giving an impromptu lecture on Eliot Wave Theory. The senior dealer is yawning. Drawing him aside, I ask about Sandersons: have they been turning us down here.

'Matter of fact they have. No drama?'

Just checking, I say.

For the next ten minutes I amble around the other desks making the same casual enquiry and everywhere, to my consternation, the answer's the same. Since early this morning Sandersons have turned us down across the board, we haven't completed one single deal with them. By the time I reach the Equities desks, Henry's reappeared.

'Give me a second, Raef,' he says.

While I was up seeing Hugh, Vance took the expected slap on the wrists from the Takeover Panel. The news is out, they've accepted that it was a genuine mistake; the Panel has given its approval for us to continue with the bid. Looking over Henry's shoulder, I see the announcement on the screen. Henry, over the squawkbox, is talking to the broker, he'll be a minute yet.

Propping myself on an unused desk, I survey the Room. Out here, even more than in his office, the memories of Daniel are strong. He was a part of all this in a way I will never be, completely devoted to the daily cry of the markets. Devoted. It's been quite a while since I had a thought about Daniel that wasn't tainted with rancour and pain. I let this one linger a moment. In my mind's eye, I see him passing through the maze of desks as I've just done; but smiling, stopping to share a joke, laughing even. They liked him, the dealers; I think it made him feel secure to know he was looking after their interests through me. And his disagreements with Vance did no harm out here. They were loyal to him too. I never realized quite how loyal until Celia rang me at the office late one night asking after him. When I said I hadn't seen Daniel she expressed surprise: one of the dealers, she told me, was sure he was in my office. After I'd hung up I went out to the nightdesk. Had someone taken a call from Daniel's wife? The senior dealer admitted that he had. And had he told her Daniel was with me? He shrugged it off, he said he'd thought he'd seen us together. It didn't seem important so I let it drop. But looking back later I realized it was the first hint to reach me of Daniel's infidelity. He'd been married to Celia three years, they already had one son, and they seemed happy enough. But something had gone wrong, and the first to know were the dealers. My own enlightenment came by accident: a glimpse of Daniel, arm around one of our

Settlements girls, that I caught through the window of a City pub. I didn't confront him at first. But there were other women: his affairs became an open secret at the bank. And it also became clear that Celia knew, and that the knowledge was crushing her. I chose a quiet moment in his office one evening, staff all gone, just Daniel and me, ties loosened, sharing a drink; a rare relaxed moment and I built up the courage to ask him what, in God's name, he thought he was playing at.

He stared into his glass. He didn't answer.

Look at Celia, I said, she's falling apart.

Did she put you up to this? he asked.

When I told him no, he finished his drink in one shot.

Stay out of it, he said.

Maybe I can help.

Yeah, you can, he said. You can help by staying out of it.

It stopped me dead. He was like that even when we were boys: cheerful and relaxed until someone crossed into his private territory, then he'd haul up the drawbridge. I knew that, but I felt I owed it to Celia to try again. So a few months later I did. This time there was no exchange. Daniel simply got up and walked out of my office, pausing to offer me three words of advice: Fuck right off. It was the last mention I made of it. Their business, I thought, not mine. Rather ironic, considering.

'How's that?' Henry steps back from the Equity

desk and hands me a note. The Dealing Room is still
in full cry.

The note summarizes the morning's trading in
Parnells: our broker has secured another two per
cent.

'Who's selling?'

Henry recounts the names: smaller institutions,
and the market-makers and some arbitrageurs
who've decided it's time to cash in. The game is
panning out just as Vance predicted. Though we
aren't there yet, the increased bid has swung the
whole momentum of the deal our way.

I guide Henry away from the desks, and we stop
beneath a row of wall-clocks. In Tokyo, Bahrain and
New York, time passes.

'What's this with Sandersons?'

'They're a bit tight with us,' he says. 'No big deal.'

'You know their Chief Dealer?'

Henry nods.

'Get hold of him. Find out if there's a genuine limit
problem or if they're just messing us around.'

He notices something over my shoulder. 'I think
you're wanted.'

I turn. Sir John, agitated, is signalling to me from
the door.

'What does that guy actually do?' Henry mutters.

I pretend not to have heard. Reminding him about
Sandersons, I move off to find out what has happened
now.

5

'We have visitors,' Sir John tells me. He's been waiting for me in the corridor, just beyond the Dealing Room's plate-glass door. He seems sober. 'Two gentlemen from the DTI.'

When he pushes away from the wall I place a hand on his arm.

'Who?' I ask.

'Skinner,' he says. 'I didn't catch the other one.'

The name means nothing to me, and that isn't what I meant anyway. As he walks down the corridor I stay at his shoulder. He explains that the two men arrived unannounced; he knows as little about it as me. The Department of Trade and Industry isn't known for sending its functionaries on social calls; the last time they came like this was the beginning of the Arnold Petrie case. In my head I run through a checklist of our clients: Who is it this time?

We enter Sir John's office and go through the introductions. Skinner's the taller of the two men, clearly the more senior, and when Sir John invites them both to sit it's Skinner who declines.

'We won't keep you,' he says. Skinner addresses his next remark to me. 'We've been instructed to make enquiries into a certain trade in Parnells.'

He consults a file and reads the details aloud.

The Johnstone deal. But the speed of this response from the DTI is unprecedented. In the normal course of things the Stock Exchange would take weeks to decide if the transaction warranted a referral to the DTI, and months of preliminary enquiries before the DTI followed it up. But to have sent two of their people in person immediately? Someone, somewhere, has pulled a string.

'We informed the Takeover Panel ourselves,' I say. 'We understood they were satisfied with our explanation.'

Skinner closes his file. 'The Department's obliged to satisfy itself on certain questions. Of course we'll keep the recommendations of the Panel in mind.'

'Who instructed you?'

He raises a brow.

'You said you were instructed to make inquiries,' I remind him. 'Instructed by whom?'

At this, Skinner looks uncomfortable. It occurs to me that he isn't actually enjoying this sudden departure from routine, he hasn't had time to prepare.

'We take our instructions from the Department, Mr Carlton,' he says finally.

His colleague flips open a briefcase. Two pieces of paper are handed to us: the details of the Johnstone deal above a paragraph of Whitehallese.

Leaning across Sir John's desk, I hit the line to Funds and Management and tell Mannetti to come down. While we wait, I try to draw Skinner out, but he responds to my questions in such vague and guarded terms that he might as well be speaking a foreign language. A language from well west of the City. He reminds me a little of Charles Aldridge.

Mannetti arrives. He keeps smiling after I've introduced him, but I can tell he's surprised. I hand him the DTI note.

Skinner asks, 'Do you trade on your own account, Mr Mannetti?'

Sir John explains that Carltons has clear guidelines for employee trading.

'Mr Mannetti?' Skinner breaks in.

'Do I trade personal?'

Skinner nods. That is his question.

'Sometimes.' Mannetti looks from me back to Skinner. 'Occasionally. Look, I didn't buy any Parnells if that's what you're getting at. Not personal.'

Most of our staff hold accounts with Carlton Brothers, it's an in-house rule that all private trading goes through us. The accounts are open to the scrutiny of our compliance department, so if any Parnells went through Mannetti's, Karen Haldane would know. Yesterday I asked her to double-check his account: nothing.

'We'll need to see the records of your account, Mr Mannetti,' Skinner says.

'What is this?' Mannetti looks disbelieving. 'You're investigating me?'

'A statement for the past six months should do initially.'

'You gotta be kidding.'

Skinner is clearly unaccustomed to having his demands questioned.

'I do not kid, Mr Mannetti,' he says coolly.

He turns aside to his colleague. Mannetti steps forward and taps him on the chest with one finger.

'Hey, smartass. Neither do I.'

Daniel used to joke that with a name like Mannetti, and coming from New York, Tony had to be mafia. Now, in the chilling moment of silence that follows, the joke seems very unfunny. The air of threat is apparent to all of us. Skinner looks like a rabbit caught in the headlights of an oncoming truck. Mannetti stares him down then steps past him, leaving without a backward glance.

Skinner doesn't seem to know where to look at first. Sir John begins to explain that Mannetti's an American, and gradually the atmosphere slides back into something like normality.

Skinner's colleague asks who else has been involved with the bid.

'Our head of Corporate Finance. A few in his team. The PR people.' I shrug. 'Take your pick.'

'Names?' Skinner says, recovering.

I tell him he's using a sledgehammer to crack a nut. 'It happened the way we told the Takeover Panel. If someone suggested it didn't, I'd like to know who he is.'

'Mr Carlton, do you trade a personal account?'

Beside me, Sir John mutters, 'This is absurd.'

But I have Skinner's measure now. He doesn't want to be here, he hasn't had time to prepare for a proper inquiry, and finally, and most importantly, these aren't his questions.

Taking my cue from Mannetti, I face Skinner square. 'I do have a personal account. I use it to invest long-term. Day-trading is a dangerous business, Mr Skinner. People get burnt. You think you're onto a winner, then you find you've backed the wrong horse.' He tried to hold my gaze, but he's wilting. 'Even very clever men come unstuck. Perhaps you should keep that in mind.'

That look comes back to his eyes, Mr Skinner, our man from the DTI, is caught in the headlights once more. I tell him to feel free to pass the message on to Gerald Wolsey.

6

Darren Lyle has called a meeting. It's common practice for the advisers on either side of a takeover to meet during the course of a bid, but most of our overtures to Sandersons have been rebuffed. Now, after the announcement of the final offer, and Vance's session this morning before the Panel, Lyle has contacted us. Vance set the terms: two o'clock in our conference room.

While I wait for them to arrive I work on the discs, copies of those I gave Hugh. Scrolling through the Shobai-Carltons deals from December, I try to see them as he might. I focus on one deal, then another. I assemble deals, break them up and reassemble. I search for patterns. I fiddle. After half an hour I've got precisely nowhere and I flick off the screen and kick back.

Odin, I think. How did Hugh do that? It worries me that he retrieved the name, but what worries me more is the ease with which the trick was done. If Hugh found it, why not some keen young programmer in our IT department? Too late now, I regret the whole Odin business. I hold my head in my hands a moment.

Vance looks in. Our friends from Sandersons are here.

The Sandersons team, Lyle at their centre, is arrayed on one side of the table; Vance, two lawyers, Haywood, Cawley and me, are seated opposite. Each of us has a folder open in front of him: dogs, marking territory. The meeting has not gone well. There was the usual speculation before the Sandersons team arrived: Haywood and Cawley almost convinced themselves that the bid was over, that the Sandersons team was coming to convey the Parnells concession of defeat. It hasn't worked out like that. Jeremy Quin, Vance's opposite number at Sandersons, has done much of the talking, mainly a recap of what's already happened. Lyle is doodling on a pad.

'Jeremy,' I say, interrupting at last. 'You're telling us the Parnells aren't conceding. Is that right?'

Quin turns to Lyle who puts down his pen.

'That's right,' Lyle says.

I ask why he's called the meeting then. What,

I say, do we have to discuss?

Lyle stares at the doodles on his pad. 'The Parnells want some light shed on the Meyers' intentions.'

Ludicrous. Cawley snorts in surprise. We're weeks into the bid, the final offer's been lodged, and now the Parnells want to know the Meyers' intentions?

'You're asking us what the Meyer Group wants?'

'We'd like to clarify the detail.'

'The Meyer Group wants Parnells,' Vance says evenly. 'How much more detail do you need?'

Quin's face remains a mask. Lyle, however, turns his head, one of those more-in-sorrow-than-in anger gestures. He couldn't look more insincere if he tried.

'Where's Reuben?' he asks Vance. 'I noticed he wasn't at the hearing this morning.'

'You lost, Darren. Take it like a man.'

Lyle grins straight back. 'I bet David Meyer really rubbed your nose in it.'

I flip my folder shut. I tell Lyle he's wasting our time.

He turns to Cawley, the youngest of our team. 'Be a good lad,' he says. 'Go fetch the biscuits.'

Cawley reddens. This patronizing insult says a lot about Darren. He's often spoken of admiringly as ruthless, but there remains a staunch and significant minority view: scum floats.

To save Cawley's embarrassment now, I make a joke of it. I pick up a pad and move behind both teams like a waiter taking orders. Forget the Law of the Jungle, this is the City: what generally prevails here is the Law of the Nursery. Lyle catches my eye as I go to the door, it seems he wants a private word. When I nod, he follows me out.

It's not the done thing for a banker to wander around a competitor's offices alone, so Lyle, plastic security pass clipped to his lapel, stays close. We skirt Corporate Finance where a few of those not working on the Parnells bid are huddled together comparing spreadsheets. They watch us out of sight. In the kitchenette, Lyle perches himself on a stool. I open a cupboard, fossicking for mugs and a tray.

'Not as easy as you thought,' he says.

It takes a moment before I realize he means the bid. I really have been on the sidelines too long.

'Darren, you haven't got a hope in hell of saving them.'

I set a tray on the bench and count the mugs. Two short. I open another cupboard.

'How's David Meyer?'

'Honestly?'

'Yeah.' He smiles with malicious pleasure. 'Honestly.'

I find the two last cups and place them on the tray. 'Always pleased with our work.'

He laughs. 'David Meyer is a wanker.'

Spooning coffee into the filter now, I only half-listen to his opinions on David Meyer. In the space of the five years since he left us, Lyle has elevated himself from the ranks of the lowly MBAs to the Managing Director's chair at Sandersons: quite an achievement.

But those at Sandersons who once thought they were his friends now find they were merely temporary allies in the onward march of his career. This isn't just standard office politics either. Lyle leapfrogged two senior colleagues in spectacular fashion to take the Managing Directorship. A deal with one of their biggest clients had gone badly wrong, the Serious Fraud Office was called in to investigate, and Lyle's two colleagues resigned in disgrace. Nobody listened, at the time, to their protestations of innocence. Since then the case has been dropped, and Sandersons are said to have paid the disgraced pair substantial severance cheques. For a while there were rumours of unrest at Sandersons, but Lyle seems to have ridden out the storm. To the victor the spoils of an unscrupulous war.

Lyle concludes a vaguely slanderous story about David Meyer.

'Anyway, he's your problem.'

'He's my client,' I corrected him.

'Same difference.'

'No, he's my client.' I turn and point. 'But he's still your problem, Darren, or you wouldn't be here.'

One of the secretaries looks in. Lyle reached over and shoves the door closed in her face. What this man really needs is a good firm punch in the mouth.

'What do you want, Darren?'

'What's on offer?'

'If you don't stop buggering us around what's on offer is a sudden close to this meeting.'

I fill the sugarbowl and get the cream from the fridge.

'Which one of you two pricks pointed the police in my direction?'

Fortunately I have my back to him. I pause. Then I nudge the fridge door shut. Cup with saucer, bowl with jug; I concentrate very hard on the layout of the tray.

'It was you or Vance,' he says.

'Me or Vance what?' I ask turning.

'One of you told the Inspector on Daniel's murder to come and see me.'

'Bullshit.'

'So, it was Vance?'

'It wasn't anybody.'

'Yeah? Then how come this Inspector knew about that run-in I had with Daniel on the Langford bid. That was what, six years ago?'

It was. And as far as I know, Vance and I were the only ones who saw the bitter acrimony that developed between Lyle and Daniel during the bid. Langford was a small insurance and investment house that often dealt through Carltons, but when we were employed by one of the big general insurers to help them launch a takeover for Langford, the people at Langford decided not to put any more business our way. Understandable; but with this connection severed, we felt under no obligation to keep up the usual Chinese Wall between our Corporate Finance Department and Treasury. Vance brought Daniel in to help us win the bid, and he proved invaluable. He knew many of the Langford managers, and even two of the board: they were all people he'd dealt with over the years. Vance spent hours with him, sessions that Daniel later told me felt like military debriefings: how did Daniel think Langford would react if we did such-and-such? Who were the main forces on the board? Were there any whispers in the market about them?

And Darren Lyle hated it. He was, and is, one of those corporate bankers who has a keen sense of his own superiority to any other forms of City life. And to find Vance turning to Daniel for advice – Daniel, who Lyle looked upon as a creature from the stinking swamp of Treasury – it hit Lyle where it hurt, in his pride.

Daniel took the brunt of Lyle's insults for weeks, then finally cracked. It happened in Vance's office: Vance had called Lyle, Daniel and me in for a meeting; we were in the last stages of the bid, a tense time. Lyle dropped one snide remark too many – a comparison, if I remember rightly, between the intelligence of the average dealer and the average mollusc – and Daniel suddenly flew off the handle. He snapped back at Lyle: Lyle replied in kind. In an instant he and Lyle were shouting at each other, trading venomous insults, while Vance and I looked on amazed. Eventually Vance intervened, laying down the law to them, and the meeting ended. But both, in Vance's estimation, had slipped badly.

Looking back, the incident was a prelude to the affair which brought on Lyle's resignation.

Lyle and Daniel, like Lyle and me, had a history.

'This Inspector's making out as if Daniel being dead helps Parnells. As if it's some great plus for me.' Darren's bulldog features crease, and he studies me. 'I got the feeling someone put that idea in his head.'

'You're mistaken.'

'I don't think so.'

'Darren, they're investigating a murder. Apparently they've heard you and Daniel didn't see eye to eye. You're running the Parnells defence. We're working to crack it open.'

'So I had your Treasurer killed. That's the big theory?' He swears.

I turn back to the tray. If Vance suspects Darren's the murderer, why hasn't he said one word about it to me? And if he doesn't suspect Darren, if all he's trying to do is cause Sandersons some problems, then he's overstepped the mark. Vance and I have to talk.

Darren asks me who Daniel's replacement is.

'Why?' I face him again. 'Someone at Sandersons looking for a job?'

Darren stiffens. 'You come sniffing around us and it'll end up in court. Poach just one of my staff.' He raises a finger in warning.

Stepping past him, I slide the door open.

'Do me a favour, Darren.' He gives me a dark look and I point to the bench. 'Bring the biscuits.'

* * *

The meeting reconvenes and immediately Jeremy Quin makes his pitch: the Meyers can have two seats on the Parnells board if they agree to stop buying.

'Two?' Vance says.

'Two,' Quin repeats.

Vance, very deliberately, makes a note of the offer. Everyone is quiet now: Sandersons' team watch Vance; along our side of the table, all eyes are on Quin. Grandmaster chess with a billion-pound prize.

'If we could have some indication of how the Meyer Group might respond,' Quin says, 'that would be helpful.' Vance remains silent. 'Do you see this as something you can recommend?'

'Frankly?' Vance laid down his pen. 'No.'

Quin nods, unfazed. Like Vance, a past master at this game. Now he suggests Vance might have a different number of Parnell board seats in mind.

'A number you'd feel comfortable recommending to the Meyers.'

Vance inclines his head. 'Twelve.'

Darren swears beneath his breath. Quin raises his brows. There are only twelve seats on the Parnells board.

'Are you suggesting we double the board?' Quin asks.

Vance, smiling, says that's not at all what he had in mind.

Darren is glowering now, one hand a white-knuckled fist on the table. The others in the Sandersons team look unsettled too: apparently they'd had some real hope for this gambit. Quin's expression, however reveals nothing. Vance offers an olive branch.

'Let's not close the door shall we? Two seats. We'll pass the offer on to the Meyers.' He makes another note, then lifts his eyes. 'Negotiable?'

Quin exchanges a glance with Darren, who hesitates before nodding.

Then Quin pulls some papers from his folder. 'And we have several queries about your valuations.' He invites one of his team, an analyst way down the table, to put Sandersons' case. The young man does so for the next ten minutes, but this is just smoke, Quin knows we won't be adjusting our valuations of the Parnells assets now; and certainly not downward. When Cawley begins a brief reply from our team Darren slaps his hand down on the table.

'That's everything, then.'

Cawley bridles, but I nudge his leg beneath the table and he holds his tongue. Vance reaches across to shake Jeremy Quin's hand.

'We'll pass on your offer.'

'Do that,' Darren Lyle cuts in.

I make the mistake of reaching to offer him my hand. Darren looks from my hand up to me, then stands and walks out. Jeremy Quin releases Vance's hand and takes mine. He has the good grace to look apologetic.

'But you'll forgive me,' he says smiling, 'if I don't wish you luck.'

* * *

'Darren Lyle is a bastard.'

'The first breach in the walls,' Vance responds smugly.

He's come to my office for a quick post-mortem on the meeting. We agree that the Meyers' increased offer has caught them flat-footed, that Quin's main purpose was to draw us out: they want to know if the Meyers will fight this one right to the bell.

'And I think Darren wanted that private word with me.' I toy with my desk calendar. 'Stephen, do you think you have some idea why Daniel was murdered?' He looks up. 'Or who killed him?'

'What?'

I push back in my chair. 'Darren's been questioned by Ryan.'

Vance absorbs this news. 'And?'

'And he thinks it was you who pointed Ryan at him. He seemed pretty particular about it.'

Vance asks what I mean. I tell him about the Langford deal.

'Ah,' he says. 'Ryan wanted to know if I was the only one who didn't get along with Daniel. Darren came to mind.'

'Why? You think he's been nursing a grudge for five years?'

Vance smiles. 'This is Darren, remember.' He drops his eyes to his notes. 'Frankly, Raef, if Darren's got Ryan breathing over his shoulder, that's Sandersons' problem, not ours.'

I take a moment with that. Then I ask Vance why he didn't tell me this before.

Embarrassed, he begins to explain that it didn't seem appropriate to speculate. 'Daniel's death.' His voice trails off. 'It wasn't the time.'

By which he means, I realize, he wasn't sure that I was strong enough to listen. Perhaps he's right. He says he's going down to see our broker, and asks if I'm coming. I gesture vaguely around my desk: work to do.

7

Alone, I return my attention to December's deals in the Franc. December. Within minutes I'm staring blankly at a screen full of numbers. Last December was the worst month of my life. Annie was in hospital. At home, Theresa and I had settled into a bitter trench warfare: long silences, punctuated by accusations and allegations intended to wound. Most, I admit, came from me. Most, but not all, and it's these other ones that have plagued me for almost three months. The coda to nearly every one of them was the same: 'Raef, you just weren't there.' Sometimes delivered sadly, and sometimes with spite, but always the same: 'You weren't there.' And here's the hard part: after nearly three months of reflection, three months spent turning over and inspecting the years of my marriage, three months of broken sleep and bad dreams, I've come to the conclusion that the accusation is just, she is right: for the greater part of my marriage I really was, as Theresa claims, not there.

Now I scroll through the Shobai deals, the wasteland of numbers. December. Never again another month like December.

I've rehearsed my excuses. That holiday to the States we'd planned, how could I let that interfere with the ICI rights issues? And her sister's wedding, it overlapped with a big telecoms demerger, what was I meant to do? Another time we were down with her parents, a rare family gathering, when Vance called me back to the office. And other times; too, too many others. Building the bank, I told her. Each incident nothing, but taken together and catalogued, they paint a picture I'm almost too ashamed to see. What in the world did I think I was doing? Building the bank with bricks stolen from my marriage? Never a selfish man in theory: only in practice.

There's a knock at the door. Henry puts his head in.

'Got hold of Sandersons' Chief Dealer,' he said. 'You were right, it wasn't just limit problems. He had orders to pull the plug on us.'

'Orders from whom?'

'From the top. Darren Lyle.'

I nod, and Henry disappears. What the hell is Lyle up to? For the time being I put it out of my mind. Thoughts of Theresa return, but these too I put to one side. Just one last time, I promise myself: the weak man's lament and ever-hopeful refuge. Then I apply myself with new vigour to the deals of December. One last time.

8

In the afternoon, Allen Fenwick calls. He's a journalist on the *FT*, one of the few in his profession I ever speak to. A minute's polite chat, then he gets down to the real purpose of the call.

'How much of Parnells have you got?'

I tell him. He suggests that the final bid of 180 won't be enough.

'Who's running the bid, us or you?'

'Okay, okay. I'm doing an interview with Bainbridge later, I thought you might do one too. Any chance?'

I rarely give interviews, and right now Gary Leicester would be apoplectic if I didn't consult with him first. A word in the wrong place and I could inadvertently move the balance of the bid against us. Apart from this, there's Daniel: Fenwick would be bound to ask about the murder.

'Maybe next time.'

He groans.

Haywood's file on Bainbridge is lying on my desk, I reach over and flip it open. 'But you might want to ask Bainbridge about some old deals of his. Grab a pen.'

I give him the three deals that show off the deplorable Bainbridge technique to best effect. He will check these deals with other sources, but at least I've pointed him in the right direction. He thanks me.

'Now, bollocks aside,' he says. 'Will the Meyers get Parnells, yes or no?'

'Yes.'

'I just spoke with Jeremy Quin. He says no.'

'Ask a stupid question, Allen.'

He laughs. 'We're getting buried in Sandersons press releases round here.'

Not surprising. If Leicester's doing his job, the *FT*'s being bombarded with our press releases too. I'm about to hang up when he asks, 'Any comment on this insider trading stuff?'

I make a sound. He reads me part of a Sandersons press release: it details the Johnstone cock-up, the slant being that it wasn't as innocent as we made out; it implies that the Takeover Panel got it wrong, and that we shouldn't have been allowed to proceed with the bid. Johnstone isn't mentioned, but my name crops up twice. Fenwick finishes and waits for my comment.

I tell him to speak with Leicester and Partners.

'Raef, if I don't pick this up someone else around here will, believe me.'

'Off the record, Allen?'

'If that's the best you can do.'

It is. I take a deep breath and give him the story,

the whole cock-up from beginning to end.

'That insider trading rubbish is just Sandersons' spin,' I say. 'I advise you not to print it.'

'Advice noted.' Not much, but with Allen the best I'll get. 'One more question,' he says.

'Make it quick.'

'We had the police around here, picking up clippings on your Treasurer, the one who was shot. There's a rumour they're chasing a financial angle on the murder. That make sense?'

'I'm not the police.'

'Rumour has it it's connected with that Shobai thing a while back. The suicide. What do you think?

'I think you're fishing.'

He laughs. I say goodbye and hang up.

Immediately I call Gary Leicester and fill him on the line Sandersons are pushing about insider trading and me. When I tell him I've already spoken with Allen Fenwick, he moans. To pacify him, I agree not to take any more calls from journalists.

Karen Haldane comes through on the intercom: she'll be free in ten minutes.

Ten minutes to kill. I take Daniel's key from my drawer and go along to his office. Since last week no one's been in here but the police and Karen, a sweet acrid smell hangs in the air. In the bin by his desk there's a pile of screwed up paper, two brown apple cores, and an empty packet of Alka Seltzer. From this office there's no view of the river; not that Daniel cared, he usually spent most of his working day in the Dealing Room. After opening the blinds, I go and thumb through the folders on his desk. Inspector Ryan and his team did a search last Friday: they said they found nothing of interest, but Ryan asked me to keep the door locked anyway. Now I sink into Daniel's chair. Empty: that's how it feels in here. I've hardly set foot in the place since November, but nothing's changed except for this: it feels empty. Daniel won't come walking through the door, waving his arms and explaining his great new idea for Treasury. There'll be no more late-night sessions together, plotting the future of the bank. All that's over now, gone for good.

Idly, I open and close the drawers: papers, clips, pens and pencils, the usual desk flotsam. Daniel wasn't the most tidy person in the world but Ryan's search has added an extra layer of disorder: loose papers are spilling from their folders and nothing's neatly stacked. The last drawer closed, I lean back and look around. This is it. The sole physical remains of one man's entire working life: a few framed documents, mementoes of deals long forgotten, hang alone one wall; a cluster of mini national flags sprouts like flowers from a square of rubber foam on the shelf; and on the desk, a photograph of Celia and his two boys. A filing cabinet, a desk and a bin. This, I know, is not the life Daniel would have chosen.

When we were boys he wanted to fly. At Eton his room was plastered with pictures of jets. But after taking his maths degree up at Cambridge, when he tried out for the Air Force, it turned out his eyesight wasn't good enough. It was the great disappointment of his life. Then came the two years in my father's old regiment, a false start, before he joined Carltons. He was a successful banker, and he enjoyed his success, but what could banking ever be to someone who'd once dreamed of jets? After joining us at Carltons, I never heard him mention flying again. Looking around his office now, I think I can feel something of what he still must have felt here: life passing unfulfilled, work a poor second best to a dream. Not an unusual story I suppose, but now, Daniel's life over, it seems so indescribably sad.

Concealed beneath the desktop there's a hidden catch, I reach back there and flick it. A slim hidden drawer slides quietly out. I'd forgotten about this drawer when Ryan came to do the search, I never mentioned it to him. It's where Daniel kept his personal documents, he showed it to me years ago when he made me an executor of his will. Inside the drawer, I find half a dozen pages. The first four detail a plan he had for cutting back the number of our dealers; it will be unpopular out in the Dealing Room, he's right to have kept it well hidden. The fifth page is in his own handwriting, jottings of numbers beneath a legal firm's letterhead. 500 K, five hundred thousand. And 1,000 C. Hundreds? He seems to have been shifting some assets around in his will. I put it aside. The last page is different – yellow paper for some reason – and the first two words stare straight up at me. Odin Investments. My throat contracts. My heart thumps in my chest. Odin. And Ryan was here. My mouth goes dry.

When Daniel mentioned the Odin deal to me last month, I warned him to leave it to me. But the conversation, like all my conversations with Daniel since November, was brief. Reading the single page now, I wonder just how much he knew. Does it matter? He certainly didn't know what I told my father he knew, and nor was he about to go public with the little knowledge he had. I lied to my father. Daniel somehow stumbled on the Odin deal, and that gave me the idea. Revenge. I meant to bring the weight of Whitehall and Westminster crashing down on Daniel's head. But even in my most poisonous dreams I never wanted it like this. I never expected him to be shot. I'm sure I didn't.

The first four pages I return to the drawer. I keep the one on Odin, and the other concerning Daniel's personal affairs. Then I push the drawer back in until the catch clicks into place. I listen for a sound outside the door. There's none, and I'm satisfied at first, then appalled.

How is it, I wonder, that I came to be a thief?

9

Karen Haldane walks between the metal shelves of our back-office filing room, touching boxes. 'August,

August, August . . . September. You want December, yeah?'

I tell her yes, the forex paperwork for December.

At the end of the narrow alley, she turns and comes back along the other side. The shelves rise floor to ceiling, the cardboard boxes filling every inch of shelf-space. Here we keep the paperwork generated by Funds Management and Treasury: dealing-slips, fax confirmations, printouts from the Reuters trading system, queries on payment details, the lot. The quantity produced on a daily basis is staggering, all of it, for a time, stored here as a manual back-up for our computer files. Standing by these groaning shelves, it's extremely hard to maintain faith in the pundits' promises of the paperless office.

Karen indicates one section with a wave of the hand. 'December,' she says.

The boxes are colour coded: red for equities, blue for money market, green for foreign exchange. I pull down the first green box.

'Who's the problem with?'

'Shobai,' I tell her. I flip open the box and immediately I'm lost again. The files inside are colour coded too.

She crouches beside me. 'Details?'

I hadn't intended to tell her, but I could waste hours tracking the deals through all these boxes and files. So I give her the details of the two deals, the dates and amounts. She glances into the box and shakes her head. Then she stands and points to a green box up on the highest shelf. I take it down.

'Why didn't Shobai back-office call me?' she asks.

I shrug: who knows?

Karen opens the box and runs a hand over the spines of the files, muttering. 'Christ,' she says.

'Something wrong?'

She pulls out some files, shuffling them. 'Not in the right order. I'll speak to Sandra later.'

Sandra, the back-office girl responsible for manual filing. Right now she has my sympathy.

Karen pulls three files from the box. 'Last week in December,' she announces. 'Spot deals in the Franc.'

She hands me one file, props the second against the box, and keeps the third for herself. She assumes she's staying, and offhand I can't think of a good reason to dismiss her. Back braced against the lower shelves, I open my file. Karen kneels by the box. For several minutes there's nothing but the sound of pages turning.

Then Karen asks, 'What did the DTI want?'

I raise my eyes. She's still busily searching her file.

'The DTI?'

'It isn't a big secret, Raef. The whole office knew within ten minutes of them walking through the door.'

Great. How long will it be before the whole City hears? I bite the inside of my lip.

'They had a few questions about the early Parnells trade.'

'Johnstone's.'

When I nod, she suddenly loses interest in her file.

'Didn't they want to see me?'

'Preliminary enquiries, Karen. I told them our compliance officer's satisfied there's nothing untoward. Okay?'

She gives me a searching look. 'Well your compliance officer might be having second thoughts,' she says.

'You said all the personal accounts were clean.'

'They are. I was thinking more generally.'

'For instance?'

'Mannetti,' she says. 'He's an experienced fund manager. He knew damn well Parnells were on the Red List.'

'He's been away.'

'And then he's conveniently on holiday, completely out of touch, when it happens.'

'Maybe that's how it was.'

'Yeah,' she says. 'Maybe.'

Like Hugh, she's suspicious of every action and motive. It makes her good at her work, but it's a trait that can grow very wearying. Besides, I know that her nose was put out of joint when Mannetti was put on the Audit Committee only months after he joined us: she had to wait two years for the same mark of trust.

'Anyway, how come the DTI came in on it so quick?'

I shrug. I tell her that if she wants to look more

closely at the Johnstone deal, to go ahead. 'But don't spend too long over it.'

A minute later I come to the end of the file. Nothing. I pick up the third file and start turning over the faxes, dealing-slips and payment details, the nuts and bolts of trade. The truth is I'm grasping at straws. Half an hour ago Penfield called to discover what progress I'd made; or rather, we'd made, he still believes I have the benefit of Hugh's professional assistance. He wanted to know if we still thought we could get to the bottom of it by Friday. I told him we were certain, as big a lie as I've told for some time. He reminded me of the consequences of failure then wished me good luck and rang off. But when he hears about the visit the DTI people have paid us, as he will quite soon, I'll get another call from him. His tone, then, won't be nearly so sanguine; in preparation I've come up here to gather evidence of the progress we've supposedly made.

My eye stops on the name in my file: Shobai. The next moment Karen hands me the details of a second Shobai deal that she's found. We look them over: one trade for five million US dollars, the other for six, nothing exceptional, the Dealing Room does hundreds just like them each week. Karen wanders around to the next aisle of shelves. It sounds like she's pulling down more boxes.

I open the third file and find the other Shobai deal almost immediately. 'Don't worry,' I call. 'I've got it.'

Laying all the paperwork side by side, I compare the details. The signature on each dealing slip is different: no two deals done by the same trader. So much for my one brilliant idea.

Karen comes back and looks over my shoulder. I ask her if she recognizes the signatures.

'Ahha. And they've both got personal accounts. Do you want me to check them again?'

I tell her it can't do any harm.

Leaning over my shoulder, she points to another signature. It's on so many pages in the file that I'd stopped seeing it. Each one's countersigned by Henry Wardell.

'I'll check all three,' she says.

Henry. We really are grasping at straws.

I drop the files back into the green box then reshelve it.

'Do I get to know what this is about? Has Shobai made a complaint? I can call them.'

I raise a finger. 'Don't. As far as anyone else is concerned, you've never heard of these Shobai deals. Check those personal accounts, let me know what you find, and that's it. All right?'

'Is this connected with Johnstone?'

She sees my surprise.

'I mean,' she says, 'how often do we get any real trouble? Once a quarter maybe? And now the DTI come calling, and you're up here, and both on the same day. Come on, Raef. I'm meant to be the compliance officer.'

215

That she is. And as our chief compliance officer her access to all parts of the bank is second only to Sir John's and mine. On Hugh's whiteboard, her name was up near the top of the list.

'If you want to help, just check those personal accounts. Discreetly.'

I lift the second box back into place, then I go around into the next aisle.

'Leave them,' she says.

I tap the Shobai papers in my pocket. 'We're all done.'

'This isn't Shobai.'

Then I notice the labelling on the shelves beside me: not 'Treasury', as in the other aisle, but 'Funds Management'. Karen crouches and reaches into the first box.

'I wanted to make a start before the DTI get serious. By the way, Stephen made a scene up here this morning. It wasn't appreciated.' She lifts her eyes. 'Could you speak to him?'

'Vance?'

She nods.

'What kind of a scene?'

She looks into the box again, eyes lowered. Tentatively, I ask if Stephen owes anyone an apology.

'Just tell him not to come up here,' she says tightly. 'He can send one of the secretaries.'

I sway back as I would from the heat of a flaring fire. Vance has really upset her. I say that I'll have a word with him, but that I won't be denying him access to this floor. She shrugs, apparently resigned to this decision already.

Resting a hand on one shelf, I look along the row of boxes. It reminds me of the Bodleian and the hours I spent researching my thesis on Price Theory. I can't even remember the title of it now, and the only thing I know about Price Theory I picked up during my stint in the Dealing Room.

'Who comes in here?'

'In here to the filing room?' When I nod, she says, 'Sandra. Me occasionally, but mostly Sandra, she does the filing. Maybe one of the other girls if there's a query.'

'Anybody from downstairs?'

'No reason to. Besides they don't have a key.'

'Who does?'

'Just Sandra and me.'

When I worked with Hugh on the Petrie case he never stopped asking questions. I'm trying to think like him now, to ask the questions he would ask, but it's harder work than I imagined.

'Karen, doesn't anyone from downstairs ever come up here?'

She pushes back her fringe and leaves her hand resting there. 'Well, back when we were working on the new systems we used to come in here a bit.'

The significance of this escapes me at first.

'We ran quite a few dummy deals, we had to see them through to the end.' She gestures to the shelves. 'But you mean more recently.'

'Doesn't have to be. You and who else? Someone from downstairs?'

She looks at me as if I'm being particularly obtuse. 'Yeah, someone,' she says. 'Daniel.'

All roads lead to Rome. I frown. She bends and rummages in the box again.

Was Daniel defrauding the bank? Though he never said it to me, I'm sure Hugh suspects it: Daniel's death and the subsequent delivery of that note to Penfield would arouse anyone's suspicions. But knowing what I do, it seems to me no more than a distinctly odd coincidence.

And I admit there's a part of me that wants to believe Daniel was ripping off Carltons. There's a part of me that cries out against him as a treacherous bastard, capable of any outrage, but all the while I know it just isn't true. He had a side to him I chose not to see, I'm aware of that. The infidelity and the womanizing, I chose not to look at it straight: his business, not mine. But the other side of Daniel, his work as Treasurer, was beyond any reproach. He was proud of what he'd achieved, and proud of his reputation for straight dealing: in fact most of his disputes with Vance arose from his failure to recognize that the direct and open approach wasn't always the best policy out in Corporate Finance. At work, Daniel was honest; something I omitted to tell both Hugh and Inspector Ryan. But now, thinking back over the past few months, it occurs to me that Daniel tried several times to broach the subject of security with me. It was on the last of these occasions that he mentioned Odin.

'Karen, when was the last time Daniel was in here?'

'Months ago. I don't know. September?' Still kneeling, she studies the files that now lie open on the floor all around her. 'That was the last dummy run through the system.'

'Did he ever ask for your key?'

'No.' She looks up. 'Do you want me to recheck his personal account too?'

I take a moment with that; then I nod.

10

Ryan steps from Vance's office into the corridor just ahead of me. He's so wrapped up in himself that he doesn't notice he isn't alone.

'Inspector?'

He lifts his head. 'I've seen your wife. I'll catch up with you later.' He disappears toward the lifts.

Vance's door is still ajar, and I slide my knuckles over it and enter to find him seated at his desk, staring into space.

'I just saw Ryan,' I say.

Coming back to himself, Vance shoots me a warning look. Apparently more bruises have been raised at this latest encounter. From what I can gather, Ryan hasn't been satisfied with the answers he's been getting from Stephen. He keeps going away then coming back for another round of questions. After giving Ryan my alibi for Wednesday night – I slept over at my father's – I seem to have slipped down the list of suspects. But Stephen has no alibi: he was working late here at the office alone. The office is fifteen minutes' stroll from St Paul's Walk: and Vance and Daniel, as the whole bank knows, did not get along.

I pull up a chair and Vance gives me the new Parnells numbers from the top of his head, but I have the impression his mind's elsewhere. While he talks, I browse through the faxes on his desk. There's one from McKinnon, he's accepted the Meyers' final offer. Vance picks up another loose page from his desk and hands it across.

It's a memo from Henry Wardell about the bond issue we placed for CTL last week. Everyone thought we'd have no trouble getting the issue away in the market, but instead we've been left with half the underwritten amount still on our books. Going by Henry's figures, our probable trading loss will be bigger than our fee. Bad news.

'The last I heard, we were going to be beating the bids off with a stick.'

'So Daniel said.' Vance points to Henry's gloomy assessment. 'Henry appears to have other ideas.'

One more headache to add to the catalogue, but by no means the worst of them. I put the memo aside and ask Vance if he's heard from the Parnells board.

'Not directly.'

He digs among the faxes then hands me the longest, from Leicester and Partners. They send us one of these each evening: a copy of everything they've got into the papers during the day, and a list of puffs in the electronic media. Vance has circled the relevant section in red. The late edition of today's *Evening Standard* carries a quote from Richard Parnell in response to the Meyers' final offer: he says he presumes the bid of 180 is a joke.

'More of the same,' Vance comments. 'Richard Parnell's going to fight it. Price isn't the issue with him, he wants the family silver kept intact.'

'The rest of the family?'

'Not taking our calls. Everything's being filtered through to them by Sandersons.'

The Parnells Board is packed with members of the Parnell family, their solidarity's been a thorn in our side all along. If we could drive a wedge between them, convince even one of them that 180's a good price, the defence would probably collapse. But so far we haven't even come close.'

'Haywood's had an idea,' Vance says. After pairing Haywood and Cawley on the bid, he's been watching over them like a father. 'He thinks he can get to Neil Parnell.'

'Haywood knows him?'

'Knows of him. Apparently Neil hunts with the Heythrop.' Vance raises a brow. 'Haywood thought he might take a day with them himself tomorrow.'

I turn this one over. At worst, Haywood will get in

a good day's hunting for his trouble: no doubt he's thought of that.

'Okay. But tell him not to make any promises. Just keep it all within the terms of the bid.'

Vance makes a note. He seems tired. There's a knock at the door and Mannetti puts his head in.

'Raef. Got a moment?'

Setting the Leicester fax aside, I ask him what's up. He glances at Stephen.

'About some possible withdrawals,' he says.

Vance offers to leave but I gesture for him to stay.

'Piedmont and Trumpton-Cave,' Mannetti tells us. 'I've just heard they're lining up beauty parades.'

'For what?'

When he pauses my stomach turns over.

'The lot,' he says.

Vance groans.

Piedmont and Trumpton-Cave are two of our five biggest clients up in Funds and Management. We run both their pension fund portfolios, and sundry other investments, for which we receive an annual fee and a share of the profits. Ideal customers. My father has the respective chairmen down to a shoot at Boddington once a year, we keep their pension fund returns vaguely in line with the market, and everybody, until now, remains happy. But if they're lining up beauty parades – inviting submissions from other City institutions which want to manage their funds – they must be thinking of leaving us. And if they take everything it will knock a gaping hole in our own Funds Management revenues. Mannetti regards me steadily.

'How soon?' I ask.

'A week. A month.' He shrugs. 'Tomorrow? They can pull out when they like.'

Turning, I glance at Stephen. He doodles glumly on his pad.

'Thanks, Tony. If you hear any more, let me know.'

Once Mannetti's gone, Vance looks up. 'Your father?'

'I'll see what he can do.'

We are silent a few seconds, pensive: this is not good news. Now seems like the appropriate downbeat moment to mention that other matter.

'I was upstairs, earlier. With Karen.'

'Oh?' He replaces the fax on the pile.

'She seemed a bit upset. You know what she's like, Stephen. It might be an idea to keep out of her way for a while.'

He regards me coolly. The shutters are up. This isn't territory into which I'd normally stray, but the relationship between these two also affects the bank.

'She asked me to ban you from the floor.'

'She what?'

'I told her there was no chance. But that doesn't mean you should race straight up there just to prove a point. Okay?'

After some consideration, he inclines his head. A thought occurs to me.

'Do you ever go into the filing room?'

'Why?'

'It's a simple question Stephen.'

'To which the answer is, no,' he says. 'And whose question was that? Yours, or Ryan's?'

It hadn't crossed my mind till now, but Ryan's investigation is probably providing useful cover for my own. Small comfort.

'What about Daniel? Do you know if he went up there?'

Vance flicks through his diary.

'Stephen?'

'Did he go into the filing room? Be serious, Raef. He didn't report to me, he reported to you. And to tell you the truth, I've had enough of this cat-and-mouse already from Ryan.'

'He's doing his job.'

'Well I'm trying to do mine.' Vance flips his diary shut. 'Any assistance would be greatly appreciated.'

He isn't happy. And in the face of this evident displeasure, my resolve to maintain suspicion on all fronts suddenly crumbles. Old habits, it seems, are the strongest. He puts on his glasses and sorts through the faxes again. I assure him, protégé to mentor, that I'll try to help him wherever I can.

11

'Pea and ham,' says my father, emptying the can into the saucepan.

The maid is off sick, and Mary Needham is busy with one of her committees. As I explain what's been happening at the bank, my father stirs the soup carefully. It is do-it-yourself night in St James's. I am in charge of the toaster.

'Lyle couldn't have been more unpleasant if he'd tried.'

'Nature of the beast,' my father comments.

He brings the saucepan across and pours the soup into our bowls. I butter the toast.

'That pair from the DTI weren't just pointed in our direction,' I tell him. 'They were shoved.'

He says he will speak to the President of the Board of Trade.

'A word in Whitehall might be better.'

He raises his eyes. 'Penfield's heard I presume. This DTI visit?'

I blow on my soup. Penfield's second call came through at five thirty. He was, as I expected, almost speechless with rage: the Deputy Governor of the Bank of England doesn't take kindly to being kept in the dark. But he seems to have decided that the DTI are the real culprits, I caught only the blistering edge of his wrath. Now I realize that all those stories about his temper weren't exaggerated. Tomorrow doesn't promise to be the best day of Mr Skinner's year. Penfield also asked to see what Hugh and I have uncovered so far. I explain this to my father too.

'And is there anything?'

'Nothing concrete. Hugh thinks he's found a few deals we should look into.'

I omit to mention that Hugh has washed his hands of the whole affair after discovering the Odin deal; my father and I have been down that road one too many times already.

'If you need some help,' he suggests, 'you can always ask John.'

I stress yet again that no one at the bank should know, not even Sir John.

'Gifford's asked us for lunch tomorrow,' he says.

I look up. I have a sense that something's being withheld. 'I can't make it.'

'Perhaps Charles might come. Nothing important.' He brings the saucepan over and refills our bowls.

Sitting here in my father's kitchen, pushing a spoon through the pea and ham soup, it's hard to recapture that momentary impression of pure menace when Mannetti threatened Skinner. But it did happen. The threat was real.

'If Gifford can let us know any more about Mannetti's record at American Pacific, I'd like to hear it.' And still stirring with my spoon, I ask a question I should have asked a long time ago. 'If Mannetti's so good, why did Gifford let us have him so easily?'

My father recites the argument: Gifford couldn't afford to have the Funds Management joint venture with us fail; there had to be someone he trusted involved, someone with a real track record. My father dabs at his lips then puts down his napkin. 'We went through this at the time, Raef.'

Yes, I think; but at the time we hadn't seen Mannetti in action.

'Are you saying he's not quite as good as we imagined?'

Worse. I'm thinking that Carltons might have been used as a dumping ground. Did Gifford use the opportunity of our joint venture to offload a troublesome senior employee onto us?

'Just see what Gifford says. Ask if there were any problems with Mannetti in New York, see how he takes it.'

My father says he thinks it'll be a waste of time, but he'll do as I've asked. 'I really do believe,' he adds, 'that John has a right to know about this fraud business.'

Old age, is this how it happens? This reversion to a subject we've already discussed has become an unwelcome but familiar pattern. When I mentioned it to Theresa last year she said my father was simply tired, that I was worrying without reason. But since then the pattern has hardened, until now the signs are there for any who wish to read them: in the person of my father, dotage has begun its slow encroachment upon wisdom.

I put our bowls in the dishwasher and I rinse the saucepan in the sink. Moving around the kitchen, I run through the arguments again, making sure he understands why Sir John can't be told.

'It has to be like that,' I conclude, drying my hands.

'If we tell Sir John, why not Vance? If we tell Vance, why not the senior traders?'

'But John,' he says.

I hang the tea-towel on the rack and face him. My father's old, but not foolish, he knows we have to draw the line somewhere.

'You're right,' he concedes at last. 'Those deals you mentioned, the ones Hugh turned up?' Here it comes, what I've been waiting for: those deals, as he knows, might be lethal. 'Were they' – he searches for the appropriately guarded phrase – 'were they of any real size?'

What he wants to know, and can't bring himself to ask, is whether Carlton Brothers is set to go the way of Barings. After so many generations of prosperity, is one torpedo going to send us down? The weight of this possibility is actually bowing his shoulders.

'They're not that big. And they're not hidden trades, they're just losses we shouldn't have taken. We can ride it out.'

'How big?'

'We can't be sure.'

He doesn't accept that. He watches me and waits.

'Probably less than ten million,' I say.

'Dollars?'

'Pounds.'

He sinks back into his chair and closes his eyes. Relief. The financial loss would have hurt, no doubt, but the shame could have finished him.

'That's only a guess,' I warn him quickly. 'And the

size of the loss won't stop Penfield from barging in on Friday. We're not out of the woods yet. Not by a long way.'

He puts his elbows on the table. 'Ten,' he murmurs. I go out to the drinks cabinet and pour two whiskies. When I return to the kitchen he hasn't moved; he's still seated at the table, one hand to his forehead. He takes his drink gratefully and we sit in silence awhile. He looks like my grandfather. He never used to, but age has chiselled out the deep family lines. To divert his thoughts, I tell him about our progress with Parnells but it takes some minutes before he finally seems to listen. Gradually the shock of relief passes.

When I tell him that Vance is sending Haywood out with the Heythrop, he raises a brow, the first sign of any interest he's shown. It seems to remind him of something.

'The meet on Saturday down at Boddington. I hope you're not going to cry off on me Raef.'

'I'll be there.'

'Good. Don't let Theresa back out either.'

Saturday with Theresa at Boddington. I have a decision to make. But not now. With a twinge of guilt I push it to the back of my mind.

He seems to have recovered, so after a minute we rise and go out to the drawing room where he puts on a record. My mother was an avid collector, classical and jazz, but I doubt if he's added even one LP to her collection: he certainly hasn't moved on to CDs. I should be at home making a few late calls, but I sense that he wants me to stay; a short while at least. When the music comes it's light and airy, Mozart, and I drop into an armchair. My father kicks off his shoes and stretches out on the sofa. Mother never saw this place, he bought it after she died, but so much of what's here, the furniture and paintings, even the clutter on the mantelpiece, is hers. And the music. But other items, like the burgundy curtains and lampshades, she'd never have chosen. These recent additions are the handiwork of Mary Needham. But they don't jar; I don't find their presence offensive. My father, I think, has been more than lucky in his women.

'I had a message from your Inspector.'

I look over. He's lying on the sofa, eyes closed.

'Ryan?'

'That's the one.' The music dances up and down the scales. 'Wants to see me apparently. I'm busy tomorrow, so he can wait till Thursday.' He turns his head and opens his eyes. 'Raef, the other night, you mentioned when you came to see me about Daniel.' We look at one another. 'I think I might have given you the wrong impression. I never told anyone.'

He never told anyone? He never did what I, at the time, intended him to do? I ask him now, tentatively, what he means.

'I was going to speak with Daniel myself. Talk some sense into him. After . . .' He waves a hand. 'Well, I never got the chance.'

Is he saying what I think he's saying?

'You didn't tell Charles?'

'No one, Raef.'

My head reels. If he told no one, my lie couldn't have had the fatal consequence I believed. Whitehall and Westminster never knew.

'I told you that Daniel was going public about the Odin deal, and you didn't pass that on?'

He turns his head. 'I wanted to speak with him myself first.'

'But what? He was murdered before you had the chance?'

'Yes,' he says. 'Raef, I promised you that Odin was strictly between you and me. That still holds.'

I nod, lightheaded, drunk with the sensation of innocence. It wasn't us. It wasn't me. Guilty of an evil intent, yes, but an intent that had no consequence. I am innocent. I am not responsible for Daniel Stewart's death. The wave of elation buoys me upward, for the first time in a week I feel free, gliding into sunlight. But then as fast as it's risen, the wave breaks. If I'm not responsible for Daniel's death, if Odin had nothing to do with the murder, if Whitehall and Westminster played no part in it; if I, thank God, didn't kill him – who did?

WEDNESDAY

1

The early years of my marriage were good. We lived in Kensington then; Theresa worked at a charity just round the corner from our flat. We had wealth, youth, good health, it wasn't hard to be happy and we were, but now all that sometimes seems like an alternative reality – not a life that was, but one that might have been. Theresa putting everyone at ease at our first big dinner party; the pair of us flying to Venice one weekend to see a Tintoretto exhibition; skiing trips to the States and fishing in Scotland, we stinted ourselves nothing. And I worked too, but I was learning more than doing, ambition spinning like a flywheel disconnected. We seemed to have so much time for each other but did we ever believe we could go on like that for ever? Perhaps in the unreflective optimism of our youth, we really did.

I remember one morning during a fishing trip up

to the Borders we rose before the rest of the party and climbed the hill behind the lodge. How long ago must it be? We emerged from the mist, sat on the grey rocks of the hilltop and watched the sun burn the mist to a thin haze. Theresa and me, and no sign of life for miles except a hawk circling slowly down the valley. Beautiful, the treeless hills and the clear sky, and I put my arms around my wife and kissed her. When we returned to the lodge the others had already left for the river, so we climbed into bed and made love and slept, and made love again. Happiness. That's what seems so unbelievable now, the pure joy.

And I just can't shake off those times, I can't shed them like a skin outgrown, hard though I've tried. If I close my eyes even now I can still hear her breathing beside me, pressing close to me on a bed in the Borders.

Don't get up. Hold me, she said.

How long ago? Fourteen years? Lying there in the quiet clear morning we seemed complete. Not fourteen years but a lifetime. Lying there on a bed in the Borders, my wife said that she loved me.

'Mr Carlton?'

The car has stopped, my driver has opened the door and he peers in at me curiously. It's still dark outside.

'We're here,' he says.

Here. Kensington; we've stopped outside Daniel's house. Bracing myself, I get out, mount the steps and ring the bell. Waiting, I turn my collar up against the cold.

After leaving my father last night I returned home to find a message from Celia: she sounded worried, so I rang straight back. Apparently Daniel's life insurers won't be paying out on his policy until they receive a full coroner's report. I assured her it was just standard practice, but God knows if I'm right. Her other concern is the will. She's learnt from the lawyers that Daniel was amending it, but he left them no signed codicil. As an executor, a friend, and probably the only person she can turn to, I've been asked to come and search his study.

'The boys are still asleep,' she whispers as we go down the corridor. 'Have you had breakfast?'

I tell her not to bother, I don't have the time. When we get to Daniel's study she opens the door and steps back.

'I appreciate this Raef,' she says.

To me, the man who wanted her husband dead.

She says she'd rather not go in there. 'Do you mind if I leave you to it?'

'No. I'll call if I find anything.'

'I'll be in the kitchen.'

The study isn't large: one book-lined wall, a large oak desk, a cabinet by the bay window, and an armchair Daniel salvaged from the attic at Boddington. Behind the door there's a pile of old magazines. The room has the same air of friendly disorder as his office but here I feel like an intruder. This is where Daniel conducted the business of his family.

After a quick circuit of the room, I sit behind his desk and work my way through the unlocked drawers. Here, instead of office business, there are credit card statements, council tax demands, electricity and water bills: the usual trail of paperwork that stretches behind every modern life like the wake from a boat. Bills and receipts, letters from solicitors, one from the RSPCA thanking the Stewart family for their donation. But no codicil. No new will.

In the bottom drawer, I find a dictaphone. I hit the rewind button and the machine whirs for a while. When it stops, I hit play. Daniel's voice. Nothing dramatic, just a reminder to himself of a phone call he has to make. It catches me raw. Suddenly, unexpectedly, a film of tears forms, and I shake my head.

'What are you doing?'

I look up. Martin, my godson. He's standing at the door, in his pyjamas, his eyes fixed on the dictaphone. I say his name and he comes and stands by the desk. He asks it again. 'What are you doing?'

I flick off the dictaphone. Martin, at last, looks at me. I ask after his younger brother.

'He's asleep.'

'Your mother's in the kitchen.'

He makes no move to go. He's ten years old, but he's always seemed quieter and wiser than his years. I could make a joke of it, spin him around and send him on his way. But somehow, with Martin, that doesn't seem appropriate. Feeling rather awkward now, I restart my search beneath his clear-eyed gaze.

'What are you looking for?'

'Your mother wants me to find some papers. I won't be long.'

He comes round the desk and stands beside me. He smells of scented soap, a child's smell that reminds me of Annie.

'What do they look like?'

'The papers?'

He nods.

'I'm not sure, Martin. There'll be some signatures on them.'

'Dad's signature?'

I glance up to find him regarding me quizzically. Yes, I tell him. Probably.

I close the last drawer, my first cursory pass over the desk complete. Martin steps out of my way as I cross to the cabinet. It has a slatted rolling door which I pull at. Locked. And there were no loose keys in the desk.

Martin says, 'Are they in there?'

'I don't know. Maybe.'

When I turn, he's climbing onto the desk. He stands and reaches up to a high bookshelf then he fumbles between the books. He finds what he wants, then climbs down and comes and presents me with it: a bright silver key.

The key fits the cabinet. Inside there are three shelves, loose papers on two of them and a heavy folder on the third. The loose papers are just more of what I've seen in Daniel's desk, but opening the folder I see at once that I've found what I'm after. Private documents: the first page is Daniel's birth certificate, and the next is his marriage licence.

'Is that them?'

I tell Martin yes, I think so.

He returns the key to its hiding place while I flip quickly through the file. The will's almost certainly here, but I can't find it immediately.

'Mum says you might come and see us,' Martin says, sliding from the desk. 'Down at school.'

'If you want me to.'

He considers this, but doesn't seem to think it warrants an answer.

'I've got to go now, Martin.'

I tuck the folder beneath my arm, pausing to squeeze my godson's bony shoulder as I pass from the study.

Out in the kitchen, Celia gives the folder a quick glance. 'I've done some bacon.'

'I have to go.'

She looks disappointed. What she wants, I know, is to talk about Daniel. And I most definitely don't.

'Well, maybe after you've found the will,' she says.

After I've found it? I'd intended to leave the folder with her, duty done. But looking at her now, I bite my tongue. Like Martin, she trusts me to help.

'Bring Theresa.' She glances over her shoulder. 'For supper? Maybe next week?'

'I'll have to check if we're free. Martin's up. He saw me in the study.'

She puts two plates in the warmer.

'He's a good kid,' she says.

I hitch the folder beneath my arm again and start to say goodbye, but she breaks in over the top of me.

'Did you know Daniel and I talked about a divorce?'

My heart sinks. I really don't want to hear this.

'You didn't, did you?' She sits, and the strange smile on her face starts to tremble. 'Can you believe it?'

'Celia—'

'All those tarts, and I stay with him. Then he turns round and tells me we should start thinking about a divorce.'

Daniel asked her? Have I heard that right?

'Do you think that was fair? Was that fair, Raef?'

I have heard it right.

'Why?' I ask.

'He wouldn't say.'

'No reason?'

'Reasons?' She opens her hands despairingly. 'He didn't want to do this, he didn't like the way I did that. Pick, pick. All rubbish. He knew it was rubbish too. He just didn't want to tell me at first.' Her hands drop to the table with a thump. She swears, something she never does. 'What does it matter now?'

A wise man would let it rest here. She needed to tell someone, she'd told me, and that would be the end of it if I wanted it to be.

'When was all this?' I ask.

'The end of last year.' She toys with the salt shaker. 'He went cold on the idea lately. Funny, by then he'd just about convinced me I'd be better off without him.'

'And he didn't say why?'

'He did, actually.' She looks at me. 'He'd got some tart pregnant. He was going to marry her.' I feel myself sway. Her eyes blaze. 'God,' she says. 'I really hated him sometimes.'

Numbness creeps over me. If Daniel meant to marry Theresa, what else would he have told Celia? But even in December Theresa never flung this one in my face. Divorce from me and marriage to Daniel?

'Have you mentioned this to Inspector Ryan?'

'He knows we were thinking of a divorce.'

'I mean about why Daniel wanted one. Did you tell Ryan that?'

'No.'

'It might be best if you don't. And I wouldn't tell him about hating Daniel either. Ryan's got a suspicious mind.'

The light of understanding dawns, Celia's lips part in surprise.

On the way down the hall I pass the boys' bedroom. At first I think they're talking together in there, but then I realize it's a man's voice. Daniel. I don't understand at first. Then I do. Martin's taken the dictaphone from the study, Daniel's dictating a memo.

Stepping outside, I suck in mouthfuls of the cold morning air.

2

There's been a change on the nightdesk. Owen and his offsiders have been replaced, but the Dealing Room looks much as it did last Thursday, the whole place in darkness save this one island of light.

'Much happening?'

'Dead as a fucking dodo.' The trader hands me the deal-sheet.

Twenty years ago our Treasury operations were just a necessary support to Corporate Finance, but nowadays the profits generated here often exceed the fees gathered by Vance and his team. The balance of power between the departments at Carltons remains reasonably equal – the constant wrangling between Vance and Daniel was an unhappy testament to that – but at other city institutions the dealing rooms have gained the upper hand, and the corporate culture has inevitably followed.

As I read the deal-sheet, the trader repeats, 'Dead as a fucking dodo.'

My grandfather wouldn't have taken kindly to this kind of thing. My father, too, regards the Dealing Room's blunt directness with distaste. But, taken in measured doses, I can't say that it troubles me. Five minutes with Darren Lyle can make me feel grubbier than any amount of time out here.

Handing back the sheet, my gaze wanders up to the restaurant. Win has come in early; he's talking to the cleaner.

'Henry's lunch,' the senior dealer says. 'Big Win's come in early to get ready. Henry's birthday today. You didn't get an invite?'

I smile and move off. Over the years Henry's birthday lunches have become occasions to avoid. Last year's ended with Henry being forcibly ejected from Annabel's at 3 a.m., swinging a half-empty bottle of champagne: the tawdry stuff of City legend.

'We'll tell Henry he's sacked then,' the nightdesk dealer shouts. As the Dealing Room door swings shut behind me, I hear them laughing.

In my office the mind-numbing slog through the numbers begins again. Patterns, Hugh said. Anomalies in patterns. But this staring at endless columns of numbers, though I plough doggedly on, I find it harder and harder to pretend that it's getting me anywhere. Maybe Daniel could have made some headway; maybe Hugh still can. But me?

I turn and stare out of the window. Theresa divorcing me for Daniel: why, after everything else, is that so hard to accept? And then a figure seems to shimmer in the glass, a gaunt face I haven't seen for years. Was there a photograph back there in Daniel's study?

Daniel's mother. She died soon after he married; I think it caught Celia by surprise when Daniel took it so badly. As far as Celia knew they were semi-estranged, all contact between them reduced to the ritual twice-yearly visits Daniel made down to Dorset:

for Christmas and her birthday. But it would be like Daniel to keep a photograph of her near at hand.

Celia couldn't have guessed how it was between them in earlier years and I doubt that Daniel ever tried to explain. And if he had, what would he have said? That he'd loved his mother? But that was such a small part of his feelings towards her, and after his father's death – in the years when he became an outer satellite of my family – so much else accrued: resentment and bitterness; hope, and hope disappointed. She wasn't a good mother to him: in any normal sense, she wasn't a mother to him at all. My father tells me she was always rather withdrawn. Buttoned up, he says, quite a statement coming from him. But however she was before her husband's suicide, that event tipped the scales of her life. She turned her back on the world. She sold up their house to pay creditors and retired to the seclusion of a small cottage by the sea. I went down there a few times while Daniel and I were at Eton, visits that I will recall as the worst holidays of my youth: nothing in that house was ever quite normal. Some days she insisted on being with Daniel every minute, never letting him out of arm's reach. On those days he couldn't even stroll down to the village shop without his mother linking her arm through his, leaning close to him and chattering with a kind of feverish desperation. By the age of fifteen he was already bigger than her, something that seemed to make it so much worse when she treated him like a child,

You must tell me, she said.

And then her fingers closed and she wasn't touching his cheeks gently any more, but squeezing them hard. There were tears in his eyes.

Promise me.

Yes.

She held him a second longer, then released him. Then she hugged him so tight he had to pull free. In the morning there were two bruises on his cheeks like purple thumbprints; livered, rimmed with red, and very dark.

Now in my office window the ghostly figures fade into shadows. Daniel, more than most of us, carried scars.

After twenty minutes, Vance drops in to tell me he's arranged a meeting with Bainbridge this evening.

'Stephen, did you know it was Henry's birthday?'

He says he spoke to Henry yesterday. 'I told him not to get too carried away.'

'What did he say?'

'He said he wasn't in the market for advice.' Vance has that look he used to get when he came to me complaining about Daniel.

'If Henry gets promoted to Treasurer, you'll have to work with him,' I say. 'Is that going to be a problem?'

'He's got the job?'

'Nobody's got the job yet.'

Vance relaxes. He isn't looking forward to the

announcement of Daniel's replacement, I see. For all their disagreements, he had a grudging respect for Daniel's professional abilities.

'Right then,' he says, taking a chair. 'Other business.'

Parnells isn't the only deal they're working on in Corporate Finance, just the biggest. Now Vance relates the state of play elsewhere. We're defending an engineering firm in the Midlands from an unwanted bid: that one's going well. There are three rights issues in the pipeline, all of them pushing hard to get their paper away before the market turns down: these, too, are on schedule. There's a management team looking for advice on an MBO, a privatization contract in Bulgaria we're hoping to win, and a host of smaller deals hovering somewhere between proposal and final signing. Vance confesses he's lost track of these smaller deals lately, but he promises to get on top of them again once the Meyers have bagged Parnells. I mention the closing date for acceptances of the Meyers' final offer: just under two weeks away now. If the Meyers don't have over half of Parnells by then, the offer lapses; they won't be permitted to make another bid for Parnells till next February.

Vance squeezes his chin. 'If we split the Parnells board, the whole pack of cards comes down. And this Ian Parnell looks promising.'

'Promising for whom?'

'The Hunt sets off at eleven. Haywood should be

on his way down there by now.'

I tell him to let me know how it goes. We seem to have reached the end of our conversation, Vance makes to rise. But then he pauses and drops back into the chair.

'One other thing,' he says. 'Inspector Ryan. How long does he plan to keep calling on us?'

'Your guess is as good as mine. Why?'

'Just wondering.'

'Perhaps Darren might keep him busy awhile.' I scroll idly through the latest from Bloomberg. 'But as long as he thinks he hasn't got the full picture, he'll be back.'

Vance gives a grunt of displeasure. I look up. I try to see what Inspector Ryan sees – a man who didn't much care for Daniel; a murderer? – but it's too hard to get past the man I know.

'Stephen, between you and me, what do you make of Mannetti?'

'Personally or professionally?'

'Either.'

He considers. 'Not entirely my cup of tea. I take it this concerns the balls-up with Parnells.'

Not exactly. What it concerns is any proclivity Mannetti might have for violence, and there's no way to approach that question except directly; but I hesitate. Hugh warned me that there might be more than one person involved in the fraud. And someone killed Daniel. Vance waits.

'Something like that.' I nod to the door. 'If you see

William or Henry out there, I'll be ready in ten minutes.'

He takes this without batting an eye.

3

The morning meeting comes as a welcome relief after my second listless trawl through the Shobai numbers. William really has the gift of the gab; he bangs on for five minutes about possible implications following the latest split between the Chancellor and the Bank of England, a subject that bores me at the best of times. Henry makes an occasional intervention, but he seems to be waiting for William to run out of steam. William finally obliges.

'Corporate bonds,' I say, and I point to Henry. 'You sent a memo to Stephen on the CTL issue.'

'It was overpriced. We've still got a boatload.'

'Your memo said almost half the issue.'

'Yep.'

He recites a list of the larger institutions which suddenly lost interest when we set the final price. I jot down the names. Then I ask Henry how much of the CTL paper he thinks he can offload.

'At the issue price? Fuck all. We start sellin', the price'll dump.'

'Okay. Keep Vance informed with what you're up to, but don't offload it yet.' I tap the list. 'We'll see if we can't encourage a few takers first.'

'Rather you than me,' Henry mutters.

Billy has been rummaging through his folder, now he hands me a chart. He points out the salient features: the outlook for corporate bonds is bleak. But when I try to pass the chart to Henry he keeps his arms staunchly folded, so I drop it on my desk.

'Same time tomorrow, gentlemen.'

They rise. William departs clutching his folder, but I signal for Henry to stay.

I glance down at the chart. 'Happy birthday.' When I lift my eyes he's grinning. 'I suppose it's too late to postpone the lunch party.'

The grin fades and disappears.

'There's twenty guys comin',' he says dismayed. 'Jesus.'

I hold up my hands. I tell him to forget that I mentioned it.

'I can't cancel it now.'

'Henry, forget it. It's your birthday, your party. The timing's not great, but we'll get through it.' I force a thin smile. 'I didn't buy you a present.'

'Put it in my bonus.'

We both laugh, a rare light moment against the week's dark backdrop. Then I ask who'll be looking after the Dealing Room in his absence.

'I'll still be here. Up in the restaurant.'

Only physically, I think. And we both know that the party is almost certain to adjourn to the pub.

'Owen can handle things,' he says. 'If there's any

major hassle, I'll come straight down.'

Not if I can help it. A drunken trader can cause serious problems in the Dealing Room, but a drunken chief dealer can cause absolute havoc. Our last chief dealer came in loaded to the gills one night and sold the Kiwi Dollar through the floor. We were still trying to explain ourselves to the Reserve Bank of New Zealand three weeks later. Once Henry leaves for lunch it will be the end of his working day: he knows it, but he doesn't want to admit it. Pride. After greed and envy, the City's third deadly sin.

We spend a few minutes discussing the outlook for the Dollar up to the weekend – long-term planning in the FX market – then Henry leaves.

Alone again, I reach over and flick on the PC screen: the columns of green numbers swim back into view. Rubbing my eyes, I reflect on how far my own pride has got me. I rest my face in my hands. Since last walking out of Hugh's office, I've got precisely nowhere with this. Nowhere at all.

I pick up the phone and dial. Two rings, then it's answered.

'Hugh, it's Raef.'

Silence. I swivel in my chair and look down to the river. A cruise boat glides slowly toward the bridge, a solitary passenger out on deck.

'I'd like to come over.'

The silence draws out; the cruise boat passes from view.

'Hugh?'

'Yeah,' he says. 'I was wondering how long it'd take you to call.'

4

The whiteboard in Hugh's office has been wiped clean. He's on the phone when I enter, and he acknowledges me with a nod. Silently he mouths the words 'one minute', so I wander over to the wall and peruse the framed tributes to Hugh Morgan's many triumphs. There are letters of thanks and commendation from the Met Fraud Squad and the Serious Fraud Office. Others bear the insignia of foreign institutions, mostly American, but some written in Arabic and French. At the far end of the wall there's a collection of caricatures, a private Rogues' Gallery of the crooks Hugh's successfully despatched: some round and jolly, others thin and pensive, nearly all of them smiling.

Hugh hangs up the phone.

'So,' he says, 'change of heart?'

I give him a chastened look. He asks if Penfield's still threatening to move in on Friday night.

'Not threatening. Promising.'

Hugh drops into his chair and leans back. He clasps his hands behind his head.

'So,' he says, and he smiles.

Unlike others of our generation, unlike me, the passing years seem to have left him largely untouched. He still looks much as he did up at Oxford, apart from the white hair, and it occurs to me now that the secret of his prolonged youth might actually be his work: unlike the rest of us, Hugh remains on the side of the angels. And he loves his job.

'You've had a go at the numbers?'

'Till my head aches,' I confess. 'No joy.'

He unclasps his hands, serious now.

'I meant what I said, Raef. You gave me some help on the Petrie fraud and I probably owe you. But I don't owe you enough to get myself compromised digging you out of a hole. I don't owe anyone that much.'

'You wouldn't be compromised.'

'That's for me to say. And if you think you're going to talk me round without clearing up this Odin Investments business first, don't bother. You could have saved yourself the trip.'

Beneath his stern gaze, my last hope of keeping Odin secret slowly withers.

'We had a visit from the DTI,' I tell him.

He makes no comment on that. He waits for my response on Odin.

'It isn't that easy, Hugh.'

'See this?' He touches a pile of documents on his desk. 'Evidence to be used in the trial of Mr Habibi. I've been to Rabat, Beirut, Cairo, other places you've never heard of, putting this together. Once I've finished my report, he'll be charged. If the prosecution do their job properly he'll be put away for a couple of years. That's real, Raef. A thief goes out of circulation for a while. The world's a little bit of a better place.'

'I understand that.'

'No,' he says quietly. 'No I don't think you do. Because you're interfering with this.'

He slams his hand down on the documents. Hard. I draw back in surprise.

'You want my help, but you don't want to give anything back. Make up your mind, Raef. Yes or no. Do I help you or not?'

I have the banker's instinct that everything is negotiable. It was a mistake, I see, to test that instinct on Hugh.

'We did someone a favour,' I tell him.

'Who's "we"?'

'The bank. Carltons.'

He gestures for me to continue.

'Nothing illegal. It had approval right down the line.'

'So what's the big secret?'

'National security.'

Surprised, he holds up his hand. 'Hang on. Back-track a little. The Odin deal, the quick in-and-out on the Franc. Carltons dropped close on four million. You knew about that from the start?'

'Yes.'

'Who else at Carltons knew?'

'No one.'

'Someone must have.'

I shake my head.

'Then how'd the deal get done?' He studies me.

The light comes into his eyes as he realizes. 'You?'

'Me.' I explain that I put the paperwork through after-hours. 'It didn't go through the Dealing Room.'

He rises from his chair, paces to the window then back to his desk, thinking.

'I guess I don't have to ask who it was that scrubbed the Odin deal off the disc then, do I?' he says.

'There wasn't any need for you to know.'

'Yeah, well now there is. Carltons deliberately dropped four million quid that went to Odin. Why?' He raises a finger. 'And before you try it, Raef, I don't want to hear any bullshit about national security or the Official Secrets Act. It's just you and me here, and it's your last chance. Convince me I can trust you or I show you the door.'

Trust. It's a gamble I've lost once too often, but this time the gamble is Hugh's.

'There was an overseas defence contract,' I tell him. 'Some consortium from the UK lodged a bid against the French and Swedes. The French got knocked out early, but the Swedes were splashing a lot of money around, it looked like we'd lost it. Then right at the close my father got word a one-off payment could land the contract.'

'That's where Carltons came in?'

'The consortium started bickering: who should pay what. My father saw the deal drifting away for no reason.' I spread my hands. 'It was a one-off.'

Hugh seems unfazed by what I've told him. He has the intent look of a man going deliberately about his daily work. 'Your father couldn't get it from the consortium in time, and I suppose he couldn't risk carving it out of the Defence Budget. So he went to Carltons?'

'This is the only time it's ever happened.'

'I'm sure,' Hugh says; but his eyes say something else. 'What did Carltons get for its troubles?'

'The consortium won the contract. My father banged their heads together and two weeks later they covered Carltons' loss.'

'Through more Odin deals against your Treasury?'

'Fees and advisory contracts.'

'For which you do fuck all, I take it.'

Feeling diminished and rather grubby, I tell Hugh he has the general idea. What I don't tell him is that it wasn't just the consortium that was grateful. I don't tell him we received a pay-off from Her Majesty's Government in the form of a privatization contract. It will be safer for him not to know.

He makes a slow circuit of the office, arms folded, staring at his feet. He doesn't like what I've told him, but if he was going to show me the door, he'd have done it by now. He stops abruptly and looks up.

'How much do you think Mahmoud Iqbal kept?'

I freeze in my chair. There's an unpleasant prickling up the back of my neck. Hugh has somehow traced the beneficial ownership of Odin. And in the next moment I see something more: I see that if Hugh knew Mahmoud Iqbal was involved, he must already have guessed the nature of this affair before I opened my mouth. He has, for the past five minutes, been jumping me through hoops.

'He's that arms trader,' Hugh says. 'Lebanese.'

I tell him, quite sharply, that I know who Iqbal is. The whole world knows who Iqbal is.

Hugh comes back to his desk. I glare at him over the papers and pens.

'Sorry, Raef. I had to be sure you wouldn't drop a pile of bullshit on me.'

I restrain the impulse to swear.

'If everyone's happy now,' I say, 'maybe we can start finding out if there's anything to that note of Penfield's.'

'No luck with the Shobai numbers?'

I shake my head.

'Not to worry. I've made an appointment with Shobai's Treasurer this afternoon.'

When he sees my surprise, Hugh smiles.

'Never doubted you for a moment,' he says.

5

At lunchtime the office is quiet. Becky's gone out for sandwiches, and strolling past Corporate Finance I find that most of Vance's team have disappeared too; it's the middle of the week, and enthusiasm for work is fast on the wane.

Surprisingly, I've had a good morning since returning from my meeting with Hugh: my paperwork's up to date, the voice-mail's answered, and I even had a chance to look at the new recommendations from the Accountancy Standards Board. My head seems to have cleared since passing on a portion of my troubles. Now I head for the lifts.

Up in Funds Management, apathy rages. A few lonely figures loll at their desks fielding lunchtime calls. There's a TV in one corner, supposedly for CNN, but just now three £100,000-per-annum men sit glued to a Tom and Jerry cartoon. A section of flooring has been lifted and two workmen in overalls are hauling up a tangled spaghetti of cables and wires. I ask how they're doing, but one gives me an ugly look so I move on. This place is much bigger now than when I worked here years ago, the warren-like maze of internal walls was stripped out last July. Bigger, but the atmosphere's somehow the same: things gone to seed, the vital force ebbing but never quite dying out. Moving on from here to Corporate Finance was like exchanging a broken-winded hack for a thoroughbred. Even the past six months' shake-up from Mannetti has done little to dispel the torpor.

'Come to pay us a visit?' I turn to find Mannetti smiling at me in a friendly way. 'You see the new cabling?' he says.

He leads me back over there, explaining the ins and outs of the new wiring. 'They'll have it done by next week. Hey,' he says addressing the two workmen. 'Done by next week or what?'

He looks like he might press the point, so I steer him away.

I tell him I'm drafting a letter of complaint to the DTI. 'Any suggestions?'

'Yeah, I've got a few,' he says. 'Suggestion one is they sack that four-eyed prick Skinner.'

'Not what I had in mind.'

'Am I meant to thank him? Don't hold your breath.' There's a wall of windows stretching down one side of the open-plan office. Mannetti perches himself on an internal ledge. 'I don't have to take that shit.'

He looks out across the river, his face profiled against the leaden sky. He has those sharp features you see in fashion magazines, a rather gay look, but striking. He's in his early forties, twice divorced, and currently walking out with one of the female partners at Slaughter and May. I rechecked the CV this morning: college in New York, an MBA from Columbia, then a quick rise through the ranks at American Pacific; he's worked nowhere else apart from there and here, an unusual record in the age of the Golden Hello.

'If it's any consolation,' I tell him, 'they asked about me too.'

'You? Shit.' He says my country is unbelievable. 'What rights do those guys have anyway? Search and destroy? Don't you have privacy laws?'

'Tony, do you want to tell me something?'

He doesn't pretend not to understand my question.

'I didn't make a cent out of it,' he says. 'I swear.'

Karen's search through the personal accounts suggests the same. Johnstone, too, appears to have made nothing from the blunder. If any insider trading went through on the back of Parnells, it didn't go through us, a fact that the DTI will be able to confirm when we finally give them access.

'I've read your report, Tony. Why didn't you call and check what Johnstone was up to?'

'No phones.' He explains that the island where he spent his holiday was set up like that. The only place connected to anywhere was the manager's house. 'I would've looked like a jerk knocking on his door every ten minutes.'

I spare him the obvious comment. A girl calls from one of the desks. Mannetti answers her question then turns back to me. I ask if he's done anything to patch up his relationship with Vance.

'I think he's talking to me. Who knows with that guy?'

'Make an effort, Tony.'

'Sure.'

But I can see by his aggrieved look that he thinks I'm playing favourites.

'I've told Stephen the same thing, Tony. You've got to meet him halfway.'

Suddenly a drill screams to life. Our colleagues by the TV start shouting at the workmen, but the workmen ignore them. Nobody seems inclined to challenge them physically, so the deafening whine of the drill continues.

I raise my voice. 'If Skinner comes back, I don't want you to speak to him alone.'

Mannetti takes a moment with that. Then he raises his own voice over the sound of the drill.

'Good idea.'

6

'You'd better come,' says Owen Baxter.

He stands in the doorway of my office, one hand on the door, a damp patch of perspiration beneath his extended arm. He looks scared.

As we go down the corridor, I ask if this is about Henry. Owen tells me that Henry and his lunch guests moved on half an hour ago. 'Fuckin' Henry,' he says.

He holds the Dealing Room door open for me.

The first thing I notice is the silence: the usual churning wave of noise, the surge and swell of voices – it just isn't there. Instead there's silence, punctuated by a few isolated voices that seem to echo. Owen breathes heavily.

'What's happened?'

He doesn't answer. When he gestures for me to go right on in, I step past him.

A few dealers wander aimlessly around the Room; two on the far side are kicking a football. Most of the others are huddled in small groups, talking, not dealing, and just near me our top four bond traders are shooting each other with elastic bands. There's a sense of things unravelling.

'No one'll touch us,' Owen says. 'Twenty minutes ago the brokers stopped hitting us; next thing the whole market's got us on hold.'

I gaze at the whole incomprehensible scene. For a moment I feel quite giddy.

'Everyone's turning us down?'

'The ones that count.'

'The clearers?'

'First to go.'

I press my fingertips to my eyes. When I open them again, heads are turning our way. The bond traders have stopped firing their elastic bands, but that other pair are still playing football. My heart hammers. The Dealing Room of Carlton Brothers has been cut free from the market: we're adrift.

Owen stays at my shoulder as I make a brief tour of the desks. It turns out my first impression was wrong, there remain a few isolated islands where trading continues: our Futures desk is still working, LIFFE, the Futures Exchange, hasn't cut us off; the Equities desk is also doing business. I ask Owen why.

'Not all the stockbrokers pulled the plug on us. Just the ones with a banking parent.' Then he lowers his voice. 'What the fuck is going on?'

I look at the equities screen. Parnells hasn't moved, but Carltons has: down. 'Where's Henry?'

'Took the lunch party to the Green Man, I think.'

'Pissed?'

'Not yet.'

He offers to call Henry back in, but I tell him if he

just finds the number I'll call Henry myself. Owen goes off to search.

I crouch by the senior equities trader. 'Show me Carltons.'

'Just looked,' he says, hitting the keys. 'Down, with a bullet.'

The figures appear and he points to the last trade: we've dropped 15p in an hour. Not good, but no catastrophe either: that could change. I stare at the screen as if this will help me understand.

Owen returns, handing me a slip of paper. 'Green Man for sure. He left the number.'

We step away from the desks. I ask him if the Americans are turning us down too.

'Americans, Krauts,' – Owen looks left and right – 'even the fuckin' Frogs.'

I make a gesture: stay calm. Then I tell him what I want him to do: no new positions are to be opened, and all our short-dated positions, our commitments out to one week, are to be closed out or rolled over.

Now, I tell him. Quickly. Before those banks still dealing with us suddenly change their minds.

'We're full on some of them,' Owen says.

'Not any more. As of now, we do whoever does us.'

Owen mentions a certain bucket-shop in Hong Kong.

'Anyone,' I tell him firmly.

The look on his face changes. It's even more serious than he thought.

'Shit,' he says.

'Put as much as you can through Futures, here or Chicago.'

'What about margins?'

'We'll sort that out later. If anyone from the Exchange queries the volume, refer them to me. Otherwise just keep closing out till you're done.'

We look around the Room. The two traders with the football have gone back to their desks; now they're talking together and glancing surreptitiously our way. As is nearly everyone else.

'Maybe you should say something,' Owen suggests.

'I'll leave that to Henry. But until he gets back, this is up to you, Owen. Don't make a song and dance of it. Just get it done.'

He gives a nervous tug on his braces. Then he thinks of something.

'What if Henry's pissed?'

'Then you've got a long night ahead of you.' I tap my watch. 'Get cracking.'

The senior equities dealer leans back in his chair, catching my eye. When I go over he points to the screen: Carlton Brothers has dropped another 5p.

'Find out who's selling. I'll be in my office.'

Passing back through the desks to the door, I nod to the senior dealers in a calm and businesslike way. I am in control. We are taking things in hand. But their manner tells me that they aren't wholly convinced, they study me searching for flaws. I can't pretend to be one of them: I haven't earned their respect. It occurs to me that, for all his faults, they would really much rather have Daniel.

7

When Henry comes to the phone he doesn't sound that bad, so I outline the situation and he agrees to get straight back.

'My office, not the Dealing Room,' I tell him. I want to see what kind of state he's in before I turn him loose out there.

Next I ring Keith Trevalyn, a director of one of the money brokers.

'Social or business?' he asks.

When I remind him that it makes no difference in his trade he laughs.

Five years ago he worked for Carlton Brothers but the parting was amicable, he's stayed in touch, and we've done each other favours in the past. The money brokers served as useful points of connection for scores of Dealing Rooms, but they're telephonic middle-men in a world that's going electronic. Whenever we meet, Keith offers the broker's usual cynical observation. 'Screens,' he says, 'don't buy lunches.' True, but neither do screens get paid a hundred thousand pounds a year: the days of the brokers are numbered. Keith Trevalyn might be looking for work very soon.

I tell him I have a small problem.

'How small?' he asks guardedly.

I explain that we're having our name turned down a little too often.

'Limit problems?'

'Doubtful. Too many full on us all at the same time.'

'Overtrading?'

A possibility, I admit, that hadn't occurred to me. But my rush of hope fades when I recall how quickly and widely the market has turned against us: too much of a coincidence.

'I don't think so. Look Keith, is there any chance you can sniff around a bit? Maybe your boys have heard something.'

'Like what?'

'Anything. A rumour, I don't know, anything.'

'Rumours? Christ, a quid for every rumour I heard in this place, I could bloody retire.'

'Keith—'

'Yeah, yeah, don't fret. I'll call you back later.' He pauses. 'Listen, if I get no joy out of my knuckleheads, I'll ring round.'

I tell him I don't want the other money brokers involved.

'Not those shits? I mean the clients. I'll try a few of the banks.'

The offer I've been waiting for. The banks, at this stage, will tell him more than they want to tell me. With or without my approval, Keith will now call them anyway, so I might as well hear the result.

I suggest two names, two of the clearing banks.

Before he can question me, I say I'll be expecting his call in half an hour. Then I hang up.

Henry arrives ten minutes later. Dishevelled, and dripping wet, he has his coat on his arm. He picks at his soaking shirt gingerly, holding it away from his chest. As he comes towards the desk, the stench of beer envelops me.

'What's up?' he says.

Deflated, I suggest he should return to his party.

He looks surprised. But then he realizes what's in my mind and shakes his head.

'One of the dickheads tipped a pint over me.' He gives another tug at his shirt. 'What's this name-problem crap?'

'How much have you had?'

'Not enough.' He smiles. 'Sounds like maybe I should've got stuck in while I could.' He nods to the ensuite bathroom. 'Any towels?'

He really does seem okay.

'Use the shower, Henry. You reek. There's a clean shirt in the cupboard.'

We hold a conversation, voices raised, between office and bathroom. I give him the sobering news. He reappears in the doorway clutching a towel around his waist, his face quite pale now. A sudden thought seems to strike him.

'Hey, this isn't some stupid birthday wind-up, is it?'

'Uh-uh.'

'Christ all fuckin' mighty.'

He steps back out of view. The shower comes on and steam billows into my office.

'When you're finished in there, get out to the Dealing Room.'

I wait but he doesn't answer, so I step up to the open door and repeat the instruction. Then I head out to find Sir John.

8

'They won't like it,' Sir John says. 'Not at all.'

Astonishment strikes me dumb at first. They won't like it? The sole redeeming feature of Sir John's arrangement was the leverage it gave us, but now that we need it he comes out with this: they won't like it?

'Nobody's asking for their opinion. Call them, tell them they reinstate our trading line, or that parcel of their shares goes to the highest bidder.'

'That's a threat, Raef.'

'If you want to ask politely, go ahead. Once they've turned you down, tell them.'

Sir John wavers a moment, his discomfort quite plain, this will not go down well with his friends at the Club. And if that cloistered world closes ranks against him he'll be out in the cold – a prospect, I see now, that terrifies him.

'Surely it's not that bad,' he protests. 'Why don't I just call round, get this straightened out quietly.'

I raise a hand; don't even think about it.

'The Dealing Room's on its knees. You start asking favours now and the market'll smell blood.'

'But I could just see, Raef.'

Between clenched teeth I name the clearing bank. 'Call them. Right now.'

'Raef—'

'Call them!'

He starts back surprised. And hurt too. It would be so much easier if I could bring myself to dislike him, but I can't. As he reaches for the phone I feel a twinge of remorse at my impulsive outburst. But when he looks at me before he dials I hold firm against his silent plea. I pick up the extension and listen.

Sir John's call is put through, and a high reedy voice comes on at the far end.

'John?'

'Matthew. Bearing up? Thought I might just catch you for a word.'

'Can I call you back John? Bit busy here.'

Sir John seems about to concede. I glare at him, mouthing the word, No.

'Well, no actually,' Sir John tells him. 'There's a situation I was hoping we could discuss.'

'Yes?'

Sir John rests his forehead in one hand. 'There's been a misunderstanding between our bods in Settlements. We're being told you no longer have any trading line open with us. Just wanted to let you know. Give you a chance to clear it up before it becomes a nuisance.'

A few seconds' silence follows; it occurs to me that a whispered conference is taking place.

'No, apparently that's right,' the reedy voice says. 'We've filled up our trading line with you temporarily. It should roll off in a few days. I really must fly, John.'

Sir John looks at me as if to say, 'What next?'

I whisper, 'Tell him. The arrangement.'

And I make a slicing gesture across my throat. This has gone beyond a gentlemanly game. After what I saw in the Dealing Room, and after hearing the clearer's attempt to drop us, I'm certain now that a deliberate punch below the belt is necessary.

I whisper it again. 'Tell him.'

'Matthew,' Sir John says. 'I wonder if you've had any time lately to look at our arrangement.'

Another silence follows, longer this time. There are definitely others at the far end, listening in.

Harris's tone becomes silky. 'The telephone's hardly appropriate. What say the Club at eight?'

I shake my head. Sir John declines the invitation. I scribble a few words on a pad and turn it for Sir John to see. He reads, then looks up at me.

'Matthew,' he says frowning, 'there appears to be a chance that the arrangement no longer suits our book. In fact it's possible the whole position will have to be unwound.'

'Unwound?' the voice blurts out. But then something, or someone, seems to check him. More silence.

I scribble another note to Sir John. Committed now, he takes a deep breath.

'If our trading line with you can't be reopened today,' he tells Matthew Harris, 'we really won't have any choice. We'll have to clear the decks. The arrangement will have to go tonight.'

Harris, regular churchgoer and respected man in the City, calls Sir John a cunt. Sir John's look darkens. His eyelids droop in a way I haven't seen for years. When I signal for him to hang up he raises a finger; one moment.

'Thank you for your cooperation, Matthew,' he says softly. 'I look forward to receiving your call before six o'clock. Kindest regards to your wife.'

Matthew Harris slams down his phone. Sir John looks up at me and smiles – a glimpse of the man he once was – and I feel, for a moment, quite ridiculously proud of him.

He leans back, readjusting his tie. 'I think we should be hearing from Mr Harris again rather soon.'

9

Many of our clients, when they run into difficulties, stick their heads in the sand. This is known around our office as the Ostrich Effect. It's the common factor behind nearly every bankruptcy we see. We had one client, a toymaker, whose line of toys was condemned by the National Safety Council in August. Micawber-like, he omitted to mention this to us and kept on producing the toys until December in the vain hope that something would turn up. By the time he stopped payment on our loan, he had a full inventory of mechanical dinosaurs, a workforce that hadn't been paid for a month, and an extremely long list of shops that had turned down his discounted wares. Vance had one of the purple brontosauruses encased in glass as a memento, and once a quarter he presents it to the member of his department who's made the worst blunder: my first year in Corporate Finance, I won it twice.

'Speak to us.' This is what we tell our clients. 'If you get into trouble, let us know.' Good advice, and some of them take it. This is the question for me now: do I take this good advice, or do I succumb to the Ostrich Effect? Do I go to see Roger Penfield and tell him what's happening, or do I cross my fingers and stick my head in the sand?

It takes me all of ten seconds to decide.

10

'You've just caught me,' Penfield says. He folds some papers and slides them into his inner jacket pocket. 'I'm making a speech over at Mansion House in twenty minutes. What's this, that note? How's Morgan getting on?'

'He'll have something by Friday.'

He hits the intercom and lets his secretary know he's on his way out. I tell him I was hoping for ten minutes of his time.

He comes over to get his coat and scarf. 'No can do, Raef.'

'It's important.'

He makes a placatory gesture. In the constant clamour for his attention, he's heard that line too many times before. He says he'll try to squeeze in ten minutes tomorrow morning. 'The City and sodding Europe,' he mutters, presumably referring to his speech. 'Déjà-vu all over again.'

He takes a quick glance in the mirror by the coat-rack.

'Important enough to cost you your job,' I say.

He continues to button his coat. He inspects himself in the mirror again.

'I trust that's not a threat.'

I remind him that with his Investigation Unit about to descend on us, I'm hardly in a position to be threatening him. He presses his rim of grey hair into place.

'Ten minutes, Roger.'

He gives me a look. Then he touches his chest as if feeling for his speech, and steps by me to the door.

'We'll walk,' he says.

On Sunday the bank was empty but now the men in grey suits are everywhere; they all bob to Penfield as we pass. It feels like I'm accompanying a cardinal down the nave of St Peter's. Not until we've crossed the Great Hall and gone into the street does he speak.

'Better here than inside. Too many ears.'

Yes, I think, and out here too many eyes. But right now I have to take what I'm given.

We turn and head for Mansion House. Keeping my voice low, I tell him my story.

'Not such a problem, surely. A few trading lines full?'

'This isn't just a few, Roger. It's damn near the whole market.'

'How many?'

'Ninety, ninety-five per cent. Our Dealing Room's like a morgue.'

Before coming to see Penfield I put my head in there again to find out how Henry was doing. Extremely sober now, he gave me a look of despair from across the room. This isn't the birthday he'd planned.

'There's a few still doing us. But not many. And the way it's looking, they won't last long either.'

'Since when's all this happened?' Penfield asks peevishly.

'This afternoon. I put out some feelers, then came straight to see you.'

His peeved look lingers; I've ruined his day. He's no doubt tracing the same line of thought I followed earlier: if our Treasury operations stay frozen out of the market, the bank will be badly destabilized; our credit rating will plummet; in the worst case, the bank might even fall. Should that awful event happen, Penfield's job will be right in the firing-line.

'You've had no credit downgrade?'

I shake my head.

'Nothing in the offing?'

'No,' I tell him.

When I explain that we're closing out as many positions as we can, he purses his lips.

A crowd of young men spills from the pub in front of us, jostling and laughing: we step down into the road to skirt round them.

'Bloody hooligans,' Penfield mutters.

In fact they're lawyers – at least one of them is, I recognize his face. He recognizes me too. And Penfield. I'm definitely not enjoying this stroll through the City.

'We can twist some arms,' Penfield says, 'but if the market's got a real reason for turning Carltons down, there's bugger all we can do long term.' He glances at me. 'Not carrying any big losses, are you?'

I assure him that our balance sheet's fine. He doesn't mention the note, but that's obviously what's on his mind.

'If you need to close out any positions tonight,' he decides, 'you can do it with us. I'll call our lot when I get to Mansion House.'

A short-term life-line, a few hours' grace: if we can close out with the Bank of England, we won't be at the mercy of the markets overnight. I thank him.

We turn into a narrow alley, pedestrians only, and halfway along he stops and looks behind. I stop and glance back too. No-one; we're alone in the alley. He takes my elbow and draws me into a recess between two pillars, where we face one another.

'You have a murdered Treasurer, a possible fraud, at least one serious complaint lodged against you with the Takeover Panel, and now this business.' His voice is low, but it quavers. He is, I realize now, simply furious with me. 'You wanted some time to sort out that fraud note; I gave it to you. You need to trade out your positions with us tonight; very well, you may. But that's all one-way traffic. Now it's your turn.' His large frame leans towards me. He enunciates the next words very clearly. 'Sort. Your. Fucking. Bank. Out.'

The blood surges into my cheeks, my heart pounds. I'll remember this moment, and I'll ensure that Penfield remembers it too. But just now I hold my tongue.

'And tell Morgan I want to see him this evening. Alone.'

He pivots, and stalks to the end of the alley, where he rejoins the stream of pedestrians. He looks like one of them now: just another grey man in a coat; something in the City.

I turn and head back up the alley.

11

At the office, my first port of call is the Dealing Room. No one's kicking a football this time. That's because almost no one's here. Each desk is the same: vacant chairs, and the few remaining dealers sitting quietly. They're gone. More than half our Dealing Room have walked out.

'Where you been?

Unbelievably, Henry actually smiles when he asks me this.

I gesture around the Room, struggling to keep the fear from my voice.

'What's this?'

He looks around calmly. 'No point everyone hangin' about spreading rumours. When they got their books square, I sent them home.'

I make a sound: relief. Henry mistakes it for displeasure.

'Hey,' he says. 'I didn't think it'd be a problem.'

I ask how our global position looks now.

He reads me our outstanding positions, the ones we haven't been able to close out or roll over: most of our interest rate exposure is covered. 'Forex, not so good,' he says.

One of the few remaining dealers calls across, 'Henry!'

Henry swivels. The dealer swings his phone like a lasso.

'They knocked us back for the fifty bucks.' Fifty million US.

'Try someone else,' Henry tells him.

The dealer watches his handpiece whirling overhead, then catches it. 'Yeah, right,' he says.

Henry gives me a look.

'If you can't get anyone to do us,' I tell him, 'forget it.'

He asks me if I intend to let the positions run. This would leave Carltons at the market's mercy, the bank would become little more than a casino chip. I don't understand Henry's smile at first. Then I do.

'You think that might be fun?'

Not fun exactly, he says, but interesting.

Traders. Vance is right, these people really aren't normal.

I reach across and tap the button marked Bank of England. 'If you can't raise anyone in fifteen minutes, call them. They'll take whatever we've got left. Interesting, we really don't need.'

'They called earlier,' Henry informs me. When I look blank he adds, 'The Old Lady. Checkin' on rumours in the market, what's happenin', blah-blah-blah. Sounded jumpy.'

'So what did you tell him?'

'Everything I know. Sweet FA.'

I ask what rumours he's hearing, and Henry recounts two wild and implausible stories. He keeps looking away, I have the impression I'm not getting the truth.

'Daniel was killed last week, Henry. That's not part of the rumours doing the rounds?'

Henry circles some numbers with his pencil, concentrating hard. It occurs to me that he's trying to spare my feelings.

'Speak to me, Henry.'

He drops the pencil. 'They reckon Daniel put some deals in the bottom drawer. The losses got too big, he was gonna be tumbled, so he topped himself.'

'Suicide?' I can't keep the surprise from my voice. 'That's ridiculous, Daniel was murdered.'

'You wanted the rumour.'

So I did. And when I recover from my surprise I turn this one over. Bad deals tucked away in a bottom drawer don't stay hidden for ever: sooner or later they explode. At a stretch, I can see how this suicide theory might have gained currency.

'And what's your theory, Henry?'

'My theory is, theories are crap.' He picks up his pencil and points to the door. 'You wanna theory, go see Billy Bullshit.'

12

In the corridor I meet Sir John. He accompanies me back to my office, explaining that Matthew Harris has phoned.

'I'm just going to see him,' he says.

I jerk my head back towards the Dealing Room. 'He hasn't reopened our trading line.'

I enter my office. Sir John stays by the door.

'He's asked for a few more hours, Raef. It's not entirely in his hands.'

'He's got till eight tomorrow morning. They trade

with us then, or we drop them in it. Make sure they understand. No extensions. No excuses.'

Sir John disappears down the corridor. Becky puts her head in.

'Stephen's just coming,' she says. 'And Allen Fenwick's been trying to get you.'

Great, I think dismally. The press is onto it already. I tell her if he calls again to refer him to Gary Leicester.

'And Mr Johnstone called again,' she says.

I give her a warning look, and she withdraws. I'm not sure I could trust myself with Johnstone just yet.

Stephen Vance, when he enters, is beaming.

'Three cheers for young Master Haywood,' he says dropping into a chair.

I am disorientated for a second, completely lost: this isn't the time for good cheer.

'Ian Parnell took a fall,' he says. 'Haywood hacked back to the stables with him.' The hunt. 'Pair of them spent the afternoon in the pub apparently. All very chummy.' Vance pauses for effect. 'Ian Parnell wants out.'

I force a smile. Vance thinks I haven't grasped his point.

'Raef, Ian Parnell wants to accept the Meyer bid. Haywood's setting up a private meeting tomorrow. If this comes off, we're home.'

'Good,' I say. 'Excellent.'

He looks at me askance. Evidently news of the freeze-out in the Dealing Room has somehow passed him by.

'Stephen, we're in trouble here. May be serious.'

Then I lay it all out for him, recounting the events of the afternoon. The only interruption he makes is when I tell him about my conversation with Roger Penfield: at his, Vance moans. Concluding the sorry tale, I ask if he has any ideas. He sinks into himself, thinking. To Vance this probably has the makings of an interesting corporate banker's puzzle. 'You need to twist some arms,' he suggests.

'Sir John's working on it.'

Vance looks sceptical. He knows nothing of Sir John's arrangement with the clearer, and I've no intention of letting him in on it now. It's the kind of deal he despises, if he heard of it I wouldn't put it past him to resign.

'Your father would be more useful,' he suggests. 'Does he know?'

'Not yet.'

He seems to read what's in my mind. 'Something like this isn't your fault, Raef. No one's going to blame you. Your father's got more clout than Sir John. Call him.'

Henry comes in. 'All done,' he says, giving Vance a quick nod. 'Old Lady rolled it over to Monday. Everyone's gone home except the nightdesk. They've got orders to watch the screens and sit on their hands.'

Then from behind his back, he produces a bottle of champagne. He asks if we'd like to wish him Happy Birthday.

The last thing I feel like, but it would be churlish to refuse. I go and fetch the glasses. Henry pops the cork, and the three of us kick back for a minute sipping champagne. We discuss the events of the afternoon, crossing and recrossing the same ground: what happened, when and why. Finally it's Vance who says what's on all our minds.

'It has to be connected with Daniel.'

Henry, loyal to the memory of the man who watched over his career, remarks that the rumours of Daniel hiding deals are just bullshit. I stare into my glass, thinking about that fraud note. Neither one of these two knows. Then Henry remembers something else.

'Sandersons were turning us down yesterday.'

'They're too small,' I say. 'This is the whole market.'

Vance sets his glass aside. 'Lyle?'

'We don't know that.'

'No,' Vance agrees. 'But he sounds to me like the number one candidate. And if it is him, I'll wring his bloody neck.'

The truth is I've had the same uneasy suspicion myself. But suspicion isn't certainty, so I tell them both not to go off half-cocked.

'So what,' Henry interjects, 'we let them screw us?'

'Leave it to me,' I say. 'There'll be some trading lines open in the morning.'

He doesn't seem convinced. He swigs the last of his drink, then rises.

'I'm sorry about your party, Henry.'

'I'm gettin' too old for that shit anyway. You did me a favour.'

Once Henry's gone, Vance and I sit silent a moment, reflecting on our troubles. Then he says, 'You know this isn't a maybe, Raef. This has got to be Lyle.'

'Not necessarily.'

'He'll use it to save Parnells.'

'This is the Dealing Room.'

'Tell that to Lyle's PR people.' Vance waves a hand. 'By the time they've finished with it we'll all look like monkeys.'

Chewing his lip, he goes over and flicks on the screen, calling up the closing price on Carltons. I see the name but not the number.

'Down how much?' I ask.

'35p on the day. Last deal a sell.'

I remark that it could have been worse. Vance flicks off the screen and watches till the shrinking star of light disappears.

'Don't worry,' he says, turning to face me. 'By tomorrow morning, it will be.'

13

'The things I'm hearing, Jesus, who wants to use the phone?' Keith Trevalyn, hands in his pockets, leans into the cold wind as we talk. We're at St Katharine's Dock, close by his office. 'I thought Carltons was meant to be having a good year,' he says.

'We are.'

He grunts. There's a metallic jangling from the yachts moored in the artificial lagoon; the wind whistles in the masts and the stays hum. We pass into darkness nearer the river.

'By the way,' he says. 'I'm sorry about Daniel.'

I nod a cursory acknowledgement. But when he asks after Celia I remind him that he said he had something to tell me.

'Yeah.' He stops at the river wall and looks out over the dark water. 'You won't like it.'

'Try me.'

'We're not having such a great year ourselves,' he says.

I'm wrong-footed a moment.

'I tell you,' he goes on, 'the way it's looking I'm not worried about my bonus these days. More my job.'

His job. Now I see where this is going. I ask him if it's really that bad.

'Reuters. Electronic dealing systems.' Still gazing over the river, he pronounces his verdict. 'We're ancient history.'

'It's possible we'll need another senior dealer at Carltons soon. If we do, Keith, you're top of the list.'

He nods without enthusiasm. 'When you called up, I thought, "Here's my chance". Then I do the ring-round. Jesus.'

'I'll help you if I can.'

'The way I hear it, Raef, that's a fucking big "if".'

A horn blasts somewhere downriver, we both turn. When I look back to him he's staring across at the far bank again.

'Okay,' he says, 'this is what I hear. The big rumour is Daniel. He was hiding deals and they blew up in his face. Suicide.' He pauses. 'That's bullshit, isn't it?'

'Yes.'

'Well that won't stop our knuckleheads from spreading it. No-one else either. I picked up about four variations on the theme in half an hour.' He looks at me. 'There's another story too. One that's real enough to get your line pulled everywhere.'

'Ahha?'

'You really don't have a clue, do you?'

'Keith—'

'The story is you reneged on a payment.'

I sway back. 'We what?'

'Some deal done last Friday,' he says, 'payment due yesterday: it didn't reach the counterparty's account.'

He gives me the details. The story is that Carlton Brothers has refused to pay a legitimate obligation to some two million pounds; not a large sum, but were it true, a betrayal of trust that would make our name dirt everywhere. If we've reneged on one payment, the reasoning goes, what's to stop us from reneging on another?

'But this is rubbish,' I say. 'A bloody lie.'

Keith tells me not to shoot the messenger.

284

'And people believe it? They don't ask me – no one's asked me – they just believe it?' I slap the river wall. I thought I'd seen the worst of the City, but this craven shrinking back from Carltons because of a lie, it plumbs new depths. I swear. Loudly.

Keith looks embarrassed. Like everyone else, apparently, he'd assumed the story was true.

'You've been badly stitched up,' Keith decides.

I thank him, ironically, for his belated vote of confidence. Diesel exhaust reaches us from a passing barge. Keith sneezes.

'Where's the story coming from?'

He takes out a handkerchief. 'All over the place. Look, I can ask till I'm blue in the face, but that's it, I won't get any more.' He blows his nose.

I have a feeling that I already know the answer to my next question, but I ask it anyway.

'Who are we meant to have reneged on?'

'I'm not sure.'

'Keith, you hauled me out here because you didn't want to speak on the phone. It's cold, and I don't have the time.'

He repockets his handkerchief, looking glum. After what he's discovered this afternoon, the attractions of rejoining Carlton Brothers have paled: he doesn't want to be the last passenger to board the Titanic. It hasn't been much of a day for either of us. He leans against the wall and studies the light on the water.

'They reckon you owe two million to Sandersons,' he says.

14

'We can forget about Shobai,' Hugh tells me. 'Their Treasurer opened the books for me.'

He's been waiting for me to get off the phone ever since the maid let him in. She's gone now, and we're alone in the drawing room.

'He showed you?'

'I spent weeks with this guy, remember. The suicide? I tell you, he doesn't want any more trouble. He showed me the lot.'

I slump into the sofa. Our best lead on this fraud thing has suddenly disappeared. I ask Hugh if he's sure.

'Raef, he went through the paperwork with me. Anyone who'd signed anything, we called in. Front and back office. I talked to a dozen of them.' He drops into an armchair. 'Nothing.'

His laptop sits alongside a folder on the coffee table; I stare at it bleakly. I've just hung up on Sir John, he hasn't had a decision from Matthew Harris yet; and Henry rang earlier to say that he'd tried trading into Sydney and Tokyo – no luck. My father, too, I've spoken with. The prognosis is grim.

'We kept looking for Shobai so we kept finding it,' Hugh explains.

'Where does Ryan fit in?'

'Okay, take Ryan. He was on the Shobai suicide. Shobai was City, Stewart's murder looks like City, so

286

Ryan gets the case. When we see him we jump to a conclusion.'

I remind him that the Shobai deal came up in his computer search.

'I loosened the parameters for the Shobai deals. Same again. I was looking for Shobai, so I found it.'

We look at each other. We have two days left, and as of this moment we are nowhere.

I get up to fix us both a drink. Hugh gives me a brief recap on the meeting he's just had with Penfield.

'What did you do? Poke him with a stick? He almost chewed my head off.' Hugh turns in his chair. 'And what's this he's saying about some other big problems at Carltons?'

I tell him to concentrate on the fraud note, to leave these other problems to me.

'You don't get it, Raef. The way Penfield's telling it, you're hanging on by the skin of your teeth. I can help, but I need the full picture. I swallowed your fancy Odin deal, but frankly, you can't afford to dick me around like that again. So,' he says. 'Let's hear it.'

I take his drink across and place it on the side-table. 'You must be sorry I ever came knocking at your door.'

'Yep,' he says. And he isn't smiling.

I return to my chair and put aside my drink. What's the point of hiding it from Hugh? After everything that's happened, I'm getting a queasy feeling that I'm not fighting isolated problems here. And if there's anyone who might be able to pick his way through the maze, it's Hugh. So as directly and as openly as I can, I tell him my story: the Mannetti cock-up; the squeeze in the Dealing Room; our difficulties in the Parnell takeover; Darren Lyle; I even mention Ryan's interviews with Vance. At first Hugh stops me every few minutes to ask a question, but gradually he falls quiet and when I finally end my story he hasn't spoken for a quarter of an hour. The only information I hold back is about Annie; that, and Sir John's arrangement.

His glass is empty now; he considers it thoughtfully.

'Jesus,' he says.

'Penfield didn't tell you any of this?'

'Not likely. He wanted the same as you: pick my brains and keep me in the dark.'

I mumble a few words of apology but he shrugs it off.

'Not the best few days of your life,' he remarks.

'Do you think it ties in? The fraud note with everything else?'

'I'm not a psychic, Raef, but sure, I'd say so.' He pauses. 'We've knocked Shobai out, okay? And Odin. That leaves just one name from those three I turned up.'

'You said Twintech was too small.'

'Look, we can't go back and start again. It's either Twintech or I've run out of ideas. I didn't give Penfield the name, if it's any consolation.'

'He agreed to stay out of it?'

'Only till Friday night. After that he'll turn Carltons upside down.' Hugh flicks his glass. 'The only reason he's not putting the cleaners through you now is it'll look bad for him. He made his big mistake when he let you put me onto this instead of his own team. Now he's just hanging on and hoping.'

Confirmation, if I needed it, that Penfield fears for his job.

'Unhappy man,' Hugh says.

I offer to fix him another drink. He declines. He flips open the folder and takes out a sheet. After studying it a moment, he remarks that Twintech has made less than two million pounds out of its dealings with Carltons. 'Not much.'

I make a sound.

'I mean not big enough for someone to get killed over,' he says. 'That's what we're discussing here, isn't it?'

'It's a possible fraud.'

'It's definitely trouble with Darren Lyle from what you're saying.'

I consider this. I ask if he thinks Ryan should be told.

'He's investigating a murder, Raef, of course he should know.' He looks as if he can't believe I've asked the question. Dropping his eyes, he adds, 'He called for a chat this afternoon.'

Ryan? This bombshell leaves me floundering. Our investigation is being filtered through to Ryan by

Penfield; and Penfield assured me that Ryan need not know who the investigators were. If Ryan finds out I'm involved, he'll erupt.

'How did Ryan hear you're working on this?'

'He hasn't. He just wants me to run my eyes over something. My guess is, the reports he's got from Penfield.' Our reports. And not knowing where they've originated, Ryan's approached Hugh for a second opinion. Hugh smiles, the irony amusing him. 'I told him I was tied up.'

Then he scans the Twintech sheet again.

'I need a dumpdown on this lot,' he says.

I lead him through to my study. After logging on and keying in the password, I give him a quick tour through our system. He leans over my shoulder asking questions. Ten minutes of instruction and he says he has the general idea.

'I have to make some calls. I'll be in the drawing room.'

He doesn't reply. He slides into the chair, fingers on the keyboard, eyes fixed on the screen. For the moment, at least, I have lost him.

The next three hours I'm on the phone, making calls. My father, from his flat, is doing the same. Influence. Pressure. There are credits in the City that pass unrecorded in any balance sheet, and now we're calling our favours in. Most of those I speak to are wary: not one of them asks me about the deal we are supposed to have reneged on. When I mention it, they sound as if I've just jogged their memories. Yes, there was some story they'd heard. No, of course they wouldn't pull our trading line because of a rumour. 'It's a lie,' I tell them. 'It's not a rumour, it's a lie.' Then I remind each of them of the particular favour he owes us. But in the space of three hours, I manage to extract just two promises to reopen the trading lines; the rest fob me off. And I can't plead. To be phoning like this already shows signs of weakness. I thank each of them with whatever courtesy I can raise, a dwindling supply as the night wears on.

In the middle of it all, Hugh appears from the study. He sees I'm on the phone, so he holds up a disc for me to see. He points to himself, then the door.

'See you in the morning,' he whispers.

I nod, and he shows himself out.

The voice in my ear keeps talking, saying he never really believed Carltons reneged on a deal; saying he'll look into it tomorrow; saying that he can't make any promises.

I assure him, politely, that I quite understand.

15

Nights are the worst. For the past three months it's usually been something in my dreams that wakes me, but not tonight. This time I simply open my eyes and stare into darkness. 'Go to sleep,' I used to tell Theresa when I woke to find her lying like this beside me. But I won't sleep now, not until I've been downstairs, made a hot drink and maybe sat for a while. After a minute I roll over and push back the bedclothes.

In the kitchen, waiting for the kettle to boil, I play a round of the Corporate Banker's favourite game: Scenarios and Outcomes. Scenario One has everything going right from now on: we get all our trading lines back, Twintech turns out to be a chimera, Hugh and Inspector Ryan both find nothing, Carltons prospers as an independent merchant bank. But somehow at this late hour, sitting in bathrobe and slippers, I can't quite bring myself to believe it. We're already too far down a different road. Scenario Two is the bid: Sandersons launches a bid and gets us, or Sandersons launches a bid and we throw ourselves into the embrace of a white knight like American Pacific. Either way my family loses control of the bank. My father, I know, is preparing himself to accept this, but the best I can manage is to let the awful possibility skate briefly over my mind. Scenario Three, the big one, is full-scale disaster: the fraud is real, the whole Odin business comes out, Ryan arrests me on suspicion of Daniel's murder, Annie is used as evidence, and the tabloids descend on my family. Even the glimpse I allow myself of this possibility starts a bead of perspiration down my neck. My hands turn moist. Please God, I think, not like that.

I take the hot drink through to the drawing room. If Scenario Three unfolds, I know what will happen.

Slumped here in the armchair I try to relax, but instead the scenes of a family tragedy I witnessed five years ago come back to me. A slow-playing tragedy in which, month by month, the Amershams, a family much like my own, was destroyed. We'd had lunch with them just a fortnight before the news first broke in the press. Bernard Amersham was talking of buying more land, expanding the boundaries of their estate: I'm sure he had no idea what was coming. A week later his son James was arrested by the DEA in the States; that was enough for one tabloid headline. The parents were certainly embarrassed, but at that stage the charge wasn't known. Only as the weeks passed, and they flew back and forth visiting their son, did it become clear how serious the problem was. James, it turned out, had invested family money in an air-freight business in Florida; and hand-in-hand with the legitimate business went a drugs distribution network covering most of the southern US. James claimed he had no idea, but the tabloids descended like a baying pack on the Amersham estate: one estate worker received five thousand pounds for her story of supposed debauches up at the big house; another sold photos taken in the Manor House bedrooms. And while these were being splashed across the tabloids, the full scale of James' investment in the freight business came to light. He'd committed nearly everything, not just his own money, but his family's. The Manor and a few hundred acres remained unencumbered, but almost every other asset was frozen pending the outcome of the DEA investigation. The investigation lasted almost two years. The Amersham saga became a running joke, a regular column in *Private Eye*.

But for those of us who watched at close quarters, there was nothing amusing in the family's fall. James' sister, furious at her parents for letting it happen, walked out; she took her trust fund and disappeared to Australia. Bernard became ill. No sooner had his wife nursed him back to health than she collapsed. And through it all the lawyers had to be paid, the jubilant press dealt with, and the American investigators answered; it was a complete and utter dissolution of their lives.

James is in gaol now. The Amersham fortune and good name has largely gone. My father and I were driving by their house last summer, and on the spur of the moment we turned in. I can still remember the look on my father's face when he realized the bent and shuffling figure putting out a sign for Teas in the Orangery was actually Bernard Amersham. 'Don't stop,' my father told me in a shocked whisper. 'Drive on.' That's what we did, straight back to the road with neither of us speaking a word.

Now, here in the darkness of the drawing room, moist hand clasping my cup, I think of my own family. And I pray. I pray with all the strength I can muster. Please God, I pray, not like that.

THURSDAY

1

'They should call any minute,' Sir John says.

My father and I have arrived at the bank to find Sir John already at his desk. On my way through, I checked the Dealing Room; the dealers on the nightdesk told me that Henry waited till Tokyo opening last night before going home. It didn't help. The lie has gone global: no one's accepting our name.

'Had a rather torrid night of it,' Sir John says, elaborating on his meeting with Harris and the others. 'They asked some very uncomfortable questions.'

'You said they're reinstating the line.' He rang to tell me at 2 a.m.

'They'll confirm it when they call. With luck, they'll get one or two others on board.'

The clearer wants to cover its back. If they support Carltons alone now, it could invite queries about the relationship between us: the last thing they want is a journalist turning up our arrangement. I'm pleased that Sir John's succeeded, but this really isn't my kind of banking – my father's either – and our congratulations are rather less than effusive. My father relates the results of his night's work: he's convinced half a dozen market players to deal with us again. I excuse myself and go back to my office.

Here I flick around the Reuters screens, checking prices: London trading hasn't opened yet, and there's no mention of Carltons on the news screens; that could change very suddenly. Gary Leicester calls.

'So,' he says. 'What's our story?'

I've spoken with him once already this morning, as soon as I woke. Like Sir John, he's had a torrid night; he's been responding to a barrage of questions from the financial journalists about the rumours.

'Just keep denying it,' I tell him. 'Anyone says they're going to print it, you can put them through to me.'

'They won't disappear.'

'They will if there's no story for them, Gary.'

He snorts. He tells me one of the broadsheets is going to run a piece on Daniel. 'Their angle is he was tied in with some City suicide a few months back. I told them it was bullshit, but they're running it anyway.'

I thank him for the warning.

'I'm not sure I can hold these guys off much longer,

Raef. If the situation at Carltons improves, they'll go away. If it doesn't . . . I do PR, not miracles.'

On that sombre note, our conversation ends.

Five minutes later my father comes to tell me that the expected call from Harris has come through. He can't keep the relief from his voice.

'They're reopening the line.'

'Who else?'

'Two more clearers.' He mentions the names.

I take a deep breath, breathing out slowly. The pressure applied by Sir John has worked, we might get through this yet.

My father says he doesn't think he can do any more, he has business at Westminster to attend to. 'None of my lot should go back on their word.' My lot, I presume, being those banks from whom he extracted promises last night. 'If they do, call me, Raef, and I'll be back at lunchtime to see how you're getting on. Unless you want me to stay.'

But I decline the offer. It will be best if we maintain the illusion of normality.

I can see he wants to say something else, but all he does finally is reach across and squeeze my arm, a gesture of affection and encouragement, before he goes.

At boardroom tables around the City our fate is being decided. But it's out of my hands now. I sit here, quite alone, and wait.

2

Activity: deals being done; numbers shouted. 8.30 a.m., and Henry and I stand in the Dealing Room surveying the scene. It's not as it was two days ago, but there is life.

'Must've been some arms you twisted,' Henry remarks.

We do a slow circuit of the Room together, stopping at various desks to chat with the dealers. There's an almost palpable sense of relief in the air: they still have their jobs; their employer, it seems, is not going under. Owen Baxter shouts a profanity and everyone laughs, but the laughter has a strained quality – they're trying too hard to be normal.

The banks which made promises to my father have come through, and Sir John's three clearers have reopened their lines. One of mine is already trading with us, and the other one's reopening its line in an hour. We look like a Dealing Room; we look, for the moment, like we're going to survive.

'This permanent or temporary?' Henry asks as we turn at the far end of the Room.

'Permanent.' I glance at him and smile. 'In case anybody asks.'

Coming back down the second aisle, we pause by the bond desk: there are two empty chairs. Henry asks where this missing pair are, but no one's seen them this morning. Henry doesn't make a scene of it, he enquires about the gilts market, then strolls back with me to his own desk.

'Those two have bolted. We'll need replacements.'

I suggest that we should wait, we can't be sure.

'I'm sure.' Henry keep his voice low. 'I heard they were sniffin' around. Yesterday must've made up their minds. Two out of how many? After yesterday, you can't complain, Raef.'

He is, I know, absolutely right. If all we've lost out of yesterday's débâcle is two bond dealers, we should be thankful.

I ask Henry to make a list of any bond dealers in the market looking for a change. He jots a note to himself. I don't tell him right now, but I've just made my decision about Daniel's replacement: it will be Henry. He's proved his mettle in the past twenty-four hours; at very least he deserves his chance. But this news can wait till Monday; in the meantime the job, and its responsibilities, are mine.

Out in the corridor I run into Vance. 'Well?' he says.

'It looks all right. The lines are opening up, we'll get through it.'

There is the hint of a smile. 'Darren's going to hate this.'

Then Vance's face changes. I glance back over my shoulder to see what he's looking at. Inspector Ryan. And just behind him, Hugh Morgan.

'Mr Carlton,' the Inspector says. 'I presume your office is free.'

3

'I could charge both of you.' Ryan points at Hugh then at me. 'Obstructing a police inquiry. Withholding evidence.'

'Evidence of what?' Hugh objects. 'We haven't got anything.'

Hugh just had time, before we entered my office, to tell me that Inspector Ryan has discovered I'm involved in carrying out Penfield's investigation. Hugh whispered that Ryan wasn't best pleased.

And I can see that myself now. Ryan has a tight rein on himself, he isn't shouting, but he's extremely angry.

'We would've passed it on if we'd found something concrete,' Hugh says. 'We knew Penfield was keeping you informed.'

'You aren't the police, Mr Morgan. Neither of you. And nor is Penfield.' He glares at Hugh. 'Didn't it occur to you that by stampeding through Shobai you might queer the pitch for us? Us, the police?'

'Shobai has nothing to do with this.'

'The gentleman at Shobai gave you their word, I suppose.'

'Daniel Stewart's murder isn't connected with Shobai. That's my professional opinion.'

'Your professional opinion cuts no ice here, Mr Morgan. Not after this cosy little operation you're been running.'

Hugh looks at the floor. I take up the baton.

'You saw the fraud note? What was I meant to do, sit on my hands?'

But before Ryan can answer, Hugh speaks again. 'Anyway why didn't the Met follow it up straight off? You got me in for the Shobai suicide, why not for Stewart?'

'For what it's worth,' Ryan says grimly, 'we thought we had the fraud angle covered. Penfield assured me he had his own investigation underway. I received a daily report.' Ryan looks at me. 'Only Penfield's report on Shobai arrived at the same time as I was taking a call from Shobai's Treasurer about Mr Morgan here's visit. I asked the Treasurer if any other investigator had been around. Apparently not.'

I take a moment with this. Then I ask Ryan if Penfield mentioned our other problems.

He nods. 'You seem to be in the fortunate habit of receiving the benefit of the doubt, Mr Carlton. That isn't something I'd rely on much longer.' When I turn to my chair he says, 'I wouldn't bother. We're going out shortly.'

The significance of this remark eludes me.

'Listen,' Hugh says. 'We're as far along with this thing as anyone would've been. Whatever we've found, you've got. Penfield's given us till tomorrow night, what's to stop us working this together? I mean, if this fraud thing's connected with Stewart's murder, and we figure out the fraud, that must help you, no?'

'You thought we might work together.' Ryan's tone is ironic.

'We crack one, we crack them both,' Hugh says.

Ryan sniffs, but he sees that what Hugh's proposing makes sense.

'If we pool what we have, we'd both stand a better chance. That's all I'm saying.'

Hugh doesn't seem so much like a trader now, more a corporate banker, wheedling an advantage. Ryan strokes his chin, considering.

'My investigation isn't a bargaining chip,' he decides. 'If you have information that might help me you're obliged to hand it over. So. Beyond what I've seen from Penfield, what do you have?'

'Not much,' Hugh says.

'How much?'

'Nothing,' I say.

Ryan studies me a moment. Then he turns to Hugh. 'You can go now, Mr Morgan.'

Hugh is taken aback. He asks if he can continue with his investigation of the fraud.

'Your arrangement with Penfield still applies,' Ryan tells him. 'But from now on, you keep me directly informed.'

Then he nods to the door. Hugh has no choice. With an apologetic shrug to me, he departs.

Ryan crosses to the window and looks out. 'Morgan knows nothing about your daughter?'

'No.'

He continues to stare out, perhaps waiting for an

explanation of why I, a suspect in Daniel's murder, have chosen to become so deeply involved in an investigation of my own.

At last he faces me again. 'There's something I'd like you to see.'

4

We take Ryan's car. After driving through the City streets, we emerge by the river and continue a short way before he slows, mounts the pavement, and parks. He flips over a small sign on the dashboard: Metropolitan Police. Then we get out.

Walking by the river wall, he asks, 'You know where we are?'

I do. We're approaching St Paul's Walk, where Daniel was murdered. There's a constant hum of traffic, and a cold breeze coming off the river. We walk side-by-side.

'Two people,' Ryan says. 'Early hours of the morning. Not much traffic – it's drizzling anyway – the drivers all concentrating on the road. It's dark. Who's going to notice us?' He leads me down the steps to the pedestrian underpass beneath Blackfriars. There are a few cardboard cartons where the tramps sleep. 'According to forensics, the muzzle was within inches of the point of entry when it was fired.' A short way along he stops and rests against the river wall.

'I've got a bank to run.'

'I'm sure they can spare you.'

This must be where it happened, where Daniel died. I shiver. Ryan asks if I'm cold.

'What's your point?'

'Let's say I'm just sharing some information. What you wanted, isn't it?' When I make no comment, he goes on in that matter-of-fact tone. 'The bullet entered at the base of the skull. Stewart died instantly.'

A sound escapes me.

'He slumped against the wall and slid down,' Ryan says.

I follow his gaze down. Beneath our feet, we're actually standing on it, there's a dark stain on the pavement. I step back.

'Considerable bleeding,' Ryan remarks.

Bile rises in my throat. I swallow, then take another step back. Turning, I breathe in the cool air from the river. Ryan watches me. I can't do or say anything for almost a minute, the brutal fact of the murder seems finally to have pierced. And that bloodstain; a part of Daniel. Ryan stands very still.

At last I face him. 'Why am I here?'

'To see.'

'So I've seen. Can we go now?'

'It's not like a balance sheet is it, Mr Carlton? Not something that a bit of fooling with the profit and loss account can put right. He's dead. Last Wednesday night someone stood here, put a gun against the back of his head and pulled the trigger. Can you picture that?'

He sees, by my look, that I can.

'Good,' he says. I go to step by him but he grips my arm. 'We haven't finished yet.'

'I've finished.'

'No,' he says. 'Not yet.'

I look down at his hand and he releases me.

'Have I been fair with you? Your wife and Stewart? Your daughter? Do you see the journalists pounding on your door?'

'I know.'

'Do you?'

'All right, I appreciate it. Is that what you want? I appreciate it.'

'It's not your appreciation I'm after, Mr Carlton.'

I can't hold his gaze. He won't use what he knows about Annie against me, I see that now. He desperately wants to discover who killed Daniel and why, but unlike nearly everyone I deal with each day he won't break the bonds of decency to achieve what he wants. He won't sacrifice two innocents – Theresa and Annie – just to get there. Could I say the same? Were I as he is, a decent man, would Theresa ever have sought solace with Daniel? And would I be standing here, as I am now, on the very spot where Daniel was murdered, and thinking of how soon I can get back to the bank? In the midst of my life, perhaps more than half of it over, it occurs to me that I'm not at all like the man I intended to be. And this man who probably doesn't even own a dinner jacket – he is.

'I'm asking for your help,' Ryan says. 'You knew Stewart better than anyone. And you know what's been going on at Carltons better than anyone. Do you understand that?'

The traffic hurries by, someone beeps a horn.

'You're in the habit of keeping things to yourself. That really isn't much use to me.'

'What do you need?'

'Cooperation.'

I glance down at the bloodstain. I tell him I'll try.

'How far do you think we are from your office?'

'Why mine?'

'The bank.' He looks pained. 'It's not a trick question. How far are we from Carltons? On foot.'

'Fifteen minutes?'

'My sergeant did it in a little less.'

Now I see what he's getting at. I tell him that he has Vance wrong. 'If Stephen says he was working, he was working. Believe me, I know him.'

'I don't mean to be rude, but you thought you knew Stewart.'

That one stops me.

'Anyway,' he says, 'Vance wasn't the only one working late at the office.'

'The nightdesk?'

'I've spoken with Baxter. No, I was thinking of someone else.' He gestures to the pavement. 'This is where Stewart was found. Does anything strike you as curious?'

He sees that I'm lost.

'Why wasn't the body dropped in the river? Sensible precaution. It might not turn up for days, Thames Barrier or somewhere. Put yourself in the murderer's shoes. You've fired the shot, what now?'

'He'd have to get away.'

'You'd have to get away from the body. In the shadow here, no traffic passing, what's to stop you from heaving Stewart over the wall?'

I suggest that a man who's just committed a murder isn't likely to be thinking straight.

'If he was a professional he would be. Or if he'd planned it.' Ryan pauses. 'And there's a third possibility. It's possible he wanted to, but couldn't. Stewart was what, about your size?'

Yes, I tell Ryan yes, give or take a few pounds: around thirteen stone.

'What can you tell me about the chef?'

I lift my head in amazement. 'Win?'

'We'll talk in the car.' Ryan glances at his watch. 'I think we've seen enough here. Don't you?'

It takes me less than five minutes to give Ryan everything I know on Win Doi: the Vietnamese background, his escape in a boat after his parents were killed, his time in a refugee camp in Hong Kong. I learnt none of this from Win himself, it all came secondhand, from the friend of Mary Needham who recommended him to me. Ryan looks mildly surprised.

'You hired him yourself?'

I explain how it happened. Mary Needham's friend works with a refugee resettlement charity, she specializes in browbeating acquaintances into offering employment to those in the charity's care. My turn came with Win. I had no idea what he was going to do. And then, when I met him, he mentioned with a nervous smile that he hoped one day to do in England what his family had done before the war in Saigon: run a restaurant. Problem solved. I took him on as a kitchen-hand at Carltons and forgot all about him. Four years ago that was, and his hard work has done the rest. Now I'm not looking forward to the day when he tells me he's leaving to start a restaurant of his own.

'Win wouldn't hurt a fly. It isn't in him.'

We pull up outside the Carlton building; the Inspector turns to me.

'Then perhaps you could explain why he keeps lying to me.'

'What's he said?'

'"I don't know." He says that rather a lot.' Ryan taps the steering wheel. 'He was here on Wednesday night. Your nightdesk, Vance, they all saw him. Vance even spoke with him. But Mr Win Doi doesn't remember. Could he have had a grudge against Stewart? Was there any bad blood between them?'

'They got along fine.'

'I imagine he's quite grateful to you for the job.'

'I suppose so.' In fact Win gives me a small present each anniversary of the day he joined us. A Vietnamese custom, he says.

'Perhaps you might have a word with him,' Ryan

suggests. 'If he's got nothing to hide, I'd like to hear a little more from him than just, "I don't remember."'

'I can try.'

'Because if there's any more trouble with this investigation, I'll be conducting the rest of my interviews down at the station.'

Eyebrows raised, he asks me if I understand. I assure him that nothing could be clearer.

5

'We're still on the skids,' Henry says.

But the Dealing Room looks to me much as it did earlier: quiet, certainly, but deals are being done at most of the desks. Henry sees my puzzlement.

'Not here.' He nods to the Equities desk. 'The Carltons share price. We're taking a bath.'

He rises, and we go across there. The Carltons share price has slid to 250 – we've dropped 75p in two days. The senior trader relates the details of the slide. 'Looks grim,' he concludes.

The number on the screen is red; the price still going down.

The trader says he's been pumping the market-maker in Carltons for information. He points to the off-Exchange screen, the order-driven market: no bid next to Carltons. 'I think he got dumped on at the top, can't get out.' The market-maker, he means.

'Can't get out anywhere?'

The trader shrugs. 'Why else's he chasing us for a bid?'

I chew that one over. If Sandersons want to make a move on us, why aren't they buying? I tell the trader to keep his ears open.

On my way to the door, young Jamie steps from the alcove beside me.

'Mr Carlton?'

I pause, one hand on the door.

'I just wanted to say it wasn't Owen's fault.' He looks downcast. Then he seems to realize that I haven't a clue what he's talking about. 'That big loss the other night?'

I remember now. But that was last week, prehistory to a dealer.

'It was my fault,' he says.

A long memory, and scruples too. Maybe this lad really isn't cut out for the Dealing Room. Opening the door, I tell him that we all make mistakes.

'Live and learn.'

Owen bawls at him from across the room, and Jamie drops his head and retreats into the alcove to fetch the custard creams.

6

Win's in the kitchen, unpacking vegetables. When I step through the open doorway he says, 'Too early, too early,' and smiles.

I prop myself against the bench. 'What's on the menu?'

He moves between the vegetable rack and the box on the floor, reciting: three entrées, three main courses, two desserts.

'Still some Henry birthday cake,' he adds, sliding open the bread bin to show me.

I find myself at a loss for a moment. I've always liked Win, and I don't want to intrude: every man has his reasons, and if Win doesn't want to speak with Ryan, what affair's that of mine? Looking at him now I couldn't be more sure that he has nothing to do with Daniel's death. But if I don't intrude, Ryan will pursue him, something I'm not sure that Win understands.

'Win, Inspector Ryan asked me to speak with you.'

If there were a noise, or any other distraction, I'd assume he hadn't heard me.

'He's just trying to find out what happened to Daniel.'

Still no acknowledgement. Win dribbles the empty box across the floor like a football, then kicks it into the pantry. He takes three chickens from the fridge.

'He thinks you can help.'

Win picks up a knife. 'He is your friend?'

'No.'

He starts to slice. 'I don't like him.'

'You don't have to like him. He just wants you to answer a few questions.'

He glances out to the restaurant where the

waitress is laying the tables. I lean back, pulling the door closed.

'What's wrong?'

Win shakes his head.

'The Inspector's not going to go away, Win. He knows you were here on Wednesday night, and he thinks you're lying to him.' I pause. 'You were here on Wednesday night, weren't you?'

He nods.

'You have to tell him.'

Win suddenly drops the knife. Hands braced on the bench, he looks at the wall. 'I don't go back Vietnam,' he says, 'I don't go back Hong Kong.'

His shoulders rise and fall. When he turns, his face is set hard, a fierce determination blazes in his eyes. So this is it, the hidden rock upon which Ryan foundered. Win Doi has no intention of returning to hell.

'That won't happen, Win. You've got a family here, a life, no one's going to send you back.'

'I don't go back.'

'No one can send you back. You've got to understand that. Ryan can't, no one can.'

Words. I see they make no impression. God knows what real horrors Win can set against them. I turn left and right in frustration.

'For Christ's sake. The only way you'll go back there is on some damn package tour.'

He looks at me. The title, Boddington and the bank, they count for nothing with Win: he sees only the man who gave him a new chance in life. But he still isn't convinced.

'You're not being accused, Win. The Inspector just needs to find out what happened that night. I've told him you couldn't be involved.'

No response. I ask him if he can at least tell me what happened.

'I come back here, twelve o'clock.'

It's like watching some wild creature moving tentatively out of the shadows.

'What for?'

'The big bowls. I bring them back.'

The giant glass bowls, I remember them from the party on the boat; full of desserts and fruit. It would be just like Win to take them into his personal charge. I pinch the bridge of my nose. The Inspector is not going to understand this at all.

'And when did you leave?'

'Maybe fifteen minute.'

'Did Vance see you leave?'

Win turns his head. 'My wife. She see me.' He explains that his wife picked him up from the boat, she helped him bring all the bowls up to the restaurant.

'Win. There isn't any problem for you then. Your wife was with you the whole time?'

'Yes.'

I could stand here the rest of the day assuring him he has nothing to fear, and still I might not reach him. I give it one final shot. I take Ryan's card from my wallet and place it on the bench. Win looks over.

'If you don't call him, he'll come back anyway. And he'll keep coming back until you answer his questions, Win. He's investigating Daniel's murder. That's his job. That's the law. But if you just tell him the truth there won't be a problem. And I think you should. I really do.'

His looks harden. I raise my hand.

'But even if you don't speak to him, no one's going to send you back to the refugee camp. I give you my word, Win. You understand?'

The chicken joints make a crunching sound as they break. I slide Ryan's card closer to the cutting board, then I leave.

7

Hugh digs through the paperwork in the box I've just taken down from the shelf. When he arrived, he said he wanted to look through the paperwork on all the Twintech deals, so we've come up to the filing room to search. I've borrowed Sandra's key.

I ask him what he'd be doing if he wasn't doing this.

'Habibi,' he says. 'Remember?'

'I mean if you wanted to give up the City. Isn't there something else you always wanted to do?'

'No.'

'Nowhere you want to go?'

He tells me he goes to plenty of places right now. 'From what I've seen,' he says, 'the grass isn't much greener. Does this have some mysterious connection with Twintech?'

Not at all. It has a connection with me, personal doubts, but nothing I wish to discuss. So I take down the last box, and crouch beside him. He's been referring to a printout on the Twintech deals; now he pushes it across the floor to me.

'The past twelve months,' he says.

A surprisingly long list. He asks if anything strikes me.

'There aren't many big amounts?'

'Correction. There aren't any.'

Looking through it again, I see that he's right. More deals than I expected, but the amounts are small.

'What else?' he says. 'See how they're paired up?'

'A lot are in-and-out the same day.'

'Most, but not all. And not every in-and-out gave Twintech a profit.' He rummages in the box. 'Take the paperwork,' he tells me, nodding to the pile he's already dug out. 'Match it up with the deals on the list. Make sure it checks out.'

'Are we looking for a dealer's name?'

'Fat chance. Whoever this is, he's no dummy.'

For the next fifteen minutes we're silent. I match the paperwork with the list of Twintech deals while Hugh rummages through the last box. Here in the quietness, amidst the dusty records, it's almost possible to forget what's happening outside: Ryan is looking for a murderer, Vance, his chief suspect, is trying to pull off our biggest deal for years, and Darren Lyle is trying to cripple us. And so far only Darren seems to be having any success. All this, while I sit up here turning pages.

Hugh finishes his search; he stands and stretches. Bending from side to side, he asks me how things ended up with Ryan.

'We went for a walk by the river.'

'A walk?'

'Don't ask.'

As I rise, the door swings open and the sounds of the back-office come flooding in. Karen Haldane. She looks from us to the open boxes scattered at our feet.

I turn to Hugh. 'Are we done here?'

Yes, he tells me, all done.

'What's this?' Karen says.

But I'm not feeling like a lecture just now. I usher Hugh past her out the door, pausing to give her Sandra's keys. She glares.

'You could've asked me,' she says.

Nodding, I pass right on by.

8

Back in my office, Hugh and I go through the

paperwork together. As he expected, it throws up no particular name.

'So what does that tell us? There's more than one person involved in Twintech?'

''T ain't necessarily so.' Hugh rocks back in his chair. 'Say someone does a deal, forgets to do the ticket. He's out at lunch when he remembers. What does he do?'

'Rings in.'

'Right. Whose signature goes on that ticket?'

I pull a face. If the dealers didn't do each other favours, the whole operation would grind to a standstill. In the normal give and take of things, it wouldn't be at all difficult to get an unsuspecting innocent to sign off a deal. I push both hands up through my hair.

'Same everywhere,' Hugh consoles me.

He opens his briefcase: more paper. He's says he's done some analysis on the Twintech deals, the losing deals are marked in red ink; beside these, the highs and lows in the market that day. I study the numbers awhile. Then I notice something.

'None of the losses are in-and-out the same day.'

'That's right. We'll make an investigator out of you yet.'

I tell him he'll have to spell it out for me.

'Okay,' he says, 'try this. The fraudster sees some price diving, so he writes himself a deal against Carltons. Then, A, for some reason he can't get the other deal written, the close-out; or, B, he thinks it's going lower so he lets it run. But when he comes in the next day the market's turned against him. He cuts the loss.'

I examine the numbers again. It makes sense.

'He kept dealing in small amounts,' Hugh speculates, 'because he didn't want to trigger a credit-check from your back-office. As long as he didn't get greedy, odds were you wouldn't notice him.'

This, too, makes sense. We have hundreds of corporate customers, there's no way we can keep tabs on all of them. We generally rely on the ratings agencies, Moody's, or Standard and Poors, but with many of our smaller clients it's easier to simply set low dealing limits: if they don't exceed these, and they pay their bills on time, we tend not to ask too many questions.

'He was right,' Hugh says. 'You didn't notice him. He's pulled nearly two million out of the bank without anyone seeing.'

'You've traced the money?'

'Destination Switzerland, by the look. He probably churns it through half a dozen places after that. Liechtenstein, the Caymans, it could be anywhere. Frankly, Raef, unless you find who's behind Twintech, the money's gone.'

I should be relieved – the amount is paltry – but what I am is angry. For less than two million pounds, the bank has been put in jeopardy; for less than two million pounds, Daniel might well have been murdered. I feel now what any decent man would have felt from the start: a deep burning rage.

'But see this?' Hugh points to Twintech's recent deals, his fingers resting on the last one. 'See the date?'

Last week. Two days before Daniel died. Twintech, it seems, bought into the CTL bond issue. I smile.

'What's up?'

I explain about the CTL paper that Carltons got left with. 'Nice to know our friend here got caught out too.' Then I notice something else: there's no close-out on Twintech's CTL deal. 'Twintech's position's still open?'

'That's how it looks,' Hugh says.

I switch on the Reuters and flick around till I find the price on the CTL bond. After the immediate sharp move downward post-issue, it's now holding steady.

'So,' I say. 'He's sitting on a loss.'

Hugh looks at me. 'You're assuming he's still alive.'

This again. Hugh, after turning it all over, has decided that Daniel was at very least a partner in Twintech. His theory is that one of the other partners had him killed. Hugh's friends down at the Met are still saying that Daniel's murder was a professional hit.

Yes, I tell him now. I'm assuming the fraudster is alive.

He considers a moment. 'I've got an idea,' he says.

9

After leaving Hugh with our IT people, I do a quick tour of the bank: in Settlements, half the girls are reading magazines, and over in Funds Management the usual atmosphere of inertia prevails. Putting my head in at the Dealing Room downstairs, I see that matters stand just as they were. I withdraw and move on to Corporate Finance. Even here the feeling is subdued. I sense the faces turning my way, searching for a sign; they're wondering if they should hang on for the half-yearly bonus, or cut their losses and jump ship now. I find Cawley and take him aside. He gives me a rundown on the state of play in the bid. Vance has gone to give a presentation at one of the big pension funds, trying to shake their Parnells shares free.

'Haywood reckons Ian Parnell's in the bag,' Cawley says.

In the bag: the kind of optimistic phrase I used to use myself when I started out in Corporate Finance. If the bid succeeds, it will boost our credibility in the market, but it won't stop Penfield. Vance, I know, would be cock-a-hoop, but all I get when I think about it is an arid rush of spite: I'd dearly love to see Darren Lyle take a fall.

I'm already halfway back to my office when I lift my head and see Gerald Wolsey coming towards me. I look around for Lyle, but it seems he hasn't come. When Wolsey offers me his hand I ignore it and walk straight past. He follows me into my office.

He seems ill at ease; not much of a consolation after what he's put us through. I ask him what he wants.

'I wouldn't have bothered you, but I couldn't seem to get through to your father. Rather busy.' He waits, but I remain silent. 'I think there's been a misunderstanding.'

'Misunderstanding?'

'Raef—'

'Mr Carlton,' I say coldly.

He looks surprised. He seems just to have noticed how angry I am. His cheeks flush pink.

'I can well understand that you might be upset—'

'Who sent you?'

'What?'

'Not that difficult a question. Who sent you?'

'If you'll just hear me out—'

'I don't want to hear you out. I heard Mr Skinner out.' I come round my desk and I hold a finger very close to his face. 'You're a worm.'

He blinks. I feel myself losing control but I don't care enough to hold back.

'This bank employs a lot of people and most of them can't afford to lose their jobs. This isn't Whitehall. We don't sit on our fat arses for twenty years waiting for a pension. Even me' – I jerk a thumb to my chest – 'I work too. Like my father and my grandfather did. That's what we do. We don't do it for the good of our health, I admit that, but I tell you what: we don't stand back and watch the lot get brought down by some bureaucratic arsehole like you.' Wolsey flinches. I point to the door. 'Show yourself out.'

The pink flush on his face deepens. 'Mr Skinner's been suspended.'

'What for? Not digging the dirt fast enough?'

Wolsey tells me that I'm labouring under a misapprehension.

'Get out.'

'I had no prior knowledge that Skinner was coming here.'

'When I need a lesson in how to be economical with the truth, I'll let you know.'

'That isn't fair.'

'And I suppose it is fair for you to join forces with Lyle and try to screw us?'

'Darren?'

'Oh, please. Spare me.'

I go back to my desk. He tries again.

'My investigators acted prematurely. I've taken disciplinary action against Skinner and I came here intending to apologize. Perhaps I shouldn't have bothered.'

Pretending to be amused rather than infuriated by this farce, I shuffle the papers on my desk.

'Carlton Brothers does have a case to answer,' he says. I make no response, and finally he goes to the door. He offers a parting shot over his shoulder. 'And if you want to start blaming someone, I suggest you look a little closer to home.'

I restrain the sudden impulse to hurl my paperweight after him. Whitehall. How do my father and Aldridge put up with these people?

Immediately I phone my father to tell him about Wolsey's visit, but he dismisses this impatiently. He asks if I've been watching our share price. I flick up the screen: another 5p down.

'Gifford's concerned,' he says.

Gifford isn't the only one. If the fall continues my father and I could be in dire financial trouble. Half our twenty per cent holding in Carltons is financed by a loan, and that loan is secured by the ten per cent of Carltons we own outright. Leverage: it cuts both ways. We need to stop the fall.

'I think we should put in a bid ourselves,' I tell him. '"Account personal".'

He greets the suggestion with silence. An attempt to support the Carlton share price will take serious money, and we both know that the one asset we could use as collateral – the only one that might make a difference – is Boddington. He asks if there's any hope the slide might stop of its own accord.

'It won't stop unless someone starts bidding.'

'I'll come over to see you at three,' he says.

Outside my window a gull soars, drifting high above the river. Carlton Brothers or Boddington: my father or me. One of us is about to have a gaping hole punched clean through his life.

When I turn back to the screen, our shares have dropped another 4p.

10

Karen Haldane missed her vocation – she should be down at the Met with Ryan. She badgered Becky so much Becky finally came in to beg me to go upstairs. 'Please Raef,' Becky said. 'She's been on my back for an hour.' Now I take the fire steps two-by-two, mentally rehearsing the sharp little speech I'll make. I have enough problems without being forced to run around at Karen Haldane's beck and call.

But Karen doesn't give me the chance to say a word. When I enter her office she says, 'Just a moment,' and walks straight out the door. I step back and watch her stroll down the corridor to Funds Management. Unbelievable. I wait in her office, brooding darkly.

She returns with a young West Indian woman in tow.

'Pauline does administration on the Alpha Fund,' Karen says, closing the door. The Alpha Fund: where the cock-up occurred. 'Tell Mr Carlton what you told me.'

Pauline looks lost. 'Which part?'

'Well, start with the instructions Mr Mannetti left when he went on holiday.'

'When Mr Mannetti left, I was with Mr Johnstone then – he did Mr Mannetti's job on the Alpha Fund.'

'The instructions?' Karen interrupts.

'Yeah, well he said he left them with some brokers.'

I ask her what kind of instructions.

'He said Mr Johnstone was just temporary, he didn't want him messing up the book. Mr Mannetti said he'd take care of all the nominee business when he got back, I should just book it through.'

Karen says, 'Mannetti left orders with some brokers before he went on holiday. Is that right?'

'Ahha,' Pauline says.

'And Johnstone didn't know?'

Pauline shakes her head. She explains that the shares passed into a small nominee account; she did the paperwork herself.

'But you must've known Parnells were in the Red Book.'

'Yeah. But when I rung Mr Mannetti he said just put it through, he'd be back in a few days. If there was problems he'd sort it out.'

'You rang him?'

'Ahha.'

Karen tells me she has the number.

Pauline shifts her weight from foot to foot. 'I just did what he said.'

I get the impression I'm missing something here. I ask why she didn't speak up earlier, back when Johnstone was fired. Pauline stares at her feet.

'She was afraid,' Karen says.

Pauline lifts her head. 'I was just doing what Tony told me.'

Karen directs a withering glance Pauline's way. Opening the door, she reminds Pauline not to speak with anyone about this, including Mannetti. Pauline bobs her head and leaves us.

I face Karen. 'Tony?'

She goes to the far side of her desk. 'Okay, he was sleeping with her.'

'And now he's dumped her and she wants her revenge?'

'He's dumped her and she's decided to tell the truth.'

'I can't believe you've brought me up here for this.'

'Mannetti's been lying,' Karen says.

She opens a folder and begins to show me the paperwork. Begrudgingly I run an eye over it. On first view it seems to support Pauline's story. Odd.

I ask Karen about that phone number.

'Fiji,' she says. 'When I tried it, I got some resort manager. He gave me the two-minute spiel on holidays in the sun.'

So about the Pacific island, at least, Mannetti was telling the truth. He wasn't in England. And if he wasn't in England he couldn't have been at St Paul's Walk last Wednesday night. I turn the whole business this way and that, trying to see it from every angle, but after a moment I give up. Whatever happened, we've taken our lumps over this Alpha Fund business already: I can sort it out with Mannetti later. Carlton

Brothers dissolving by the hour, I have greater and more immediate concerns.

'I'll have a look at it on Monday.'

'Monday?' She's appalled.

And then as if summoned, Mannetti appears on the doorway.

'Private party?' he enquires.

He flashes a grin too, and looks about to enter but he's picked an extremely inappropriate moment to apply his boyish charm. Karen rolls her eyes. I excuse myself, explaining that I have some rather serious business to attend to downstairs.

11

Vance has just returned from his presentation. The Corporate Finance team spends hundreds of man-hours each year doing the rounds of the institutions, talking them out of their money or drumming up support. This time it's support for the Meyers: Sandersons has been equally busy on behalf of Parnells. Tinker sessions, Vance calls these presentations, a fair description: each one a door-to-door sales pitch, the salesmen dressed by Armani.

Vance is talking with Cawley when I enter his office.

'Success?' I venture.

Vance suggests to Cawley that it might be an idea to grab a sandwich, and Cawley takes the hint and goes. As soon as the door closes, Vance's carefree look evaporates.

'Another presentation like that, and this bid is dead in the water.' He gets to his feet. 'They didn't want to hear what the Meyers have got planned for Parnells. They wanted to hear about us. Carltons.'

'The share price?'

'Every damn thing. Is it true the DTI are investigating us? Did Daniel leave any deals in the bottom drawer? Are the police looking here for the murderer? Everything.'

He opens his copy of the *Evening Standard* and drops it in front of me. In the business section, speculation on the fate of Carlton Brothers has displaced the Parnells takeover as the lead story. There's a picture of Daniel lifted from last year's annual report. A cold ripple runs up my spine.

Frowning, I drop the paper into the bin. I ask Vance how much we already have of Parnells.

'Forty-five per cent. Postal acceptances won't get us there. We've stopped dead.' He says that he's had no luck with Bainbridge either: now we're relying absolutely on Ian Parnell breaking ranks with his family. He rubs his forehead. 'Even Reuben's angry, he's asking what the hell's happening here at Carltons. And do you know what? I honestly can't tell him.'

'It isn't easy for any of us, Stephen.'

'Bloody Daniel. He couldn't even die without making trouble.' Then he realizes what he's said. He bows his head. 'Sorry.'

I tell him it's all right. But it isn't. It's not what he's said that disturbs me, it's his whole manner: this tenseness isn't like him at all. And it's more than just the bid. I'm starting to wonder if there might not be something behind Ryan's suspicions. Not murder, I don't believe that, but there's definitely something going on with him. Twintech?

Haywood pokes his head in. 'Ian Parnell's here.'

Vance straightens, instantly alert. 'Is he selling?'

Haywood laughs. 'Give him a chance. He wanted lunch, so I brought him over. I'll bring him in.'

When Haywood returns and ushers Ian Parnell, my first impression is of weakness: Ian's handshake is limp and his chin recedes. He's dressed like Haywood, an expensive pinstripe and a quiet tie – if I saw him in the street I wouldn't look twice. Vance asks how the Hunt went; Haywood draws Ian Parnell into the conversation, but Ian's distracted – he has other concerns just now than the field. If his uncle, or Darren Lyle, found that he'd come over to see us, they'd lynch him. Eventually Vance mentions Parnells.

'We'd rather hoped your uncle might have found time to see us.'

'My uncle,' Ian murmurs, dismissive. We wait, but Ian isn't inclined to elaborate. He turns to Haywood. 'Are we going to eat?'

Vance tells Haywood to show Ian around, adding that he might join them after lunch.

The moment the door closes Vance raises a brow.

'Sounds like a split?' I say.

He swivels left to right in his chair. 'He wants to sell or he wouldn't be here. But he might need some encouragement. How did he seem to you?'

'Weak.'

'Too much money too young.' Giving me a wry look, Vance adds, 'Not a hard and fast rule, of course.'

A few more moments' thought, then he slaps his hand down on the desk with real force. I lift my head in surprise.

'We're not going to lose this,' he says. 'Not to Darren bloody Lyle.'

12

At two o'clock Celia Stewart arrives unannounced. I'm perched on the edge of Cawley's desk when I see Henry approaching with her; he must have gone out to reception to sign her in. An odd silence descends. Everyone's gawking at Celia, but pretending not to. She's dressed in a bright red jacket and skirt; and she's smiling too, no one's idea of the heartbroken widow. Henry explains to me that Celia's come to get the personal effects from Daniel's office. 'I've gotta get back,' he says, jerking a thumb towards the Dealing Room. He wants nothing to do with this.

Walking her down the corridor, Celia asks if I've found Daniel's will yet. I grimace. The folder's still in my office, unopened.

'It's okay,' she says. 'You must've been pretty busy.'

I unlock Daniel's office, and she passes in. She stops in the middle of the room.

'There's a few pictures on the desk,' I say. I'm not sure what Inspector Ryan would think of this visit, but he need never know. 'Have a look in the drawers, too, there might be something.'

She seems in no rush. She runs a hand over the bookshelf. 'Do you remember when he started here?' She looks back over her shoulder. 'He brought a new book home every day. Like a kid.'

Her hand slides from the books. She crosses to the desk and opens the drawers, searching them one by one.

'I'm meant to be seeing the lawyers later,' she says. 'I suppose I can cancel it.'

The will: it occurs to me that this is really what she's come for. I tell her that if she can wait ten minutes, I'll look through the folder now. She nods, still searching the drawers. After considering several items, finally all she takes from his office are the pictures.

In my office she stands at the window while I pore through Daniel's folder. When I come across their marriage licence, I glance up. Celia's gazing out at the City. Marriage: who ever knows? I recall when Stephen Vance's marriage ended. They'd come down to Boddington the month before, a summer's weekend, with their boys. Happy, relaxed and laughing, everything sunny and fine. A month later Vance and I were looking through some valuations in his office. 'How's Jennifer?' I said. He didn't even raise his eyes. 'We're getting a divorce.' Just like that; the bolt crashing from an unclouded sky. And then Celia and Daniel. The trouble between them was quite open, it seemed merely a question of when the final separation would come; but it never did. Their marriage, foundering and rudderless, never actually went down. And Theresa and I?

I return my attention to the folder.

After five minutes' search, I find the will. This is a moment I've been dreading. I glance quickly over each clause, praying Daniel won't send us further suffering from the grave. To my immeasurable relief, I actually feel something like gratitude to Daniel for sparing us, there's no mention of Theresa or Annie. It's dated the first week in January.

'When did Daniel tell the lawyers he was rewriting the will?'

'December.' Celia turns from the window. 'Is that it?'

There's a catch in her voice, she's clearly been dreading this moment as much as me. She doesn't know who Daniel intended to marry, but she knows there might be a name other than her own on the will.

'You and the boys are the sole beneficiaries.'

I hand it over. She looks from the will back to me, then she has to sit down.

'I knew it'd be all right,' she says. 'I knew it would be.'

Her cheerful bright red clothes, and the smile: all a front. She's actually on the verge of tears. Embarrassed for her, I drop my eyes. Daniel. The pain he caused.

And then I see it: the edge of a yellow page jutting from the folder. It's the colour that catches my eyes, the same as that paper I found in Daniel's hidden drawer, the page describing the Odin deal. While Celia dabs at her eyes, I pull out the page. A row of numbers appears. I draw it out further, and now letters appear right to left. When the whole word's revealed, I just stare.

'Shall I take it?' Celia says.

I look up. She's holding out the will.

'Sure. I'll drop the file around later.'

As I rise and come around the desk to show her out, I glance down again at what I've found. It's still there. I'm not imagining it. Black letters on a yellow page and the word underlined: Twintech.

I need to find Hugh Morgan.

13

'This was where?'

'In his personal papers. A file from his study at home.'

Hugh bites his lip, studying the yellow page. We're

outside the IT office at the back of Settlements, he's taken off his jacket and loosened his tie. Still examining the page, he leads me inside.

'His wife knew it was there?'

'No.'

Hugh takes a slip of white paper from his jacket on the chair, and hands it to me. A list of numbers.

'Familiar?' he says.

But it's much more than familiar: it's an almost identical list of deals to that on the yellow sheet I've just given him. We look at one another. Finally I flick the white page. 'What is it?'

'The deals Twintech put through during the last twelve months.' He takes the white list back from me, and holds the two pages side-by-side. 'You're sure you've just found this?'

I tell him Celia left five minutes ago, the folder's still lying open on my desk.

'Daniel never gave any indication he was up to something?' he asks.

'Never.' But Daniel, as I know too well, had no trouble keeping a secret when he chose. I tell Hugh that too. 'But he didn't need the money. I don't get it.'

'You don't have to,' he says, raising the page. 'This more or less proves it. Daniel was Twintech.'

'Then who sent the note to Penfield?'

'I don't know.'

'We can't be sure Daniel was Twintech.'

'True.' He lifts the yellow page. 'But how else do you explain this?'

We both look at the sheet. What, I wonder, would Ryan make of it?

'But Daniel couldn't have been the only one in on it,' Hugh decides. 'Someone killed him.'

'A partner?'

'I'll have the programme finished in five minutes.' He hands back the yellow sheet. 'Hang onto it. When I'm done, I'll call down.'

I can see this sudden discovery doesn't sit well with Hugh. He drops into his chair and starts work on his computer programme: the trap. Hugh's big idea.

14

Becky asks where I've been hiding. 'Calls?' she says. 'You want them alphabetical?'

Standing in the doorway, she recites: Penfield's called twice, Fenwick, Leicester and several others; nothing from Darren Lyle. I ring Penfield and brace myself.

'Well,' he says sarcastically, 'managed to find a minute, have we?'

'Hugh thinks he's found a name.'

There's a pause. 'Yes?'

'We're pretty sure it's been done through a company called Twintech. He's still working on it.'

'How bad?'

The big question, the one that will decide Penfield's own fate. If Carltons can take the loss on the chin,

Penfield will ride out any subsequent inquiry; but if the loss isn't containable, if the Bank of England has to intervene publicly, his head goes on the block.

'Containable. The losses aren't a problem.' I can actually hear him breathing. 'Less than two million,' I say.

'First decent news you've given me all week.'

'Roger, we need more time to find out who's behind it. A few more days.'

He erupts. 'Time!' A string of expletives follows, coupled with some very pointed advice. I hold the phone away from my ear. Twice I try to cut in, but each time he roars over me. 'Have you seen your bloody share price? Have you?' he shouts. 'Because the BIS have; I've been on the bloody phone to them for half an hour assuring them you're not going down. Do you hear that? Close of trade Friday night!' He slams down his phone.

I sit dazed a moment. Any hope of reprieve from Penfield is gone, but it wasn't much of a hope anyway. What's really unnerved me is his mention of the Bank of International Settlements: the central banker's Central Bank simply can't be ignored; not by Penfield, and certainly not by us.

I hit the intercom and ask Becky to have Gordon Shields come up. 'He's been trying to get you too,' she says.

I'm not at all surprised.

Gordon, when he arrives, is agitated but under control. Just. 'Finally,' he mutters. He makes his displeasure clear by a look, then he sits and spells out our capital position: our deposit base is haemorrhaging; we're moving perilously close to a breach in capital adequacy. Gordon delivers this information in a voice leaden with foreboding. I suggest some possible asset revaluations, but he tells me this is just playing at the edges of our problem.

'If you can't stop the fall in Carltons' share price,' he says, 'we won't stop the withdrawals.'

'The BIS have been onto Penfield. We've been noticed.'

Gordon groans. We discuss the situation a minute longer, but it's obvious that we're both equally helpless in the face of the falling share price. He says he feels like he's walking through a nightmare. I'm beginning to know the feeling only too well myself. Finally he leaves, going back to manage the decline in our fortunes as best he can.

Alone for a moment, I try to collect myself. My grandfather used to say that behind every crisis there was always someone who'd lost his head; and by that definition, we're moving close to a crisis. Gordon isn't a man who rattles easily, but he's rattled now.

So now where are we? We still have no idea who murdered Daniel, and Carltons, following this week's endless troubles, is starting to crumble away. Ryan still believes the murderer is in the bank, Hugh thinks Daniel was part of the Twintech fraud, and Penfield, God help us, is sending in his Investigation Unit tomorrow night. Our problems won't be solved by unmasking the fraudster, not now. This whole thing has been pushed from behind closed doors into the marketplace. If Penfield were to publicly give Carltons a clean bill of health, even that wouldn't save us.

What the market wants to see is a real financial commitment from someone; what the market wants to see, as always, is cash. I jot some numbers on my pad; cross these out, and guess again. How much, I wonder, is Boddington actually worth?

15

My father tugs at his earlobe, and nods occasionally to show he's still listening. When I mention the BIS, and repeat Gordon's opinion that we'll be in breach of Capital Adequacy by Monday, he frowns. Then I find myself faltering. We've yet to speak a word on the subject, but we both know there's only one question to be decided between us: do we risk Boddington and make an attempt to save Carltons, or do we let the bank go without a fight?

I take a breath, about to raise the subject, but my father interrupts.

'Penfield's been onto me. There's a possibility of a merger.'

It stops me dead. 'Not Sandersons.'

My father looks horrified. 'God no. American Pacific. I've just left Charles over there with Gifford.

I looks like he might be amenable.'

It leaves me floundering a moment. Instead of being at the forefront of this whole business, as I'd thought, I'm actually several paces behind.

'When's all this happened?'

'I couldn't get hold of you, Raef. Nothing's decided yet. I thought it was best to be prepared though.'

'Is Penfield pushing this?'

'Charles and I raised the possibility with him earlier this afternoon. He said he was already thinking along the same lines. A merger, I mean.'

So Penfield already knew about this when he chewed my ear off.

'How's this been left with Gifford?' I ask, put out. 'What's Charles discussing with him? The price?'

'Raef, they're just preliminary discussions. We can't even be sure Gifford will want us after this.' He nods to the Reuters. The slide in Carltons continues.

My face flushes hot with anger and shame. This is a measure of how far we've fallen: a year ago Gifford would have paid a substantial premium to get us, but now Charles Aldridge is over there pleading, cap in hand. Suddenly we need a big brother.

'I think there's an alternative.'

'Yes.' He inclines his head. 'But do you agree a merger with American Pacific would be best, should the alternative fail?'

As usual, the oblique approach.

'It wouldn't be a merger,' I tell him. 'We'd be lucky if Gifford let us keep our name on the door.'

'It's a fall-back position.'

'It's a surrender.'

'Raef,' he says. 'Please.' Lines form across his brow. I ask him how much we're talking about.

'We can discuss that. For now I just need to know that you agree.'

I cross to my desk and sit down. Somehow this whole business seems unreal. This is Carlton Brothers we're discussing here. A week ago this was one of the few remaining independent merchant banks in the country. A week ago I was getting ready to leave for the party on the boat, and now my oldest friend is dead, and here I am with my father discussing how best to manage the Carlton family's departure from the City. But this is actually happening. Worse, I have to admit to myself that my father's probably done what's best. We can't just hang on and hope. If Gifford can be convinced of our worth, we'd be well advised to cut some kind of deal with him while we still have an asset to sell. I squeeze my temples.

'All right,' I concede. 'If all else fails, I agree. We merge with American Pacific.'

Unexpectedly, a lump rises to my throat. And when I look at my father I see that he too is quite shaken. The magnitude of the decision, of what it means for our family, penetrates deep.

'If all else fails,' I repeat, more firmly. 'But first we try the alternative.'

He nods. 'Boddington,' he says.

We look at one another. Then before he has a chance to muster his objections, I launch into my argument: I say that if we act fast we might raise ten million against the estate; I say that once the market sees us buying it will give everyone pause. He cuts me off in mid-flow.

'I've already done it, Raef. I've raised twelve million.'

I stop and stare.

'Boddington, and a few other odds and ends.' He tells me who's lent us the money: another British merchant. He misunderstands my silent response. 'It was the best I could do, Raef.'

'No.' I shake my head. 'I mean, excellent. Twelve.'

'Twelve, and a touch more.' He hands me a slip of paper and I read the number: almost twelve and a quarter.

I look up. 'You're sure about this?'

He names the broker we use for our personal dealings. 'We've got credit for the full sum.'

'I meant about Boddington. You're sure you want to put it on the line.'

He points to the slip. Not an answer, but the best I will get. God knows what it must have cost him to reach this decision.

'One other thing,' he says. 'The bidding can't be done by committee. Even a committee of two. I'm leaving it in your hands.'

'That isn't necessary.'

'I believe it is, Raef. This is moving too fast now.

You have a feel for these things. I don't.' He stands. 'Believe me, if I thought there was a better way . . .' He spreads his hands. If he thought there was a better way he would never have risked Boddington.

'When do we expect an answer from Gifford?'

'We're at his place for supper. Will you come, Raef?'

I look down at the number again: twelve and a quarter. Boddington. Without argument, my father has placed the most important thing in his life completely and utterly in my care. The foundations of the relationship between us seem to shift, and a new weight settles on my shoulders.

'I think we should have some cut-off figure in the Carltons share price,' he says. He points to the slip in my hand. 'You try to stop the fall with that. If you succeed, well and good. If you don't, I think we should have a cut-off.'

'Then we merge?'

'If Carltons drops to our agreed figure, then we do everything in our power to sell to Gifford.'

A fair suggestion. I can't object to this. Once I've spent the twelve and a quarter buying Carltons shares, we'll have shot our last bolt. If our share price continues to slide, we either agree a merger with Gifford or face financial annihilation; that, or a takeover by Sandersons.

Then I realize something else: if we sell out to Gifford, we can redeem the pledge against Boddington. No doubt my father's thought of this too.

I tap the Reuters, the last trade in Carltons was at 245p.

'What figure were you thinking of?'

He considers. 'How does 200 sound?'

'Make it 195.'

'If it touches 195,' he says, 'we sell out. Family rules.'

Family rules, I agree. Strictly between him and me.

16

'Bid,' I say to the broker down the line. 'Yes. Bid, as in buy. And I'm not averse to letting the market know it's my family. Stay on line. I'll put you on the squawkbox.'

I hit the button and put down the phone.

'Still there, Raef?'

'I'm here. I can't see my bid up on the screen yet.'

But then up it comes: 245p. It stays there five seconds, then disappears.

'You're done at 245,' the broker tells me.

One hundred thousand shares at 245p. Plus stamp duty.

'Bid 243,' I say. 'Another hundred.'

I watch the screen. The bid flashes up, but almost at once the broker comes back.

'You're filled at 243.'

The bid on the screen winks out.

Brutal confirmation, if I still needed it, of just what

we're fighting. Everyone wants to get out of Carltons. Against this I have the rather meagre weapon of twelve million pounds.

'Bid again,' I tell the broker. '241 for a hundred.'

I have to be careful how I do this. If I keep bidding in small amounts, and dropping the bid, I might cause the thing I want to avoid; but if I stand at one price, and fight with everything I have, what happens when I run out of ammunition? It's the kind of judgement I generally left to Daniel.

Remembering this, I call through to Becky and tell her to have Henry come down.

By the time he enters I have a bid on of 239, and I've already spent a million pounds. I outline the situation briefly, not revealing how limited my resources truly are.

'Mm. I've been watching it,' he says. 'Billy's done Carltons' chart.' Carltons' Chart: a graph of the recent history of our share price. In the eyes of chartists like Billy, a sure fire predictor of future performance. 'One line goes down till it hits two hundred, then splits.' He gestures with his finger. 'A black line bounces back up. A red line keeps going down.'

'I thought you didn't believe in charts.'

'Five million idiots can't be wrong. Not in a market.'

I ask if he thinks I should wait till it drops then defend the price at 200.

'No way. Put your name about. The market sees you buyin', there might be second thoughts.' He nods to the screen. 'I wouldn't piss around with small lots.

Put a decent bid in every 10p fall. Make it look like you're serious.'

I speak to the broker, changing the amount on the bid.

'Maybe it's none of my business,' Henry ventures, 'but I would'a' thought there'd be some friendly support, you know, for Carltons.'

I remind him of the salvage operation in the Dealing Room midweek. We've blown all our favours.

'Ah,' he says, nodding.

I'm expecting him to leave, but he doesn't.

'That Inspector Ryan keeps comin' back here,' he says. 'Everyone's wonderin' why he's so interested in us. Owen's runnin' a book on who gets arrested.'

'Is he now?'

'I'm fifty to one. Vance is down to even money.'

'Tell Owen that if he doesn't close that book, he's fired.'

Henry smiles at first, then he sees that I'm serious. He takes another look at the screen.

'If the Meyer bid comes unstuck,' he says, 'Carltons won't even pause for a breather at 200 on the way down.'

The broker shouts over the box: I've bought a million and a half more Carltons at 239.

17

239, 234, 229. Nerve-racking: I know what that

means now. A million and a half pounds every 10p fall, but the fall's slowing as word gets around. After the deal at 239, Brian McKinnon came through on my private line to check on the rumour he'd heard: was I buying? 'Confirmed,' I told him. He asked me if I knew something I didn't. 'Well,' I said, 'I know that 239's a bargain.' He laughed and hung up.

Now, approaching close of trade, my bid of 119 sits on the screen beside someone else's offer of 229. The price has sat untouched for almost quarter of an hour: the market has paused to reconsider. I'm beginning to hope.

Vance will not be arrested. I keep telling myself that. Because if he is, Henry's right, the bid could well fall apart. And if the bid falls apart, the cascade of sellers in Carltons could well turn into an avalanche. Twelve million pounds won't save us then. I think about my father and Boddington. Piece by piece, bid by bid, I've committed the estate to this struggle for the bank's salvation. Now, a third of the money gone, a growing doubt comes to me: what right do I have to be doing this? If we open negotiations with Gifford at once, we'll get a better price for Carltons than if we wait. And Boddington would no longer be at risk. But the bank would go; and I can't bring myself to surrender the bank.

The broker shouts, 'Seller at 225.'

Immediately the offer appears on the screen. I watch and wait, but nothing more happens. The minutes pass slowly. We've almost survived the day.

Then I think of Annie; of Annie and my wife. Where are they? Are they safe? I don't even know that. Here am I, staring at a screen, wringing my hands over the fate of Carlton Brothers, and where they are, and how they are, God only knows. And isn't this exactly what Theresa told me she hated? Even before Annie came, didn't she say I'd let my whole life be devoured by the bank? In December – the month of our personal Somme – she hurled in my face the bitter accusation that by the time she slept with Daniel, she'd already lost me to Stephen Vance. I laughed then, in derision. Staring at the screen now, reflecting on the years of my marriage, that derisive laughter seems very hollow. It's true what Theresa said: there really is more than one kind of unfaithfulness.

'You're done at 219.'

I lean forward and hit the button. 'Bid 209. Same amount.'

My bid appears on the screen. Leaning back, I fold my arms, and close my eyes for a moment. Just at the edge of sense now, I smell the subtle musk of my wife's perfume.

18

Inspector Ryan followed me around the Dealing Room. We stop by a desk, and I enter Twintech's name into our Dealing System.

'Hugh's confident,' I tell him.

He lifts his mobile phone to his ear and waits for Hugh's okay.

Apart from Henry and the nightdesk, the dealers and salesmen have all gone home. With many of the trading lines still closed, it's been a quiet day for them. My own trading day ended with the 209 bid untouched: the sellers of Carltons are definitely reconsidering. But tomorrow the game starts anew. More than half my ammunition spent, I'm not looking forward to the morning.

When Ryan came to see if we were any further on with the fraud, Hugh sent us both down to the Dealing Room. 'Raef'll explain the trap,' Hugh told him. And that's what I do now – quietly, so Henry and the others can't hear.

'Once a deal's done, the trader enters the deal here,' I say, pointing to the keyboard and screen.

Ryan interrupts, his mobile still held to his ear, and gives me Hugh's message from upstairs. 'Morgan says, "Okay, next one".'

I scrub Twintech's name from the deal-screen and move on to the next desk. Ryan follows.

'If someone enters Twintech down here, it'll go through to Hugh's screen upstairs. All lights and bells. That's how he's programmed it.'

'And then what? You and Morgan come racing down and make a citizen's arrest?'

'We contact you.'

'Naturally.' He gives me a look. 'What makes you think he'll trade tomorrow?'

'The open position in CTL. If the market turns against him, he'll cut the loss. That's what he's always done.'

'And you're sure the market will turn against him tomorrow?'

'Reasonably.'

He doesn't press the point. We test the last two desks, and after getting Henry's okay from upstairs Ryan repockets his phone. On our way out the door, Henry calls across the room, asking if we need any help. I wave; no thanks.

'I went up to see Mr Win Doi,' Ryan says, stepping after me into the lift. 'Apparently he went home early.'

'He's afraid you're going to send him back to Vietnam.'

Ryan does a double take.

'Just an idea he got into his head,' I explain. 'But it might pay you to reassure him.'

Ryan thanks me for the advice. I'm not sure if he's being ironic.

Settlements, like the Dealing Room, is quiet: three girls remain, they stand by the fax machines, chatting, and Hugh's installed himself by the door.

'Good news,' he says as we approach. 'Nothing got put through in Twintech's name this afternoon. The positions still open.'

Ryan props himself against Hugh's desk.

'Penfield's talking as if your bank might be in real trouble,' he says to me.

I glance over my shoulder: the girls, I decide, can't hear us.

'I'm not a banker,' Ryan goes on, 'but if the Deputy Governor of the Bank of England's concerned, I'd say there's genuine cause.'

'We'll survive.'

'Whether you survive or not isn't my worry, Mr Carlton. I'd like to know what, if anything, Daniel Stewart's murder has to do with your problems.'

'It hasn't helped.'

'Meaning?'

I turn to Hugh. This seems to be the time to mention the Twintech note I found among Daniel's papers. But Hugh's look checks me.

'Listen,' I say, facing Ryan again. 'It's not only Daniel. We've had the DTI onto us, trading problems, this fraud note, it builds up. We've fallen out of favour. Daniel's murder's become a useful peg for the market to hang rumours on.' I repeat with more hope than conviction, 'We'll survive.'

Ryan gestures to Hugh's PC. 'Is there much chance of this trap coming off?'

'If the market moves against him,' Hugh says. 'Sure.'

Ryan's mobile rings, he steps away and holds a brief conversation, voice lowered. Hugh taps impatiently at his desk, I get the impression he wants to speak with me alone.

Ryan's conversation ends. 'The moment you get anything on this,' he points his mobile at the PC, 'I want to be told.'

'Was that about Stewart?' Hugh asks.

'Someone known to us left the country in a hurry last Thursday morning,' Ryan says. 'It's a possibility.'

'Who?'

'Known to us, the police, Mr Carlton. Now, if you'll excuse me.'

He hurries out to the lifts.

'Known to us?' I turn to Hugh. 'What's that supposed to mean?'

'Not our problem.' Hugh watches Ryan through the glass wall; he disappears into the lift. 'I'm having second thoughts on that Twintech list of Stewart's. Have you got it here?'

I take it from my pocket and hand it to him. He examines it, thoughtfully.

'You said there was some kind of note on Odin too,' he says.

Odin. Again. I thought we'd settled this. 'I don't know why Daniel was murdered, Hugh, but it wasn't because of Odin. All right?'

'Have you still got that note?'

'Hugh, it's not part of this.'

He regards me steadily.

19

I take Daniel's Odin note from the drawer of my desk. Coming out of my office, note in hand, eyes down, I walk straight into Vance. He hurries by me, talking over his shoulder as he goes into his office.

'Ian Parnell's staying the night in town. I've offered him a room on Carltons.'

He's already on the phone, dialling, when I put my head round his door.

'He accepted?'

Vance grins. 'He not likely to win any IQ awards, I can tell you that. He seems to think Haywood's his new best friend.'

'Is he going to sell?'

'We'll put the thumbscrews on him tonight.'

'Where?'

'The Savoy. You free?'

Tonight I'll be dealing with wider concerns than young Ian Parnell. But I wish Vance good luck. If he can shake Ian Parnell's holding free, the Parnells defence will fall apart, the Meyers will win the bid, and Carltons, after a calamitous week, will begin to look like a bank again. Hope abounding.

Upstairs, I hand Daniel's note on Odin to Hugh. Hugh places the yellow Odin page side-by-side with the yellow Twintech page I found among Daniel's papers. The layout of the two pages is identical.

'You said Daniel would have told you about Twintech if he wasn't involved in some way,' Hugh reminds me. 'You were sure if he'd come across it accidentally, he would have brought it to you.'

'I'm sure he would have.'

'What if it wasn't accidental?'

I look up.

'What if he was doing what we've been doing?' Hugh says. He touches the Odin page. 'He did it once before, didn't he?'

'An investigation?'

'Ahha.'

'He would have told me.'

Hugh taps the Odin sheet. 'After this? Put yourself in his shoes. He found the Odin deal, he thought he'd uncovered a big problem and took it straight to you. What did he get? A pat on the back? Well done, Daniel, you've just saved the bank several million quid?'

After a moment I realize he's actually waiting for an answer.

'I told him I was aware of the situation.'

'Anything else?'

There was, and remembering it now I see what Hugh's getting at. It feels like curtains being drawn back, and light pouring in.

'I told him I didn't need his help. I told him to stay out of it.'

'You told him to stay out of it.' Hugh echoes. 'And he was your Treasurer.'

In fact I told Daniel rather more than this: I warned him that he'd already done quite enough meddling in my affairs. My affairs. And if Daniel found Twintech after that?

'So let's say Stewart still didn't like the look of the Odin deals even after you told him to lay off,' Hugh says. 'Then he thinks to himself, if Odin got through the system, could there be any others? He does a trawl, just like I did. That'd be reasonable, wouldn't it? He was Treasurer, he had responsibilities.' Hugh raises one yellow page. 'Bingo. He finds Twintech.'

Which would explain why Daniel was asking Karen about weaknesses in our system: not to exploit them, as we'd supposed, but to plug the gaps. And the disorder in the folders up in the filing room: knowing Daniel's talents in that direction, how hard would he have found it to get hold of Sandra's key for a few hours?

'Who was he going to tell?' Hugh says. 'You? Uh-uh. You'd already warned him off Odin.'

'That was different.'

'Maybe from where you're sitting.'

Hugh puts the pages side-by-side again and we inspect them. I think of Daniel at home in his study during the last weeks of his life, inspecting the same pages. He didn't want to rob Carltons, he thought someone else was. But who could he tell? If he told Sir John or Vance, it would come back to me. And if he told Karen Haldane, he'd have known she couldn't resist confronting me directly. Finally I figure it out, why Daniel couldn't tell me.

'I was Daniel's number one suspect. He thought I was Twintech?'

'At a guess,' Hugh says. 'At least he thought you were part of it. Like Odin.'

'And that note Penfield got? From Daniel?'

Hugh puzzles things out loud. 'He'd have tried to

nail Twintech down. Only he'd have had one big advantage over us. The Dealing Room. He knew the place inside out. And say he uncovered the person or persons behind Twintech.' He looks at me. 'Now what happens?'

'The fraudster killed him?'

'It's over a million pounds, Raef. Maybe not much to you, but you've got plenty down there in Treasury who wouldn't be on a hundred thousand a year. Someone thought the stakes were big enough for a murder or it wouldn't have happened.'

We are silent a moment; pensive. Daniel's murder is the one incontrovertible fact in all this, the one wrong that can't be glossed over or put right. And he died trying to help Carltons.

'Thanks, Hugh.'

'For?'

'You could have done your speculating while Ryan was here.' I pick up Daniel's Twintech sheet. 'I don't think I could have explained why Daniel didn't bring this to me.'

'I'm sure you'll think of something.'

I will? He reaches for his jacket.

'Hugh, I thought we'd agreed Odin was private.'

He points to the Twintech sheet. 'That's not Odin. And this is just a reprieve. If we haven't cracked this by tomorrow night, Ryan gets told.'

Friday night. We get this sorted out or it blows up in my face tomorrow night. I bite my tongue. I pick up the Odin page, folding it into the Twintech page, then I pocket them both. Hugh flicks off his PC. At the far side of the room, a fax whirrs quietly into life.

20

'You want to sell the CTL paper?' Vance says.

'I don't just want to Stephen. I am.'

Ten minutes ago I instructed Henry to start selling tomorrow morning. Evidently Henry thought Vance should be informed, they've come to oppose me together.

'Why?' Vance asks.

'Stephen, it has to be sold. No arguments.'

'A lot of people bought that paper in good faith. What do we say to them when they see us baling out?'

'It'll dump,' Henry remarks. 'Through the floor.'

Exactly what's needed to spring Hugh's trap. But Stephen and Henry have very good reasons to try and stop it from happening. Our customers, the ones who bought CTL, will be furious. We told them the CTL bond was good value. 'Buy,' we said. And now, a very short while later, we're getting set to offload. Some of them will be looking for blood.

I walk around my office hitting switches. 'We made a mistake. Let's cut the loss and get out.'

'Cut the loss?' Vance sounds appalled. 'We won't be cutting a loss, we'll be cutting our own throats. How long do you think it'll be before we can shift any paper again?'

'Dump CTL tomorrow and we won't make budget in Treasury this month,' Henry says. 'No way.'

I turn out the last light and they follow me into the corridor, still pressing their case. I'm starting to wonder if there isn't something more to their pleas than conscientious concern for the bank. Someone killed Daniel. And if Hugh's latest guess is right, it wasn't because Daniel was involved in Twintech, but because he found someone else who was. The way the Twintech deals have been spread across a number of markets, Hugh's quite sure it must be someone senior. A junior trader just wouldn't have the opportunity to deal that widely. Henry? Vance? I step into the lift, then turn to face them.

'The debate's over. Tomorrow morning the CTL paper gets sold.'

They look at one another dismayed. The lift door closes.

Daniel, I think, why didn't you just tell me? All this time I've not quite been able to accept him as the fraudster, he wasn't like that. Not dishonest with money. But I never expected this. He was investigating the whole thing, and he never breathed a word of it to me? Those last few months of his life, what must it have been like for him? He suspected me, but he couldn't be sure. And so he worked on alone, unaided, to try to get to the bottom of Twintech. Now I lean back against the wall of the lift, clutching my briefcase. I wanted him to suffer. I hated him, and I wanted him to suffer. Revenge. That's what I wanted. Not for my family, not even for Annie, but for me. And now this. All that time, those weeks that I nursed my hatred and plotted revenge, what was Daniel doing? He was working for the good of the bank. He didn't know it, but he was trying to help me.

The bell rings, the lift doors open, and I stand here gazing across the empty foyer. I make the last connection. He was murdered because of what he was doing. Daniel died because he tried to help me.

21

At eight o'clock I arrive at Eric Gifford's flat in the Barbican. Charles Aldridge, my father and Gifford: all three of them are here. There's a pall hanging over the room: talks, apparently, have not gone well. While Gifford takes a call in the adjoining room, my father brings me up to date.

'Gifford's not convinced. He wants some assurance he won't be investing in a bottomless pit.'

'He wants to drive down the price, you mean,' Sir Charles observes.

I ask if any price has been mentioned. My father mumbles something about preliminary figures. I don't like the sound of that, so I repeat my question.

'We're not in a position to dictate terms, Raef. The way things stand, 220's a reasonable number.'

'220?' I look at him in disbelief. 'Last year he was floating 350 past us. 220?'

'The situation's changed, you must see that.'

'We approached him,' Aldridge reminds me.

And that, of course, is the problem. Gifford holds the whip hand. It doesn't matter that Carltons has the same staff as a year ago, or that in nearly every material particular, we're unchanged. What matters now are the indefinables, confidence and trust: without these, we're nothing. A bank only in name. We're not beating off Sandersons as I feared last weekend; we're imploring American Pacific, anyone, to say they still want us.

Gifford reappears. The three of them take up their interrupted conversation, and my father tries to draw me in but I find the whole business too depressing. I go and stand at the full-length window, looking out over the City lights. So this is it, I think. More than two hundred years after our first move into banking, the Carlton family is preparing to withdraw. If our share price stays over 195 tomorrow, the withdrawal won't happen immediately; but with Gifford's urbane East Coast voice droning behind me, the City spread out below, it comes to me that Carltons has reached some kind of natural turning. I stare out. I sip my drink. My grandfather's ambitions for Carltons will never be realized. Not Sir John's fault, or my father's, I realize that now. It's just that the world has moved on, and away from our kind of banking. London's no longer the financial world's centre of gravity. I was born two generations too late. I hear Charles Aldridge asking Gifford to look at the figures once more. This really is too dismal for words.

'How did it go?'

My father. Arms folded, he stands beside me, looking down on the City. Behind us, Gifford's still busy with Sir Charles.

'We're down to half our funds. Last trade 219, but the fall's slowing.'

'We can't change the number, Raef. Not now.' The agreed 195 he means, the trigger for the sale of Carltons to Gifford. Presuming, of course, that Gifford can finally be persuaded to buy. Not the certainty we'd imagined.

'No,' I agree. 'We can't change it.'

'I noticed the 209 bid wasn't touched.'

I swirl the ice-cubes round my glass. My father has spent the afternoon glued to a dealing screen, waiting for the single trade at 195. This realization descends on me like a dark, drizzling cloud.

'Can I ask a question?' I glance back over my shoulder: Gifford and Sir Charles are still talking. I face him. 'Do you want to get rid of the bank no matter what?'

'It isn't like that Raef. How could anybody plan for what's happened this past week. I couldn't. You couldn't. Our responsibility's to salvage what we can.'

'What if we can salvage the bank? What if I stop the slide before it hits 195? We've still got a bank.'

'Badly weakened.'

'But still ours.'

He purses his lips. 'We've agreed the figure, Raef. I'll stand by that.'

'If I stop the slide now, we'll keep the bank, but lose Boddington. We won't have the funds to redeem your pledge.'

Rather pale now, he inclines his head. Whatever the cost to him, he'll stand by his word. Edward Carlton has a strength I never suspected, and I feel beneath the warring emotions of this moment a real stirring of pride. My father is an honourable man. He takes my arm to guide me back to rejoin Eric Gifford and Charles, but just then my mobile rings. Hitting the button, I step aside.

David Meyer. He wants to know what is happening on Parnells. And he wants to know now.

22

When I ask for Stephen Vance's room the Savoy concierge points to the lounge. 'He's just gone through.'

I find Vance seated at a table in there. He's alone, considering his drink.

'Where are Haywood and whatsisname?'

He starts, lifting his head. 'I thought you weren't free.'

'I wasn't. Where are they, upstairs?'

'In the room.' Vance takes a sip from his drink. There's a good scattering of people here tonight; most of the tables are taken. A man in black tie plays the piano. I sit down and try to relax.

After fifteen more minutes at Gifford's flat, I couldn't endure any more of his grindingly reasonable objections to the possible merger. He's sensed that we need him, and he's doing everything possible to screw down the price. He intimated that it might be best if the Carlton family severs its ties with the bank immediately. He even suggested that if the merger were to go ahead, Charles Aldridge might be a useful interim chairman. I didn't bother to wait and hear what he had in mind for me. And it might not come to that anyway. That's what I tell myself. I want, even at this late stage, to hope.

'David wants to know what's happening.'

'Bloody man.'

'Can I tell him we've bagged a Parnell?'

Vance turns his head, glancing towards the empty doorway.

'Tell him to get off our backs,' he says.

'He's worried.'

Vance gives me a look. He says that David Meyer's not alone. His finger traces the rim of his glass. 'You can let him know we're making progress. We might have something concrete for him tonight.' He takes another swig, emptying his glass.

David Meyer won't be happy with the brush-off, but I find myself slipping quite easily into Vance's downbeat mood: my session with Eric Gifford has prepared the way. To hell with David bloody Meyer, I think. I order a drink, and another for Vance. Here we are, once again, in the Savoy lounge. We must have been here scores of times over the years, sometimes with clients but often just the two of us; a quiet drink on those rare evenings when work was put to one side. And suddenly that's what I seem to want now, not to discuss Parnells or David Meyer, but to regain some personal connection with a friend.

With my grandfather gone, and Daniel, Stephen Vance is the one man left who understands what I feel for the bank. But I don't want his sympathy. I don't know what I want really. Maybe it's just that with the sword of Damocles hanging over us, I want to be reminded of those early years when I worked in Corporate Finance. Vance drove me hard then; I drove myself hard; I had something to prove. If the dreary summing-up must be made, it was during those years that I did my best work. Pride. Is that all this is? Perhaps what I want is to be reassured by Vance that I have actually achieved something, anything at all, in my career.

Looking around, I remark that not much changes. Vance brought me here for the first time many years ago after I'd led the Dyer defence, my first big success.

'I'm thinking of getting a lawyer,' he says, voice lowered. At the tables to either side of us the other patrons are engrossed in their own conversations.

'What kind of a lawyer?'

'One that'll get Ryan off my back. He's contacted Jennifer.' His ex-wife. 'He's digging around in my private affairs. I don't like it.'

'When was this?'

'She phoned this afternoon.'

I tell Vance that if it's any consolation, Theresa's been contacted too.

Vance makes the connection, he looks shocked. 'The man must be out of his tree.'

'He's thorough, Stephen, that's all. And he's not convinced you're telling the truth about last Wednesday night.'

'Jesus Christ,' Vance mutters.

'I told him that if you said you were working late, he could take your word for it.'

'I bet that went down a bundle.'

'A lawyer's not going to stop him.'

'It might slow him down.'

I look at Vance curiously after this unguarded remark. It reminds me of something else Ryan said.

'Stephen, do you remember when Ryan went and interviewed the Meyers?'

'Mm?'

'You told him Daniel had a run-in with David Meyer.'

He shrugs; no big deal. 'What if I did? They had an argument, I thought I should mention it to Ryan.'

But he knows very well what I'm getting at. Maybe David Meyer did have an argument with Daniel, but David Meyer has arguments with everyone, that's his nature. And even if he did, why tell Ryan? Vance couldn't seriously have believed David was involved in Daniel's murder. Telling Ryan that story just caused us problems and pointed Ryan in the wrong direction. Stephen Vance is not being absolutely straight with me.

Our drinks arrive. There are some familiar faces around the lounge, a few from the City, but mercifully no one comes over to see us. Why am I questioning him? That's not why I've come. I've been spending too much time with Hugh Morgan. Trying to lighten things now, I remind Vance of the time we brought Arnold Petrie here. Petrie made a complete ass of himself, the particular highlight was when he ordered his steak tartare well done. I've heard Vance roar with laughter at the memory of that night, but now he barely smiles.

I give up. Time for me to bow out gracefully and go home. Vance has Ian Parnell upstairs, the bid in the balance, and Inspector Ryan breathing down his neck. He doesn't need sitting here getting gently pie-eyed, and waxing lachrymose about the good old days.

The porter comes and tells Vance that his guests have arrived.

I look to the door, expecting to see Haywood and Ian Parnell. Neither one of them is there. Vance rises.

'Stay. Finish your drink,' he says. 'Haywood's got him on a string: there's not much you can do to help. I'll call later.' He follows the porter away.

Great. Here I am, alone in the Savoy lounge late

at night, staring into my drink. This wasn't how the night was meant to end. Unneeded by Vance and his team, that wasn't how my career was meant to end either. I seem to have reached some kind of significant new low-point in my life. I've lost my oldest friend, who it seems was one step away from marrying my wife before he died; I am not the father of my own child; I have nearly lost the bank, and in the only work in which I've ever achieved anything, I find that I've suddenly become surplus to requirements. Step forward the Honourable Raef Carlton.

I finish my drink and head out.

'Mr Vance,' the porter calls across me in the foyer. 'Your key?'

Vance and his guests, I see them but it takes a moment to register. Vance returns to the desk and picks up the key. Then he sees me. He turns ashen. I take his arm and lead him away a few paces.

'What the hell is this?'

On the far side of the foyer, two attractive young women stand waiting for Vance and the key. They smile at me.

He shrugs my hand off and I grab him again.

'Christ,' he whispers hoarsely. 'They're not for me.'

Stephen Vance, my mentor, the corporate banker's banker, can't look me in the eye.

'Get rid of them.'

'You want to win the bid? This is part of the price.'

'It's too high.'

Stung, Vance rounds on me. 'You've been out of

the business for three years. Raef. Don't give me any lectures.' He glances left and right, but no one's within earshot of our angry whispers. 'For the last three years I've busted a gut doing things the old way. And every year the bonus gets a little bit smaller.'

'In a moment you'll be telling me right and wrong don't come into it.'

He pulls free. 'I don't like it any more than you do. But this is the business now. Do you think Lyle would balk at this? Do you think he'd even notice there was a question here? The City's changed.'

I look to the women, then back to Vance. I lean towards him, our faces are very close now.

'Something's changed,' I say quietly.

He stiffens. For a second I think he's going to take a swing, I've never seen him look more angry. But at last all he does is turn and walk away. The women join him as he passes, he doesn't speak a word to them: two tarts and a banker. Stephen Vance, my sometime mentor, has just become the most expensive pimp in town.

FRIDAY

1

No call from Vance. There were plenty of other calls before I fell asleep: from my father, Hugh Morgan, Ryan, the journalists and fund managers, but none from Stephen Vance. Now when I wake the first thing I do is reach for the phone and call him. But he's switched off his mobile, and at his home I get the answering machine. Crawling out of bed, I check the clock: 6.30 a.m. I ring my driver, then drag myself into the shower. During the next twelve hours the fate of Carlton Brothers will be decided.

Downstairs, eating toast, I make more calls. Gary Leicester hasn't heard from Vance either, he wants to know if there's anything new he can feed the press. I tell him he'll have to keep pushing the same line, Vance should be in contact soon. Next I call Gordon Fields: his wife answers; she says he's already left for the office. Good old Gordon. I consider calling Sir

John, but decide against it. He can't help us now, and my father has probably spoken to him anyway.

I drop my plate into the sink and drink my orange juice. No postponements now: if the market doesn't finish us first, Penfield's Unit moves in tonight. That, or Hugh traps the fraudster.

I put down my cup and grab my briefcase. Then out in the hallway, on the doormat, I find an envelope. I pick it up and turn it over as I open the door. Raef, it says. The handwriting's Theresa's, but there's no address and no stamp. Pulling the door right open, I look out: the pavement's empty both ways.

In the car I flick distractedly through the *FT* for ten minutes, trying to concentrate: Carlton Brothers has received a dishonourable mention in the 'Lex' column this morning, there's speculation, yet again, on a possible bid from Sandersons. There's a short piece on the Meyer bid, too, but nothing new. Finally I put the paper aside and take the envelope from my pocket. It's years now since I received a letter from my wife. She used to send them all the time when we were engaged and first married; New York, Singapore, everywhere I went, I'd find them waiting at my hotel when I returned from the day's work. But nothing for years, and now this. A hard knot forms in my stomach. I tear the envelope open.

Three pages.

Raef,
    I wanted to talk with you on Wednesday

night – really talk, not argue – but there we were again, squabbling, and I didn't get a chance to say what I meant. I hope you don't think this is too cowardly a letter. It's just that I can think first, and write what I mean, instead of meeting you and getting into another stupid quarrel. I'm sick of all that, I think we both are.

I'm sorry. That's what I want to say most of all. I know I've told you before, and I know being sorry can't change one bit of what's happened, you have every right to hate me, but it's true, Raef, from the bottom of my heart, I'm sorry.

It's stupid to try and explain, so I won't, but there are some things I've been thinking about that I wanted to tell you. I've thought about us a lot lately, about our marriage and how it was before all this. Raef, I don't write this to hurt you, but those last few years before Annie was born, I really was desperately unhappy. When we married I knew you had plans for the bank, I just never realized it would mean I wouldn't see you for weeks at a time, or that when I did see you, you'd be too tired to do anything but sleep. (God, I sound like my mother.) Anyway, I can't pretend I liked it. And when you kept putting off having children, that made everything so much worse. I went to see a doctor. Clinical depression, he said. He recommended a psychiatrist, but I never went. I never told you that, did I?

I read those last few lines again. The things we glimpse but refuse to see. Clinical depression. My wife.

I know that doesn't excuse anything, but it might help you understand how the rest of it happened. What I told you about Daniel was true too. It wasn't an affair, it was just the one time, he was drunk, and it was my fault, not his. You know how weak he was sometimes. He never came near me again, except if Celia or you were there. I think he was as ashamed as I was. Even after Annie's diagnosis, when Daniel went to the hospital for the tests, he could barely look at me. He told me he'd do whatever he could to help save Annie, but that was all. After he'd done that he'd walk away. He wasn't Annie's father. He said that, and it's true, Raef. In any way that matters, you're Annie's father.

Now Daniel's dead, and that still seems completely unreal. Celia's asked me to go to the funeral, but if you're going, and you don't want me there, let me know. And I think you should go, Raef. Even after this terrible mess, he would have wanted that.

I don't want us to finish like this, Raef. I don't want us to finish at all, but if you want a divorce I won't make it difficult. I've been seeing the press reports about Carltons and I spoke to your father this morning. He didn't say much but I could tell he was worried. I don't need an answer by Saturday – about the divorce, I mean – you've got enough to think about right now. But later, when things are quieter, we'll have to talk.

The last thing I wanted to say was about Annie. None of this is her fault. I couldn't forgive myself if she grew up thinking she wasn't wanted, and I'm afraid that might happen if you're not sure what you feel about her. If we get divorced it won't matter so much (I'll never stop you seeing her, though) but if we try to stay together I've got to be sure you want Annie too. It just wouldn't work otherwise, I think you realize that. I've made some terrible mistakes, Raef. There are so many things I'd change if I could, but the truth is – and I hope you can understand it – I wouldn't change Annie for the world. But if you can't understand that, it would be wrong of us to even try to stay together.

But I do want to try, Raef, I'm sure of that. If you can somehow bring yourself to forgive me, and if you can still love Annie, that's what I want most of all, the chance to try.

Anyway, when things are sorted out at the bank, I hope you'll think over what I've said. Please think it over carefully, Raef. There's nothing else to say.

All my love,
Theresa.

I read the letter twice. Theresa. I think. Theresa, how in God's name can I trust you? Daniel meant nothing, yet you bore his child. You meant nothing to him, but he was ready to divorce Celia? I slip it into my pocket. The words are ashes. Outside the first pedestrians are hurrying to their work, the streetlamps glowing orange in the morning dark. Rain falls in torrents on the passing umbrellas. It will be weeks yet before the first signs of spring.

2

'Don't look so worried.' This from Hugh Morgan, who has nothing riding on the day but his fee. I remind him of that, and he laughs. 'You chose the risk business,' he says, 'don't blame me.'

The lift opens and we go through to Settlements where his PC's set up where we left it yesterday. I ask what else he needs.

'Keycard for the door.' Hugh looks around. 'Coffee machine?'

I point to the far corner. 'I'll get Becky to bring a card up later.'

He sits and runs through the procedure, miming the actions. 'Right. So one of the girls comes in here with the deal-slips. I take a look – no Twintech – I give them back. She takes them to be processed, I drink my coffee.' Hugh grins up at me. 'Fine.'

'Karen might start badgering you. If she does, send her down to see me.'

'She sounds like a pain in the arse.'

'Compliance. Part of the job description,' I say. 'Gordon knows you're here; he's told the senior girls.'

Hugh wants to check his trap one last time, so I give him my mobile number and go down to the Dealing Room.

Henry and several other dealers are already in. I select an empty desk and punch Twintech into the system. Hugh rings immediately: everything's in order. I delete Twintech's name.

'What's the problem?'

Henry. I turn to find him at my elbow. 'Nothing.' I pocket my phone. 'A glitch with the IT people. They've sorted it out.'

Henry glances at the screen, now blank. 'Dow's up thirty points. Should give the Footsie a leg up.'

'And Carltons?'

'Can't do us any harm,' he decides. 'You still buying?'

'Depends on if anyone wants to sell.'

'Oh, there'll be sellers,' he assures me dryly. 'Don't worry about that.'

As we walk towards the door, I ask him if he's seen Vance.

'He's not in yet. By the way, I heard a whisper he's got something up his sleeve on the bid.'

'Don't worry about what he's up to, just make sure the CTL paper gets offloaded when the market opens.'

I look up. Win's looking down at us through the

glass wall of the restaurant; he's dressed – the first time I've seen him like this – in a suit and tie. He sees that I've seen him, but he doesn't move. I wave. He gazes down unsmiling.

3

Win looks solemn, solemn and grave, not like himself at all. His dark suit is several sizes too big for him.

'I have the meeting,' he says levelly, 'for Mr Ryan.'

'You met Ryan?'

Win shakes his head. He explains that he'll be meeting Ryan at nine o'clock.

I don't quite know what to say. In Win's mind the forthcoming meeting seems to have taken on a deadly earnest aspect. Perhaps I should call Ryan to warn him.

'You don't have to wear a suit, Win.' Win frowns. 'It's good, though,' I say. 'I'm glad you decided to see him. It's the right thing. You won't have any trouble.'

'Mr Carlton. I say everything?'

'Sure, you've got nothing to hide.'

'He ask me who I see here.'

I tell Win not to worry. 'Ryan already knows Vance was here that Wednesday night. The nightdesk, too. Don't worry.'

'Miss Haldane?' he asks hopefully.

I've been edging back to the door but this stops me dead.

'Karen?'

'She ask me was the party good. She come here,' he gestures to the kitchen.

No mistake, it was Karen; but what does this mean?

'Did she say what she was doing?' I ask.

Win turns his head.

'Had she just arrived from somewhere? Was she on her way out? She must have said something, Win.'

'Working,' she say.

'That's it?'

He nods. Ryan won't like this when he hears. I don't much like it myself. Win sees my concern, he asks if I still think he should tell the Inspector. I would dearly like to tell him not to, at least until I've had a chance to figure this out. But after all of yesterday's pieties about having nothing to fear from the truth, I'm trapped, hoist by my own petard.

'Win, whatever he asks, just answer as best you can. You've got nothing to be afraid of.'

'This will make trouble for her.'

'Tell the truth and everything will be all right.'

This trite little homily brings a crooked smile to Win's face. Life, it seems, has taught him an altogether different lesson.

4

Karen Haldane is watering her plants.

'Karen.'

'Just a minute.'

She goes from the pot on her window-sill to the flourishing rubber-plant in the corner, mug in hand. She concentrates hard as she pours, the thin trickle comes with painful slowness. I've interrupted her early-morning routine. She finishes and places the mug back on the window-sill.

'What are you going to do with Tony?' she asks.

'I'm not here to discuss Mannetti.'

'Haven't you read my memo? It wasn't Johnstone's fault, I've interviewed Pauline again, it was Tony.'

'Karen, where were you last Wednesday night?'

She pauses. 'What?'

'Last Wednesday night. You weren't at the party on the boat.'

'No.'

'Where were you?'

She seems momentarily wrong-footed. 'Wednesday?'

'Yes,' I say. 'Wednesday night.'

She picks up her diary and flicks through it, but I have the impression she isn't looking too closely. At last the diary snaps shut.

'I was here.'

'Doing what?'

'Watering the plants.' She drops the diary onto the desk. 'I was working, Raef. I've been told that's what I'm paid for. Is that a problem?'

'Did you mention it to Inspector Ryan?'

'That I was working late?'

'Karen, did you tell Ryan you were here on Wednesday night? Yes or no.'

She hesitates. 'No,' she says at last.

I really don't understand this woman. And I wonder how Ryan is going to react when he hears. Badly, I imagine.

'He didn't ask me. Why should he?'

'Don't play games.' I point. 'You knew he was on Stephen's back just because Stephen was here on Wednesday night.'

'That's different.'

'How?'

'Stephen hated Daniel.'

The blunt firmness of this judgement sets me back on my heels.

'He didn't hate him,' I say.

She takes off her glasses and presses her fingertips to her eyes. 'Yes, he did. He hated him. I never told Ryan that, how much Stephen hated him. I didn't think anyone would want me to. I didn't think you'd want me to, Raef. I still don't.'

I'm suddenly lost, all at sea. What's she telling me, that she actually believes Stephen killed Daniel? I cling to the few facts I know like a drowning man to the wreckage.

'Last Wednesday night Karen, Win Doi saw you here. And he's just gone down to see Ryan. On past form, you can expect Ryan knocking at your door within the hour.'

She drops her hand. There are dark rings around her eyes, and the eyes are puffy and red.

'Karen, do you want to tell me anything before he arrives?'

'He might not come.'

'Don't kid yourself.'

She sits down, telling me she'll deal with it when it happens. I glance up at the clock: the market's just about to open, I need to get my bid in right now. Heading for the door, I warn her, 'This isn't finished.'

'Where's Stephen?'

'No idea. And I wouldn't worry too much about him. You've got your own problems, Karen.'

For the first time in years she doesn't answer me back. She sits there quite still, looking down.

5

'Bid 210,' I tell the broker.

'What's the big rush?' he calls over the squawkbox.

I glance at the dealing screen: no prices up yet. Settling into my chair, I ask him what he's hearing in the market. He gives me three minutes on everything that might have an impact on the Carltons share price: a general overview, then specific information picked up from his contacts. Apparently the City pubs were buzzing last night.

'So what's the consensus?'

'No consensus. The big boys are staying out of it

till they see which way it breaks.'

The best news I've had for quite a while. The buying I did yesterday had raised serious doubts in a few minds, Carltons is no longer the one-way bet it appeared.

'Bid 210 for how much?' the broker asks.

'Up to two million. But let me know how it's going.'

I flick the switch, and swivel in my chair. Outside the clouds are lifting, a few shafts of sunlight slant down. Friday morning. This time last week I was up in the boardroom, and Sir John was breaking the news of Daniel's murder to me. Seven days. As Penfield said, a long time in the City.

There's a knock at the door. Sir John.

'Well,' he says, coming in. 'Quite a stir.'

I begin to apologize for not keeping him as informed as he might have expected. In fact for the past two days I've had a job finding him: he keeps disappearing from his office. He waves a hand, dismissing my apology.

'So where are we?' he says, coming around the desk.

I tell him the market hasn't opened yet, but that I have a bid in, ready. He enquires about yesterday's trading, and I explain the position.

'Anything I can do Raef?'

'Becky's being swamped by calls. Perhaps she could redirect some of them your way.'

'Journalists?'

'Fund managers, brokers, the whole bloody market.'

He smiles encouragingly.

The broker speaks to me over the box. Sir John, to my mild annoyance, makes no move to leave. When I finish with the broker, I reach for some papers in a purposeful, businesslike way. But Sir John still doesn't take the hint. Worse, he wanders across to the sofa and sits down. He senses my displeasure though.

'This won't take a minute, Raef.' His elbows rest on his knees, his hands clasped. He seems to be building up to something. 'I wanted to tell your father first, but I suppose he'll know soon enough.' He raises his eyes. 'I'm retiring.'

Retiring. The word goes echoing around my mind. Retiring. Sir John, at long last, is retiring. I've been waiting for this moment every day for the past three years, waiting and hoping, but all I do now is stare at him in silence. The bank's on its knees, I'm fighting with every weapon I can find, and Sir John, years too late, is retiring. Thanks, I think. Thanks a million.

'I can imagine what you must think. It hasn't been easy for me either, Raef, these past few years.'

'For you?'

'Who could take me seriously as MD with you waiting in the wings?' He opens his hands. 'Nobody's fault.'

It catches me oddly. I've never thought of it from his point of view before.

'I won't make an announcement' – he nods to the screen – 'not until this is all over. But I thought you and your father should know.'

'What brought this on?'

'The past few days. Daniel. Intimations of mortality, I suppose. I started wondering if I really wanted to spend the remainder of my life swearing into a telephone.' He gives me an uncertain look. 'I've not been much use to you with all this, have I? And before. Your father wanted to be sure you were ready. I never meant to stand in your way, Raef.'

He is, I realize, absolutely sincere; and before this moment I never saw it. How much else of my life have I passed through blind? What else, even here at the office, have I failed to see? Sir John's head is bowed.

'Not your fault,' I say.

He looks up, immensely relieved. He asks if I'm sure there's nothing he can do.

'Just take those calls for Becky.'

A great burden seems to have been taken from him. Absolution. He comes over and shakes my hand.

'Offer of 220,' the broker calls, 'against your 210 bid.'

Snapping back to the present, I hit the switch. 'Okay.'

Sir John leaves, saying he'll come and see me later.

Now I take yesterday's deal-sheet from the drawer and check the numbers: around six million pounds left, I confirm the exact number with the broker.

'If we finish that,' I tell him, 'I'll have some more transferred over.'

A blatant lie, but at this stage a little disinformation won't do Carltons any harm.

Then I ring through to Henry and get his assessment of the market. He puts me through to our senior equities trader who gives me a second opinion. The trader is about to pass me on to Billy, but I tell him not to bother. It's too late to be trawling for opinions now.

On the screen my bid stands at 210. My father, somewhere, will be watching.

6

Time passes with the flickering numbers. After an hour my bid's still 210, and the offer's down to 213. I've bought two and a half million pounds' worth of Carltons, absorbing small parcels, but it doesn't feel like yesterday. As the broker predicted, the institutions are waiting for something to break. I flick across to the bond screen. CTL is falling; falling fast. Henry might have misgivings, but he's following his instructions to the letter. The person or persons behind Twintech won't be feeling too well just now.

When I phone Hugh upstairs, he's still cheerful but there's no sign of the trap being sprung. Then Becky brings me a cup of tea, there's a lull in trading, and I walk around the office, cup in hand.

Karen Haldane, I decide, has deliberately deceived Ryan. But why? She implied that there was something between Daniel and Vance, something it might be better the Inspector never heard. Was that the truth? She's the last person I ever thought I'd doubt, but my faith in her has been badly shaken.

Who wins? This was always Hugh's big test. When I worked on the Petrie case with him, this was the measure he laid over every dubious transaction: the web of lies was impenetrable, the only way of really telling what happened was to ask that one simple question. Who wins?

But here I just don't see it. Karen was at the office on Wednesday night, but that's a long step from murder. And what motive could she have? And Vance was here too, but I can't see him involved with Daniel's death either. Then the blindingly obvious hits me. I stop and put down my mug. Karen and Stephen, they were both here. I brace my hands against the desk, thinking it through. Inspector Ryan is adamant that Vance knows more about Wednesday night than he's saying. And after a minute I'm almost sure of it. Stephen Vance doesn't want Ryan to know what he saw here that Wednesday night; and what Stephen saw here that Wednesday night was Karen Haldane.

Becky's voice comes over the intercom. Stephen Vance has arrived.

7

'It's done,' Vance tells me. 'We've got it.' He makes this announcement in a flat, dead tone, devoid of emotion. That's how he looks too, completely drained. 'Young Parnell's just signed. Haywood's got him in my office if you want to see him.'

I turn my head; no.

This should be a great moment. The Meyers have bagged Parnells, we've beaten Darren Lyle, Carltons have won. But instead of an eruption of high spirits, a round of back-slapping and mutual congratulations, we look at one another awkwardly, both unsure of what to say. We know the price of this victory.

'I'll get Leicester to arrange the press conference for twelve,' Vance says at last. He glances at his watch.

This is ridiculous. Rising, I offer him my hand. 'Congratulations.' He seems doubtful, but he reaches across. 'I overstepped the mark last night,' I tell him. 'I was out of order.'

'Right on target actually.'

'Forget it.'

He releases my hand. 'I'd rather not,' he says.

At this curious remark, I raise a brow.

'Lesson learned, and all that.' He pushes a hand up through his hair. 'Christ. What a night.'

'Sit down.'

He slumps into a chair and takes a moment with himself. Strong, brilliant, able, I thought I knew all the adjectives for Vance. But this is a new one: wretched. He looks absolutely awful.

'I came back downstairs to see you.'

'The Savoy?'

He smiles wearily. 'You were going to get a piece of my mind.'

'I thought I had.'

'There was more. Thank God you'd gone. I ended up at the bar.'

'You don't owe me an explanation, Stephen.'

'No.' He pauses. 'I owe you an apology.'

The broker speaks over the box, I turn the volume down.

'Accepted,' I say.

He nods, but I can see this isn't over with him yet. The real score he has to settle is with himself. For the first time it isn't just respect and admiration I feel for Stephen Vance, it's sympathy. He's a man of flesh and blood like the rest of us; like the rest of us, he can sometimes err. But this isn't the time for reflection or regret: there's still work to do. And Vance, being what he is, puts his feelings aside now. He reaches for his briefcase, in an attempt to move us on.

'I thought we might invite Lyle over for the press conference.'

The vanquished at the victory dance. I tell him it sounds like an entertaining idea.

He runs through the other calls we have to make: the Stock Exchange, the Boards of both companies, Gary Leicester and several others. I wait till he's finished.

'Stephen, Win saw Karen here last Wednesday night. Ryan's taking his statement.' It's a second before he absorbs this news, but when he does, he looks stunned. 'You knew she was here that night, didn't you.'

He stares into space. 'Win?'

'She went down for a sandwich. He was bringing a few things back from the party on the boat.'

Vance raises a hand to his eyes.

'Stephen, if you saw her, why didn't you just say? Ryan's been crawling all over you, is this what you weren't telling him?' He doesn't answer. 'Stephen?'

'Stay out of it, Raef.'

I come around the desk. 'Karen's going to tell Ryan that you hated Daniel's guts. She seems to think it was more than just professional differences between you two.'

No answer. Breaking into the silence comes the broker's voice from the squawkbox. I keep my eyes on Vance. I didn't think it was possible for him to look much worse than when he first came in, but now he does; not just drained, but haunted.

'Stephen, who killed Daniel?'

He closes his briefcase. 'The press conference is at twelve,' he says. We look at one another a moment, then he gets to his feet and walks out.

I feel giddy. Behind me the broker keeps calling my name.

8

I'm late. Since the public announcement of Ian

Parnell's sell-out, the Carltons share price has steadied. I've left Henry in my office watching over my bid, while I skip out to the press conference. I had a quick word with Hugh before leaving: still no luck on Twintech.

Allen Fenwick loiters in the corridor outside the conference-room, smoking a cigarette.

'Kept this one quiet,' he says.

He thought he had the inside running on the Meyers bid, and now he's miffed. When he asks for an interview I tell him to try me again later then I step past him inside. The TV lights are blazing. Up on the podium, a cluster of microphones half-screens David Meyer: he's taking questions from journalists in the front row. Reuben and Stephen Vance are just to one side of him. Ian Parnell has apparently decided that discretion is the better part of valour: he's nowhere in sight. As I shuffle along the rear wall the institutional investors and lawyers in the back row crane round to offer their congratulations and shake my hand. Carlton Brothers, it appears, is no longer an untouchable: we've been washed by the sweet waters of success. A pity Penfield isn't here to see the change in mood.

Cawley, Haywood and the rest of the bid team are assembled in the back corner. A magnum of champagne is doing the rounds, the celebrations have started already. Declining the proffered glass, I turn my attention to the performance up front. The crowing of the cocks, that's what Vance calls these occasions: the banker's answer to the athlete's victory lap. Nothing of substance is achieved, but the victor has a chance to preen and strut. Here David Meyer's in his element. He fields most of the questions, only occasionally referring one to Vance or Reuben. Stephen looks better than he did when he left my office, but not much. I catch his eye as he answers a question but he looks away. Others won't be so easily evaded. Win is already back in the restaurant: Ryan can't be too far behind.

There's a stir over by the door, and I turn to see Darren Lyle coming in. For a man who's just had the rug pulled from under him, he looks remarkably sanguine: he must be dying inside. Most men in his position would retire to lick their wounds in private, but not Darren. He's decided to accept Vance's invitation to come and watch us crow. Proof, if any were needed, that Darren Lyle has a freakishly thick hide. The journalists see him; one of them stands and asks if Darren would like to make a comment.

'Sandersons are pleased to have extracted maximum benefit for the Parnells shareholders,' Lyle answers. The usual banality of defeat.

The journalist follows up with a question on Sandersons' appeal to the Takeover Panel. To this Lyle smiles and raises his hands.

'No comment,' he says.

A ripple of laughter goes around the room, then attention returns to the podium where David Meyer is talking again.

Lyle comes across, running a gauntlet of hollow commiserations, before he reaches me. We shake hands. It almost chokes him, but he offers his congratulations. I savour the moment. Then I ask if he's got a minute for a private word, and he follows me into the adjoining room where I close and lock the door.

Apart from the chairs, the whiteboard and the overhead projector, the room is empty: here we can talk in private.

'Ian Parnell, eh?' He pulls up a chair and sits down, legs stretched in front, hands in pockets. 'I always said he was a prick.'

'Win some, lose some.'

'Spare me the bullshit, Raef. If the Takeover Panel had done their job, you wouldn't've got a look-in. That was Sir John, right? His mates on the Panel?'

I keep my face blank. Darren glares.

'Shit,' he says. 'The old silver-spoon brigade.'

I offer to get some champagne for him to take back to the wake at his office. He tells me to fuck off.

Then I pull up a chair. Lyle and me in the aftermath of battle. It brings back memories. Working together under Vance inevitably forged a bond of shared experience. Certainly we've attended more than our share of wakes together. I know exactly how it will be back at his office: everyone involved in the unsuccessful defence of Parnells will gather over a few drinks, and the post mortem will start; what went wrong. By early evening they'll all be ducking for cover or looking for someone else to blame. Lyle has a miserable time ahead of him, but after the trouble he's caused us I really can't dredge up much sympathy.

'We've been filing 212s all week.' A 212, a request to the Registrar for a shareholder's name. When Lyle looks surprised, I add, 'For Carltons.'

'Bully for you.'

'What's that, another no comment?'

He gives me a look. 'Am I missing something? You're filing 212s. Wonderful. So you find out who's buying Carltons. Call me a slow learner, but that doesn't look to me like your problem. I mean, you've got problems, but finding out who's buying? What do you want to do, send them a thank-you card? Jesus.'

'Why did you pull our trading line?'

'When?'

'Tuesday.'

He takes a moment, remembering. 'You weren't the only ones. We had a fuck-up in IT last weekend. Things went wrong on Monday, so we wound back on Tuesday. Not just with you. Why?'

'Have you reinstated the line?'

'I can check.'

'Don't bother. The line went out on Tuesday and stayed out. Darren—'

'Hang on, hang on.' He rises from his chair. 'I came over to shake hands and say 'well done'. No hard feelings, and all that. Instead I'm getting a fucking interrogation?'

'Darren, is Sandersons lining up a bid for Carltons?'

He stops, dead still, his eyes on mine. Then after a few seconds, he smiles. Not a fake smile either, he's actually amused.

'You're filing 212s to find out if we're buying?' he says, finally figuring it out. He leans over and claps me on the shoulder. 'Dream on.'

'You're not buying?'

'Read my lips. We're not buying. Never have been. Never intended to.' I shrug his hand off, then stand. He lays his other hand on my chest. 'Not yet, golden boy.'

He tries to shove me back but I swipe his hand aside. Now he points at me.

'You know what I never liked about you? You were always so damn cock-sure. Just gliding along, everything laid out for you. Just keeping your nose clean and wafting up to the top. Nothing to stop you.'

'There's the door.'

'But this isn't quite that easy, is it.' He rises malevolently, enjoying himself now. 'The golden boy hasn't got a fucking clue. You got Parnells, yeah, great. But your bank's fallen off a cliff, and you haven't got a fucking clue.'

'If you're behind it Darren, I'll break your balls.'

He hoots in derision. I feel the blood rush into my cheeks.

'What are you going to do?' he says. 'Report me to your old man? To Vance?'

'How about I just have you done for slander.'

'Whoa.' He draws back, feigning surprise. 'Me?'

'There's a rumour we reneged on a two-million-pound payment.'

'Is that right?'

'A payment to Sandersons.'

His brow creases and he shakes his head sadly. 'Fucking rumours,' he says.

The muscles tighten in my shoulders. I sway forward, dizzy with the effort of control.

'Get out.'

His grin fades, and his look hardens now into one of raw belligerence. Our eyes lock.

'Who pointed Ryan at me?' he asks. 'It was Vance, wasn't it.'

'I'm not Ryan's confessor.'

'You reckon I should be done for slander? An accusation like that in the middle of a bid from Mr Clean himself, and I should be done for slander?' He swears at me with real venom. At my sides I feel my hands clench into fists.

'The pair of you should be flushed down the friggin' toilet. You and him both,' he shouts.

His face is red and so close to mine that I can see a crooked vein on his temple pulsing. The act is over: losing the battle for Parnells has cut him to the quick. I count the pulse-beats up to three.

'Who killed Daniel?' I ask quietly.

He stares at me a long moment. Then he nods, just to himself at first but more vigorously as he turns left and right. 'Who killed Daniel?' he mutters. 'Who killed Daniel?' Bending, he picks up a chair and hurls it across the room; it clatters into a stack of chairs in the corner. Then he faces me again, chest heaving, 'Me. I killed Daniel. Is that what you want to hear? Well, back luck. I didn't kill Daniel, I don't know who did, and to tell you the truth, I don't bloody care.' He raises a finger. 'But if my name gets waved under Ryan's nose once more you and Vance are going to need lawyers.'

'What about Wolsey?'

He checks. 'Have I missed something here?'

'You and Wolsey worked together. Your committee.'

He looks at me blankly and I get a queasy hollow feeling. My mention of Wolsey has him genuinely perplexed. This isn't an act. I am a voyager suddenly robbed of his compass. Is it possible he's telling the truth, that Sandersons never intended to buy into us?

'You're full of shit,' he says finally. 'Open the door.' He gestures towards the door leading out to the corridor. He has no intention of running the gauntlet of the press conference a second time. I go to the door and unlock it. I want this man out of here.

'And tell Vance I'll see him with Quin tonight,' he says. The Bankers' Association do. His head drops. The thought of exchanging chit-chat about his defeat over a tray of canapés has deflated him.

As he steps past I clutch his elbow.

'Darren. You ever come here again and I'll have you thrown out on your ear.'

He jerks his arm free, the full vigour of his anger suddenly returned. Lifting his head, he looks me straight in the eye.

'Your blue-blood family, arsehole,' he whispers, 'is history.'

9

Returning to my office, I find Henry lounging in my chair, his feet on the window-sill.

'Going nowhere fast,' he informs me over his shoulder. He drops an empty crisp packet into the bin. 'Your bid's 202,' he says, 'the offer's 205. You've picked up dribs and drabs.'

He swivels around and hands me the deal-sheet. He doesn't know it, but I'm down to the last million pounds.

I hit the switch on the squawkbox. 'Pull the bid back to 200.'

We watch the number change on the screen: mine still appears to be the only bid. Henry asks how the press conference went, but I have other matters on my mind.

'Could you find out if Sandersons pulled their line on anyone apart from us last Tuesday?'

'Sure.'

'Now?' I say.

Once he's gone, I punch up the CTL bond price: stationary; it's stopped moving down. I ring through to Hugh who tells me there's still no sign of Twintech.

'He's clocked up a decent loss though.'

'So I see.'

'If he's got any sense, he'll close out. And by the way,' he says, lowering his voice, 'Ryan appeared fifteen minutes ago.'

'Where is he, with Karen?'

'As a matter of fact he is.' Hugh sounds surprised. My guess was a little too astute. 'Should I know why?'

'I'll explain later.'

After hanging up, I doodle on my pad.

Darren Lyle is a liar, I know that. But I worked with him long enough to be able to read his signs. Put the reneged-payment rumour aside. He really was indifferent about Wolsey, but why? Have they had some disagreement? It doesn't add up: there'd still be some flicker of interest when I mentioned the name. And if Lyle hasn't been, and never intended to be, in the market for Carltons, why would he want Wolsey to destabilize us? And that odd visit from Wolsey yesterday: I was definitely too hasty there, accusing when I should have listened. Even a lie might have given me a clue.

I am still doodling when Henry returns.

'It wasn't just us,' he says. 'Sandersons' system

crashed, some kind of IT problem.'

'When I asked you to check the other day, you said it was Lyle's doing.'

'I got it wrong.'

I make a sound. So Darren was telling the truth here too. Henry waits by my desk, and my eyes wander to the screen.

'What do you think will happen if I take the 205 offer?' I ask him.

'Not much. There's been sellers all the way down. They see your bid comin' up, they'll hit it.'

'So the price'll keep falling.'

'I doubt it. You in there buyin', the Meyers gettin' Parnells.' He examines the screen. 'I'd say the worst of it's over. The price'll just ride with the market awhile. It's found a level.'

The price has found a level. Over a third of our capitalization wiped out, Boddington in hock, and now the Carltons share price has found a level. Excellent. Sound the cracked trumpets.

The broker calls over the box: he has someone interested in bidding 195, just behind me.

Henry nods, his assessment confirmed. 'It won't fall out of bed now.'

A rather bleak consolation. In the space of twenty-four hours I've poured Boddington away. I've kept the bank under my family's control; I've done what I set out to do, but I have, in the process poured Boddington away. I wonder where my father is right now.

There's a sharp rap at the door. Inspector Ryan looks in.

In the voice of a man who means business, he says, 'Where's Vance?'

10

The press conference is over. The journalists are all milling around, looking for a quote or a glass of champagne. I beckon to Vance over their heads. While I wait for him to break free, Reuben Meyer approaches. He shakes my hand and thanks me.

'What now for you?' he says. 'Holidays?'

If only. I try to smile. He tells me David also appreciates the work we've done, then he moves back into the thinning crowd where he's buttonholed by Gary Leicester. They look pleased. Everyone looks pleased. The Meyers got what they paid us to get for them, and even Reuben in the end doesn't give a damn how it was done. Another satisfied customer.

A minute later Vance joins me, and I lead him back to his own office.

'Ryan's there,' I tell him. 'With Karen.'

He takes this news in silence. He appears to have the weight of the world on his shoulders. When we enter his office he goes straight to his desk and sits.

Then he says to Ryan, 'I can have my lawyer here in twenty minutes if you care to wait.'

Ryan looks at me but I stay put. I want to hear

this myself. He returns his attention to Vance.

'Mr Vance, your lawyer can't stop me from arresting you. And if I'm not satisfied with your answers this time, that's what's going to happen. Now,' he faces Karen, 'did you see him here that Wednesday night?'

She nods.

'I beg your pardon?'

'Yes,' she says.

Ryan turns to Vance. 'And you saw her?'

Vance doesn't reply.

Ryan sighs. 'Miss Haldane, did he see you here?'

'Yes.'

'And you talked together, didn't you say?'

She nods again.

'More than once?'

'Twice.'

Vance drops his head. He knows what Karen's like: she won't tell Ryan an outright lie. If Stephen wants to remain silent now, he's on his own.

'Do you recall the time of these conversations?'

'Not exactly.'

Karen glances at Stephen but he keeps his eyes averted. I wonder if Ryan senses the undertow here.

'Once at around eleven thirty. The next time later.'

'Sometime after 1.00 a.m., isn't that what you told me?'

Yes, she says, but she's not sure exactly.

'It was after you spoke with Mr Win Doi in the restaurant. And he's quite certain that was just after one. I think we can be reasonably sure.' Ryan turns. 'Mr Vance. Perhaps you'd care to tell me why neither of these conversations appeared in your statement.'

Stephen maintains a stony silence.

'In fact,' Ryan reminds him, 'there was no mention at all of Miss Haldane's presence here that night. Should I read anything into that?'

'You're wasting your time,' Stephen says quietly.

'No, Mr Vance. You're wasting my time. And if it continues, we'll be walking out of here together, you and I, and you won't be coming back for quite a while. How will that look on your CV?'

'For God's sake,' Karen takes a step towards the door.

'We're not finished yet, Miss Haldane,' Ryan tells her.

She stops. She turns back and waits, arms folded, a picture of barely restrained fury. It's more than an undertow now.

'Now, Mr Vance,' Ryan says, 'I'd like to hear your version of those two conversations. Take your time.'

We all watch Stephen. He's quiet for several moments, then he looks from Ryan to Karen. 'Speak to my lawyer,' he says.

Ryan stiffens.

'For Christ's sake,' Karen says angrily, stepping forward. 'Just tell him. I've already told him anyway.'

Stephen looks at her in dismay. 'Why?' he says.

'Was I meant to perjure myself?'

'Miss Haldane,' Ryan breaks in. 'If you don't mind.'

Stephen seems thoroughly confused now. Ryan, I notice, is studying him closely.

'Everything?' Vance asks.

Karen's belligerence fades; she's gone beyond anger. 'Just tell him, Stephen,' she says.

Vance peers at her. And the way he peers at her gives me a sinking feeling.

'Yes,' he tells Ryan finally: 'we spoke twice.'

Ryan asks him to elaborate.

'Personal,' Vance says.

'You spoke about Stewart, Mr Vance. Please. Let's not waste more time.'

I feel a cold tingling up my spine. They were discussing Daniel that Wednesday night? And both of them have tried to conceal it? Voices pass along the corridor outside.

'I asked Karen if she'd like to go somewhere. Dinner, a club – ' Vance waves his hand vaguely – 'somewhere. She turned me down and we had an argument.'

'The subject of which was Stewart,' Ryan suggests.

Vance nods unhappily. I look at Karen: her face is turning pink, and a queasy understanding begins to glimmer.

Vance directs his next remark at Karen. 'Things were said that weren't meant.'

Ryan consults his notepad. 'You said you wanted to throttle him.'

'A figure of speech.' He's clearly taken aback. 'No one could have taken it seriously.'

Karen makes a sound in her throat, and Vance looks at her in surprise.

'The second occasion you spoke,' Ryan says, 'sometime after one?'

'I went back up to apologize. She was upset.'

'How upset?'

A little, Vance replies.

'How could you tell she was upset?'

'That's how she seemed.'

'Nothing in particular?'

'No.'

This exchange means nothing to me, but Ryan glowers when he receives Vance's final answer. He gets to his feet.

'She was bawling her eyes out, Mr Vance.' He thumbs his own chest. 'I know, because she told me. You know, because you saw her. Now do we carry on this conversation here, or do you want to keep playing silly buggers?'

Vance doesn't know which way to turn. Finally his gaze settles on Karen. He says her name.

'For Christ's sake,' she murmurs.

And then I know. The way he's said her name, and how he looks at her now; the way she can't bear to face him. Ryan knows too, he'd have to be a blind man not to see. He studies the pair of them darkly. He appears to feel no embarrassment for Vance. How many times have I sat in the same room with Karen and Stephen – at the same table – and never seen it? Stephen Vance looks dreadful, completely stricken.

He is in love. Karen Haldane, just as obviously, isn't.

Ryan says to Karen, 'You were crying because of Stewart?'

Vance stands. He tells her not to answer. 'We'll get you a lawyer.'

She rounds on him. 'Shut up!'

He flinches. The colour drains from his face, it's almost too painful to watch.

'Don't you get it?' she says to Ryan. She points at Vance. 'This stupid bastard thought it was me. He thought I killed Daniel.' She looks at Vance. 'Didn't you?'

Vance doesn't have to answer, his baffled look says it all. Karen swears.

'And why would he think that?' Ryan asks.

She hesitates. But she's said too much now: there's no turning back. Finally she seems to realize that.

'I was crying because Daniel dumped me.'

There it is. Karen and Daniel. But by now it doesn't surprise me, since the first mention of Daniel I'd half seen it coming. And if I'd thought about it, I could have seen sooner, back when Karen told me Stephen hated Daniel. Why did any man hate Daniel?

'When was that?' Ryan asks.

'December,' she says bitterly. 'The twelfth.'

'So what upset you on Wednesday night?'

'When Stephen asked me out, I turned him down. He started shouting about Daniel. And Daniel was at the party on the boat,' she adds flatly. 'That too, I guess.'

Ryan asks Vance how long he's known there was something between Daniel and Karen. Vance tells him since the middle of last year.

Ryan gives it all some thought. At last he points at Karen. 'You didn't come forward, because you thought that once you opened your mouth you'd incriminate him.' He jerks his thumb at Vance.

Karen can't hold Ryan's gaze; he seems to have hit the bullseye; she thought it was Vance who killed Daniel. On the Thursday morning, each must have remembered words said the previous night and drawn their own unwarranted conclusions. He was protecting her by sending Ryan after the likes of Lyle and David Meyer. And she was protecting him by keeping her mouth shut. Neither one of them is a murderer.

Vance sees what's happened. He sits and buries his face in his hands. Through the mesh of his fingers he begins to apologize.

'Save it.' Ryan glares at Vance, then at Karen, and he finishes with me. Each one of us, in our own way, has deceived him. 'You fucking people,' he says.

He stalks out.

Vance looks up at Karen and opens his hands, a gesture of supplication. She swears at him and turns on her heel. I go after her, striding down the corridor.

'Karen!'

She stops by the Ladies.

'I need to ask you something,' I say, catching her up.

'Not now.' She turns and pushes open the door.

I clutch her arm. 'Were you going to marry Daniel?'

She tugs her arm free and steps inside.

'Were you pregnant?'

A split second she looks at me, then the door slams closed in my face. But in that split second, I see.

11

'The broker reckons the bidder behind you's getting ready to take the 203 offer,' Henry tells me. He gets out of my chair and I drop into it, glancing at the screen and the deal-sheet. Almost no one's hit my 200 bid for the past hour. 'I reckon he's right,' Henry adds.

He repeats his assertion that the price has found a level.

'It might get to 220,' he says, 'but that's it.'

He brings me up to date with CTL: apparently some of the institutions are threatening to boycott the next issue we bring to market. A worry that can wait.

Then Henry goes off to check on the Dealing Room.

Alone now, I turn this whole thing over. It was Karen: not Theresa, but Karen. When Daniel told Celia he'd got someone pregnant, that he was going to marry her, that was the truth. It wasn't what I thought, a convenient cover while he sorted things out with Theresa. It was Karen all along. And the same with the will, that page I found in his hidden drawer. I pull it from my own drawer now to check. 500 K. 1,000 C. Not K for thousands. Not C for hundreds. Their names: Karen and Celia. But then Daniel changed his mind: he didn't rewrite the will, and instead of marrying Karen, he dumped her. The twelfth of December. Within weeks of finding out about Annie. What was it, the shock? Did Daniel suddenly realize something about himself? Did he finally discover, so very late in the day, what it actually means to be a husband and a father?

Daniel. Jesus, Daniel, I think. Why?

All those women, the craving of affection that needed such constant reaffirmation, did he see the truth at last? His mother might be dead, but he had his own family. He was already loved.

The broker calls over the squawkbox. '200–203, your bid.'

I swivel in my chair and study the clouds. Had Daniel really turned over a new leaf? Once the shock of Annie had worn off, might not the old habits have reasserted themselves? Even Daniel couldn't have known the answer to that, but I find that I want to believe it, that he was strong enough, that it might really have happened. And Karen. What kind of private hell has she been through these past few months? Somehow, even in the act of returning to his family, Daniel managed to wreak destruction. To the very end he retained his strange blighting gift in these matters of the heart.

Bringing out Theresa's letter, I read it once more. It goes right into me now, every word. Could this be the truth?

I hit the switch on the squawkbox. 'Is this price going anywhere?'

'Nowhere.' Friday afternoon, and the market is winding down for the weekend. 'There's a good-sized bid just behind you,' the broker says. 'If he gets tired of waiting, he might pay up. I told Henry.'

And what then? The Carltons share price will hover between 200 and 220, and my family will retain control. The bank, badly weakened, will maintain its short-term independence. And something else: we will not have the funds at our disposal to redeem my father's pledge; Boddington will pass out of our hands.

Henry returns. I leave him watching over my bid, and wander down to the Dealing Room where the usual Friday afternoon torpor has taken hold. Half the equities desk has left to celebrate with the Corporate Finance team, and the lads on the proprietary trading desk are getting set to join them. Just days ago, the market shutting us out, it was all so very different. Now the only visible scars remaining from that battle are the two empty chairs on the bond desk. I doubt that even Daniel could have handled it any better, a real tribute to Henry. The traders have played no part in the Meyer bid, but it seems to be the only subject of conversation out here, everyone bathing in reflected glory. I pause for a word at the bond desk: they inform me that our name is dirt in the bond market right now, our dumping of CTL has not been appreciated. After completing a circuit of the Room, I go on up to Funds Management.

Here the story's the same, the weekend has already taken hold. Trevor Bailey, our top fund manager, comes over for a word.

'I'll tell you the truth,' he says. 'I didn't think Vance could pull it off.'

'Never in doubt.'

He laughs. 'So what now for Carltons? Onward and upward?'

He regards me from the corner of his eye. With our share price where it is, we're vulnerable, and Trevor's seen these situations too often, he knows the score. We've survived an horrendous week, far and away the worst in my career, but it's still too early to say if the goring we've taken won't attract predators. By Trevor's look, I see that he thinks it will. I tell him not to fret, he'll still get his bonus.

'Tony around?'

Trevor says he hasn't seen him, and I retreat before he can ask any more questions.

Hugh sees me through the glass wall as I pass Settlements. He makes a sign with his fingers: nothing.

The bank, this place, it's been so much of my life, maybe more than it should have been, but walking along the corridor to the Boardroom now, I feel strangely detached. The ties that once held me so firmly have loosened. Inevitably, after all that's happened this past week, things have changed. A minute later I circle the Boardroom table and study my grandfather's portrait. Why have I come in here? To ask myself, What would he do? I used to ask that question quite often, but today it seems faintly absurd. He was a good banker, he had a fine career, a good life, but now his life, and his world, have both gone. Studying the dark picture now, I consider just what it is I really owe to the living and the dead.

12

'Unchanged,' Henry tells me as I pull up my chair. '200–203, your bid.'

I thank him and he heads out to the Dealing Room.

Checking the deal-sheet, I find I've only two hundred thousand pounds left in hand.

'Lose my bid,' I tell the broker. 'How does that leave you?'

'195–203. Frankly, Raef, the bid's not a problem. That offer's going to be taken any minute.' The price, he's saying, is about to rise.

I hit the switch again.

'Sell fifty thousand at 195.'

'What?' He's astonished. He asks me to repeat my order, he's not sure if he's heard it correctly.

I repeat it.

'This guy'll pay 200,' he advises. 'You want me to try him?'

'Sell at 195. Now!'

I turn and watch the screen. A few seconds later it happens.

'You're done for fifty at 195,' the broker tells me.

On the screen, the 195 winks off, then on again. The deal has gone through. I have triggered the agreement with my father.

I count the seconds. Before I reach ten, my private line beings to ring.

'Raef, it's traded at 195. Did you see?' My father's voice is tense; slightly broken.

'I saw.'

'I'll call the board, then contact Gifford.'

There is a hesitancy in his voice I hadn't expected. As though he's asking my permission. Head in hand, I agree that will probably be best.

'Raef?'

'I'm still here.'

In the pause that follows I hear him breathing. 'I never wanted this Raef. I'm sorry.' He rings off and I hang up the phone.

Once Gifford buys us we'll have the cash to redeem the loan against Boddington; the family estate will stay in our hands. But not Carlton Brothers. Not the bank. I watch the screen: the bid has already risen to 200.

More than a century and a half after our arrival, the time has come for the Carlton family to make its unceremonious exit from the City.

13

Trading in Carltons is suspended. 'Pending further announcements on merger talks between Carlton Brothers and American Pacific,' the Reuters newsflash says. I just had time to warn Sir John before the calls started coming in: journalists, competitors, clients, some to question and some to gloat, but the general reaction is one of regret, it seems I'm not the only one who thinks something of value is being lost. Several of the older callers mention my grandfather.

When I told Sir John, he took the news surprisingly well. His first concern seemed to be that I might not be given the chance to run the merged business, a possibility that had also occurred to me. He enquired about the possible sale price too: his options in Carlton Brothers have taken a sudden turn for the better. I left him fielding calls in his office.

In my own office now, I do the same. There's one from Penfield.

'This doesn't change my mind,' he says. 'The Unit still goes in tonight.'

All charm. I assure him that wasn't the purpose of the proposed deal, then I add the usual cant phrases about this being a good deal for both parties.

'Next thing I know you'll be telling me it's a merger, not a takeover.'

'Would you like to see Gifford?'

'He's booked in here for a courtesy call at five,'

Penfield tells me. 'He might not be too pleased to find a fraud investigation underway at Carltons. I take it he doesn't know yet?'

'Not from me.'

'Would you rather he heard it from us?'

Roger Penfield wants the merger to go ahead smoothly. Any problems we have in the Dealing Room will be more easily absorbed into a larger capital base, and being completely cynical about Penfield's motives, American Pacific's involvement will blur the supervisory lines of responsibility: the Bank of England, at worst, will be able to spread the blame.

'That might help,' I say. 'I'd appreciate it if my name didn't come up.'

Penfield seems pleased with how this is all turning out. He tells me to leave it to him.

The phones are still pealing when Vance comes in. He smiles crookedly, I can see he's tipsy, but he isn't drunk. Celebrating the Parnells victory with his team, I suppose, and drowning his private sorrows over Karen.

'I don't know if I should be angry you didn't tell me,' he says, 'or pleased with how well I taught you to keep your mouth shut.' He regards me askance. 'Is it congratulations?'

'Ask me again this time next year.'

'Ah,' he says nodding. 'Like that.'

But he offers me his hand anyway, and we shake. Last night at the Savoy seems a long time ago. Like Sir John, Vance has a stack of options in Carlton

Brothers, and this merger will enable him to cash them in early. I ask what he's going to do now that he's rich.

'Retire and play golf with Gordon.'

'No chance.'

'No, maybe not,' he agrees smiling. 'What about you?'

And what about me? Where do I go now? Do I really want to stay on waving the Carlton family flag over territory no longer our own? And if I did, how long would it be before colleagues and clients began pointing me out to each other as the man that was, yesterday's banker, the last of the Carltons, kept on as living relic by Gifford's good favour? I could sail, I've always said I wished I had the time for a long trip. But after two or three months, what then? I can't retire down to Boddington, I'm too young. Besides, where I want to be is here, right here in the City, and what I want to be doing is the work I was bred for: banking, it's too much a part of what I am.

'You don't have a bloody clue,' Vance says. 'Do you?'

We both laugh. I ask him if he'll do me a favour and speak to his people in Corporate Finance.

'American Pacific's got nothing in Europe,' I say. 'There won't be any jobs on the line.'

Vance says he'll pass on the good news. My private line starts ringing and Vance heads for the door.

'One other thing Stephen.' He looks back. 'Did you

ever really think Lyle had anything to do with Daniel's murder?'

Rather shamefaced, he turns his head from side to side.

'Pointing Ryan away from Karen?'

'Not one of my brighter ideas,' he confesses.

Reaching for the phone, I tell him I'll catch up with him later.

It's Charles Aldridge on the line: my father's asked him to call and let me know when they're meeting at Gifford's flat to settle terms. I explain that I might be a while.

When I step out of the office, Becky's frantically answering calls, and putting everyone on hold. In the corridor, clusters of employees have formed to consult, jarred from their late-Friday torpor. They fall silent as I hurry by, spectators at the Changing of the Guard.

Up in Settlement, Hugh has his head down, reading the *Evening Standard*.

'So,' he says, without glancing up, 'big news.'

There's a row of empty styrofoam cups at his elbow, and a ring of orange peel. His PC screen looks exactly as it did when I left him first thing this morning. Hugh Morgan has had enough.

'Things moved pretty quickly.'

'Yeah,' he says. 'I noticed.' He closes the paper. 'Parnells too. Big day all round.'

There's an undertone of sarcasm here: Hugh's not at all sure I've been straight with him.

'We only started speaking with Gifford seriously a couple of days ago. We just decided to go ahead with it this afternoon.'

He gives me a dubious look. 'What now? You retire and take up charitable causes?'

I gesture to the screen. 'No luck?'

'Uh-uh.'

The trap remains unsprung and our time is almost up. I lost Daniel, and now I've lost the bank, while this fraudster – Daniel's possible murderer – remains free. I want him. Gazing at the empty screen the realization steals over me like a physical thing, my cup of sorrow and anger finally brimmed. I want to find this bastard. I need to find him. And when I've found him I mean to choke him, and with careful steady blows, I will nail his lifeless body to the wall.

'I've got some questions,' Hugh says.

One of the girls comes and hands Hugh some paperwork: he scans it quickly then passes it back. He nods towards the coffee machine, and I follow him over. He doesn't seem in much of a rush. He makes himself a coffee, then we wander over to the corner by the IT room and prop ourselves against an abandoned table. The girls carry on sending faxes and working their keyboards. There are no big bonuses or options packages at stake in Settlements: provided they don't lose their jobs, nobody here gives a damn who owns Carltons.

'I did some ringing round,' Hugh says. 'You've been

buying Carltons in the market, and now you're getting out?'

'That's right.'

He asks if I'd care to explain.

It's over now; we're at the end. After keeping so much from Hugh, I at least owe him this much. So I tell him what happened. The tale comes out slowly, an elegy for the last days of Carltons, the story of how my father put Boddington on the line and I refused the sacrifice. Like an idiot, I begin to feel quite proud of my own good deed.

When I finish, Hugh considers. 'How well does your father know you?'

'Well enough.'

'Ahh,' he says.

He finishes his coffee and steps away from the table. I reach over and take his arm. I ask him what he means.

'Forget it, Raef.'

But I don't want to forget it. I ask him again.

'It's just a thought,' he says. 'But could your father have guessed what you'd do if he put Boddington on the line for you?'

I don't understand at first. Then I do. Hugh has laid his unsentimental measure over the situation: who wins? My father wanted to keep Boddington, I wanted to keep Carltons: who won? Hugh's suggesting that my father might have manipulated me into surrendering the bank. Suddenly unsteady, I lean back against the table.

'No,' I say.

'Just a thought.' Then he smiles. 'Look on the bright side. Once you've cashed in your chips, you'll be able to afford my fee.'

He gives me a friendly pat on the shoulder. When he cracks the old joke about even paranoids having enemies, I manage a weak smile.

Then it happens. From across the room, the sound of a high-pitched beeping. Everyone turns from their work to look. Before I can register what's happening, Hugh strides back to his desk. I follow a few paces behind.

The PC screen flashes wildly. Hugh flicks off the sound and we stare at the monitor. Twintech, it says; and just below this, Desk No. 4.

Hugh asks Sandra if any deal-slips have come up in the past ten minutes. She shakes her head. He punches a key, the beeping stops and the screen goes blank.

'Let's go down.'

We take the fire stairs at a run. Hugh calls back over his shoulder, asking me who belongs to Desk No. 4.

'Fourth from the right, far side of the Room,' I tell him.

'Proprietary desk?'

I don't answer. I picture the Room, counting along the imaginary desks. I don't want to believe it.

Downstairs, we race to the Dealing Room door, then we pause while I swipe my card. The lock clicks and Hugh shoulders the glass door open. I tug at his coat-tail.

'Careful.'

Inside, many of the desks are empty, most of the traders have escaped early for the weekend. Still trailing Hugh, I count the desks right to left as we cross the room. Desk No. 4 is the one feared. As we draw near, Hugh glances back to me.

'Empty,' he says, dismayed.

But it isn't. When we reach the desk, a face rises from the far side of the console, smiling.

Hugh turns to me, brow raised.

'Did you bring the champagne?' Henry says.

Henry. I don't want it to be him, but it is. I grip the back of a chair. 'Has anyone else been at this desk in the past few minutes?'

'Just me,' he says. 'Why?'

Beneath his hand, I notice a small pile of deal-slips. I ask him to give them to me. He looks at me uncertainly, so I reach over and take them. He asks me what's wrong, but I flick through the deal-slips without answering. Twintech. The CTL deal's in the middle of the pile. I pass it to Hugh.

'Do I get to hear the big secret?' Henry says, becoming annoyed. 'What's up?'

Hugh looks at me and nods. Twintech's position in CTL has been closed out, the trap is sprung, and here we are, at long last, with Henry. Why?

But before I can ask Henry that question, he says, 'Owen's gone, if you want to see him.'

'Owen?'

'Those deals.' Henry points to the deal-slips. 'I just punched them through for him. He left ten minutes ago.' Henry turns from Hugh back to me. 'Now do I get to hear the secret?'

'All those deals were his?' Hugh asks.

'Yeah. He was holding the fort on the proprietary desk. He just left.'

Hugh glances at me. This sounds like the truth.

'Where to?' I ask Henry.

Henry doesn't know. He asks me a second time what's wrong.

'Probably nothing. We just need to speak with Owen.'

Henry doesn't buy that. 'Anything to do with this merger?'

I wave the question aside. 'Listen Henry, can you track Owen down? Don't let him know I'm looking for him, but find out where he is, and come and tell me.'

I head for the door, Hugh close behind me.

Henry calls out, 'Where'll you be?'

I answer over my shoulder. 'The tape room.'

14

Hugh drapes the headphones around his neck. 'I get the feeling you've had an idea. Care to share it?'

I run a hand over the row of shelved tapes, searching. The tapes are stacked chronologically, neatly labelled, and I find the one I'm looking for almost immediately. While I'm loading it into the machine, Hugh asks if I've forgotten our agreement.

'Penfield was going to get the fraudster's name as soon as we found it,' he says. 'And the name's Owen, right?'

Putting on my headphones, I push Play. Hugh lifts his own head-phones into place.

'The nightdesk tape,' I say. 'From last Wednesday.'

We watch the tape go round. The tapes are voice-activated, and timed: the digital timer ticks over as we listen.

Owen: Check the Sporting Index.

'Owen,' I tell Hugh.

Owen: They're showing 330-360 for the second innings.
Other voice: Yours, big time.

They laugh. The timer says 11.00 p.m: too early. I fast-forward to after 1.00 a.m. Then I hit Play again, and turn up the volume.

Jamie: Hello. Carlton Brothers.

'Jamie,' I say to Hugh. 'Graduate trainee.'

Hugh bends forward, listening. The reel-to-reel hisses softly.

Other voice: Jurgen?

Jamie: He's not here. Owen's on tonight.

Other voice: Who's that?

Jamie: Jamie. Owen'll be back in a minute.

There's a pause.

Other voice: Dollar/Yen?

Jamie: Who's this speaking?

Other voice: Chris Yeoh, Bank Bunara, KL. What's your Dollar/Yen?

Jamie: Just a sec.

Other voice: Haven't got all day, lah.

Jamie: Can you call back?

Other voice: Call back, bu'shit! I ask for Dollar/Yen, you give me a price, lah. Look in Dealer's Handbook.

Another pause. Hugh turns to me and mutters, 'Pleasant guy.'

Jamie: Can you show a side?

Other voice: Dollar/Yen.

Jamie: Sec . . . We offer five dollars at sixty-two.

Other voice: Fuck off! 55–60 I make you, Dollar/Yen. 55–60, my price. Hit me.

Jamie: Nothing there. Thanks.

Other voice: Off Yen! . . . You show me now. Dollar/Yen two-way price. Hey!

Jamie: 52–62.

Other voice: Very funny. I show you 55–
60, you show me 52–62. You good dealer.
Very quick, lah.

The tone is suddenly more friendly. I have a feeling
I know what's about to happen.

Jamie: Yeah.

Jamie actually laughs. A nervous laugh of relief,
he thinks it's all over.

Other voice: Ten point spread, should be
good for a hundred dollars, lah. Should
be.

Now the dealer from Bank Bunara laughs, and
Jamie, completely lulled, joins in.
Jamie: Yeah.
Other voice: Hundred yours! . . . I send
you the fax.

There's a click, and then silence; it really is over
now. I stop the tape.

Hugh takes off his headphones, and turns to me.
'It was a stitch-up,' he says.

I nod. Owen's unusual lapse is explained: as Jamie
tried once to tell me, it wasn't Owen's fault, Jamie
made the mistake.

Hugh asks if we lost much on the deal.

'That's not what worries me.' I tap the timer: 1.24 a.m.

Then I rewind the tape till I find the last time Owen speaks: 1.03 a.m. Next I wind forward past 1.24 a.m., searching for the next time his voice comes. Finally I locate it.

> Owen: Brad? Owen. Put me on your box. I
> need to see everything you get in Dollar/
> Yen.

His voice has a desperate edge. He's speaking to a New York broker, getting ready to trade out of the 100 million dollar position young Jamie has landed him with.

Hugh lowers his headphones. 'Owen's back.'

I take off my headphones and point to the timer again: 1.47 a.m.

'He's back,' I agree. 'But where the hell has he been?'

15

Jamie sits head bowed, one hand on his headphones, and listens. As the tape plays we watch him turn red. When the timer hits 1.24 a.m., I stop the tape. For a while Jamie just sits there, then he peels off the headphones. 'Am I fired?'

'Where was Owen while this was going on?'

Jamie tells us it wasn't Owen's fault. I repeat my question.

'He said he was going for a leak. We couldn't find him.'

'What happened after they stuffed you?' Hugh asks.

'Dollar/Yen tanked. Those bastards dumped it everywhere, it really wasn't Owen's fault.'

'Who went to look for Owen?'

'Me.'

'Where did you look?'

'The toilets.' Jamie gestures to the door. 'All along here. The offices. Up in the restaurant.'

'You couldn't find him?'

'No. I went back to the desk, it was pretty crazy.'

Hugh asks how long it was before Owen showed up.

'Ten minutes?' Jamie says. 'Not long, anyway. It felt like hours.'

He studies his hands. This is, without doubt, the worst moment of Jamie's short career.

Hugh looks at me over Jamie's head. Silently he mouths the question, 'Where's Owen?'

I ask Jamie that.

'I don't know. I think he said he was going skiing somewhere for a few days.'

'Where? The Continent?'

'Yeah. I think he said Switzerland.'

Hugh swears softly. Jamie repeats that the mistake was his fault, not Owen's.

'I don't want to get him in trouble,' he says.

I tell him not to repeat a word of this to anyone. He's still apologizing for his mistake as I show him out the door.

'Lad should consider a career change,' Hugh remarks, when I come back in. 'Too pleasant for this business.'

'Switzerland,' I say.

Hugh considers. 'Owen's on the proprietary desk, isn't he, he could dabble wherever he liked from there. And he gave Henry the Twintech slip just now. And he went missing at the same time Daniel was murdered.'

I slap my forehead. 'That night. Hell. Wednesday night, he was only looking after the nightdesk because Daniel put him there.'

'So?'

'Daniel said it was for something else, some stupid deal Owen'd done.' I groan, seeing at last what I've been missing all along. 'If Daniel suspected Owen was involved with Twintech, if he thought Owen was my patsy in the Dealing Room, what else would he do? He couldn't sack him without alerting me.'

Hugh sees what I'm getting at. 'So Daniel shoved Owen onto the nightdesk to keep a better eye on him?'

'Owen was isolated there. He wouldn't have any chance to do what he just did with Henry. He couldn't cover his tracks.'

Now I swear. Hugh ponders a moment.

'If Owen guessed Daniel was onto him,' he says,

glancing at the timer, 'he had a motive as well.'

We look at one another. Henry comes in, knocking at the open door.

'They think Owen went home.' He hands me a slip of paper. 'That's his number and address.'

The address is in Notting Hill Gate. Henry's still waiting for an explanation as we rush past him out the door.

16

'Flat battery,' Hugh says, switching off his mobile. 'We can't wait.'

Sliding open the glass partition, I hand Owen's address through to my driver. We'll have to tell Ryan later.

We go up the Strand, and Piccadilly, to Hyde Park Corner, then up to Marble Arch. I speak my thoughts aloud, but all this while, Hugh stays silent. Passing Lancaster Gate, he suddenly asks me what Owen Baxter's like.

'A good trader. Not someone I'd have over for dinner.'

'Violent?'

'You mean can I imagine him shooting Daniel?'

He turns his head; not what he meant. 'Did I ever give you my Couchet arrest story?' he says. He leans back in the seat. 'It was in Paris. I ferreted away at Monsieur Couchet's accounts for six months, I thought I'd finally nailed him. When we got the order for his arrest, I tagged along with the gendarmerie.' He screws up his face at the memory. 'They didn't want me there. They thought I was up to something with Couchet. They told me that later. It was *"quelle dommage"* and *"beaucoup apologies"* later.'

'What happened?'

'We went trooping up to his flat, me and three gendarmes; they knocked on his door. Couchet invites us in. Old man, over seventy, the first time I met him he was charming. Next time he had a lawyer and accountant with him, and after that it was all downhill. Anyway, the gendarmerie told Couchet why they were there.'

'To arrest him.'

'Right. He'd ripped off some pretty big fish; he knew his number was up. But when they told him he was under arrest he just looked like "no problem". He asked if he could get a few things first.' Hugh repeats it to himself. 'A few things.'

'Like what?'

'A gun,' Hugh says. 'When he came back out of his study, he tried to shoot me.'

I look at Hugh. The memory has turned him white, he isn't joking.

'You weren't hit?'

'Not me. One of the gendarmes. In the spine.' Hugh turns and looks out at the traffic rushing by. Sweat beads on his brow. 'Seven years ago. And he's still in a wheelchair.'

We turn up by Queensway. The remainder of our journey passes in silence.

17

Owen's house is a Victorian terrace at the end of a row.

Crossing the street, Hugh suggests that I stay out of sight for a moment. 'If he sees you on the security camera, he might not open the door.'

Sweat has broken out on his face again. He points to the neighbouring doorway and I go and stand there. Hugh rings Owen's bell, he presses it twice before Owen answers.

'Yes?'

'Mr Baxter?' Hugh says. 'I'm from the council. We've adjusted the tax-band in this street downward, I just need your signature.'

Owen doesn't reply. After a few seconds Hugh looks across at me, and I signal for him to push the doorbell again. When he shakes his head, I step out from my hiding-place. He gestures angrily for me to go back, but then the door suddenly opens, and there Owen is. Owen focuses on Hugh first, then he looks up and sees me. The scene freezes: me looking at Owen looking at me. Before Owen can recover, Hugh rams his shoulder hard against the door. There's a crunching noise and someone bellows in pain.

I move fast, following Hugh through the breach.

In the hallway we find Owen bent double, hands over his face and swearing. There appears to be blood.

Hugh looks at me apologetically.

'Fuck,' Owen says. 'Fuck.'

Still bent double, he turns and stumbles down the hall, a trail of red droplets forming on the pale wooden floor behind him. We follow him into the kitchen, Hugh keeps asking if he's okay.

Owen hangs his face over the sink. 'You broke my fuckin' nose.' He snorts blood.

Hugh wets a tea-towel, Owen snatches it and starts dabbing. This isn't working out as we'd planned.

'Owen,' I say. 'This is Hugh Morgan. He's an investigating accountant. He has a few questions for you.'

'Jesus H. Christ! Questions? What about my fuckin' nose?' Owen splashes his face. He doesn't sound quite so bad this time.

'Concerning Twintech,' Hugh puts in.

Owen pivots and stabs a finger in Hugh's direction. 'That was assault. I'm gonna do you for fuckin' assault.' Blood trickles from both nostrils, but the nose doesn't look broken. When the blood touches his top lip, he swears again and turns back to the sink.

Hugh fetches a roll of kitchen towels from near the bread bin. For the next few minutes we watch Owen tear off sheets as he tries to stanch the flow of blood. The kitchen smells of detergent. All the shiny black surfaces have the look of being lifted from a magazine, a bachelor's idea of good taste. Expensive enough, but this is one life that a million and a half pounds could have changed. Finally Owen faces us again, holding a crumpled sheet to his nose. He says he's going to find a doctor.

'You're going nowhere,' Hugh mutters.

Owen lunges at him. Hugh darts around the table. When I step between them, Owen tries to jostle me aside.

'Get out of my fuckin' house,' Owen shouts, pushing me.

And right then something in me gives way. I grab Owen and drive him backwards; he slams into the fridge door. I hold him there, my hands on his throat, and I begin, quite deliberately, to throttle him. His eyes open wide. He kicks, but I just keep squeezing. Hugh shouts my name, but that doesn't touch me either. Owen clutches at me, struggling. I have him in my hands, the man that killed Daniel. Steadily I squeeze.

And the next moment I'm on my back, Hugh has his knee planted on my chest, and Owen's slumped at the table, holding his throat and trying to breathe.

'Jesus, Raef,' Hugh says.

Lifting his knee from my chest, he casts an anxious glance at Owen. I sit up. Owen coughs and tries to swallow. Blood drips from his nose. Hugh brings over the roll of kitchen-towel and puts it down at Owen's elbow.

'Fuck,' Owen says. When he asks for water, Hugh fetches him a glassful.

After a few seconds I get to my feet. My hands, I notice, are trembling. All that rage, where did it come from? Hugh points to the far end of the table, and I go and sit there, a good distance from Owen. Owen drinks his water and towels his nose, glancing nervously my way.

'Are you all right?' Hugh asks. He seems to have recovered.

'What the fuck is this?'

'We told you,' Hugh says. 'Twintech.'

Owen doesn't respond. He dabs at the blood. I produce the list of Twintech deals from my pocket, and Hugh takes it and smooths out the page. He reads the numbers aloud. After half a dozen deals, he stops and looks at Owen. 'Twintech,' he says.

'And there was one went through today,' I add. 'This afternoon in CTL.'

Owen holds the kitchen towel to his nose, saying nothing.

'Owen, why did Daniel put you on the nightdesk last week?'

'Bananas,' he mumbles through the towel. 'I got caught long in that stupid banana market, some idiot dumped two barrowloads in reception.' The same reason Daniel gave me: Owen, bored, got involved in one of those dealers' games. When it went wrong Daniel sent him onto the nightdesk as a punishment.

'So where did you disappear to on Wednesday night?'

Owen goes to the sink, his back to us. 'Nowhere,' he says. He turns on the tap and says something about calling a doctor. But he doesn't mean it this time, the fight seems to have gone out of him. He knows it's serious now. It looks like he might even be thinking.

'We've listened to the tapes. You went missing between 1.03 and 1.47 a.m.'

'Because I'm not on the tapes doesn't mean I wasn't there.'

'We've spoken to your colleagues. You weren't there.'

Owen faces us again, a fresh towel to his nose. 'Maybe I went for a leak. Last Wednesday, I mean give me a break.'

'They couldn't find you in the building,' Hugh tells him.

'They didn't look hard enough.'

'They couldn't find you because you weren't there. You were gone for threequarters of an hour.'

He tilts his head right back, eyes to the ceiling. But there's no fresh blood on the towel. I have the impression he's simply buying a few seconds in which to think. When he drops his head again he says, 'So we took a loss, big fuckin' deal. We came out square on the night.'

'Inspector Ryan isn't interested in how much money the bank lost,' Hugh says.

Owen does a double take. 'You what?'

'He questioned everyone on the boat that night,

from the party. You weren't there, so he didn't question you.'

'What is this bullshit?'

Owen takes the towel from his nose, he's stopped bleeding. I rap the table and he looks my way.

'Daniel was murdered that night. Right around when you went missing.'

'Hey,' he says raising his hands. 'Hey. Nothin' to do with me. No fuckin' way.'

'The Bank of England knows about the Twintech fraud. And Inspector Ryan's waiting to hear from us.' Tapping a forefinger on the table, I conclude, 'If you have any kind of explanation Owen, now's the time.'

A cornered rat could not look more frightened. His bravado deserts him completely now, he steps forward and drops into a chair. He rests his elbows on the table, puts his hands to his face and swears. Blood begins to trickle from his nose again, he lifts his head and looks around helplessly. Hugh hands him another towel.

'It wasn't a fraud,' Owen says, wiping the blood. 'It was a systems check.'

Hugh snorts. 'A what?'

Behind his bloody towel, Owen mutters, 'Ask Aldridge.'

For a second the world tilts, everything knocked completely askew. Charles Aldridge and Twintech?

'Why come breaking down my fuckin' door?' Owen whines.

When I look at Hugh he's shaking his head: he

doesn't believe Owen's story. Recovering, I tell Owen that he'd better explain.

'Explain what? He asked me to put through some deals. Keep it quiet, he said. The audit committee needed to check our systems.' Owen is all wide-eyed innocence.

'Daniel wasn't told?'

'Search me.'

'Who chose Twintech's deals?' I ask.

'Listen, what is this shit?'

'And you reported the deals to Aldridge?'

Owen nods. Then he pauses as if he's just figured it out: the reason for us bursting into his house like this, and for all these questions. 'Jesus, he was telling you guys, wasn't he?' I turn to Hugh, he's watching Owen carefully now.

'Shit.' Owen suddenly stands, his chair topples over. 'If he wasn't I'll kill the bastard.' He thumps the table with his fist and the fruit bowl jumps. Not a very convincing display.

Hugh says, 'You didn't explain where you were that Wednesday night.'

'He called me. Aldridge. He wanted to meet me.'

'At St Paul's Walk?'

'No fuckin' way. Down at Cannon Street. He didn't show up, so I went back to the office.'

Hugh tells him he'd better think of something a little more believable before he sees Inspector Ryan. Owen's mouth drops open.

Hugh nods to the phone in the hallway. 'No skiing

this weekend. You want to call and cancel?'

Gutted. Owen is absolutely gutted. The terrible reality has descended on him at last: after twelve months of pulling the wool over everyone's eyes, he's finally been caught. He stands gaping, then like a sleepwalker he wanders out to the hall. We watch him phone.

Lowering his voice, Hugh says, 'Worst piece of acting I ever saw.'

'You think he's lying?'

Hugh rolls his eyes. 'The man's a crook, of course he's lying. What else can he do?'

'What about Aldridge?'

'Bollocks. You employed me to catch your fraudster.' He points to the hall. 'That's him. And if you ask me, he's probably the murderer too. But once we take him down to Ryan, my job's over. Whatever else Ryan or Penfield can shake out of him isn't my concern.'

Perhaps not, but it might well be mine. I ask Hugh if he'd consider staying with this for a couple more days.

He looks at me very directly. 'No,' he says.

I see there's no point arguing, he's had enough of this case. Enough too, I suspect, of me.

'And by the way. The next time you want to choke someone to death, leave me out of it.'

We hear Owen's conversation ending. I rise, asking if Hugh minds taking Owen on alone.

'I've got some business to sort out with my father.

Take Owen in my car, you'll have the driver.'

Owen overhears this as he returns from the hall. 'Take Owen where?' he says.

A thin line of blood trickles from one nostril. Hugh picks up the kitchen towels and shoves them into Owen's stomach.

'The Met,' Hugh says. 'Close your eyes, you can pretend you're in Geneva.'

Once they've gone, I call my father. He's still with Eric Gifford, coming to terms on a final price for Carltons.

'We'll need your signature too, Raef,' he says. He adds that he's taking Gifford to the Bankers' Association function tonight. 'We should have an agreement in principle ready by then. If you sign it, we'll make the announcement there.' He sounds dejected. He doesn't mention the likely price, and I don't ask.

'Is Charles with you?'

'Went home ten minutes ago. He'll be there tonight though.'

I wish him luck with the negotiations, then ring off. Running out into the street I whistle down a passing taxi.

18

Who wins? The question came to me quite suddenly in the midst of Owen Baxter's explanation. Who wins?

Charles Aldridge lost out to Sir John in the contest to run the bank after my father retired; but now he stands on the brink of the Chairmanship. And that story of Owen's about checking our systems, far from being implausible as Hugh imagines, I can see just how it might have occurred. Aldridge thrives in the shadows. Say he approached Owen, wined, dined and flattered him, then made a suggestion in that confidential way he has. 'The Board has a problem we think you can help us with. Discreetly.' Owen, being what he is, would bite. But after a few weeks he'd realize something was up, a systems check wouldn't need to go on that long. So then what? Could Aldridge have implied that for convenience' sake Twintech's profits might be held in a Swiss account? An account controlled by Owen? Or could it be even simpler? Could he have just paid Owen to do what was required? Either way, what did Owen have to lose? If the deals were discovered he'd explain, as he has done, that he thought it was a system check ordered by Aldridge. Provided the money was still there, and he handed it back, he could gamble on riding out an investigation. He might even have deluded himself that Charles would stand by him.

Or is this all completely crazy? Charles Aldridge? Maybe I've just been spending to much time with Hugh.

Charles presses the buzzer and I shoulder his door open.

'In the study, Raef,' he calls.

At the far end of the hall I turn, and he beckons me in. He's at his desk, pen in hand, phone to his ear, so I stand by the shelves and wait. It's much like my father's study at Boddington: leather-bound books, floor to ceiling, a big work desk and a few armchairs. A gentleman's room. Sir Charles puts down the phone.

'Gifford's screwing us on the price,' he says.

He starts to give me a blow by blow account of how negotiations have gone. I raise a hand.

'Owen Baxter's been taken to see the police.'

He pauses. 'Owen who?'

'Baxter. One of our dealers. He's been up to no good.'

Charles frowns. He asks me how bad.

'Not too bad. And it's capped. Don't worry, it won't scupper the deal with Gifford.'

He lets out a long breath. I study him for a moment, my father's old friend. But that's all I see: Charles Aldridge.

'He's named you as an accomplice.'

He lifts his head, surprised. The surprise turns to amusement. 'How interesting. And did he name anyone else? Your father perhaps?'

'Just you.'

'Well then.' He closes a file. 'What do you suggest? Can he afford to fight a slander action?'

'He's been taken to see Inspector Ryan.'

Charles' eyes widen.

'It's possible Baxter had a hand in Daniel's murder.'

'One of your own dealers?'

'It's possible. Look, Ryan can figure it out from here. I just thought I'd let you know. It might help if you get down and have a word with him before Owen says his piece. Nip the lie in the bud.'

He agrees that it might be a very good idea. He asks me to give him a moment, he just wants a quick word with Sir John.

While he calls, I step out into the hall to wait. If Owen had accused me of complicity in the fraud, I wonder how I might have taken the news. Not well, I expect. Not well at all. But then again, Charles Aldridge isn't me. A minute later he comes out to join me.

'John'll give himself an ulcer one day,' he says.

We go to the front door, but as he steps out I turn back.

'Left my briefcase. Won't be a second.'

And a second is all I have in his study. I scoop up the case from under the chair where I left it, then I cross to his desk and hit the last-number redial on the phone. The number flashes up in the crystal display. A number I know; but not Sir John's.

'Raef?' Charles calls.

I lift the receiver and replace it gently, then I hurry back out to the hall. I tell Charles he'll have to make his way to the Metropolitan Police on his own.

The taxi driver turns to me. 'Where in Whitehall?'

'The DTI.'

I give him the address then lean back, continuing to turn it all over. Who wins? Owen, if it all went smoothly, would end up with a nest-egg in Switzerland. But it didn't go smoothly: Daniel was killed. Last Thursday morning, with Inspector Ryan and his crew descending on the bank, and the news of Daniel's murder filtering out, Owen would have realized he was in very serious trouble. And then the dive in CTL. No wonder he was departing for Switzerland.

And Charles Aldridge, my father's friend, the Carlton family's confidant: how did it take me so long to see?

I call Becky on the taxi driver's mobile and ask for Johnstone's number. I'm still on the phone to him when the taxi stops outside the DTI. At the end of our conversation I offer Johnstone his job back, and he accepts. I give the driver a tenner then I go up to find Gerald Wolsey.

19

It will all be over soon. Coming home from Whitehall it was drizzling, but now the rain drums against my bedroom window like pellets of ice. Hugh called fifteen minutes ago, he's on his way here. He tells me he has a big surprise.

Showered and changed, nothing more to put on

but my bow tie, I lie on my bed and sip my whisky. Tonight I will sign the papers. Tonight the Carlton family will make its unexpected departure from the City. I can face that now. Leaning across to the bedside drawer, I dig out a framed photograph of Theresa and Annie: it was taken in Annie's first summer. She is just a baby here, cradled in Theresa's bare arms. The picture propped on my thigh, I study it, sipping my drink. These days Theresa has more lines, and Annie's much bigger: she's a child now and still changing. But this won't ever change, what I see now in the picture, the thing I never noticed all that time: Annie has Daniel's eyes.

When the doorbell rings, I put the picture aside and go down and let Hugh in.

'Owen's with Penfield and Ryan,' he says, watching me fix my bow tie. 'Penfield says he'll see you tonight.'

'Is he sending in the Unit?'

I glance at Hugh's reflection in the mirror. He turns his head.

'I told him I'd been right through it,' he says. 'Twintech's closed out now. That's it.'

So with Penfield, our account's clean at last.

'Do you know how lucky you were?' He sees my twisted smile in the mirror, and laughs. 'No,' he says. 'Really.' He sits on the arm of the sofa. 'Your friend Owen would have lined up Twintech for a big one in the end. One big hit, then he'd have been in Rio and you'd have been down the pan.'

I take a moment with that one. Could Owen have

done it? Maybe. He already had our systems accepting Twintech as a legitimate client. And that, compared with our current disaster, would have been cataclysm. The whole bank could have disappeared into the maelstrom. Nobody in their right mind would have bid 10p a share for us, let alone 210; Boddington would have been sold to cover our borrowings; everything, absolutely everything, would have gone. In the mirror I watch Hugh's world-weary smile.

My bow tie finished, I face him. 'What's the big surprise?'

He takes some papers from his coat and hands them to me. I sit on the sofa.

'We got it wrong,' he says.

The pages he's given me are photocopies: grainy black and white images of photographs. The subject of each is the same, a sleeping body, each picture taken from a different angle. There's a lot of shadow. And there's one close-up of the man's face, but I don't recognize him. I lift my eyes.

'Daniel's murderer,' Hugh says. 'I got a friend at the Met to do me some copies.'

I look down, then straight up. 'Who is he?'

'Axel Dortmund. And not is. Was. German. Now deceased.' Hugh points to the pictures. 'The arrest went a little bit wrong.'

I study the pictures more closely. Axel Dortmund, I realize now, isn't sleeping, he's dead, and what I mistook for shadow is actually blood. An unbelievable quantity.

'A professional bad guy from Berlin,' Hugh says. 'Ryan was tipped off that he'd been in the country for a flying visit. Less than a day. It happened to coincide with Daniel's murder.'

'What about Owen?'

'He didn't pull the trigger. I tell you what, though. If Ryan hadn't found this guy,' Hugh points to the pictures, 'things wouldn't have been looking too bright for Mr Baxter at all.'

I ask how Ryan can be sure it was Dortmund.

'Ballistics match up. They dug a bullet out of St Paul's Walk. Fired from the same gun Dortmund was using on the German police when he was killed this morning.' He glances down.

'This Dortmund was a professional killer?'

'He was a dope,' Hugh says. 'A thug. The police were trying to arrest him on some racketeering charge.'

'Ryan thinks he was paid to kill Daniel?'

Hugh tells me Ryan was pursuing that line of inquiry with Owen when he left them.

'None of my business now,' he says. 'Thank God.'

We study the pictures. Daniel's murderer. The man who pulled the trigger. Hugh makes a macabre comment on the German police force's interviewing technique, but I don't feel much like smiling just now. Because now, for the first time, I see the whole thing complete.

Hugh stands to go, he looks exhausted.

'I haven't thanked you yet,' I say.

He waves it off. When I rise he places a hand on my shoulder. 'I think this leaves us all square with favours, Raef. The next time you've got a problem, deal me out.'

He means it too. He's not looking quite as young as he did a week ago. Going to the door he tells me what he saw of Owen's interview with Ryan. But he has none of his usual enthusiasm. He seems to be winding back, withdrawing himself emotionally from the whole affair by slow degrees. He's done what I asked, cracked Twintech, and now all he wants to do is go home.

'I promised Ryan I'd get back there tomorrow,' he says. 'Make sure Owen's statement adds up.'

Out on the pavement, I offer him a lift but he's not going towards the City. My driver opens the car door for me. I shake Hugh's hand.

'Anything you need, Hugh.'

He smiles. Hugh Morgan has heard this kind of promise too many times before.

Then as I'm stepping into the car, he touches my arm.

'I'm sorry you lost the bank,' he says. 'I really am.'

He's still standing there on the pavement as we pull away. My head falls back in the seat and I close my eyes.

I'm sure I've done right not to compromise him. This time, I'm sure, there really was no need to tell Hugh Morgan the truth.

20

The noise from the party is a steady hum, the City's big-hitters at play. While waiting for the coat-check girl to return with my token, Roger Penfield appears at my side. He looks smug.

'Quite a story,' he says. 'Mr Morgan certainly knows his business.'

I ask him if he's seen my father.

'They're waiting for your signature before they make the announcement. He's with Gifford.' Then he lowers his voice. 'I've kept this Owen Baxter thing quiet. I thought it could wait till after the announcement.' By which he means that he doesn't want the merger derailed. 'No objections?'

No, I tell him. No objections.

The girl hands me my token and Roger leads me inside.

It's one of the livery halls, the coat-of-arms and other paraphernalia of the company are draped from the walls. Gothic carving sprouts everywhere, and three giant chandeliers hang from the ceiling. The champagne has been flowing for some time, and conversation is loud.

Roger plucks two glasses from a passing tray. 'To a successful conclusion to the day,' he says.

Mercifully someone catches at his elbow, and before Roger can free himself I slip away into the crowd. The City worthies really have turned out in force. I see Sir John locked in conversation with two clearing bank chairmen, and at the far side of the room Vance and Darren Lyle are sharing a private word: the transition at Parnells, I expect. Neither one of them is smiling. As I make my way through the crush I'm stopped three or four times and asked if the rumour is true: will there be an announcement tonight on the terms of the American Pacific–Carltons merger tonight? I tell them they'll have to wait and see.

Then I spot Eric Gifford and my father. They seem relaxed, slightly detached from the crowd, they haven't seen me yet. As I move towards them, a hand shoots out and takes my arm.

'Is it congratulations,' Brian McKinnon says, 'or do I shed a wee tear?'

'I did warn you not to bale out.'

He swears good-humouredly. Drifting back into the crowd, he says we'll talk later.

When I emerge from the ruck, Eric Gifford greets me hand extended. My father, peering past me, asks if I've seen Charles. I shake my head.

'Well,' he says, indicating a rear door, 'let's get this done then, shall we?'

The room we enter is like a private ante-chapel to the main hall. It has a table, chairs, a large empty fireplace and more Gothic carving. A French clock ticks on the mantelpiece. My father takes out some papers and lays them on the table.

'We've come up with something in principle. Read it through, Raef. See what you think.'

Gifford offers to leave for a minute. My father tells

447

him that won't be necessary.

But as I reach for the papers I say, 'If you wait outside Mr Gifford, we'll call you in when we're ready.'

Gifford goes without demur.

'Raef,' my father says, suddenly concerned, 'you agreed to this.'

'How much is he offering for Carltons?'

'It's on the last page.'

But instead of pawing through the papers, I wait for an answer.

'Two shares in American Pacific for every one in Carltons,' he says.

'Cash value?'

'At today's rates, 218.' Two hundred and eighteen pence a share for Carlton Brothers. And days ago we were trading well over 300. 'The way things stand, Raef, it's a fair price.'

'Does Charles think so too?'

'His recommendation's there.' He points to the papers. 'The first page.'

I read Aldridge's recommendation. It's hedged round with provisos and qualifications, but the general thrust is unmistakable: sell now at 218. I turn the page and read the conditions on the general agreement: my father's retirement is to be effective immediately, Aldridge will take over as interim chairman, and I must resign within a month. Sir John, too, will step down. My finger pauses on the name of Carltons' Managing-Director-in-waiting.

'You saw this?'

He looks over my shoulder. 'Evidently Gifford thinks more of him than you thought.'

Yes, I murmur. Evidently.

The Managing-Director-in-waiting is Tony Mannetti. Suddenly the golden boy, Gifford's anointed. I spend a minute on the final page, the price, and Gifford's agreement to make a general offer in the market at Monday opening. Below this are the empty places for the signatures: me, my father, Gifford and two witnesses. Everything is impeccably prepared.

I put the agreement aside. 'I'd like a word with Gifford.'

'You will sign it, Raef?'

Will I? I suppose even now I could stop it going through. But I don't want to. Not now. When I nod, he rests a hand on my shoulder. I suggest that maybe Vance and Penfield could be the witnesses, and he goes out to find them. Immediately Gifford comes back in, he must have been waiting outside the door. He crosses to the table and sits opposite me, tugging at his shirt cuffs beneath his dinner-jacket. The hum of the party seems distant.

'Not an ideal situation,' he remarks. 'Your father's a persuasive man, though. Aldridge, too.'

'Charles Aldridge is with the police.'

Gifford pauses. 'Somebody in trouble?'

'Yes,' I say. 'Charles.'

He draws back.

'He's been accused of involvement in a fraud.

449

Apparently one that's been going on for some time.'

'Accused by whom?'

'One of our dealers. Owen Baxter.'

Gifford looks perturbed. He asks if I'm taking the accusation seriously.

'Baxter's been using a dummy company to rake money out of our Dealing Room. About one and a half million pounds. Yes. I'm taking it seriously.'

'Are the losses capped?'

'Funny,' I say. 'I was about to ask you the same thing.'

There's not even a flicker. As a liar, he's in a different league to the likes of Darren Lyle.

He opens his hands. 'I'm sorry?'

'We've traced Twintech to source.'

For the briefest moment I see that I've pierced his armour. But then it's gone, and he's laying his hand on the agreement.

'If there's been a fraud, that would constitute a material change in Carlton Brothers' circumstances. You realize that.'

'Whose idea was it?' I ask.

He folds his arms. He tells me that in the light of this new information he might have to reassess his bid.

'Oh, I'm sure you will.' I pick up the agreement. 'Because at 218 a share, it's a steal.'

'Your father disagrees.'

'My father doesn't know what I know, Mr Gifford. Not yet. But if you wish me to tell him, I'll oblige.' I toss the agreement back onto the table. Gifford regards me steadily. 'You'll have to change the number.'

He doesn't flinch. He tells me he's not sure what we're discussing. How in the world didn't I see this? Whitehall and Westminster? What do those two places have to teach a New York banker about duplicity?

'A revised bid,' I tell him. 'A change in the terms of the merger.'

'In the light of this fraud?'

'Among other things. You pay three American Pacific shares for one Carltons, Mr Gifford, or the deal's off.'

He murmurs that the idea is ridiculous.

I point to the unsigned agreement. 'Ridiculous, Mr Gifford, is taking someone like Tony Mannetti and making him the Managing Director of a bank like Carlton Brothers.'

'He's a professional.'

'Of a kind. So professional that our compliance people couldn't figure out how he'd managed to make such a complete balls-up over Parnells. Why he went on holiday, leaving orders for a share purchase that nearly scuppered the Meyers' bid. I expect you noticed what that reference to the Takeover Panel did to our share price?'

'I'm not answerable for your employees. And if the agreement's unacceptable to you, I don't see that we have anything further to discuss.'

'We can discuss who Tony Mannetti's really been working for since he joined Carlton Brothers,' I say. 'Me or you.'

Gifford rises from his chair and turns to leave.

'If you don't sit down,' I tell him quietly, 'you're going to finish the night in a police interrogation room. Take your pick.'

He faces me again. But he doesn't sit.

'Twintech,' I say. 'Does the name ring a bell?'

'Make your point.'

'Twintech was the vehicle for the fraud. Twintech was being run by Owen Baxter, and Owen Baxter was being run by Charles Aldridge. And Aldridge – ' I point – 'was being run by you.'

Gifford smiles. 'Really?' he says, shaking his head.

I could happily knock his gleaming teeth down his throat. But instead I stand and begin a slow circuit of the room. 'You wanted Carltons, but you knew that without the agreement of my family – my father and me – you had no chance. So you approached Charles Aldridge. Or he approached you?' I look at Gifford. He makes no comment. 'Together you came up with a way to shake us loose. Mannetti was a Trojan Horse. With one stupid deal he made both our Funds Management department and Corporate Finance look ridiculous. And in the meantime I was chasing my tail with Twintech.' I stop by the fireplace. 'It wasn't Daniel who sent that anonymous note to Penfield, was it? It was you.'

'This is absurd.'

'Do you know Gerald Wolsey?'

He says the name means as much to him as my story.

'He's with the DTI. When their inspectors came calling, I thought it was Wolsey doing the dirty work for Darren Lyle. I spoke to Wolsey two hours ago. He's quite adamant it was Aldridge who caused the visit.'

'This seems to be a roundabout way of saying that you're not selling.'

'Oh, but I am.' I return to the table and place a hand on the agreement. 'Three American Pacific for one Carltons.'

Gifford reminds me of Carltons' closing price this afternoon: 203. I lean towards him.

'You had Daniel murdered, Mr Gifford. What's it worth to you not to spend the rest of your life in gaol?'

He doesn't so much as blink. He remains quite still.

'I presume I had a motive,' he says, as if humouring me.

Motive. What was it that Hugh said way back at the start of this? His friend at Scotland Yard? Love or money: the only two motives for murder.

'Twintech was your failsafe,' I say. 'The bomb you were going to explode under us if you couldn't shake us free any other way. But Daniel found Twintech. And Owen.'

'That gives your Mr Baxter a motive. Not me.'

'But what if Owen told Daniel the same thing he's

telling us now? A systems check? Speak to Aldridge?'

Gifford holds my look.

'Or simpler. Owen panicked when he found Daniel was onto him, and that panicked Charles Aldridge. Charles sent the panic up the line to you.'

'I see,' he says, smiling again. 'And then I shot him.'

Far from unsettling Gifford my speculation appears to have convinced him that I don't know enough to cause him any harm. And the truth is, he's right, I don't. There isn't one bit of this that can be pinned on him directly. Not only did he not pull the trigger, but all the rest of it went on at one remove as well. Mannetti, Owen Baxter, even Aldridge, he's built up the separating layer like a fortress. And he's done more than just that: with Aldridge's help, he's set Owen up to be arrested for the murder – sooner or later Ryan would have heard that tape; and by sending that anonymous note to Penfield, he's ensured that Twintech's been uncovered, and that Owen has named Aldridge. His allies, though they don't realize it, are being cut free. Gifford's surprised by what I've uncovered, I'm sure of that. But he isn't frightened. Plausible deniability: he has it in spades.

And so I deal my ace from the bottom of the pack.

'No,' I say. 'You didn't need to shoot him. You hired Axel Dortmund for that.'

It catches him clean, his mouth opens in surprise. The name of the murderer: I know it, and Gifford doesn't know how. There's absolutely no doubt in my mind now.

I move around the table. 'Daniel's murder, what was that to you? A successful piece of opportunism? Another chance to stick the knife into Carltons while you set Owen Baxter up?' My voice is low and hoarse. A flicker of real fear passes over Gifford's face. 'After what you've done, do you think I'm going to let you stroll away with Carlton Brothers for 218?'

He grips the back of the chair. With a visible effort he holds himself steady.

I lean in, very close to him now. 'You pay up, or I take the statement I have from Axel Dortmund, and I give it to Inspector Ryan.'

Fear. He doesn't go to pieces – that's not how he is. But I see the fear at the back of his eyes. Given that I've somehow tracked Dortmund down, this lie about the existence of a statement is quite plausible to Gifford. And it's reaching him that I'm in deadly earnest.

'And if that doesn't bother you,' I conclude, 'I'll walk out of this door right now, I'll get up in front of everyone there – and that's everyone you'll need if you ever want to do business on this side of the Atlantic again – and I'll tell them what I know. And Mr Gifford, if you think you can survive a court case, I promise you, in the City you'll disappear without trace.' I drop my pen onto the unsigned agreement. 'Three for one. Change the number, and sign it.'

He looks down at the papers. In cash terms, an

extra 109p for every share in Carltons. All up, it will cost Gifford's bank just over one hundred million pounds. He looks to be trying to puzzle out some way of struggling free from the snare; trying and failing.

'What happens to the statement?'

Not a confession, he's too sharp for that; but a tacit admission of guilt.

'It's with my lawyer. If I happen to have a mysterious accident, he knows what to do with it.'

'I'll have to consult my board.'

'You can call them after we've made the announcement.'

'They'll object.'

'Then you'll have to convince them, won't you.'

His board, as we both know, is completely his creature; they'll do as he says. And as he turns my proposition over, the fear seems to leave him. He thinks he's getting my measure now. I'm not the zealot he feared, all I want is more money. I'm a banker just like him.

He touches the agreement. 'And what guarantee do I have that this is the end of the matter?'

I lean down close to him, and I say it very quietly. 'My word is my bond.'

He makes a sound, and I look at him. He is back there where I want him, uncertain, and a little afraid. There's a sound at the door. He glances over his shoulder.

'Change the number and sign it before they get back, Mr Gifford. Or you're done.'

He hesitates. The money doesn't worry him. American Pacific spent almost a billion dollars on acquisitions last year, not a cent of it from Gifford's pocket. No, what worries him is me; he's not sure that I can be trusted. But whether he trusts me or not, he has no choice here. Slowly he seems to realize that. Eric Gifford, Daniel Stewart's murderer, is screwed.

He picks up my pen, amends the number, and signs. A minute later, my father enters with Vance and Roger Penfield.

21

'What the devil happened?' My father whispers it from the corner of his mouth.

We're standing side-by-side on the platform. In front of us the room has fallen silent, everyone facing Gifford who's stepped forward to make the announcement.

I raise a finger to my lips.

Later, I say.

Then we listen. Gifford makes it brief. Speaking through a fixed smile, he recounts the virtues of Carlton Brothers: tradition, a sense of fair play and integrity, the usual City roll-call. He dwells a little longer on the qualities of American Pacific. The upturned faces, the City worthies and their wives, all nod. There's a ripple of applause when he mentions the name of someone in the room. I notice Vance and Penfield off to one side: having seen the amended price, they're watching Gifford with bafflement, waiting for some explanation as to why he's thrown so much money away. When Gifford nears the end of his announcement, he lowers his voice and hurries over the terms of the agreement. At the news of my father's immediate retirement, and my departure within the month, heads turn our way. There are whispers, but no one's really surprised: a changing of the guard was inevitable. The whispering dies as Gifford comes to the real matter of interest, the only question that ever counts here in the Square Mile: how much has he paid?

Finally it comes.

'The consideration for which,' Gifford says, 'shall be three ordinary class shares in American Pacific, for every one in Carlton Brothers.' And immediately he steps down from the platform.

Some at the back haven't caught the figure, but down at the front people turn to each other and give free rein to their surprise. Gifford, politely but firmly, is shouldering his way to the exit. The murmur grows. It's dawning on everyone that the humbling of the Carlton family hasn't turned out quite as expected.

Penfield senses the mood: he steps onto the platform and shakes my father's hand. 'Well done,' he says. 'Congratulations.' Polite applause starts, and a few voices call their own congratulations from the floor. My father looks at me, still uncertain. When we shake hands, there's more applause. I lean forward.

'I'll see you at home later.'

Stepping down from the platform, I make my way through the crowd to the door. Everyone wants to shake my hand. I smile and smile, and shake hands and keep moving. As I pass from the throng, Vance's voice rises behind me. He calls on my father to make a speech.

I turn, and my eyes meet Vance's over the sea of heads. He gives me a dry, somewhat doubtful smile, then lifts his glass in a private toast above the crowd. Later, I know, he'll want an explanation: as with Hugh, he won't get one.

My father begins his speech, the last rites of Carlton Brothers. With a parting nod to Vance, I turn and leave.

22

The house seems more empty than ever. My weekend bag sits unzipped at the foot of the bed, the wardrobe doors are open, and I still haven't finished packing for tomorrow. The day has been every bit as bad as I expected. And now, at 12.00 p.m., my father has finally arrived. He climbs the stairs calling my name.

'In here,' I answer. 'The bedroom.'

A moment later he's standing in the doorway. I swing my feet over the edge of the bed and sit up.

'Gifford's not taking my calls,' he says.

I rise and cross to the wardrobe, searching the drawers for another pair of thick socks. I remark that Gifford's probably halfway to New York by now.

'Shouldn't be surprised,' my father says. 'Not the way he left after the announcement.'

Turning, I lob a pair of rolled socks into the bag. My father sits. I bring out a jumper and some vests and drop them into the bag too. Then I shut the wardrobe doors and zip the bag closed.

'What happened, Raef?'

'He was underpaying.'

'That's not what I asked.'

I study the zip a moment. If it was just Gifford I'd have no hesitation, but what do I tell my father about Charles Aldridge? How do I explain that he's been betrayed by a friend?

'Gifford paid the right price. I suppose we can't leave it at that?'

I look up. He turns his head, eyeing me steadily: he wants an answer. Sliding the bag across to the door, I tell him this will have to be family rules. He nods and waits. There really is no avoiding this.

'Gifford was behind the Twintech fraud,' I say. 'And that cock-up that landed us in front of the Takeover Panel. That too.'

He just sits there. For a moment I wonder if he's understood. But then he says, 'Johnstone?'

'No. Tony Mannetti said it was Johnstone. But Mannetti's been working for Gifford all along. The

Managing Director's office at Carltons was Mannetti's pay-off.'

My father looks appalled.

'It gets worse,' I warn him.

'Eric Gifford. Why?'

'He had to shake us free. Mannetti's deal in Parnells made Carltons look bad in Funds Management and Corporate Finance. If that didn't work, he had Twintech up his sleeve. He was battering away on all fronts.'

He can't take this in. 'Gifford?' he says again.

'Eric Gifford. Our American friend.'

I lean against the doorframe now, arms folded, giving him a minute to recover. And I look at him. Suspicions. Bats in the twilight.

'But we approached him,' he says, confused. 'He wasn't the instigator, we were.'

'I wasn't.' When he looks up sharply, I add, 'And I'm not so sure that you were either.'

He turns this over. His face clouds. 'Charles?'

'Remember last Saturday night at Boddington. After the shoot? Who was it that said Lyle was going to take a run at us?'

'But he was.'

'No he wasn't. Lyle never had any intention of bidding for us. But as long as we thought Lyle was behind our troubles, we weren't looking anywhere else. I had my eyes off the ball.'

'You said it was Lyle spreading that rumour.'

'About reneging on a payment? Fair enough, that

was Lyle. But that was much later. He was just getting in on the act. He wanted to stop the Meyers' bid. He saw us on our knees so he put the boot in. Darren at his best.'

My father shakes his head. Not Charles. Not his friend. He reminds me that it was he himself who invited Gifford down to Boddington last Sunday. And it was then that the first overtures were made.

'Think back,' I tell him. 'You know how Charles operates. Are you sure you weren't responding to any prompts? Over the past few weeks, or months maybe, are you sure Charles wasn't pointing you in a certain direction?'

He reflects a moment. And what he remembers bows his shoulders. My guess was right.

'Last Sunday wasn't the beginning,' I say. 'It was the end of Charles' efforts to have you open the door to Gifford.'

And then I take him through every little detail of the operation piece by piece, all the problems we've had this past week. I tell him what Karen found on Mannetti, and how Hugh trapped Owen Baxter. I take him right up to my final meeting with Sir Charles this afternoon. I explain that when Owen named Charles, a lot of small things seemed to click. Charles, naturally, dismissed the charge out of hand; in fact he barely acknowledged the accusation. Why should he? Who was going to take the word of a suspected murderer over his? Plausible deniability. But then he made that call. And who was the first person Charles rang after being told of Owen Baxter's arrest? Eric Gifford. And at long last the picture fell into place. I went to see Wolsey: not only weren't the inspectors sent by him, he also had nothing to do with that scene at the Select Committee hearing. Charles Aldridge again. I contacted Johnstone too, he confirmed what Karen had found. And finally, at the livery hall tonight, I had my five minutes with the man himself: Gifford. The only thing I don't mention to my father is the tie-up with Daniel's murder. The way he looks, pole-axed by what Charles Aldridge has tried to do to us, that final piece of knowledge can wait.

When I finish, he seems shattered. He looks at me, eyes moist. 'Raef,' he whispers.

That's all, just my name, but then I know. The last vestige of doubt finally clears. Charles Aldridge, I'm certain, was not acting in concert with my father. Unburdened, I go and lay a hand on his shoulder.

'We could inform the Exchange,' he offers, shaken. 'Undo the agreement.'

'And lose Boddington?'

He nods.

'No,' I say. 'Let is stand.'

He drops his head. It will take him a long while yet to come to terms with the betrayal.

'And tonight you told Gifford you'd discovered what he'd been doing?'

'That's right,' I say. 'And when I told him, he paid up.'

He considers this. 'Penfield told me they've found Daniel's murderer,' he says.

We look at one another. I'm tempted to tell him, but he really isn't strong enough just now. I've done right to withhold this part of the story. Later will be quite soon enough.

'I heard.'

He drops his head again. Beneath his breath he speaks Charles' name.

And what comfort can I offer him? An assurance that the fierce pain of the betrayal will settle in time to a dull ache? The hope that something may yet be discovered to prove me wrong? The truth is that nothing anyone said now could help him. The blow has fallen, and all he can do is endure; endure and wait for time to carry him on.

I offer to phone Mary Needham, she could meet him in St James's. He turns his head. He says he'll see her at Boddington tomorrow. We seem to have reached the end of things so I bend to pick up my bag.

'When we first heard Daniel was murdered,' he says, 'you thought the Department was involved, didn't you.'

I stop, very still. I thought we could avoid this, but if we can't, I'm not going to lie.

'Yes,' I say.

'Because of Odin?'

I nod. Because of Odin, I say.

He regards me directly; he suspected, but now he

knows. 'Raef, you told me Daniel was going to blow the whistle on Odin.'

'Yes.'

He hesitates. 'Was that true?'

I feel myself sway.

'No. No, it wasn't.'

'You said,' he goes on warily, 'you said we might have to do something about him.'

'Yes.'

His look goes right into me. He seems to be grappling with himself, unsure of just how much he wants to know.

'If I told them down at Westminster. Whitehall,' he says. 'In the Ministry. . .'

Again I nod. If he'd told his colleagues the Odin deal was about to come into the open, anything might have happened. An arms contract with the hint of a Defence slush fund in the City, the award of a privatization tender to the bank which did the Odin deal; by the time the media had finished with it, senior Cabinet and Whitehall members might have ended up in court. And what might they have done to defend themselves from that? Murder?

Now I gird myself. There's one more question to be answered: why? Why did I do it? Why did I tell my father the lie? Why did I try to throw Daniel to the sharks? The truth, suddenly it seems so very precious.

But the question remains unspoken. He simply rises and comes and touches my arm. He looks ill.

'It's over with,' he says. Not a word of rebuke, but the sorrow in his eyes is deeper than oceans.

Reticence? Wisdom? Or perhaps, somehow, he's pieced it together. Standing by my bag I listen to his footsteps going slowly down the stairs.

SATURDAY

1

Boddington, late morning. Horseboxes are arriving down near the stables. I stand on the front lawn and watch them unloading. When the hound-lorry comes, the horses whinny and stamp, the hounds bark with excitement. My father, in his scarlet coat, steps from the house with the Master.

'Can't change your mind, Raef?' says the Master, nodding to the stables.

'No thanks.'

We stand surveying the scene below. Some riders are mounted, the horses turning tight circles, but most stand to one side talking with the followers. Behind us there's the sound of hoofs on the gravelled drive as more of those hacking up from the village arrive. The Master excuses himself and heads down.

'Theresa's getting Annie rugged up,' my father says.

And he looks at me. He arrived early this morning but so far no mention's been made of our conversation last night. Gifford called from New York an hour ago to confirm his board's acceptance of the price. It seems this whole thing really is over.

Mary Needham comes out with the stirrup cup, my father takes the tray.

'Coming down?' she asks me.

'I'll wait for Theresa.'

They set off down the hill, two dark trails forming behind them in the wet grass. I wander up past the walled garden to the churchyard. Margie's dressed her husband's grave, the flowers are garishly bright against the tombstone. When I open the church door, the pigeons flutter then resettle in the belfry. It smells musty and damp, I pause and touch the stone font. I was christened here; and my father and grandfather. And Annie too. My footsteps sound loud and hollow as I walk down the aisle. There are Carltons on both Rolls of Honour by the pulpit, and beneath my feet there's a stone slab bearing the inscription: LORD BELMONT. HIS USURPED LANDS RETURNED TO HIM ON THE RESTORATION OF THE KING. And then our family motto: LOYAL IN ADVERSITY. Everything here, the church and the house, Boddington, it means so much more to me now than I ever thought it could: here, without question, I belong. Now I sit in the choir stalls and thumb through the *Book of Common Prayer.* 'For Those At Sea'. 'The Churching Of Women'. Hearing a sound, I turn to the door. Theresa. She's standing by the font.

'I saw you.' She gestures back. 'From the house.'

'Where's Annie?'

'Margie's taken her down to see the horses.' She comes down the aisle, studying the corbels and plaques she's seen a hundred times before, her gaze wandering left and right. She's wearing jeans and wellingtons, there's a soft swishing noise as she walks. By the front pew, she stops.

'You got my letter?'

'Yes.'

'I didn't mean it to affect any decision about the bank, Raef.'

'I know that.'

'Truly.'

Turning my head, I promise her that the sale of the bank wasn't influenced by the letter. 'My decision,' I say.

She looks relieved. She sits then, and we gaze past one another, neither one of us knowing how to start. We've been married more than ten years; we've shared intimate secrets; we've been as close as two people can possibly be; and yet now even the simplest words fail us. All those things I'd planned to say, all those speeches I'd rehearsed in my mind, in her presence they seem utterly pointless. Is it the same for her? But finally I hold fast to this: I don't want to go back to where we were. Together or apart, we have to get on with our lives.

'I spoke with Vance this morning,' I tell her. 'I asked

him if he wanted to leave Carlton Brothers and come and help me set up another bank.' Theresa faces me. 'He said he'll think about it. It won't be like Carlton Brothers. Something much smaller. A boutique. Just Corporate Finance.'

'Raef. No one's trying to stop you.'

'It's my life, Theresa.'

'I know that,' she says.

I look at her. And then I ask her my question. 'Does that change anything? What you wrote in the letter?'

'I never wanted you to give it up, Raef. All I wanted was some balance. Time for Annie and me.'

'I promise.'

'No.' She checks herself then. Her eyes glisten. 'Am I whining already?'

I shuffle awkwardly out of the choir stall. Theresa stands as I approach.

Who in this world can claim a past that throws no shadows? We two are in the middle years of our lives now; there have been things done that can't be put right; but when Theresa takes my arm and leans into me, I feel that for us, and for Annie, there is hope. And in this moment I think of Daniel too. What was it that he asked of his life? What strange and endless yearning did he try, so unsuccessfully, to fulfil? Not like me, the realization of my grandfather's dreams for the bank. Not like Theresa, the desperate desire for a child. But there was something, I understand that now, a burning dissatisfaction inside, a craving for affection and love that brought so much pain in its wake. And for Daniel there will be no second chance. With part of the money I've extracted from Gifford, I'll set up trust for Celia and their sons: Daniel can't be brought back, but I think he would have appreciated this mercenary revenge. Wherever he's passed to, I pray that it might help him find peace.

But for now I press my lips to Theresa's head. I touch her cheek, and I hold her very close.

By the time we get down to the stables, the riders are all mounted, the horses milling now, ready for the off. My father notices us standing with the followers, Theresa holding my arm. He smiles and touches his crop to his cap. I pluck Annie from the ground and set her on the stone wall, an arm encircling her waist. She points to the horses.

'Granda,' she says.

The horses' bits jangle; they toss their heads, snorting steam into the cold morning air.

And then the huntsman lifts his horn and blows: he blows long and hard, and the pure sound of an English winter goes pealing out across the valley. Theresa's grip on my arm tightens; the hunt moves off. As the horses canter by, I look at Annie. Her mouth is open: she's spellbound by the world opening before her, and she laughs. It will never be the same, I know that now. It will never be how it was. Sometimes, I suppose, I'll forget, and for a few fleeting moments she'll be mine again utterly. But not always. For the rest of the time I imagine it will be just like this: though I'll love her with all my heart, she'll remain both mine and his. And yet somehow that no longer seems an insufferable burden. Life is strange. My daughter, my beautiful daughter, she turns and looks up at me now, her eyes shining, lit with wonder and delight. Who could deny her? I will never deny her. All too late for Daniel, I forgive.